# MURDER ON THE DOWN LOW

Also by Pamela Samuels Young

*Every Reasonable Doubt*
*In Firm Pursuit*
*Setup (LAndmarked for Murder* anthology*)*

**Pamela Samuels Young**

# MURDER ON THE DOWN LOW

Murder on the Down Low
Goldman House Publishing
ISBN-13: 978-0-9815-6270-4
ISBN-10: 0-9815-6270-1

Goldman House Publishing
P.O. Box 6029-117
Artesia, CA 90702
www.goldmanhousepublishing.com
www.pamelasamuelsyoung.com

Cover design by Marion Designs

Author photo by Sir Harrison Photography

**Printed in the U.S.A.**

*For my sister-friends whose support went
way beyond the call of duty,*

*Olivia Smith, Russana Rowles, Sharlene Moore,
Donna Lowry Reid, Jewelle Johnson, Cynthia
Hebron, Nichelle Norris, and Bettie Lewis.*

# Chapter 1

$\mathrm{D}$r. Quentin Banks was a man's man. The kind of guy other men liked being around. Handsome, but not a pretty boy. Wealthy, but not a showoff. Versatile enough to host a fundraiser one night and chill out with his buddies over a game of dominoes the next.

Standing outside Exam Room 5, the doctor scanned the chart of the first patient he was scheduled to see after his lunch meeting. His office suite in the Horton Medical Plaza was tastefully decorated with muted walls and dark slate tile. Colorful prints of jazz musicians lined the long, bright hallway. The place was classy, but not over the top. Just like Dr. Banks.

He checked his watch. It was almost eleven-thirty. Time to leave. The doctor closed the chart and dropped it into the plastic casing posted at eye level outside the exam room. He strode into his private office, locked the door, then retrieved a throwaway cell phone from his desk.

"I'm about to leave," he said. "The President's Suite, right?"

It was always that cut and dry. He was a happily married man who did not have the time or the need for emotional connections. His lunch meetings were all about the sex.

The doctor slipped out of his white coat and hung it on a metal rack. Casually but impeccably dressed, he wore a khaki-colored shirt and black slacks made from an expensive linen fabric. The kind that didn't wrinkle much. He was forty-two years old, just shy of six feet, and a hearty 215 pounds. He had the build of an aging ex-football player. Not nearly as lean as in his prime, but thick and firm enough to advertise that he still hit the gym on a regular basis.

After telling his office manager that he'd be back by one-thirty, Dr. Banks took an elevator to the parking structure. He eased his black Jag onto Hillcrest Street. At the light, he turned left on Manchester Boulevard and headed for the northbound ramp of the 405 Freeway.

Without question, Dr. Banks was one of the best OB/GYNs in Southern California. From the day he had applied to Howard Medical School, he had vowed to return home to Inglewood to set up shop. And despite the sacrifices, he'd kept his word, turning down opportunities that were far more lucrative, in terms of both prestige and compensation. Having a predominantly black and Latino patient base meant keeping late office hours and working one, sometimes two, Saturdays a month. The people he served couldn't afford to take time off from work. Not even for medical care.

When he wasn't working, the doctor cherished his family life. Though he now lived just a few miles from his childhood stomping grounds, in many respects it was a world away. View Park was a haven for L.A.'s black elite. Professionals with six and seven-figure salaries who actually liked the idea of having neighbors who looked like them. The doctor's residence spanned five thousand square feet and had a full-length basketball court, a circular swimming pool, and a guesthouse. The Mrs. was a stay-at-home mom who loved her job as wife and mother to their two sons as much as she loved her husband. All in all, life was good.

The doctor pulled his Jag to a stop in front of the Marina Marriott on Admiralty Way, hopped out, and took a ticket from the valet. He felt invigorated by the very thought of the treat that awaited him. Dr. Banks rotated his lunch meetings among different hotels in the area. His favorite was the much more elegant Ritz-Carlton just up the street. As he crossed the hotel lobby, he tossed the cell phone into the trash, then made a mental note to switch locations for next week. He was many things. Sloppy wasn't one of them.

When Dr. Banks reached the hotel room, there was no need to knock. The door was always left open just a crack. He could not risk being seen with his lunch date for even the few seconds it would take to open and close the door.

As usual, the main room of the spacious suite was empty. His lunch sat on a sterling silver room service tray on the coffee table in front of the couch. He'd have the turkey sandwich, root beer, and Caesar salad after his *other* hunger had been satisfied.

Stepping over to the large picture window, Dr. Banks stared across the street at the sailboats lolling in the Marina. Maybe he'd buy himself a boat.

He walked back to the couch, undressed, and slipped into the white terrycloth robe left waiting for him. Another part of the ritual. Dr. Banks sank down onto the couch and for the next five minutes, fell into a deep, calming meditation. The more intensely he fantasized about what awaited him in the adjoining room, the longer and harder his erection grew. He reached down and gently stroked himself, then picked up the condom on the end table and slipped it on.

Dr. Banks entered the bedroom and nodded at his lunch date, who sat naked in a velvet club chair, a sly grin stretched across his bearded face. Clarence Mitchell was his youngest son's soccer coach. They had been *hooking up* on a semi-regular basis for over a year.

Clarence stood up, showing off a solid, mink brown body. "Good to see you, man," he said, smiling.

Dr. Banks didn't respond, his growing excitement over what was about to occur more internal than external. The two men awkwardly embraced, then let go. Extended foreplay or professions of love were unnecessary. They saved that for the women in their lives.

Clarence walked over to the bed. Following close behind, Dr. Banks discarded his robe and prepared to treat himself.

Just over an hour later, as he exited the freeway, Dr. Banks heard his cell phone ring. He glanced at the caller ID before picking up.

"Hey, beautiful," he said into the phone.

"Hi, honey," his wife chirped back. "I'm catching a movie with Karen tonight. The kids are with my parents."

"Have a good time."

Diana was always good about making sure he knew her precise whereabouts, and Dr. Banks appreciated that. Now that he was free for the evening, the thought of arranging another hookup with Clarence crossed his mind, but he quickly dismissed the thought. He was not a greedy man. He never prowled for sex and the thought of going to a gay bar disgusted him. Only gay men did that, and he wasn't gay.

His lunchtime excursions were just a freaky little hobby. Nothing more. Nothing less. He was a fanatic about safe sex and always chose partners who were family men with as much to lose as he had. Dr. Banks even required his sexual partners to periodically produce written proof that they were HIV negative, and he gladly did the same. He loved his wife too much to demand anything less. In the twelve years since he'd said *I do*, there had only been five other men besides Clarence.

Dr. Banks turned left into the parking structure, made his way to the second level and backed into a stall that bore his name in neat block letters. He hummed his favorite Temptations song, *My Girl*, as he took off his shades and clipped them onto the sun visor.

Pushing open the car door, Dr. Banks planted his left foot on the ground at the same moment that a bullet pierced his cheek, just below his right eye. The force of the shot sent his head hurtling backward, then slowly forward, as a splash of crimson darkened the car's pristine beige interior.

As the second and third bullets entered his neck and chest, Dr. Banks' body fell sideways toward the open car door. His hand reached out for something to grasp, but found nothing to break his fall.

In what looked like a slow motion videotape, Dr. Banks tumbled onto the dirty garage pavement, head first.

# CHAPTER 2

Vernetta Henderson could not remember the last time she'd seen Mt. Moriah Baptist Church crammed with so many people. Crowds this big only showed up on Easter Sunday or right after some natural disaster. Like a 7.0 earthquake or a hurricane like the one that nearly wiped New Orleans off the map.

A lone tear inched its way down Vernetta's right cheek, but she didn't bother to wipe it away. Another one would replace it soon enough. She peered over her shoulder for the umpteenth time, praying that she'd spot her best friend, Special Moore, somewhere among the mourners. Instead, she saw Jefferson, her husband, slip in and take a seat on the back pew.

*Where in the hell was Special?* She was taking her cousin's death pretty hard, but Vernetta couldn't believe Special would actually miss the entire funeral.

In the pulpit just a few feet away, the testimonials were going into overkill now. Another twenty or so people were lined up along the church's east wall, waiting for their chance to speak. A petite white woman with curly red hair had already been at the microphone way too long.

". . . and when we first joined the D.A.'s office," the woman sniffed in a mousy voice that matched her appearance, "Maya and I would work late into the night. And whenever I needed help with one of my cases, she would always stay to help me out." The woman paused to blow her nose, blaring right into the microphone. "I couldn't believe it when I found out she had pneumonia."

*Pneumonia. Yeah, right.*

Vernetta closed her eyes and tried to shut out the anguish that felt like it was oozing from her pores. Maya Lavelle Washington was not supposed to be dead. Not at thirty-two. The comforting presence of the friend sitting to Vernetta's left made it a little easier to cope with the pain. Nichelle Ayers held Vernetta's hand in a grip so tight it nearly cut off her blood supply. Every two seconds she blubbered something incoherent and dabbed at her cheeks with a wadded up Kleenex.

The woman at the microphone stopped to honk her nose again, and the willowy Reverend Jones seized the opportunity, making it over to her in two long strides. He gave her shoulder a sympathetic squeeze, then waved up the next person in line.

Just over two years ago, they had all celebrated Maya's thirtieth birthday with a blowout party at The Savoy in Inglewood. Maya had danced so hard her press 'n curl had poofed into a kinky afro by the time the last guest departed. Afterwards, the four of them—Maya, Special, Nichelle, and Vernetta—buzzed from way too many strawberry margaritas, headed over to the Denny's on Jefferson, where they drank coffee and hot chocolate and laughed until daylight. That had been the last really good time they had all shared together. Three weeks later, Maya found out about her illness.

Nichelle's cries had turned into hiccupping sobs now, which was only to be expected. Nichelle was so emotional Vernetta often wondered how the girl was able to function as a lawyer. She had barely lasted two years at the City Attorney's Office in West L.A. before throwing in the towel. Nichelle was a more-than-competent prosecutor. She just had a bad habit of letting her heart cloud her legal judgment. Every defendant Nichelle was assigned to prosecute, she wanted to set free. Her current law practice was limited to preparing living trusts and helping people through the probate process. Now she could feel sorry for her clients *and* get paid for it.

J.C. Sparks, the woman on Vernetta's opposite side, shifted in her seat. J.C. was a colleague of Maya's who had been just as much of a fixture at Maya's bedside as they all had been during the final weeks of her life. Vernetta could see that J.C. was struggling to maintain her composure. In her line of work—she was a detective with the infamous LAPD—J.C. saw death on a regular basis. Tears weren't in her job description.

A portly Hispanic man stood before the microphone now, praising Maya's *pro bono* work for a homeless shelter in Watts. Vernetta listened without hearing, her thoughts now focused on the mountain of work that awaited her back at the offices of O'Reilly & Finney, one of L.A.'s top law firms. Lately, her professional life had been nothing but drama, drama, drama, and she was not looking forward to more of it come Monday morning.

A commotion emanating from the back of the church wrenched Vernetta's attention away from her work woes. When she turned around, she saw Special stalking down the center aisle, her arms swinging wildly with each step. Special was tall and curvaceous, with a fun, outrageous personality to match. But today, she looked haggard and borderline anorexic. Her eyes were swollen and red from crying and her long thick hair was mussed together in a scraggly bun.

To everyone's amazement, including Vernetta's, Special sidestepped two ushers, shrugged off a funeral director and charged straight into the pulpit. The mourner who was speaking stumbled aside as Special snatched the microphone from its stand.

"Everybody thinks Maya died from pneumonia," Special said, choking back a sob. "Well, she didn't."

Vernetta shot out of her seat and was at Special's side in a flash. "What're you doing?" she whispered, covering the mike with her hand. "Don't do this!"

J.C. followed after her, and the two of them formed a tight half circle around their distraught friend. Reverend Jones took a half step toward them, but froze when J.C. shot him a cop glare that didn't require any verbal instructions.

"People need to know the truth," Special replied in a weak but angry voice.

Nichelle had also joined them, which was a surprise considering how much she hated confrontation. She stood off to the side, still dabbing her eyes with the tattered Kleenex.

Vernetta placed a hand on Special's shoulder. "Maya's family doesn't want people to know."

"I'm her family, too," Special replied stubbornly. "And I think they should know."

A muffled clamor drew all eyes to the front pew. Maya's mother slowly rose to her feet. Pearl Washington was a young woman. Just over fifty. But the weight of her daughter's death had added a good ten years to her otherwise flawless face.

"Special's right . . . " Mrs. Washington said in a weathered voice that had Maya's feminine raspiness. "People should know. Let her speak."

After a long, uncertain moment, J.C. took a step back. It took another few seconds before Vernetta reluctantly did the same.

As the congregation waited, Special dropped her head as if she had suddenly lost her nerve and was searching for it on the floor. But in an instant, she straightened into a lofty, almost regal pose.

"Maya wasn't just my cousin," Special began, fighting to control her emotions. "She was like a sister to me. And she shouldn't be lying in that casket. The only reason she is, is because somebody deceived her. And it would be a crime to deceive all of you."

She stopped and rubbed her right eye with the heel of her hand. "Maya didn't die of pneumonia. Maya died of AIDS. And Eugene Nelson was the man who infected her."

An elderly woman gasped from the back row, and a teenager sitting up front cupped his mouth with both hands.

"Maya didn't know that Eugene was gay or on the down low or whatever you want to call it," Special continued, ignoring the waves of shock ricocheting through the church. "Eugene needs to pay for what he did. And I promise you . . ." Her lower lip began to quiver and for a second it seemed as if she would not be able to go on. "I plan to make sure that he does."

Special let out a loud, agonizing wail as her three friends rushed over to her. Reverend Jones waved frantically at the pianist, whose fingers hit the wrong keys, then broke into *Amazing Grace.*

Vernetta wasn't sure what emotion she felt as they escorted Special from the pulpit. But she didn't blame her friend for what she had just done. It didn't make sense for Eugene to be walking around looking like the picture of health when Maya was dead. *What was God's lesson in that?* Special was absolutely right. Eugene had to pay.

As a matter of fact, they had already come up with a plan to make sure that he did.

# CHAPTER 3

Vernetta felt her breath catch as she watched Maya's casket descend into the ground. A whimpering Nichelle held hands with Maya's mother. This time, even J.C. couldn't hold back her tears.

It was barely sixty degrees. Cold in L.A. for March. Vernetta scanned the cemetery grounds, hoping to spot Special someplace in the distance.

"I've already looked," J.C. whispered into her ear. "She's not here."

When the church service ended, Special had insisted on driving to the burial site alone. They had tried to follow her in J.C.'s Range Rover, but lost her in the long funeral procession. *So where is she?*

Reverend Jones said a final prayer and several mourners formed a haphazard line to extend condolences to Maya's mother.

"I can't believe Special didn't show up," Nichelle said, her cries having finally tapered off.

"She's having a hard time," J.C. reasoned. "She'll be alright."

J.C. wore her hair short, with just enough perm to enhance its natural curl. Her slimming black skirt and leather pumps showed off long, muscular legs. She was a pretty woman with flawless chocolate skin. She wasn't one of those female cops who hid her femininity, but she didn't flaunt it either.

Vernetta linked her arm through Nichelle's, more for her own comfort than her friend's. Nichelle was of average height, barely five-six, with a thick, brick house frame. She was always stylishly dressed and wore her size fourteens with the swagger of a runway model. The color, print and design of her clothes always separated her from the crowd. Today she donned a flower-print dress that was tapered at the waist with yellow rhinestones along the collar. She said funerals were already too depressing, so she never wore black.

Looking down at her black pants suit, Vernetta wished that she had worn something colorful. Her shoulder-length hair was pulled back into a tight ponytail. Other than her favorite bronze lipstick, she hadn't bothered to put on any makeup.

"We should head over to the repast to help out," J.C. said.

They trudged toward J.C.'s SUV and were almost there when Nichelle abruptly stopped and pointed. "There she is!"

Special was sitting alone on a stone bench at a gravesite adjacent to Maya's.

"It's just not right," they heard Special mutter as they approached. "It's not right for that man to be walking around without a care in the world."

"I'm sure he cares," Nichelle said, unable to be anything but sympathetic. "He's hurting as much as we are. He loved Maya, too."

Special shot Nichelle a look meant to wound, if not kill. "He didn't love her enough to tell her he was out screwin' men. *He* should be the one in that casket, not Maya."

Vernetta sat down next to Special and pulled her close. "We need to get over to Maya's place. Where's your car?"

Special raised a limp hand and pointed to her decade-old Porsche several yards away. She pulled her keys from her purse and dropped them into Vernetta's lap. "You drive. I'm lucky I made it here alive."

"You guys ride back with Special," J.C. said. "I'll meet you at the house."

As J.C. drove off, Nichelle struggled to stuff herself into the backseat of Special's Porsche. Vernetta had just started up the engine when Special flung open the passenger door and charged out of the car. "What the hell is *he* doing here?"

Before Vernetta could cut off the engine, Special was halfway to Maya's gravesite, where Eugene stood staring down at her casket.

Special was jabbing her finger in Eugene's face by the time they caught up with her.

"Why didn't you come to the church?" Special demanded, giving him no time to answer. "Because you're a coward and a murderer, that's why."

Eugene looked anxiously over his shoulder. He seemed disoriented and had a disheveled look about him. His eyes were sunken, and he needed a shave. His black shoes, brown slacks, and tieless green shirt did not match.

"I didn't come because I knew you would make a scene." He sounded as defeated as he looked. "You don't have to keep doing this, Special."

"I hate you!" She was sobbing now and pounding his chest with feeble punches that seemed to do little damage. Eugene took a single, controlled step backward but did not bother to otherwise protect himself from Special's blows.

Vernetta slid between them and clutched Special by the wrists. "None of this is going to change anything, Special. Let's just go."

She jerked free and charged at Eugene. "You're a murderer, you know that? You're a goddamn murderer!"

Eugene closed his eyes and looked away. "There's nothing I can say, so I'm not going to even try. I loved Maya as much as you did, I only wish that—"

"You didn't love her!" Special spat at him. She was about to strike him again when Vernetta grabbed her from behind and hauled her several feet away.

"Take her to the car," Vernetta said to Nichelle, handing Special off like a rag doll. Her tirade had sent Nichelle into another crying fit. The two of them were now bawling uncontrollably.

"You're going to pay for this!" Special yelled back at Eugene as Nichelle dragged her toward the car. "I swear on Maya's grave, you're going to get yours!"

Vernetta studied Eugene's pained expression. Even in his rumpled state, he was a striking man. She could still remember Maya's excitement after meeting him at a singles' retreat sponsored by a friend's church. "Fine, successful, *and* saved!" Maya had bragged to her friends over dinner. "I've finally met my soul mate."

Eugene proposed nine months later, and they had all celebrated Maya's lucky catch.

Vernetta could think of nothing to say to Eugene so she turned to leave.

"Could I talk to you for a minute?" Uncertainty filled his voice. "If there's anything I can do to help out. . ." His words trailed off. "If Maya's mother needs anything, would you let me know?"

"We'll take care of anything she needs," Vernetta snapped. She had never gone off on the man the way Special had, but she wasn't about to give him the impression that she had even an ounce of sympathy for him.

She was about twenty feet away when Eugene called out to her again. She stopped and waited as he hurried over.

"Uh, what do . . . um . . ." He looked down at his hands as if he didn't know what to do with them. "People still think Maya died of pneumonia, right?"

The resentment Vernetta had been carefully holding in check teetered on an eruption. She took a second to compose herself. "So it's still all about you, huh, Eugene? You and your deadly little secrets."

"No, I . . . uh . . . I just wanted to know." He looked down again and kicked the grass with his foot. "If people know, it's fine. I just . . ."

"Well, you know what?" Vernetta's lips eased into a wicked smile. "Everybody knows Maya suffered from AIDS and everybody knows that you infected her. In fact, Special stood up at the funeral and announced it to the whole congregation."

Vernetta chuckled softly to herself as she turned away, relishing the horrified look on Eugene's face.

The brother wasn't on the down low anymore.

# CHAPTER 4

As much as she hated funerals, J.C. actually enjoyed the gathering that followed. The repast was a shot of anesthetic for the soul. A chance to eat, laugh, and reminisce. If only temporarily.

Several people greeted her as she stepped into Maya's living room. The two-bedroom home in the middle-class Leimert Park neighborhood had a cheery, homey atmosphere. Even without the bright peach walls and the chocolate wood trim, it still would have felt that way. Maya's spirit permeated the place.

Making her way to Maya's kitchen, J.C. offered to help, but three older women from Mt. Moriah shooed her away. Seeing strangers take charge of Maya's kitchen left her with an uneasy feeling.

J.C. had easily bonded with Maya after testifying in a murder case Maya was prosecuting. Her friendship with Vernetta, Special and Nichelle began during the latter days of Maya's illness. At first, J.C. felt like an outsider, but the three women soon welcomed her into their sister-circle.

Nichelle and Maya had attended Loyola Law School together. Vernetta became part of the group as a result of being Special's best friend. She wondered what would become of their friendship now that their anchor was gone. J.C. had never made friends easily, particularly not with other women. Growing up with a name like Johnine Cleopatra Sparks hadn't made things any easier.

J.C. grew anxious as she watched the crowd of strangers traipsing through Maya's front door. She wandered from the living room into the tiny dining room. A dinner table draped with Kente cloth was stacked with the kind of food that the normally health-conscious Maya rarely indulged in. An oval platter was piled high with fried chicken, while large metal tins held thinly sliced roast beef and ham. There were two big bowls of macaroni and cheese, plus large Tupperware containers with potato salad, collard greens, fried cabbage, and hot water cornbread. J.C. counted six sweet potato pies and three pound cakes. All of her favorite dishes. And she had no appetite for any of it.

She decided to head to the backyard and was relieved to see Special and Nichelle come through the back gate. Special no longer looked angry enough to bite somebody, and Nichelle finally seemed all cried out.

"Where's Vernetta?" J.C. asked.

"We dropped her off at home," Nichelle replied. "She's coming over with Jefferson."

They each found a folding chair and formed a small circle away from the other mourners. Special sat on the edge of her chair. "We're still going through with our plan, right?"

Nichelle and J.C. looked at each other, then nodded.

Nichelle pulled a fresh Kleenex from her purse and loudly blew her nose. "So when should we talk to Maya's mother?"

"Let's do it tonight," Special said. "She's going back to Detroit Monday morning."

Nichelle shook her head. "No way. Not on the same day she buries her only child."

"How about tomorrow?" J.C. suggested. "After church." The women again consented with silent nods of the head.

"You think she'll do it?" Nichelle asked.

"If she doesn't, we'll just have to convince her otherwise." Special sounded confident that she could. "Eugene has to pay."

J.C. felt torn about what they were planning to do. She should've objected when Special first came up with the idea. It was too late to jump ship now. She heard her cell phone ring and pulled it from her purse. Flipping it open, she saw that the call was from her partner, Detective Gerald Jessup. J.C. found a deserted corner of the backyard.

Seconds later, she hurried back to her friends, her pulse racing.

"I have to run over to a crime scene in Inglewood," J.C. said. "Somebody just murdered a doctor in broad daylight."

# CHAPTER 5

Exactly twenty-four minutes later, J.C. turned her Range Rover off Manchester onto Hillcrest. The Horton Medical Plaza was bustling with police activity. Yellow crime scene tape roped off the driveway leading into the parking structure. A crowd of onlookers watched from across the street, craning their necks and pointing. J.C. parked between two police cruisers and climbed out.

As she neared the entrance to the building's parking structure, she eyed the young officer charged with logging everyone into the crime scene. J.C. could tell from his body language that he was about to give her flack. It was the same thing over and over and over. She waited until she was within arm's reach of the rookie before flashing her badge.

"Homicide." Her curt greeting silenced his lips, but his eyes flashed disbelief. A female homicide detective in L.A. was rare enough. A black, female dick was about as common as a unicorn strolling down Crenshaw Boulevard.

J.C. gave her name and unit number, then waited as he wrote it down on his clipboard.

"Second level," he mumbled, then lifted the tape high enough for her to slide underneath.

Inside the parking structure, J.C. spotted a stairwell and took the steps two at a time. When she got to the second level, she saw several men, most of them in plainclothes, crowded around a black Jaguar in the northwest corner of the structure.

Lieutenant Donny Wilson was the first person she recognized. As usual, he had a bite-sized Snickers bar in one hand and a cup of coffee in the other.

J.C. owed her rank as a detective after only six years on the force in large part to Lieutenant Wilson. One of the Department's first black officers to rise to the rank of lieutenant, he had experienced his share of discrimination and felt compelled to protect other minorities and women from similar abuse. He had taken the time to school J.C. not only on proper police procedures, but the politics of climbing the blue ladder.

"What's going on?" J.C.'s two-inch heels placed her at eye-level with her boss.

Lieutenant Wilson took a sip of coffee, which he drank any way it came: hot, cold or in between. He had a thick, but toned body and a gruff exterior that camouflaged a soft side few knew he possessed. "The vic got it once in the head. Another in the neck and a third in the chest."

"I'm surprised you're here," J.C. said. "Is this guy somebody important?"

He took a bite of his candy bar. "Let's just say he has friends in high places. And one of 'em is the mayor. He donated big bucks to the mayor's last campaign."

J.C. examined the black man sprawled on the pavement in a pool of his own blood. He was casually dressed, but the expensive leather of his shoes and the style and fabric of his clothing advertised not just wealth, but class. "What do we know about him?"

Before Lieutenant Wilson could respond, Detective Jessup, J.C.'s partner for the past four months, answered for him. "Dr. Quentin Banks. OB/GYN. Has an office on the fourth floor. Married with two kids. Owns what his nurses describe as a mansion up in View Park. Very successful practice."

Detective Jessup was a young, wannabe police chief. When he wasn't talking about himself, he was usually being an all-around pain. Unlike most people in law enforcement, Detective Jessup loved telling people he was a cop. He claimed to be writing a screenplay about a black detective and a Hispanic drug dealer. A hip-hop version of *Beverly Hills Cop*. He wanted Fat Joe and Jamie Foxx to star in it.

"So, did anybody see anything?" J.C. asked.

"Yep, and here it is." Detective Jessup flipped open his notepad and held up a blank page. "At least fifty people are standing across the street over there, but nobody saw a thing."

Lieutenant Wilson's cell phone rang and he stepped away to answer it. J.C. crouched down to examine the bullet wounds, which wasn't easy to do in her tight-fitting skirt.

Detective Jessup knelt down beside her. "You think gynecologists ever get tired of staring between women's legs?" He inspected J.C.'s exposed thigh through the slit in her skirt.

"I don't know, Gerald. You ever get tired of being such an asshole?"

"You should start being nicer to me, you know. Once my movie gets produced, I can get you a job as an extra."

J.C. stood up. "You have major issues."

The lieutenant finished his call and loudly drained his cup. "Ahhhhh," he said, with exaggerated satisfaction. "What a meal! I don't understand why anyone would pay four dollars for a cup of supposedly gourmet coffee when you can get the same thing for just over a buck at 7-Eleven." He tossed the empty cup into a trashcan near a wall scarred with graffiti.

"So what do we think happened here?" J.C. asked.

"Wasn't robbery. That's for sure," Detective Jessup replied. "The guy had more than three hundred bucks and several credit cards on him, and they're still there. Looks like a hit to me."

The crime scene tech walked up carrying a heavy metal box. J.C. liked Chester Dowd because he never made her feel like she didn't belong. Short and round with sandy blond hair, he was undisputedly the Department's best.

J.C. watched as he conducted a cursory examination of the body.

"Anything important you can tell us at this point?"

Dowd scratched his temple. "Maybe. Remember that shooting two days ago, about six miles from here?"

Shootings weren't exactly uncommon in L.A. J.C. tried to recall which one he was talking about.

"That engineer killed outside the Ramada Inn on Bristol Parkway," Dowd said. "Another well-dressed black guy. Shot in the head and chest three times. Small caliber gun. Probably a twenty-two."

J.C. took a step closer. "Yeah?"

"This one—and this is just my initial take—looks a whole lot like that one."

"So, what're you saying? You think the murders are connected?"

"Maybe," Dowd said, "but that's not my job. That's something *you* gotta figure out."

# CHAPTER 6

After leaving Maya's repast, Vernetta found herself plodding down the twelfth floor hallway at the offices of O'Reilly & Finney. There wasn't the usual hubbub of activity typical of a weekday, but a fair number of attorneys were still chained to their desks at seven o'clock on a Saturday night.

Easing into the chair behind her desk, Vernetta frowned at the bright red message light on the telephone. She turned on her computer, then picked up the phone and punched in her voicemail password.

*You have sixteen new messages.*

With a loud sigh, she dropped the telephone back into the cradle. *What was she even doing here?* She had hoped to get a head start on next week's workload, but no matter how much she got done tonight, there would still be more to do Monday morning. That was the worst part of her job. You could never catch up. There was always another lawsuit waiting in the wings.

Vernetta had recently been passed up for partnership and her passion for practicing law was slowly ebbing away. Just getting dressed in the morning and coming into the office was becoming more and more of a chore.

During the past few weeks, she had given serious thought to leaving the firm. Perhaps it was Maya's ordeal and the realization that life was too short to waste time doing something you didn't absolutely love. But she wasn't a quitter. She was bound to make it on the next go-round. She would evaluate her career options *after* she made partner.

"Oh, good. You're here." Jim O'Reilly, the firm's managing partner, who used to be her staunchest supporter, stood in the doorway of her office. *Used to* being the operative phrase.

After a sexual harassment case spiraled way out of her control, their relationship had become strained. And there didn't seem to be anything Vernetta could do to fix it.

"Did you get my voicemail message?" he asked.

"Uh . . . no, I didn't." Vernetta sat forward in her chair. "I've been out most of the week. I was just about to listen to my voicemail now."

O'Reilly grimaced. "I left that message two days ago. I also sent you an email. Didn't you have your BlackBerry with you?"

She didn't respond. It wasn't like O'Reilly to berate her. "I had a death in the family," she said, not feeling at all like she was telling a lie since Maya felt as close as family.

"Sorry to hear that."

The old O'Reilly, the one who'd been her mentor and friend, would have inquired further.

"I had an out-of-office message on both my voicemail and email."

"I guess I wasn't paying attention. You should always check your messages. Even when you're on vacation."

Vernetta disagreed, but wisely held her tongue.

"Anyway," he went on, as if he had better things to do, "Honeywell has an employee who's been abusing family leave. I gave them a quick answer, but promised that you'd get them a memo with some additional steps they should take. They need it by Monday afternoon."

It annoyed her that he'd made that promise without checking her schedule first. This assignment was something a second or third year associate could easily do.

"Doesn't Haley do work for Honeywell?" Vernetta asked. "Can't she handle it?"

Haley was the only associate at the firm she truly loathed. Not long ago, the brainy, blond bombshell seemed to be on her last leg, her arrogance and backstabbing ways having alienated every senior associate in the Department and a few partners, too. But somehow, she had managed to clean up her act and transform herself back into Ms. Superstar Associate.

"Haley's swamped. So, can you get it done?"

It bothered Vernetta that O'Reilly was asking her to do junior associate work. She still hadn't figured out how Haley, who had just finished her second year of practice, had wormed her way into O'Reilly's good graces. Now, it appeared that O'Reilly had Haley's back. Not hers.

"Sure," she said.

The phone rang as O'Reilly walked out.

"I was hoping you didn't pick up," Jefferson said. "I figured you'd be on your way home by now."

Vernetta transferred the receiver from one ear to the other. "You know how it is. Once I turn on the computer, my butt gets stuck to the chair."

Jefferson chuckled. "I wish I could find just one employee with your work ethic." He owned a small electrical contracting company, and lately, he had more work than his small crew could handle. "You doin' okay?"

"Yep," Vernetta said, though she wasn't.

"Sorry I couldn't stay longer at the repast, but we're way behind on this project." Jefferson's company was under the gun to finish work on a new condo complex in Torrance.

"That's okay. I had my girls with me."

"So when are you coming home?"

Vernetta thought about the Honeywell assignment, then looked at the computer screen and saw a long list of unopened email messages. Even if she read all of them now, there would soon be more to replace them. It had been a mistake to think she could get any work done tonight. She didn't have an ounce of energy left. She would come in extra early on Monday and bang out the memo.

"Now," she said, turning off the computer. "I'm coming home right now."

# CHAPTER 7

Eugene shuddered with apprehension as he approached the double glass doors leading into the vestibule of Ever Faithful Missionary Baptist Church. It had been a while since he'd attended church. But when life got too heavy, it was the only place Eugene knew to go for help.

An instrumental version of his grandmother's favorite hymn wafted from the speakers. The memory brought a smile to his lips. An attractive woman walking his way assumed Eugene's smile was intended for her. When she smiled back, he looked away.

About two dozen people, mostly women, were scattered about the vestibule. No matter what direction he turned, he met enticing female eyes that told him any one of the stylishly dressed women could be his for the asking. *The women in L.A. are so damn desperate.*

Eugene's thoughts went to Maya. He loved her and had wanted to give her the world. But instead, he had destroyed Maya's world.

Except for Lamont Wiley, a paralegal at his law firm, his hookups with men had been brief, insignificant excursions. Each one followed by a vow that there would not be another. He had usually been careful to wear a condom, but he obviously had not been careful enough.

For several months after asking Maya to marry him, Eugene had committed himself totally to her. She was the first and only woman he truly believed he could spend the rest of his life with. But seeing Lamont at work day after day made it next to impossible to break things off with him.

A tall, good-looking man, Lamont could charm the pants off his white coworkers one second, then quickly slide into hip-hop mode with the effortless ease of a stoplight turning from red to green. The attraction between the two men had been instantaneous, though both had been slow to act upon it. Unlike Eugene, Lamont had never dealt with women and had made it clear that he was looking for a serious relationship.

Standing in the church vestibule now, Eugene felt burdened with guilt. Why had the new AIDS drugs left him feeling strong and healthy, but allowed Maya to whither away? Even Lamont remained healthy and HIV negative. God obviously wanted him to live the rest of his days with the guilt of Maya's death.

Eugene entered the sanctuary and took an aisle seat near the back of the church. As the pews slowly filled, he decided to make a run to the men's room before the service began.

The north wing of the church had been renovated since Eugene's last visit. As he made his way inside, he took a second to admire the restroom's new marble floor and silvery-black granite countertops. Just as he was finishing up at the urinal, a handsome black man with short wavy hair entered the restroom. He had to be in his mid-forties, but Eugene could tell even through his conservative blue suit that he was in excellent physical shape. The man greeted Eugene with a friendly smile.

With one lingering look, Eugene knew. He quickly zipped up and hurried over to the sink to wash his hands.

"I haven't seen you here before," the man said. His body faced the urinal, but his eyes were on Eugene.

"Haven't been in a while." Eugene hoped that his clipped response conveyed that he did not welcome prolonged conversation.

"Well, welcome back, brother. I'm Derek. Derek Stevens."

"Eugene Nelson."

"Hold up a minute." Derek stepped away from the urinal, his pants still unzipped, briefly exposing himself.

Eugene needed to leave. Now. He grabbed a couple of paper towels from the metal box on the wall and quickly dried his hands.

"Bishop Berry really puts down the word," Derek said, as he washed his hands. Their eyes met a second time and Derek smiled that smile again. "And there's a pretty cool men's group here you should consider joining. If you'd like to hear more about it, give me a call." Derek reached inside his breast pocket and pulled out a business card.

Eugene looked down at the card, glad to have someplace else to rest his eyes.

"And if you're interested in investing, I can help you out with that, too. I'm a broker with Morgan Stanley." Derek was putting it all on the table. Before Maya, Eugene would have jumped at the opportunity.

Eugene headed for the door.

Derek followed him into the hallway, where an attractive woman dressed in a designer suit stood waiting. "This is my fiancée, Latrice. We're getting married in November."

Latrice beamed and swooned at the same time.

Now Eugene knew without a doubt that God was speaking to him. Maya had worn that same look of adoring pride every time Eugene nervously introduced her to men from his past. But there would be no more lies. And no more life on the DL. As Eugene made his way back to his seat, he tossed Derek's card into a metal trashcan.

Bishop Berry's sermon turned out to be exactly what Eugene needed. Not preachy or condemning, but thought-provoking and compassionate. His message—*God Is Talking, Are You Listening?*—seemed tailor-made for Eugene. By the time the ushers passed the offering, Eugene was ready to toss his entire wallet into the plate.

When Bishop Berry extended an invitation to join the church, something lifted Eugene from his seat and before he knew it, he was floating down the center aisle to enthusiastic handclapping, hearty nods, and a few pats on the back.

"Welcome, brother." Bishop Berry gave him a hug. "Welcome to the Ever Faithful family."

Eugene stood facing the congregation as tears poured from his eyes. After more applause and *amens*, an usher showed Eugene and two other new members into a small room to the right of the pulpit.

A woman stood waiting for them. "I'm Belynda Davis, head of the New Members Ministry. I love this church and you will, too."

Belynda went on to tell them about the classes they would be required to attend before their membership became official. Eugene didn't hear a word she was saying. The woman wasn't just beautiful, she had a radiance about her. The same glow that had attracted him to Maya. She even had Maya's smile.

Eugene took a long, deep breath. Not only had God given him the strength to resist Derek, He put another beautiful woman in his life to help him stay focused. When Belynda concluded her presentation, Eugene walked up to her.

"If you don't mind, I'd like to hear a little more about those church groups you were telling us about." Eugene treated her to a smile that had wooed almost as many men as women. "If you don't have plans after church, I was wondering if you might be willing to join me for brunch."

# CHAPTER 8

Vernetta, Nichelle, and Special, gathered around Maya's small kitchen table as Maya's mother busied herself at the stove, preparing her famous Kitchen Sink Omelet.

Nichelle had come up with the name because Maya's mother used anything she could find to toss into it. The omelet's real kick was the combination of jack, mozzarella, and cheddar cheeses. Whenever Pearl Washington came to town, they looked forward to breakfast more than any other meal she prepared for them.

Mrs. Washington dished omelets onto three plates, then leaned back against the kitchen counter watching them devour her cooking. There was an awkward silence in the room as everyone tried to pretend not to notice Maya's absence.

"You're not eating?" Nichelle asked.

"I haven't had much of an appetite lately," Mrs. Washington said. "I'll have something later."

Vernetta pulled out a chair for her. "Why don't you join us at the table?"

As Mrs. Washington took a seat, Nichelle swallowed a big forkful of her omelet, then cleared her throat. Even though they had rehearsed what she was about to say, Vernetta could tell she was on edge. "Mrs. Washington, there's something important we'd like to talk to you about."

Mrs. Washington raised her right hand. "Girls, I don't think I'm up to talking about Maya's personal affairs just yet. She already told me that she named you as her trustee, Nichelle. I'm fine with that."

Nichelle tried to smile. "No, it's not about Maya's affairs," she said gently. "But it's important that we discuss this before you head back to Detroit."

Mrs. Washington wrung her hands. "Okay."

Nichelle reached for her orange juice and took a sip. "I know Maya told you she had no idea Eugene was sleeping with men," she began. "And while he didn't know that he was HIV positive, he—"

"We don't know that for sure," Special interrupted. "He lied about being gay. He probably lied about that, too."

Vernetta placed a hand on Special's arm and gave her a look that told her to cool it.

Nichelle took another sip of orange juice. "As I was saying, even if he didn't know he was HIV positive as he claims, he still put Maya's life at risk by sleeping with men and not telling her that he was bisexual."

Special cut in again. "There's no such thing as bisexual. You're either straight or you're gay, and we know what Eugene is."

"May I please finish without you interrupting me? This is hard enough as it is." Nichelle didn't get upset often. But when she did, people usually backed off. Even Special.

Nichelle turned back to Mrs. Washington. "What I'm trying to say is, we don't think Eugene should be allowed to get away with this."

Mrs. Washington frowned. "He already did. My baby's dead."

Nichelle stabbed at her omelet with her fork. "Mrs. Washington, we want to file a lawsuit against Eugene, but we can't because we're not related to Maya. We want your permission to sue Eugene on your behalf."

Mrs. Washington glanced around the table. "A lawsuit? A lawsuit for what?"

"For wrongful death."

"I can sue him for that?"

"Yes, you can," Special said eagerly.

Mrs. Washington pressed her hand flat against her chest. "I don't know if I have the strength to go through something like this. And getting money from Eugene isn't going to bring Maya back."

Special touched her aunt's forearm. "It's not just about the money, Auntie Pearl. This lawsuit will attract a lot of publicity. It's going to send a message to other men on the down low that they can't do what Eugene did."

Mrs. Washington retied the belt of her robe. "I don't have any money to pay a lawyer."

"Nichelle's law firm will be handling the case on a contingency basis," Vernetta explained. "If they win, her firm will collect a third of the award." Vernetta wished *she* could handle the case. But her specialty was employment law and O'Reilly & Finney took very few cases on contingency. With partnership on the line, she needed clients who could pay by the hour.

Mrs. Washington massaged her forehead. "I don't know about this, girls. I don't know if this is the right thing to do."

"Auntie Pearl," Special said gently, "it wasn't right that Eugene took Maya from all of us. The law says you can sue people who wrongfully cause someone's death and we want you to sue Eugene."

Mrs. Washington's sister entered the room. Mavis sported a colorful scarf around her head, knotted in the front. She was ten years older than Pearl, but it barely showed. Vernetta could see a definite resemblance between Special's father and his two sisters.

"I've heard everything these girls have been saying," Mavis said. "They're right. That boy should pay. In my book, what he did amounts to murder any which way you look at it."

Mrs. Washington rose and gripped the back of the chair for support. "I don't know, girls. It's God's job to punish Eugene, not ours."

Special huffed and was about to say something when Vernetta kneed her underneath the table.

Mavis ambled past them and opened the back door of the kitchen. "Pearl, that boy could walk around here for another fifty years infecting I don't know how many women with that stuff." She stepped out onto the porch and lit up a cigarette.

"If the lawsuit these girls are talking about stops one man from doing this to another woman," Mavis said from the open doorway, "or if it encourages one woman to look more closely at the man she's about to lay down with, then it'll be worth it. That's how you should look at this, Pearl."

Mrs. Washington sat back down. "I can't hang around here sitting in a courtroom all day. I've been here almost three months taking care of Maya. My leave of absence ends next week."

"It'll be close to a year before the case gets to trial," Vernetta said. "You'll have to come back for your deposition, but even that won't happen for a few months."

"The three of us are going to split the court costs," Special volunteered. Both Vernetta and Nichelle gazed at her with something less than affection, knowing she didn't have a dime to contribute.

"What court costs? How much is this going to cost?"

"Not that much," Nichelle said. "It only costs a couple hundred dollars to file the complaint. We'll need to take Eugene's deposition and hire an expert witness. That'll be a few thousand dollars, but we'll get that money back after we win."

"A few thousand dollars?" Mrs. Washington said, alarmed. "And what if you don't win?"

Each of the women waited for the other two to field that question. When no one did, Vernetta spoke up. "The way I see it, even if we lose, we still win. This case is going to attract loads of publicity. If we save even one woman from getting involved with a man like Eugene, then it'll be well worth whatever we have to spend."

Mrs. Washington nodded for the first time. "Well, what would the lawsuit say and what—"

"I have a draft of the complaint right here." Nichelle pulled a folder from her purse, took out a thick document, and handed it to her. "Most of this stuff is legal jargon. Basically, you'd be suing for wrongful death and intentional infliction of emotional distress."

Mrs. Washington scanned the first few pages, then got up from the table. She moved the frying pan from the stove to the sink and began scrubbing it with a brush.

After several nerve-racking minutes, Mrs. Washington set the frying pan down on the counter and turned around to face them.

"You're right," she said, the doubt gone from her face. "Go ahead. Sue that boy."

# CHAPTER 9

The Monday after Maya's funeral, Special watched raindrops pelt the window outside her office. She raised her mug to her lips, then pulled it away, surprised that her coffee was now cold. She had just refilled the cup in the breakroom a second ago. *Hadn't she?*

The clock on the corner of Special's desk told her it was almost eleven o'clock. She'd been spacing for nearly an hour. Special knew that the rage she felt was not healthy, but she couldn't restrain it. An only child like Special, Maya had been more like a sister than a cousin. They spent every summer together as kids, celebrated birthdays that were only days apart and shared a special closeness their mothers noticed before they could talk.

Everyone thought that her volatile mental state was caused solely by Maya's death. In reality, she'd been wrestling with more than that. Special had become obsessed with the possibility that Clayton, her new man, might not be all that he appeared.

She turned away from the window and picked up a framed photograph of the two of them at Venice Beach. Clayton was an engineer for a defense contractor in D.C. They'd met several months ago at a National Urban League convention. Despite the difficulties of a long distance relationship, they'd become pretty serious. But if a brother like Eugene was gay, how could she know for sure that Clayton wasn't? He didn't look or act suspect, but that didn't mean a thing.

After all, she *had* been fooled before. Not long after finding out about Maya's illness, she had experienced her own HIV scare. It started when a coworker sent her a link to a website for men on the down low. When she browsed through the pictures of the handsome, masculine-looking brothers, she couldn't believe what she was seeing. None of them looked effeminate in any way. Hell, she would've been open to hooking up with half of them based on their looks alone.

She was just about to close the disgusting site when the photograph of a sexy, shirtless man practically jumped off the screen. The name underneath his picture identified him as Charles, but Special knew him as Ronald. Not Charles. They'd met at the Black Ski Summit in Vail and after returning to L.A., they'd had a short, but intense relationship.

She could still recall the one night they'd carelessly neglected to use a condom. At the time, her only fear had been pregnancy, not HIV. Later, after seeing Ronald's face on that website, she became paralyzed by the possibility that *she* might be infected. She had confided in Vernetta, who insisted that she get tested right away. It took ten days for her to gather the courage, and to her relief, she was HIV negative.

There was a knock on her office door, but Special didn't hear it.

Her coworker, Araceli Gonzales, stuck her head inside. "Didn't you hear me knocking?"

Special jumped, spilling coffee onto her leather desk blotter. "I guess I was daydreaming." She reached for a wad of napkins from a drawer and started wiping up the mess.

"Are you ready?" Araceli asked. "We have to do the dry run in fifteen minutes."

Special squinted. "Dry run? What dry run?" Special worked as a manager for Telecredit, having recently been promoted to the Credit Services Department.

"Wednesday's meeting with Citibank. Remember?"

Special flipped the pages of her desk calendar. "I completely forgot."

Araceli sighed. She had been covering up a lot of Special's screwups lately. "You know the proposal better than I do. You can just wing it."

"No, I can't. I'm here, but I'm not *here*, if you know what I mean."

Araceli's expression softened. She closed the door and took a seat in front of Special's desk. "I know your cousin's death was really hard on you, but everybody's starting to talk. You're either mad all the time or in tears. And this isn't the only meeting you've forgotten. Maybe you should take some more time off."

Special sighed. "I don't have any more vacation time. I used it all up helping my aunt take care of Maya."

"I'm sure you can get an unpaid leave."

*"Unpaid?* I'm already behind on my rent as it is. And don't even mention my credit card bills."

"I'll handle it this time," Araceli said, standing. "But this is the *last* time."

When she left, Special went back to gazing out of the window. Both Ronald and Eugene needed to pay for their deceit. She'd had no success tracking down Ronald's ass after seeing him on that website, but she had Eugene squarely in sight. Suing him was just the warm-up act.

She turned away from the window and dialed a five-digit extension. "Are we still on for tonight?" she said, when her coworker, Eddie Chin, picked up. A senior at University of Southern California, Eddie worked part-time in the Information Technology Department and was the troubleshooter for Special's group.

"Yeah, but like I told you, I'm only going to walk you through it. You've gotta actually do it yourself."

"You've told me that a million times," Special replied. "I'll see you at eight at your place."

Special hung up and smiled. Eddie was helping her plan a nice big surprise for Eugene. It was just too bad she couldn't be there tomorrow morning to see the look on his face when it arrived.

# CHAPTER 10

Nichelle collected three folders from her desk, then headed for her law firm's main conference room, just east of her office.

She was a total ball of nerves, realizing that she had done things in precisely the wrong order. Instead of approaching Maya's mother about suing Eugene, she should have first sought the approval of her law partners. She'd put off talking to them because she wasn't sure how they would feel about filing the wrongful death lawsuit. But she couldn't delay this discussion any longer.

Russell Barnes was already seated when Nichelle walked in and plopped a thin folder on the conference table. Her other law partner, Sam Howard, who would be the tougher sell, was late as usual. The three partners met every two weeks to discuss firm expenses, new cases, anticipated billable hours, and any other issues related to the administration of their six-person law practice.

"I have something I want to discuss before we go through our regular agenda." Nichelle opened one of the folders, then inhaled and hoped her good luck, hot pink pants suit didn't fail her.

Russell nodded but didn't look up from the brief in front of him. He was a solid family man who abandoned a lucrative partnership at one of L.A.'s mega firms to spend more time with his family. He arrived at the office at the crack of dawn, but rarely worked past six.

Nichelle heard Sam approaching and her stomach fluttered. You could hear him a mile away. He was the size of a linebacker and walked like he had tree stumps for feet. A well-regarded litigator, he spent several years at the District Attorney's office prosecuting everything from white collar crime to capital murder cases. He was smart, persuasive, and fast on his feet. When it came to women, though, he was a complete imbecile. He couldn't spell romance, and *cheap* should have been his middle name.

Unfortunately, Nichelle had made the mistake of sleeping with him, and their relationship had never been the same. Her mother's words still reverberated in her head every time she remembered their disastrous three months together. *Never sleep where you eat.*

Sam sloshed into the room carrying a folder sloppily stuffed with papers.

"Hey, everybody." He squeezed into a chair that was not intended to accommodate a man his size.

Before their little tryst, Sam had always greeted her by name, stretching out both syllables like it was poetry. Now, he only spoke to her when necessary and never by name. Nichelle doubted he would be treating her this way if *he* had dumped *her*. So far, Russell didn't know about their little fling and she was thankful for that.

"Okay, let's get started," Sam said.

"As I was about to tell Russell," Nichelle began, "I have a wrongful death case that I want to take on contingency."

Sam glowered at her. "You don't even litigate anymore. And you barely billed thirty hours a week over the past couple of months."

Nichelle reminded herself to stay calm. "Sam, you know my friend, Maya, was ill and I—"

"Yeah, yeah, I know all that. And I don't mean to be unsympathetic, but you need to find some paying clients. This *is* a business."

"C'mon, Sam," Russell prodded. "Let's hear about the case first."

Nichelle focused her attention on Russell. "I want to file a lawsuit against Eugene Nelson."

Sam scowled at her. "Who's Eugene Nelson? And you better be getting a retainer large enough to cover all the court costs."

"I'll be paying the court costs from my personal funds." Nichelle paused, knowing her next words would be met with staunch resistance. "Eugene Nelson was the fiancé of my friend, Maya. He's the one who infected her."

"You have to be kidding!" Sam pushed his chair back from the table with a loud screech. "You're not using this firm to play a game of female revenge against this guy. That case'll be kicked in a week."

Russell remained quiet, which usually meant he agreed with Sam.

"Just hear me out," Nichelle said. "I think this case will lead to future work and perhaps a whole new practice area for me. Take a look at this." She slid two sheets of paper across the table.

Russell started reading his copy. Sam ignored his.

"According to the Centers for Disease Control, HIV infection is the leading cause of death for African-American women between the ages of twenty-five and thirty-four," she said. "And believe it or not, the rate of AIDS diagnosis for African-American women is *twenty-three* times the rate for white women."

She handed them a copy of a *Newsweek* article with more disturbing stats. Sam ignored this one, too. "The majority of these women are contracting HIV from heterosexual sex."

"Are these numbers actually true?" Russell asked, as he picked up the *Newsweek* article.

"Yep. It's scary, isn't it?"

"You're darn straight. I have three daughters."

"More than a million people are living with HIV in the U.S. and nearly half of them are African-Americans. And it's estimated that a quarter of a million people are infected but don't even know it."

"Just tell me one thing," Sam snarled. "How is this going to bring in some billable work?"

"Just hear me out, Sam. This next document," she slid another page toward them, "is an article from the *New York Post* about a woman who won a two-million-dollar verdict against the man who infected her."

"And how much of that award did she actually collect?" Sam scoffed. "I don't even have to read the story to tell you. Zero. She got squat, because the guy probably didn't have a dime to begin with and if he did, he more than likely hid it long before the verdict came in. The Goldmans got a thirty-three-million-dollar verdict against O.J. Last I heard, they're still trying to collect."

Nichelle had anticipated this argument. "Well, Eugene *does* have money and I'll be filing the necessary documents to freeze his assets as soon as the lawsuit is filed. And you're forgetting that this case is going to garner a lot of publicity for the firm, and ultimately some paying clients."

Russell nodded, which gave her encouragement. "The media's going to eat this case up and I intend to milk it."

"You don't even like trying cases," Sam pointed out.

"I'll like trying this one. I'm doing it in Maya's memory."

"I told you!" Sam fired back. "It *is* all about revenge."

"Yes," Nichelle admitted, growing frustrated. "There is a revenge factor here. I don't like the fact that Maya is dead solely because she was sleeping with a guy who never told her he was running around screwing men." Both men flinched. That was the closest thing to a curse word they'd ever heard Nichelle utter.

"This is a legitimate practice area worth exploring. Look at these numbers." She pointed to the *Newsweek* article. "There's no one locally or even nationally who's recognized as an expert in handling these types of cases. I, or *we*, could become the experts."

Finally, she detected a glint of interest in Sam's eyes. "But you don't know anything about wrongful death law."

"It's not rocket science. Anyway, my friend Jamal is going to help me on a *pro bono* basis. You've met him. He works upstairs at Russana & Rowles. He went to law school with me and Maya."

Sam frowned. "Isn't that guy gay?"

"Yeah, and what about it?"

"Isn't he going to take some flack for handling a case like this?"

"Frankly, I think it might add a little credibility to the case to have a sharp gay black man like Jamal on the defense team. He wants to do this for Maya, too."

Sam finally examined the papers Nichelle had given him. "When are you going to find the time to do the legal research, draft the complaint, and—"

"The complaint's already written." She pulled two copies from her folder and handed them to her law partners. "And here's the press release I'm planning to send to the media."

Russell quickly perused both documents. "I like it. It'll get the firm's name out there."

Sam took his time reading the materials, then looked up at her. "Fine, but you just better make sure you know what you're doing. I don't want this firm getting hit with a malpractice lawsuit."

"That won't happen." Nichelle was smiling inside and out.

She had just swayed the toughest jury of her career. Who said she wasn't a litigator?

# CHAPTER 11

Vernetta checked the fuel gauge of her Land Cruiser and cringed at the orange light signaling that she was about to run out of gas.

She zoomed down the 405 Freeway, trying to make it to Irvine in time for an important meeting. She'd overslept, a rare occurrence since Jefferson was usually around to wake her up. But he had an early appointment and left the house before five.

If she stopped to fill up, she would definitely be late. With less than five miles to go, she prayed that she would make it.

The dog and pony show Vernetta was rushing off to was something clients were making law firms do more and more of these days. Even law firms with a reputation like O'Reilly & Finney's. Instead of handing over a new case based on an existing relationship, companies were requiring firms to compete for the work. Whoever made the best pitch won the case.

She pulled into the parking lot of Vista Electronics at a much faster rate of speed than the posted five-mile-an-hour limit and swerved into the only open stall, which was marked "car pool." Grabbing her briefcase and purse from the passenger seat, she ran all the way to the lobby entrance, then slowed to a forced stroll the minute she stepped inside.

Haley and O'Reilly were sitting in the north corner of the lobby. *Thank God.* The meeting hadn't started yet.

"Good morning." Vernetta concentrated on replenishing her air supply.

Haley checked her watch, then smiled up at her. "You certainly cut it close." Haley had striking looks—high cheekbones and those pouty, model lips that a lot of women paid for. Men routinely salivated when Haley entered a room.

"It's hard to predict the traffic on the 405." Vernetta took a seat next to O'Reilly and opposite Haley.

"You've got that right. That's why I always add at least thirty minutes to any trip that involves the 405."

Vernetta fought the twinge of annoyance that seemed to surface whenever she was in Haley's presence for more than five seconds.

A sexual harassment case that they had jointly litigated had not been a pleasant experience. After Haley's backstabbing ways had been exposed, she apologized and extended an olive branch of friendship. Vernetta's instincts told her not to trust the girl and her gut had been right. Within weeks of Haley's sympathetic overture, she was up to her old treacherous tricks again.

"You guys ready to wow 'em?" O'Reilly stretched his arm along the back of the couch. He looked as cool and confident as he always did. "This wage and hour lawsuit could be an important case for the firm. It'll involve more than twenty-five Vista facilities across the country."

In other words, they could bill the heck out of the client.

An African-American woman in a dark suit greeted them and handed out visitor's badges. Vernetta pegged the woman to be in her mid-thirties. "I'm Sheryl Milton, Director of Human Resources."

She led the way to a conference room where the Assistant General Counsel for the Labor and Employment Group and two staff attorneys were waiting. The AGC began by briefly describing a lawsuit they expected to be served with any day.

When he was done, O'Reilly handed out a summary of cases O'Reilly & Finney had successfully litigated for Vista Electronics in the past, then described his extensive experience with wage and hour lawsuits. "And here with me," he said, pinning his gaze solely on Haley, "are two of our firm's brightest associates, Haley Prescott and Vernetta Henderson."

"I'd like to hear your strategy for litigating the case," one of the staff attorneys said. The question was directed at Vernetta, but Haley snatched the ball and ran with it.

"Being able to coordinate a large amount of information is crucial in a wage and hour matter," Haley began. "As the junior associate and the cheapest attorney in the room, most of that grunt work will fall into my lap." Haley smiled and everybody chuckled. Except Vernetta. Haley was using her feminine appeal to the hilt. Her clothes were professional, but acceptably sexy. A pink silk blouse accented her charcoal grey suit. A long pendant fell right at the crest of her cleavage.

"It's crucial to get in as soon as possible to conduct interviews with the employees to tie them down on the number of overtime hours they claimed to have worked." She leaned forward, planting her forearms on the table. The move revealed just a glimpse of a lacy pink bra. "If the plaintiffs' attorney gets to them first, they're going to exaggerate their hours. So the first thing we would do is interview everyone in the proposed class as soon as possible."

"Sounds good," the Assistant General Counsel said.

"There's a new case out of the Ninth Circuit that should be a big help in fighting class certification." Haley went on to explain an incredibly complicated decision. Vernetta hated to admit it, but even she was impressed.

The Assistant General Counsel smiled at Haley like he wanted to screw her. So far Vernetta had yet to say a word. That wasn't good. She needed to get her foot in the door.

Just as she was trying to figure out the right place to insert herself, the HR Director threw her a lifeline. "Ms. Henderson," she said, "tell us a little bit about your wage and hour experience."

"I've had quite a bit." Vernetta was about to describe a case where she had obtained a dismissal when her cell phone started ringing. And ringing and ringing and ringing. As everybody waited, staring at her, she fumbled around inside her purse, desperate to find the thing and turn it off.

She finally spotted it buried beneath her makeup bag. The second she turned it off, her mind went blank. She couldn't remember the last thing she had said or what question had been posed. Just as the silence threatened to blow up the room, O'Reilly opened his mouth to speak, but once again, Haley took charge.

"Vernetta and I have worked pretty well as a team," she lied. Haley clasped her hands and leaned forward again, giving the men another glimpse of her fancy pink bra. "Maybe I can tell you something about my colleague's experience."

# Chapter 12

J.C.'s eyes burned with fatigue. For the last three hours, she had been pouring over the files from the shootings of Dr. Quentin Banks and Marcus Patterson, the engineer gunned down days earlier outside the Ramada Inn.

People who complained about doctors' handwriting had never tried to read a handwritten crime scene report, J.C. thought. At least doctors could spell. After examining all of the evidence, she still wasn't buying the crime scene tech's theory that the two murders were connected. But she also wasn't ready to dismiss the possibility either. Both men were shot in broad daylight with a small caliber gun. Both appeared to have been ambushed and both were successful family men with no financial problems, no history of drug abuse, no known enemies and no run-ins with police.

Wolfing down the remainder of the steak sandwich she'd picked up at the Quiznos a block from the station, she hurriedly drank the last few drops of her Sprite. She had a three o'clock appointment at the home of Dr. Banks and needed to leave right away if she expected to make it on time.

Thirty minutes later, she turned off Slauson onto Corning Street and hopped out of her Range Rover. J.C. had only knocked once before the door opened and she was invited in. Gospel music played softly in the background and a dozen or so people milled about the living room.

The teenager who greeted her apparently assumed that J.C. was there to pay her respects. "Come in," the girl said, not bothering to ask her name.

J.C. stepped just inside the doorway, but did not go any further. "I'm here to see Mrs. Banks? I'm Detective Sparks. With the LAPD."

The girl's numb expression came to life. "My aunt's in the den."

An even larger group occupied couches, stools, and folding chairs in a room the size of a small banquet hall. The girl introduced her and Diana Banks rose from the couch, shook J.C.'s hand, then led the way to her husband's study. Her sister, Patricia, followed.

"You have a beautiful home," J.C. said once they were behind closed doors.

Diana managed a weak smile. "We just finished remodeling the kitchen three weeks ago. Quentin was very proud of this place."

Mrs. Banks had the graceful presence of a kept woman. Every strand of her dark brown hair was in place. Her French manicure looked freshly done and she'd taken the time to put on lipstick. She was wearing blue jeans and a simple white blouse.

J.C. settled into a chair that felt like sitting on a bed of cotton. Diana and Patricia sat across from her behind a small oak coffee table.

"First, let me apologize for having to bother you at a time like this," J.C. said, "but I need to talk to you while everything's still fresh in your mind."

Diana nodded.

"When was the last time you spoke to your husband?"

"About five minutes before he was killed." Diana's voice quivered. "I called to tell him I was going to a movie." She pulled a handkerchief from the pocket of her jeans and wiped the corner of her eye.

Patricia reached over and squeezed her sister's hand.

"Was he at the office when you spoke to him?"

"I called him on his cell. It sounded like he was in the car. But I didn't ask."

"What time was it?"

"It was exactly one-twenty-one," she said. "I remember because I had a nail appointment at two and I checked the time before calling him."

"Did he tell you where he was headed?"

"No, but his office manager later told me he was returning from lunch."

"Any idea where he had lunch?"

Diana inhaled. "No."

"Were there any friends he regularly met for lunch?"

"I don't think so. He often came home, except on Saturdays."

"Can you think of any reason someone would want to kill your husband?"

Tears fell from Diana's eyes. "My husband didn't have an enemy in the world. You couldn't find a man with more integrity."

Something in her sister's body language said she disagreed with that characterization of her brother-in-law. J.C. would follow up with her later. She had been a cop long enough to know that spouses rarely knew everything they thought they did about their mates. "I hate to ask this next question, but did your husband use drugs?"

Diana chuckled. "No. He wasn't even much of a drinker. When we socialized, he'd have a single glass of wine or brandy and that was it."

J.C. covered a few more questions then asked for a picture of the doctor. Diana opened a built-in cabinet and pulled out a heavy photo album with the words *My Family* embossed in gold across the front.

"They're some nice close-up shots on both of these pages," she said, handing the open album to J.C. "You can pick out one you like."

J.C. felt a pang of sadness as she scanned the photos. There was nothing but pride on Dr. Banks' face. What a storybook life they had led. She selected a photograph taken last summer during a family vacation in Cancun.

J.C. closed the album. "Do you mind if I attend your husband's funeral service?"

Diana hunched her shoulders. "Not at all."

Patricia spoke for the first time. "You don't think the killer would show up there, do you?" Except for their differing hair styles, the two women could have been twins.

"It's been known to happen, but you shouldn't be concerned." J.C. stood up. "Here's my card. Please call me if you think of anything helpful."

"Why don't you go back into the den," Patricia said to her sister. "I'll show Detective Sparks out."

When they reached the front door, instead of saying goodbye, Patricia stepped outside and escorted J.C. down the walkway.

"I'd like one of your cards, too," she whispered.

J.C. pulled out a business card and handed it to her. She'd been right. Patricia knew something. "Is there anything you'd like to tell me?"

Patricia shot a worried glance over her shoulder. "Yes," she said hesitantly, "but we can't talk now."

J.C. started to speak, but Patricia raised a finger to her lips.

"I'll give you a call." She turned and disappeared through the front door.

# CHAPTER 13

Special entered Eddie Chin's studio apartment on McCarthy Street, just north of the USC campus, and plunked down her laptop on one of the four card tables scattered about the room.

At work, Eddie usually dressed in slacks and short-sleeve shirts. Special was surprised to see him in an oversized white T-shirt and sagging jeans. From the neck down, he looked like a pint-sized rapper.

"Okay, let's get to it." Special looked around for a place to sit. The stuffy little apartment was a jumble of squares and rectangles in bright orange, pea-green, and sunshine yellow. Vintage Ikea. There were five or six metal folding chairs, but each one held stacks of books and magazines. Eddie could afford three desktop computers and two laptops, but no couch.

A faint smell of mildew seemed to emanate from the area that housed Eddie's rumpled futon bed. Special didn't even realize they still made futons. If he hadn't been a computer nerd she would've made some smart-ass crack. But weird guys like Eddie were supposed to live in places that looked like high-tech junk yards.

Eddie thrust out his hand. "Payment please."

Special was hoping to talk him down, but seeing the look on his face, she doubted she would be able to.

"Uh . . . I need to talk to you about the price, Eddie. I was wondering if you could—"

"It's seven hundred dollars and I'm not taking any IOUs," Eddie snapped. "Computer hacking is a felony. You're lucky I'm even willing to do it this cheap. I've already put a lot of time into this. I stayed up until two last night working on it."

"You said it would only take a few hours."

"Well, I was wrong. I'm used to working with stateful inspection firewalls. That law firm has proxy firewalls."

Special started to ask what the hell he was talking about, but let it drop.

"And if you don't have cash," Eddie continued, his hand still extended, "the deal's off."

Since when did Eddie get so assertive? At the office he barely spoke above a mumble and rarely looked anyone in the eye.

Special reluctantly pulled an envelope from her suede Prada bag. "Here," she said, slapping it into his hand. She had borrowed three hundred dollars from Vernetta and the rest from her father. "But if this doesn't work, I want my money back."

"It'll work. I've already pulled up the law firm's email list. Have a seat."

"Where?" Special scanned the room. "You don't even own a couch."

"I didn't get a chance to fold up my futon," he said, apologetically. He picked up a stack of magazines sitting atop a stool and set them on the floor. "You can sit on this."

Eddie took a seat in front of one of the computers. Special watched as he connected a series of cables from her laptop to his much larger desktop version.

"With all the computers in here, why'd you need me to bring mine?"

"'Cause I don't want any forensic evidence on my computer."

*Forensic evidence?* "Look, Eddie, I need you to drop the *CSI* lingo and speak English. I thought you said they wouldn't be able to trace anything back to us."

Eddie's left cheek twitched. "Not *us*. You. If something goes down, I had nothing to do with this."

"But you said—"

"Just calm down. I have everything under control. I'm just being extra careful. They won't be able to trace anything back to you or me because I'm using my neighbor's AP."

Special's forehead creased.

"AP means access point." Eddie typed a series of key strokes. "That's—"

Special held up her hand. "Don't even bother explaining. How long is this going to take?"

"As long as it has to," Eddie grunted. "So don't start rushing me."

Computer nerds were so temperamental, Special thought. "You got anything to eat?"

"Yeah, help yourself. I don't get room service here."

Special wanted to thump him in the head, but instead got up and maneuvered the obstacle course that led to the kitchen. It was barely big enough to house Eddie's toaster, microwave oven and a refrigerator the size of a hotel mini-bar. When she opened the refrigerator, a rotten smell assaulted her nostrils.

"Did something die in here or what?" she mumbled to herself.

She spotted two Chinese takeout containers and a dried-up slice of pizza. She closed the door and opened the only cabinet. She found a bag of Fritos and popped a couple into her mouth.

"Ugh! These are stale!"

"Shhhhh!" Eddie said. "I'm trying to work."

Instead of returning the bag to the cabinet, she tossed it in the trash.

Special walked up to Eddie and peered over his shoulders. "So what are you doing now?"

"I'm setting up the programs and systems to test." Eddie looked up and smiled warmly at her. He obviously got off on this stuff. "I'm basically casing the joint," he continued, in lecture mode. "Before a bank robber robs a bank, he makes a trip to check everything out. That's basically what I'm doing. Scanning the law firm's network. This stuff takes precision, home girl."

*Home girl?* Special sat down on the stool and crossed her arms. "So where's your TV?" She scanned the room.

"Don't have one." Eddie never took his eyes off the computer monitor. "Ruins the brain cells."

Special searched for something to read. Everything she picked up was either a computer magazine or a comic book. She took an emery board from her purse and began filing her nails.

"Now, I'm spoofing your address so they can't trace anything." Eddie appeared to be enjoying his own play-by-play. "And once I'm through doing that, I'm going to hack into their email system."

After another twenty minutes, Eddie yelped with glee. "We're in!" He hopped up. "Everything's set up. All you have to do is type in your message."

Special pulled a piece of paper from her purse and sat down in front of the monitor. She had stayed up past midnight working on the precise wording of her message. She had rewritten it at least ten times.

Eddie turned his back to her.

"What are you doing that for?"

"I don't wanna know what you're typing," Eddie said. "I'm the best hacker there is. But if I ever have to take a lie detector test, I'll be able to say I had no idea what kind of message you were sending."

"Whatever." Special pecked the computer keys. "So this email will go to every employee in the firm at exactly seven tomorrow morning, not just the attorneys, right?"

"Yep." Eddie still had his back turned. "Everybody at the firm who has an email address will receive it. Even employees at offices in other states."

When she finished typing the message, she scrolled up to the subject line and typed "Important Alert—Read Immediately!" She read through the message three times to make sure everything was spelled correctly.

"So can I send it?" Special asked excitedly.

Eddie gave her a thumbs up.

As Special clicked the send button, a devilish smile lit up her entire face.

# CHAPTER 14

Jefferson blinked in confusion as he peered down at his wife, who lay sprawled on the couch watching TV.

"You're home before ten. Did your law firm burn down?"

Even after a long day at the office, Jefferson usually found Vernetta reading a brief or giving her fingers a workout on her BlackBerry. Not decked out in her favorite sweats watching a rerun of *The Bernie Mac Show*.

"For your information, I've been home since four-thirty." She waved her hand from side to side, motioning for him to get out of the way. "Move. You're blocking the TV."

He stepped aside, then scanned the coffee table. It was littered with an empty bag of Cool Ranch Doritos, two Almond Joy wrappers, and a half-empty Strawberry Snapple bottle.

Jefferson picked up one of the candy wrappers. "Are you okay? Did somebody die?"

Vernetta answered his wisecrack with narrowed eyes. "Very funny." She sat up and stretched. "Just another wacky day at the wonderful offices of O'Reilly & Finney. I couldn't take it. So I left."

Jefferson plopped into an adjacent chair and started untying his work boots. "So what happened?"

"Nothing out of the ordinary. Just more crap from Haley. She basically showed me up at a very important client meeting. Let's just say *she* came off looking like the senior associate, not me."

"I don't know why you let that girl get to you."

"She doesn't get to me."

"Sounds that way to me."

Vernetta shrugged. "So how was your day?"

"Same old, same old." He kicked off his boots, laced his fingers behind his neck and sank down in the chair. "How's Special doing? Any better?"

"Nope. I talked to her earlier today. I don't think she'll get a peaceful night's sleep until Eugene gets hit by a bus."

"That's understandable." Jefferson yawned, which made Vernetta do the same about three seconds later. "That brother better be glad he didn't date one of my sisters. Special has a right to be hot."

"I'm okay with her being hot, but I'm beginning to think she may need professional help. The idea that Eugene could possibly live another fifty years is killing her."

"If I were him, I'd be packing up and moving out of state 'cuz Special ain't about to forgive or forget."

"I think she will," Vernetta said, "in time."

Jefferson stuck out his hand. "Bet."

"Bet what?"

"Bet she goes after him."

"Special is all talk. Her anger will pass."

"No way. Special's the kind of woman who won't rest until she gets her revenge. Don't forget about that guy whose tires she slashed. All he did was cheat on her."

"I really regret telling you about that," Vernetta said. "She was young and crazy when that happened."

"And now she's older and crazier. You should tell that brother to pack up and get the hell outta Dodge."

"She'll be alright."

"If I had to be on your bad side or Special's, I'd choose you any day."

"You act like she's going to start stalking him or something."

"I wouldn't put it past her." Jefferson stood up and picked up the trash from the coffee table. He couldn't stand untidiness. "What's for dinner?"

"It depends. What are you cooking?"

He smiled down at her. "I want you to know that I resent that bait-'n-switch scam you pulled on me."

Vernetta laughed. When they first started dating, she regularly treated him to home-cooked meals. Now that they were husband and wife, home cooking was reserved for special occasions.

"You women are experts when it comes to deception," Jefferson said. "That's how I know your girl's got something off the hook in store for that dude Eugene."

# CHAPTER 15

Marvin Dobbs drummed his fingers on the table and wondered what was keeping Nathaniel. A loud group of unruly students cheered at the two flat screen TVs hanging over the bar at the Trojan Horse Grill across from the USC campus. Monday night basketball always brought in a nice crowd.

Just then Nathaniel "Breakaway" Allen entered the bar. A slight buzz whizzed about the room as eyes turned and fingers pointed. Nathaniel wasn't even a Trojan yet, but people treated the young running back like he was a million-dollar player in the pros.

Nathaniel slapped his books on the table where Marvin was sitting. "Hey, dawg. What up?"

Before Marvin could answer, a busty blond pranced over and purred at him. "Hi, Nate. I hope you can make my party tonight."

*Who had time to party on a week night?* The lust glistening in the woman's eyes disgusted Marvin. If Nathaniel had given her the go-ahead, she probably would've spread her legs and let him do her right there on the table.

*If you only knew,* Marvin thought.

Nathaniel promised to drop by, then pulled the girl into his lap and started feeding her lines Marvin hadn't heard since junior high.

Marvin didn't have time for this nonsense. For the past six months, he had been tutoring Nathaniel, a student at Fox Hills Junior College, so that he would have a head start on his course work when he transferred to USC in the fall. But Marvin had his own school work to get to if he planned to graduate in June. Of course, English and biology weren't the only things on their agendas tonight.

Finally bored with the girl, Nathaniel booted her from his lap. "Let's get over to the library, dawg."

As they made their way to the door, Marvin's eyes were drawn to a jock sitting at the bar. *Damn!* The guy had just *clocked* him. Marvin knew the man would keep his secret, just as Marvin would keep his. Still, he hated being exposed.

Marvin listened to Nathaniel rattle on about himself as they trudged across campus.

"A sports reporter from the *L.A. Times* is interviewing me next week," he bragged. "They've got their eyes on me for the Heisman Trophy."

Marvin nodded like he was impressed, but he really didn't give a shit. He hated sports.

They climbed the steps of Doheny Library and took the elevator to the stacks on the fifth floor. They found a deserted area of the library near the back. Marvin plugged in his laptop while Nathaniel dumped his books on an adjoining desk and pulled out a notepad and pen. It wasn't likely that they would be interrupted. Thanks to the Internet, few students took the trouble to traipse to the library. But if some librarian happened to interrupt, at least it would look like they were there to do work.

Marvin hit the switch which controlled the lights in the left quadrant of the floor and the area went pitch black. He made his way back to the desk, careful not to bump into the book cases. Without discussion, Nathaniel unzipped his fly and Marvin dropped to his knees.

When they were done, Nathaniel callously pushed Marvin away. More and more now, Nathaniel turned cold within seconds of coming. But Marvin didn't care. He had something that Mr. Big Man On Campus couldn't resist.

"We ain't doing this no more!" Nathaniel growled as he hurriedly zipped up his pants. "And I don't feel like studyin' tonight."

Marvin didn't respond. They'd been hooking up for close to four months now. Every other week, Nathaniel proclaimed that it would be their last time. Then, a week later, he would call, begging to see him again.

"Whatever, man," Marvin said.

"No, I'm serious this time. This is getting too risky. I got somebody else. An older dude. He has a place where we can kick it without getting caught."

Fear rose in Marvin's throat. Nathaniel had never mentioned having anybody else before. Flipping on the lights, Marvin watched as Nathaniel grabbed his books and stalked off.

Marvin hated to admit it, but he had fallen in love with Nathaniel. He knew he would always be the man on the side, but he didn't care. He was exactly what Nathaniel needed, a partner who was masculine enough to never raise anyone's suspicions about his sexual preference and discreet enough to keep his mouth shut.

After leaving the library, Marvin headed back to the apartment off Vermont that he shared with his girlfriend. Jana was nice enough, but she didn't turn him on. Sex with most women bored him and it took all the mental energy he could muster to force himself to get off. With Jana, it was easier than with some, but still nothing he looked forward to. But she was safe because she trusted him completely and didn't ask a lot of questions.

When he opened the front door, he saw her sitting on the couch in a pink, frilly teddy.

*Damn.*

"Hey, sweetie. I was waiting up for you."

He gave Jana a quick peck, then headed into the bathroom and turned on the shower. She followed after him, throwing her arms around his waist and standing on her tiptoes to give him a wet kiss on the back of the neck. He could feel the two sunny side-up eggs she had for breasts pressed against his back. She was a beautiful girl. She was a beautiful redbone with long thick hair. But she had the body of a twelve-year-old boy. Marvin preferred men, not boys.

"I missed you, sweetie," she squealed in an annoying, high-pitched voice. "Did you miss me?"

Marvin did not bother to turn around. "Of course."

He pulled away, lifted his T-shirt over his head and stepped out of his jeans.

Marvin resigned himself to having to make love to her, but he needed a few minutes alone to psyche himself up for it. He turned around and kissed her pancake-flat breasts, then ran his hand between her moist little stick thighs.

"I see you're already nice and wet for me." He rewarded her with a long, passionate kiss. "Why don't you go pour me a glass of wine and wait for me to finish my shower so I can give you what you need?"

Jana grinned excitedly and scurried away. Marvin stepped into the shower and turned on the water as hard as it would go and soaped himself down. He hoped Nathaniel didn't have another dude. He did not want to lose him.

Back in the bedroom, Jana had turned out the lights and placed scented candles on both nightstands.

"Here's your wine, sweetie."

Marvin took the glass from her and chugged it down, wishing he had asked for something stronger. He sat back against the headboard as Jana did a cat crawl from the foot of the bed and took him into her mouth. Her blow jobs did absolutely nothing for him. He closed his eyes and thought about Nathaniel. That image immediately brought him to life.

"That's my good boy," Jana cooed, taking credit she didn't deserve. She slipped out of her teddy and was about to climb on top of him when he turned away and pulled a condom from the nightstand.

"Sweetie, I already told you, we don't have to use protection anymore. I'm on the pill and we've been together long enough to trust each other."

That made the third time this month that Jana had protested when Marvin reached for a condom. He'd be able to come faster without it, but he wasn't about to play Jana's little game. She was on academic probation for the second time and would almost surely be kicked out of school next semester if she didn't get it together. Getting pregnant would mean child support payments for the next eighteen years. He wasn't about to fall for that.

Marvin tore open the condom wrapper with his teeth, slipped it on and gave the girl what she wanted. He never took his eyes off the clock on the nightstand. It took her exactly seventy-eight seconds to come. He didn't bother to.

The next morning, while he lay in bed, Jana ran out for coffee and croissants. Neither of them had classes on Tuesdays, so Jana had dubbed Tuesday mornings their *cuddle time*. Marvin had gone along without a fuss. They usually spent the morning watching movies recorded on TiVo. It was one of the few times that Marvin actually enjoyed Jana's company.

Despite his indifference, Marvin knew that he might actually end up marrying the girl. Having a wife who was as trusting as a two year old would make things much simpler. As long as he paid the bills, pampered her with flowers and expensive gifts, and dicked her good a few times a month, she would have no complaints. He could keep Nathaniel on the side and they could all live happily ever after.

Marvin heard the front door open and slam shut. Jana bolted into the bedroom, a stricken look on her face. She was panting like someone in need of a respirator. She had a copy of the *L.A. Times* in hand, but no coffee or croissants.

Marvin sat up. "What's the matter?"

Jana held up the newspaper and pointed to a large headline across page one. "Somebody shot him." Her face crumpled into tears.

"Shot who?"

"Your friend. Nathaniel Allen. He's dead. Somebody shot him last night."

Marvin tried to stand up, but his equilibrium was way off kilter. The floor actually seemed to be swaying. He grabbed the newspaper from Jana and read the first paragraph, then read it again. When he finished the entire story, he dropped the paper on the bed and brushed past Jana into the bathroom.

Marvin locked the door and turned on the shower to drown out the sound. Then he sobbed.

# CHAPTER 16

Eugene drove his BMW into the underground parking garage at Ramsey & King and turned off the engine. Everything was going well in his world and he refused to believe it was anything but the grace of God.

He'd seen the doctor the day before and his T-cell count was still strong. He'd been taking a combination of several new AIDS drugs which gave him a lot more energy. He'd also given up beef and pork and limited his alcohol intake to red wine. He was basically turning into an all-around health nut.

Eugene had actually enjoyed his first new members' class at Ever Faithful on Monday night and was feeling as if his life was finally back on track. And Belynda was absolutely incredible.

For the first time in his life, he felt comfortable enough with a woman to tell her everything about his past. His attraction to men, his promiscuity, even Maya's death. Belynda had listened without comment, clearly in shock at first. But later, she told him she truly believed that he was ready to commit himself to God. The fact that he was being so honest with her was proof of that. If God could forgive him, so could she.

Turning off the engine, Eugene pulled his cell phone from his shirt pocket and dialed Belynda's number. He couldn't believe how he had connected with her on such a strong, spiritual level in just two short days. They had talked on the phone for nearly three hours after brunch on Sunday, and last night after class, she had invited him over to her place.

When Eugene heard Belynda's voice on the phone, he grinned. "I just wanted to be the first to tell you good morning. I really had a nice time last night."

"So did I," Belynda said. They had read Bible verses, then gone for a long walk at Fox Hills Park. Belynda was deeply religious and did not believe in sex or even intimate kissing before marriage. With everything going on in his life, Eugene welcomed her rules.

"I'm wearing that lapel pin you gave me." He glanced down at the small, gold circle with a mustard seed glued to the center.

"I didn't expect you to wear it to work." Belynda was obviously pleased.

"I plan on wearing it everywhere I go."

"Just remember what it represents," she said. "If you have faith the size of a mustard seed, God will do the rest."

"You have no idea how much your support means to me. I just wanted to let you know I was thinking about you. I'll call you later."

Eugene opened the car door and removed his jacket from the back of the headrest. His buttoned-down Hugo Boss was the most expensive suit in his closet and wearing it always made him feel like a million bucks.

He stepped off the elevator onto the twenty-first floor and waved at the receptionist, a Filipino chick who had been hitting on him since the day he'd joined the firm.

"Good morning, Marci."

She frowned and turned up her nose.

*What was that about?*

He strolled down the hallway, past cubicle after cubicle where the secretaries sat. Either he was being paranoid or all of them were shooting him hateful looks. When he passed an older black woman who'd always been chatty with him, she rolled her eyes. The woman in the next cubicle looked away.

*What was going on?*

When he reached his office, his secretary wasn't at her desk. He set his briefcase down and turned on his computer. While it was booting up, he checked his voicemail.

"Hey, man, call me as soon as you get this message. It's extremely important." It was Liam, an associate in the Tax Department. The urgency in Liam's voice concerned him. Liam was the only openly gay associate in the firm. His partner was HIV positive. They had spent many hours talking about Eugene's situation.

He dialed his coworker's extension and Liam picked up on the first ring. "Have you read your email?" Eugene sensed panic in Liam's voice.

"No. I just turned on my computer."

"Well, you should check it. Right now."

"What's going on?"

"You'll see in a minute. I'm on my way down."

Eugene typed in his password and waited for access. There were ten new email messages. He opened the one that read, "Important Alert—Read Immediately!"

When the words of the email hit him, he felt like someone had bashed him in the head with a baseball bat.

> *Did you know that your coworker Eugene Nelson is a murderer? His beautiful fiancée, Maya Washington, recently died after a long, painful battle with AIDS. Eugene's story about her dying of pneumonia is a big, fat lie. Maya died because Eugene is a closet homosexual who failed to tell her that he was HIV positive. Maya would be alive today if Eugene had told her he was running around having sex with men. Do you really want a liar and a murderer working at your law firm?*

Liam charged into his office just as Eugene finished reading the message.

"Are you okay?" Liam closed the door.

Eugene's cheeks burned with rage. He did not deserve this. How could he continue to show his face around the firm? Now the nasty looks from the support staff made sense.

"Did everybody in the firm get this email?"

Liam nodded and sat down. "I think so. Who could've done this?"

Eugene knew exactly who was responsible. He had no idea how the crazy bitch had been able to hack into his law firm's computer system, but there was no doubt in his mind that Special was the culprit. No one else held this kind of animosity toward him.

Two weeks before Maya's death, Eugene had tried to visit her in the hospital, but Special had stood in the doorway, blocking his path, loudly threatening to call security if he didn't leave. Special was the only reason he didn't show up at Maya's funeral. He couldn't handle another angry confrontation. Their altercation at the burial site confirmed that he had made the right decision not to attend the church service.

Before he could figure out what he was going to do, his telephone rang. The mailroom had a package for him, but the messenger insisted that Eugene, not his secretary, had to sign for it. Eugene didn't have time for this right now, but then he remembered that he was waiting for some confidential documents from a client.

He told Liam to stay put and took off for the mailroom. This time, he ignored all the evil looks from the secretaries.

Eugene scribbled his name on a clipboard and rushed back to his office. As he tore open the envelope, he noticed that it wasn't from his client. His face clouded after he read the first few words.

"Are you okay?" Liam put a hand on Eugene's shoulder. "What is it?"

It took a second for Eugene to respond. "Maya's mother is suing me," he said, fighting back tears. "For wrongful death."

# CHAPTER 17

The day after her big fumble at Vista Electronics, Vernetta was headed out for a late lunch when she ran into Haley and O'Reilly in the lobby of their office building.

"Hey, Vernetta," O'Reilly beamed, "great news. We got that Vista Electronics case. And we owe it all to Haley." He gave her a fatherly hug. "The Assistant General Counsel said he'd never met such a sharp young lawyer."

Haley glowed up at O'Reilly, then treated Vernetta to a more modest smile.

Vernetta tried to fight it off, but pure jealousy made her stomach churn.

"We just had lunch at Spago to celebrate," Haley announced. "I dropped by your office to invite you, but you weren't there."

Vernetta could not hide her disappointment. She was part of the team. They should have postponed their little celebratory lunch and waited for her.

"I had the lobster salad." Haley splayed her fingers and pressed her palm against her belly. "And it was fantastic."

"We're getting together at three for a planning meeting," O'Reilly said. "Are you open?"

O'Reilly should have checked with her before scheduling the meeting. He was treating *her* like the junior associate. "Yeah, I'm open," she said and walked away.

Vernetta ate a dry turkey sandwich at her desk and pouted. After about fifteen minutes of feeling sorry for herself, she decided to shake it off. If she were going to make partner, she couldn't let things like this get to her. Haley was jockeying for lead on this case, and Vernetta would just have to jockey her out of the way.

The meeting with O'Reilly and Haley was in less than forty-five minutes. Vernetta pulled a legal pad from her desk and started making a to-do list. The key to handling a wage and hour lawsuit was getting organized at the beginning. She began drafting a detailed litigation strategy.

The time flew. Fifteen minutes before three, Vernetta made her way to O'Reilly's office. She wanted to get there before Haley so she could have a little bonding time with the boss. When she reached the doorway she found the two of them sitting at his side table, already fully engaged.

O'Reilly waved her inside. "Come on in. Vista Electronics is anxious to get going with this case. A messenger dropped off these payroll records this morning. We've been taking a look at some of them."

Haley gave Vernetta a look that told her in very clear terms that she was prepared to do battle. If Vernetta had any doubts about Haley and O'Reilly's relationship, she didn't anymore. It was clear that Haley was now holding down the top spot on O'Reilly's list of favorite associates. If Vernetta wanted her title back, she would have to fight for it.

She pulled out a chair and sat down, hoping her concern didn't show. Opening a folder, Vernetta took out several sheets of yellow legal paper with her handwritten notes. "I started preparing a case plan."

"Great," Haley said. "So did I." She handed both of them a three-page, typed document. "We can just combine our ideas. I guess you didn't have time to type up anything."

Vernetta smiled. "No, I had time." She pulled copies of a six-page document from another folder Haley hadn't seen.

It pleased her to see Haley's red cheeks turn even rosier. "Let's go over your document first," Vernetta said.

An hour later, after they had shared their respective ideas, it was clear who had the superior legal knowledge. Haley's document was not nearly as comprehensive as Vernetta's. Haley had never handled a wage and hour case before. Vernetta had. O'Reilly gave both of them several follow-up tasks and appeared to conclude the meeting. But Vernetta wasn't leaving before Haley and Haley apparently had the same idea.

After O'Reilly mentioned an upcoming conference call, they finally left together.

"I forgot to mention to O'Reilly that we could probably use a first-year associate on the case," Haley said.

*Why? So you'll have somebody to boss around?* "It's a little early to make that decision. The three of us and a team of paralegals should be able to handle everything for the time being."

"Okay. Sorry you weren't able to join us for lunch."

Something in her gut told her to keep moving, but she ignored the warning. She stopped and faced her colleague. "I'm surprised that I missed you. I was in my office all morning. When did you drop by?"

"Oh . . .Well, I asked my secretary to go look for you. Maybe you were in the ladies' room."

"I didn't leave my office until I ran into the two of you." Vernetta stared in a way that she hoped communicated that she knew Haley had intended to exclude her.

"I don't know how she could've missed you. Sorry about the mix-up."

Since their offices were on opposite ends of the floor, Vernetta turned to leave.

"This should be a fun case to work on," Haley called out after her.

Vernetta did not bother to look back. "Sure should be."

# CHAPTER 18

"Why didn't I get a call last night?"

J.C. had not wanted her words to sound so angry, but there was no way to take them back now. Detective Jessup was talking to a USC campus security officer outside the Trojan Arms apartment complex. He continued his conversation, ignoring her.

J.C. stood there, arms folded, waiting for him to finish. It was important to keep her temper in check. Her partner got off on getting her riled up.

The Trojan Arms student apartments were located directly across from USC. The scene was complete chaos. Cops, crime scene techs and campus security fought over turf while more than a hundred looky-loos milled about the parking lot of the 32nd Street Market across the street. The crowd was a combination of scared-looking, white college students and the black and Hispanic residents who lived in the low-income neighborhood surrounding the prestigious university.

When the security officer left, Detective Jessup turned to J.C. "Now what were you saying?"

"You should've called me."

"And you should've called *me* before you went over and interviewed that doctor's wife." He waited for a reaction, but J.C. didn't give him one. "Saw your notes. Looks like you didn't get much from her. I could've helped you pose better questions."

J.C. took a second to carefully craft her response. Anger turned him on, so she couldn't go there. "You were out of the office when I did that interview." She reached out and patted his shoulder. "Just keep me in the loop next time, cowboy. Okay?"

She saw Lieutenant Wilson getting out of a police cruiser and took off in his direction.

"Anybody know where the closest 7-Eleven is?" The lieutenant was chomping on a Snickers. "I need a dose of java. Bad."

A young campus security officer eagerly responded. "Not sure about a 7-Eleven, but there's a gourmet coffee house across the street."

"I ain't paying four bucks for a cup of coffee," Lieutenant Wilson barked.

The security officer shrank away.

"I don't like this," the lieutenant said as J.C. walked up. He cracked his knuckles, then flexed his fingers. "This is murder number three in less than a week. They're a couple of rumors hitting the streets that could make it a long, angry spring in L.A."

"What rumors?" J.C. asked.

"We got one report that a Hispanic gang, 18th Street, might be behind the shootings. Either the Crips or the Bloods, depending on who you believe, screwed 'em on a drug deal so they're gunning down black men. Figured they'd get more attention shooting prominent black guys."

"And the other rumor?"

"The Klan. A white hate group. Some hick white boy gone mad. Take your pick."

"So what do you think?"

"The gang thing sounds believable."

Detective Jessup joined them. "Good morning, Lieutenant."

Lieutenant Wilson barely nodded.

Detective Jessup envied J.C.'s relationship with their boss and tried everything he could think of to get on Lieutenant Wilson's good side. All he needed to do was stop being a jerk.

The two detectives followed the lieutenant over to the body of Nathaniel Allen, sprawled outside the entrance of the apartment complex.

A man wearing a navy blue T-shirt with the words *Crime Scene Investigator* plastered across his chest in white block letters joined them. "So what do we have here?"

Detective Jessup responded even though the question wasn't specifically addressed to him. "I think we have a—"

"Don't say another word." Lieutenant Wilson waved his hand high in the air. "Hey, Officer," he yelled to a uniformed cop a few yards away. "How did this reporter make it past you?"

The officer's face blushed with embarrassment.

The reporter grinned as two other officers approached. "What gave me away?"

"I can smell your kind," the lieutenant said. "Now get the hell away from my crime scene."

Lieutenant Wilson turned to Detective Jessup. "Media Relations and only Media Relations talks to the press. You got that?"

Detective Jessup took a step back. "I didn't know he was a—"

"I don't want to hear what you didn't know. It's your job to know."

J.C. was enjoying this.

"Now go fetch me some coffee. Two creams, three packets of sugar. Real sugar. And it better be from 7-Eleven."

J.C. chuckled to herself as Detective Jessup slithered off.

"What're you smiling at?" the lieutenant griped. "You didn't know he was a reporter either."

J.C. started to defend herself when everyone's attention turned to a tall, red-headed man desperately trying to get past the yellow crime scene tape.

"I need to know what's going on!" the man shouted.

The lieutenant shook his head. "There goes his bank account."

"Who's that?" J.C. asked.

"A scum-sucking agent. He was waiting in the wings to orchestrate Allen's break into the pros."

J.C. felt her cell phone vibrate. She answered it and heard the voice of Patricia Kilgore, the sister-in-law of the second victim, Dr. Banks.

"Sorry, I didn't call you earlier, but we've been busy with funeral arrangements. I was hoping you might have some time to talk."

"Sure." J.C. heard anxiety in Patricia's voice. "I can head over there now."

"No," she said quickly, "not here. Can you meet me in the Marina in an hour?"

# CHAPTER 19

J.C. sat on a long, cushioned bench in the waiting area of the El Torito Mexican restaurant on Admiralty Way, ten minutes early for her meeting with Patricia Kilgore. J.C. was more than anxious to hear what information the woman might have about her murdered brother-in-law.

"Detective Sparks?"

J.C. looked up to find Patricia standing in front of her. J.C. stood and extended her hand. "Thanks for coming."

Patricia looked even more like her sister than she had during their initial meeting. She was a thin woman with short reddish-brown hair.

The hostess showed them to a table with a view of the marina. A waiter appeared seconds later.

"I'll just have a Coke," Patricia said, when the waiter attempted to hand her a menu.

J.C. started to order a salad, then changed her mind and chose the crab enchiladas.

"Thanks for calling me," she began, once the waiter left. "Your brother-in-law's case has been pretty baffling for us. Any information you could provide would be helpful."

Patricia slowly exhaled. "It's been hard for Diana. Quentin was her world."

"I can imagine." J.C. wanted her to get to the point, but knew she had to be patient.

"What I have to tell you is something I've never shared with anyone," Patricia said. "Not even my husband. And I don't want anyone to know that this information came from me."

J.C. hoped that she would not be forced to betray the woman's trust. "Okay. Go ahead."

"I'm not saying that this has anything to do with Quentin's murder, but you said *any* information could be helpful."

J.C. encouraged her along with a nod.

Patricia paused for a long while before continuing. "I think my brother-in-law had a lover." She fiddled with her napkin. "And I think his lover was a man."

J.C. tried not to visibly react. "And what makes you think that?"

"I don't just think it. I know it."

J.C. waited for her to continue.

"Several months ago, I saw him at this Indian restaurant on Melrose. He was having dinner with a very attractive man who looked to be in his early thirties. I just sensed that something was up. When I walked over to their table to say hello, both of them acted as if they'd been caught stealing."

Disappointment flooded J.C.'s face and she fell back against the padded booth. What Patricia had just said was not enough to support her accusation.

"And that's not all," she said hurriedly. "I started following him."

J.C. sat forward again.

"Nearly every Saturday he'd go to a hotel during the lunch hour. I followed him three different times. The first time he went to the Marina Marriott right up the street. Another time the Ritz-Carlton. The third time it was the Airport Hilton on Century."

"Did you actually see him with another man?"

Patricia shook her head. "I hung out in the lobby after Quentin went in and waited. About an hour and a half later, he walked out. And all three times, about fifteen minutes after Quentin left, so did another attractive, well-dressed black man. The same man I saw him with at the restaurant."

J.C. was intrigued but not totally convinced. "I'm sorry, but you're going to need more than that to convince me that they were lovers."

"On three different occasions Quentin walks into a hotel in the middle of the day and leaves ninety minutes later? What else could they be doing?"

"Do you even know for sure that they went to the same room?"

"No. I never followed Quentin up there. I couldn't run the risk of him seeing me."

J.C. pursed her lips.

"There's no reason for two grown men to be hanging out in a hotel room in the middle of the day," Patricia insisted. "I checked and there were no conferences going on at any of those hotels on the days I saw them. Quentin was on the down low. I just know it. He'd always been a little suspect as far as I was concerned. He was just too darn perfect."

J.C. wondered how much of what Patricia was telling her was the result of jealousy over her sister's picture perfect life. "Did you ever share your suspicions with your sister?"

Patricia laughed softly. "Of course not. That would've killed her. Anyway, I doubt Diana would've left him."

Again, J.C. wondered about Patricia's motives.

"I didn't know what to do." Patricia reached for her water glass. "So I didn't do anything except pray that the man had the decency to wear a condom."

# CHAPTER 20

Equipped with a detailed description of Dr. Banks' alleged lover, J.C. drove the short distance to the Marina Marriot.

She took a seat at the bar to the left of the entrance and quietly observed the activity. Windows that stretched to the ceiling sent surges of sunlight into the lobby. Tall leafy trees created a tropical atmosphere.

J.C. ordered a Sprite and mulled over which of the three clerks at the registration desk she should approach. After a few minutes, two of the clerks left, leaving a young black woman alone at the desk.

When J.C. flashed her badge, the clerk's eyes rounded into quarters. "I can't talk to you without getting my manager's permission first." J.C. pegged the girl to be in her early twenties. "And he's out at the moment." She enunciated her words like a speech major.

J.C. ignored her reticence. "I have just a couple of questions. Off the record." There was no such thing as off the record as far as cops were concerned, but people always seemed to loosen up a bit when she said that.

"Do you recognize this man?" She placed the photo of Dr. Banks on the counter.

The woman's eyes signaled recognition, but her lips remained zipped.

"So, you *do* recognize him."

The clerk looked around furtively. "We're trained to protect our guests' privacy. I could get in trouble for talking to you."

"I promise you won't get in trouble. Just tell me what you know."

Her eyes swept the lobby again, then she leaned across the counter and dropped her preppy tone. "That brother's on the D-L. He marched his ass in here at least one Saturday a month just before noon and went straight to the President's Suite where his boy was waiting on him."

"His boy? How do you know someone was waiting for him?"

"Because I checked the other guy in. He was the one who always registered and ordered lunch. Two turkey sandwiches, two root beers and one Caesar salad. Every single time."

"How do you know what they ordered?"

"My friend Miguel told me. He works in room service and delivered the food to their room. Every time he rolled his cart in there, the other guy was dressed in nothing but a robe." She arched an eyebrow.

J.C. pointed to the photograph of Dr. Banks. "Did this man ever check in at the desk?"

"Nope."

"Then how do you know he went to the same room as the other guy?"

She leaned in even further, her head nearly touching J.C.'s. "The third time he came through, I followed him onto the elevator and he got off on the same floor as the President's Suite and headed in that direction." She raised both eyebrows this time as if to say, *case closed*.

"So when they came back the following month, I knew what was up. I remembered the time they'd finished before, so I timed my break so I could walk past the room around the same time this guy," she jabbed a finger at the photograph of Dr. Banks, "should have been coming out. And guess what? He did."

J.C. was finally beginning to believe that Patricia may have been right about her brother-in-law.

"This guy was nice looking for an older guy," the girl said, referring to Dr. Banks, "but the man he was meeting? Straight up fine. I checked him in, so I got to see him up close and personal. He gave me some story about being a songwriter and coming to the hotel because it helped with his creativity. He had a laptop under his arm, but I doubt he ever turned it on. It's a shame." Her lips puckered in disgust. "Men just aren't men anymore."

J.C. eyed the name on the girl's badge. "Hey, Tisha, can you check your records and tell me the name the man checked in under."

Tisha straightened up real quick. "Excuse me, but I need this job. If you want that information, you better come back with a subpoena."

# CHAPTER 21

I hope you know how lucky you are to be married to a secure brother like me."

Vernetta leaned back in her office chair and smiled at the sound of her husband's voice on the telephone.

"If you had some sexist, insecure dude," Jefferson said, "he'd be down there banging on the law firm door, telling you to get your ass home and cook him some food."

It was almost nine and Vernetta still had another hour's worth of editing on a discovery motion. She balanced the phone between her ear and shoulder and continued typing. "I know how good I've got it. I'm the luckiest woman in L.A."

"Yeah, yeah, yeah. I just called to tell you I picked up some Thai food."

"Great. I'll be leaving soon."

"Well, hurry up. I'm horny."

"Why can't you say something romantic, like *I really miss you* or *I can't wait for you to get home so I can make mad, passionate love to you.*"

Vernetta heard him chuckle and could imagine the grin on his face. "You know I ain't with all that mushy stuff. That's why you love me. 'Cuz I keep it real."

Forty-five minutes later, Vernetta had finished putting the final touches on the motion. She had almost made it to the elevators, but took a detour to the ladies' room. As much as she wanted to get home, she couldn't ignore the call of nature.

Making a right off the hallway, she pushed in the door of the ladies' room. Haley was standing in front of the mirror applying lipstick. The color was a shocking red, which provided way too much contrast against her white skin.

"Working late, too?" Vernetta asked, walking up behind her. She figured she should at least attempt to have a civil conversation with the girl. "What case is keeping you so busy?"

"Oh, uh . . . I uh . . ."

She waited for Haley to respond. Her nervous reaction made Vernetta wonder if there might be reason for concern. Had Haley been busy undermining her again? As far as she knew, nothing big was cooking with the Vista Electronics case yet.

"Nothing important," Haley finally said. "I just decided to spend some time catching up on some new case law."

*That's bull.* "Really? That's quite a luxury. I'm usually too busy to spend time on work I can't bill. We need to get you some new assignments," she said playfully.

Haley smiled, then tucked a loose curl behind her ear. "Oh, I have plenty of work. But it pays to keep up with the latest cases. O'Reilly said my explanation of that new Ninth Circuit decision was one of the reasons we won that Vista Electronics case."

"We probably would've gotten it anyway," Vernetta retorted. "We already do work for the company and the Assistant General Counsel loves O'Reilly." *Why was she letting this girl get to her?*

"And now, thank God, he loves me, too." Haley dropped her lipstick into her purse. "Turns out he belongs to the same country club as my father."

*Whoop-dee-doo.* She had given it a try and Haley had only confirmed that it wasn't worth it to even pretend to be her friend.

Vernetta found an empty stall and was glad to find Haley gone when she came out. The girl was always throwing around her family connections. Vernetta was not going to concern herself with Haley's antics tonight.

O'Reilly approached as she was waiting for an elevator. He rarely worked this late. When their eyes met, she saw the same guilt-ridden look that had glazed Haley's face.

"Working late?" Vernetta asked for the second time that night.

"A lawyer's work is never done." He half grinned, then transferred his black briefcase from one hand to the other.

They waited in silence for the next elevator car. O'Reilly was Mr. Personality. Day or night. Vernetta had rarely seen him this tight-lipped. The elevator opened and they rode to the lobby without conversation. When they entered the parking garage, O'Reilly didn't bother to say good-bye.

Vernetta found it strange that both O'Reilly and Haley were working late. Her mind went back to the possibility that the two of them had been working on something pertaining to the Vista Electronics case. *Were they excluding her again?*

As she started up her SUV, she dismissed the thought and scolded herself for being so paranoid.

# CHAPTER 22

Eugene woke up Wednesday morning just before seven with the hangover of all hangovers. He had hoped that the last twenty-four hours had simply been a bad dream. But the shock and embarrassment of the email and the wrongful death lawsuit rushed back to him the second he opened his eyes.

When he arrived home the night before, he had indulged in the one activity guaranteed to ease his pain. Getting blasted. Eugene wasn't much of a drinker, so it didn't take much. After a half pint of Cognac, he could barely stand up. So much for his health kick.

He'd stumbled out of bed in the middle of the night to take a leak and thought about calling Belynda, but decided that he had already burdened her enough with his problems.

An explosion of sound coming from the alarm clock startled him. Eugene reached out to shut it off, but couldn't seem to find the right button. Each shrill buzz felt like a gong pounding inside his head. He finally hurled the clock across the room, denting the wall and shattering it into several pieces.

Eugene stared at the ceiling as he relived the previous day's events. Once Liam left his office, Eugene pulled himself together and decided to face things like a man. He made an appointment with the managing partner of the Corporate Law Department and marched into his office with his head held high. He could handle the lawsuit, but Special's vicious email was another story. Computer hacking was a federal crime. He wanted the firm to deal with that.

Eugene tapped on the office door of Charles W. Benton.

A ruddy-faced man in his mid-sixties, Benton was an introvert who enjoyed drafting contracts more than talking to people. "Have a seat," Benton said.

"No, thanks." Eugene closed the door. "I won't be here that long." He felt an odd sense of power standing over the rich, balding white man. He was actually surprised at how calm he felt. As he peered down at his superior, he was glad he'd worn his Hugo Boss.

"I have a couple of requests." Eugene was careful not to stand so close that Benton might deem him a physical threat. "First, I'd like to take a three-month leave of absence. There are some personal matters that I need to attend to." He would leave it at that. He wasn't about to try to explain away the vile email, and he was glad Benton knew nothing about the lawsuit. Yet.

Benton nodded, seemingly relieved. "I don't think that'll be a problem." He steepled his chubby fingers.

Eugene figured they would eventually ask him to leave the firm. Especially if the lawsuit was widely covered by the media. Ramsey & King valued its reputation more than anything else. His preemptive strike let them off the hook. He had no intention of returning, but he wanted to keep his options open. Just in case.

Benton picked up a silver pen and gently tapped it on the desk, a sign that he was just as uncomfortable with this conversation as Eugene. He was a straight-laced Mormon with eight kids. No telling what he'd thought after reading Special's email.

"I'm not asking for a paid leave, but I'd like my medical benefits to continue."

Benton adjusted his wire-rimmed glasses. "That shouldn't be a problem either."

"My next request—" Eugene stopped to clear his throat. He hated even acknowledging the damn email. "I want to make sure the firm plans to pursue charges against the individual who sent that email. I have an idea of who may be responsible."

Benton nodded. "We've already retained an investigator who's a specialist in computer forensics. You should pass any information you have over to Todd in IT. We're obviously concerned about the vulnerability of our communications system."

Eugene was glad to hear that. Special probably had no idea how much trouble she was in. At the height of his rage, Eugene had wanted to call her, but Liam had talked him out of it. The legal system would deal with her.

Back in his office, Eugene prepared a status memo regarding each of his cases, which took him about two hours to complete. He packed a few personal items and walked out, ignoring everyone he passed. Even his long-time secretary had given him the cold shoulder. That had hurt more than anything else.

Now, as he lay in bed, Eugene realized that his job was the least of his worries. Leaving the firm had been on his mind lately because of the impact of stress on his disease. He could easily afford to take several months off before looking for another job. He had an MBA from Wharton, a Stanford law degree, and was in great shape financially, with a year's salary sitting in a money market account and four times that in stocks and bonds. The home he purchased in foreclosure was practically paid for and he owned a four-unit apartment complex.

Eugene sat up, lifted his laptop from the nightstand and logged onto the Internet. Liam had given him the name of a friend who worked at the Gay and Lesbian Center in L.A. Eugene was hoping the organization might be able to refer him to a good lawyer who would be as outraged by the lawsuit as he was.

He pulled up the organization's website, jotted down the address, then hopped out of bed. After a bowl of instant oatmeal with chopped bananas and a quick shower, he noticed that his hangover had all but disappeared. His spirits had lifted considerably by the time he hopped into his BMW. He popped in a Angie Stone CD, hit the garage door opener, and backed down the driveway.

It was not until he had almost reached the street that he saw the mass of black dots scattered about his driveway. He threw the car into park and jumped out without turning off the engine.

"Goddamn it!" Dozens of tiny nails were embedded in his tires.

He circled the car in an angry rage, gingerly dodging the nails. All four of his tires were ruined.

Eugene pulled the car out into the street and parked it along the curb. He took his BlackBerry from his briefcase and fumbled through his electronic phonebook until he found Special's name and number. Maya had insisted that he have the numbers of the people closest to her in case of an emergency.

He was trying to get right with God, but he wasn't about to turn the other cheek. If Special wanted a war, he would give her one. He dialed the first three digits of her number, then stopped. There was no way he would be able to have a civil conversation with her, so why even try? He thought about calling Vernetta, then dialed Nichelle's law office instead.

She picked up on the second ring. "You need to tell your buddy Special to lay off." Eugene tried to sound calm.

"What are you talking about?" Nichelle asked.

"She hacked into my law firm's computer system and sent a vicious, defamatory email to everybody in the firm. I'll send you a copy. And she also tossed nails in my driveway, ruining my tires."

Nichelle gasped. "How do you know Special had anything to do with any of that?"

"The same way *you* know she did," Eugene snarled. "I'm not going to call the cops this time only out of respect for Maya. But if she keeps fucking with me, I won't be the only one defending a lawsuit."

Nichelle didn't say anything.

"And your lawsuit is bullshit," Eugene said. "I loved Maya. I wouldn't have purposely—"

"*You* made the decision not to tell Maya about your other life and *you* infected her. That's negligence any way you look at it."

Nichelle's haughty tone surprised him. She was usually pretty non-confrontational. Of all Maya's friends, he liked her the best.

"We'll let a judge decide that," he replied, then hung up.

Eugene pulled his Auto Club card from his wallet, dialed the 800 number and requested a tow truck to take him to the nearest tire store.

# CHAPTER 23

Later that evening, Special and Nichelle sat at the bar of Magic Johnson's T.G.I. Friday's restaurant in the Ladera Center, staring up at the television screen.

"How much longer before they run your interview?" Special asked anxiously.

Nichelle spread her hands. "I have no idea."

"Don't take this the wrong way, girlfriend, but what did you wear?"

Nichelle rolled her eyes. "I know how to dress, okay?"

Special only hoped so. At the moment, Nichelle was wearing leopard-skin jeans and a black chiffon blouse with way too many ruffles.

J.C. slid onto the stool next to Nichelle. "Where's Vernetta?"

Special yawned. "Couldn't make it. Billable hours."

"How's everything going with you and Clayton?" Nichelle asked.

"Okay, I guess. But it's not easy dating a man who lives way across the country."

"I thought Vernetta was fixing you up with Jefferson's cousin," J.C. said.

Special flicked the air with her hand. "That man wasn't even out here a week before some hoochie secretary at his office snagged his ass. It's Vernetta's fault. She took too long to set it up."

Nichelle laughed. "Girl, you—"

"Shhhhh! This is it!" Special seemed more excited about the story than Nichelle. "Hey, Keith," Special called out to the bartender, "can you turn up the volume for just a sec?"

The bartender hit a button on the counter and the anchorman's voice drowned out the soft jazz from the restaurant's speaker system.

> *In one of the first such cases filed in L.A. county, a local attorney is being sued for wrongful death for allegedly infecting his fiancée with the AIDS virus.*

The anchorman tossed to a reporter in the field who gave a brief summary of the lawsuit. A photograph of Eugene filled the screen.

"How'd they get that picture?" Special asked.

Nichelle smiled. "Eugene's law firm website."

The three friends watched in rapt attention as the scene switched to Nichelle's office.

Special squeezed Nichelle's arm. "You look good, girl!"

Nichelle sat behind her desk dressed in a conservative, dark blue pinstriped suit. The camera moved in for her sound bite.

*African-American women are being stricken with the AIDS virus at a faster rate than any other group. And the majority of these women are being infected through heterosexual sex. They are innocent victims who know nothing about their men's secret homosexual lives. One of my closest friends, Maya Washington, died because of her fiancé's deceit. The purpose of this lawsuit is twofold. First, to obtain financial compensation for Maya's family, and second, to let Eugene Nelson and other men like him know that they can't endanger women's lives and get away with it.*

"You go, girl!" Special cheered when the report was over. She gave Nichelle a high five, followed by a big hug.

"Nice publicity," J.C. said. "How'd you swing that?"

"A friend of mine runs the assignment desk at Channel 2. I have interviews with two radio stations tomorrow."

"Cool!" Special beamed. "I hope this case gets so much publicity Eugene can't even find a closet to hide in."

"I heard you've been pretty busy lately." J.C. leaned forward over the bar to make eye contact with Special. "I got a call from Eugene earlier today."

"He called me, too," Nichelle said. "I already read her the riot act."

Special picked up her Long Island iced tea and took a noisy sip. "I have no idea what y'all are talking about."

"Special, you better back off," J.C. warned. "And you better hope nobody saw you toss those nails in Eugene's driveway and that his firm isn't able to trace that email back to you. I promised him that you weren't going to bother him again."

"Wasn't me." She picked up one of the nachos they had ordered and crunched on it.

"Eugene sent me a copy of that email," Nichelle said. "How in the world did you even come up with such a spiteful idea in the first place?"

"That man is a pathological liar. That's part and parcel of being on the down low."

"Just leave him alone, or I'll arrest you myself." J.C. signaled the bartender and ordered a Sprite. "So what's the next step with the lawsuit, Nichelle?"

"Eugene has to answer the complaint. But I wouldn't be surprised if he tries to get it dismissed."

Special stopped mid-crunch. "He won't be able to, will he?"

"I doubt it. At least not this early on."

"Good. I can't wait for you to put that boy on the witness stand." She pointed a finger at the now-muted TV screen. "At least that brother right there got what he deserved."

J.C. looked up and saw a photograph of Nathaniel Allen, the star running back at Fox Hills Junior College, flash across the screen.

"Special!" Nichelle glared at her. "How can you be so mean? The man was murdered."

"I know for a fact that brother was on the down low, too. No telling how many women he infected."

J.C. put down her Sprite. "What did you say?"

"You heard me. That brother was all up in the closet."

"How do you know that?" J.C. asked.

"You know Shawnta, my braider at the Emerald Chateau? Well, she knows this guy named Donte who was one of Nathaniel Allen's boys. Or I should say, *girls*."

Nichelle folded her arms over her ample bosom. "I don't believe that. You think every guy you meet is gay."

"You don't have to believe it. Shawnta didn't believe it either until Donte showed her a picture of the two of them together."

"A picture of two men together doesn't prove anything," Nichelle said dismissively.

"It does when it's taken with a hidden camera and shows two you know whats. Shawnta told me Donte was in the shop yesterday crying like a baby."

"He must've really loved him," Nichelle said sadly.

*"Loved him?"* Special crinkled up her nose. "Hell, nah. Donte's a major whore. He was waiting for that boy to win the Heisman trophy and go pro so he could confront him with the photographs. He kept extra copies of 'em in a safe deposit box at Bank of America. Donte was crying over all that blackmail money he won't be getting."

"That's awful," Nichelle said.

"It is what it is."

J.C. drained the remainder of her Sprite and hopped off the bar stool. "Gotta go."

"Already?" Nichelle said. "They should have a table for us soon."

J.C.'s face glowed with excitement. "I think Special may've just given me some information that might help me solve not one murder, but three."

# CHAPTER 24

Nichelle arrived at the O'Reilly & Finney offices just before seven o'clock the following night. Vernetta had agreed to help Nichelle work out a trial strategy for the lawsuit against Eugene. Wrongful death wasn't her area of expertise, but she knew lots of tricks of the trade that might be useful at trial.

"So Jamal isn't helping you?" Vernetta asked.

Nichelle pulled a stack of cases from her satchel. "Nope. His managing partner vetoed that. They're concerned about the type of publicity this case is likely to attract."

"Well, you've got Sam."

"He's not about to help me. He doesn't even think we should be suing Eugene. But don't worry. It's been a while since I litigated, but I have a pretty good handle on everything. I just wanted to bounce a few ideas off of you."

They discussed several recent negligence and wrongful death cases involving HIV and AIDS and made a list of the legal elements Nichelle would need to prove. It was close to nine when they finally decided to pack up.

"I need to drop off a document for O'Reilly's secretary," Vernetta said. "I'll be right back."

When she reached the secretary's cubicle, she heard laughter coming from O'Reilly's office. Male laughter *and* female laughter. She stood there, eavesdropping through the closed door.

Vernetta saw the doorknob turn and dashed into the secretary's cubicle and pretended to be writing a note. When she turned around, Haley was standing behind her, white as a sheet.

"I . . . uh . . . I was . . . just looking for a document in O'Reilly's office," Haley volunteered.

Vernetta had not asked a question, so her unsolicited explanation made her sound guiltier than she looked.

Her blond hair was mussed and her red lipstick was smeared to the left of her lower lip. Haley noticed Vernetta examining her untidy state and quickly wiped her mouth and raked her fingers through her hair.

"O'Reilly forgot to give me some documents I needed for the Vista Electronics case," Haley offered, again without solicitation.

*But he hasn't left the office yet.*

Vernetta's mind raced. *Was O'Reilly stupid enough to be messing around with Haley? And here in the office of all places? Men were such knuckleheads when it came to sex.*

"Which documents were you looking for? I might have copies."

"Uh . . . the . . . oh, never mind. It's late and I'm exhausted. I better be getting home."

"Are you okay, Haley?"

"Yeah, of course." She ran her fingers through her hair again. "Why do you ask?"

"You just seem a little flustered."

"I'm fine." She started walking away.

"Good night," Vernetta called after her.

Haley turned back and flashed a syrupy smile. "Good night to you, too."

Vernetta was dying to charge into O'Reilly's office and bust him. He was probably inside with his ear pressed to the door. Instead, she scampered back to her own office.

She closed the door behind her and rushed over to her desk, her heart beating wildly.

"What's the matter?" Nichelle asked.

"I have the gossip of the century."

"Do share."

"You know that little witch, Haley?"

Nichelle nodded.

"She's messing around with the managing partner."

"And how do you know that?"

"I just caught them."

Nichelle stood up. "You caught them? Here? In the office?"

"Yeah—I mean no. I didn't actually *see* them. But I heard laughter coming from O'Reilly's office and then Haley walked out with her hair messed up and her lipstick smeared."

Nichelle sat back down. "I don't think that evidence would hold up in a court of law, counselor."

Vernetta plopped down behind her desk. "I'm telling you, he's screwing that girl. I could tell by the look on her face. The same guilty look both of them had when I saw them here late a couple nights ago."

Nichelle apparently wasn't buying it. "That doesn't make sense. He would not take the risk of messing around with her in the office."

"We're talking about sex," Vernetta said. "Men take stupid risks for a five-second orgasm all the time."

"If they wanted to mess around, why wouldn't they go to O'Reilly's place? Or hers?"

"Haley lives in the same apartment building as two other associates. And O'Reilly has a live-in girlfriend." O'Reilly's significant other was a fortyish interior decorator whom everyone at the firm was predicting would finally get him to the altar.

"Well, it's not like they couldn't afford a hotel."

Vernetta shrugged. "I can't explain why they're screwing around here. I just know they are." The firm had a strict policy prohibiting dating between employees in a direct or indirect reporting relationship. Partner-associate liaisons were a definite no-no.

Nichelle stubbornly shook her head. "I just can't see O'Reilly being that stupid."

"I can," Vernetta said adamantly. "Those two are having an affair. I just know it."

# CHAPTER 25

Special circled the lower level of LAX for the third time, trying to keep an eye on the car in front of her and dial her cell phone at the same time. Clayton had promised to call the minute his plane landed. His flight was obviously late. Special just needed to know how late.

"Whatever happened to a human being answering the friggin' phone?" she said out loud, as an automated voice gave her a menu of options. She had to make four selections before finally learning that Clayton's plane wouldn't be landing for another twenty minutes.

Special found a spot in the short-term parking lot across from the Delta terminal. She was glad to have the additional time before Clayton arrived. She'd been on edge all day long and knew she had to get her act together. She was excited about seeing him, but still hadn't been able to quell her concerns that her man might be a fraud.

She reached underneath her seat and pulled out her worn copy of J.L. King's book, *On the Down Low: A Journey into the Lives of "Straight" Black Men Who Sleep with Men*. Over the past month, she had devoured the book and then scoured the Internet for anything else she could find about men on the down low.

She'd also read two books on the subject written by women, *Faith Under Fire: Betrayed by a Thing Called Love* by LaJoyce Brookshire, and a book written by J.L. King's wife, Brenda Stone Browder, *On the Up and Up: A Survival Guide for Women Living with Men on the Down Low*. Special's heart went out to those sisters. She was determined to learn from their mistakes.

She turned on the overhead light, quickly flipped to Chapter 13 of King's book and reread it for the umpteenth time.

In this chapter, King described various categories of DL men. Some were quintessential family men and presented themselves to the public as the ideal boyfriend or husband. If she were right about Clayton, he would probably fall into that group.

Turning the book face down on her lap, Special closed her eyes and leaned back against the headrest. She had been back and forth all morning long, mulling over the factors that said Clayton might be perpetrating. Then, minutes later, she would come up with a longer list that contradicted each one of them.

She checked the time on the dashboard clock, turned the key to the alternator position, inserted her Queen Latifah CD, and hit track seven. Queen Latifah's remake of *California Dreamin'* had a way of chilling her out better than three glasses of Merlot.

Thirty minutes later, Special slowly drove along the airport walkway, leaning her head down to peer out of the passenger window, hoping to spot Clayton. She stopped at the sight of a wiry man in a bright, flower-print jumpsuit and a closely cropped auburn Afro. He was prancing down the sidewalk with a pronounced feminine gait.

"Now that's what I'm talking about." Special watched the man swing his hips from side to side. "Why can't you down low assholes give a sister a sign like that brother right there?"

She pulled over to the curb, rolled down the passenger window, and called out to the man. "You lookin' mighty good in that outfit, my brother. Go on with yo' bad self!"

The man stopped, put his hands on his hips, did a slow pirouette, then sashayed on down the sidewalk.

Special was still laughing when Clayton knocked on the driver's window, causing her to jump so high she almost hit her head on the roof of the car. She threw open the door and fell into Clayton's arms.

"Miss me?" he asked, pulling her to him.

"Every day and every night," Special said.

Clayton was only wearing jeans and a T-shirt but he still looked hella sexy. He tossed his bag into the backseat and they took off. He held her right hand as she drove and leaned over to kiss her at every traffic light.

"I can't wait until we get to your place," Clayton said. "I've missed you so much, and I'm horny as hell."

Special blinked. Down low brothers supposedly had unusually strong sex drives.

Clayton started going on and on about some project at work. He stopped when Special turned into the Ladera Center.

"Where we going?"

"I need to make a Starbucks run."

"I'm tired as hell," Clayton complained. "Can't you make some coffee when you get home?"

"If I get a couple extra shots of caffeine, I'll be all hyped up." She reached over and gave his upper thigh a quick pat. "I just wanna make sure I have enough energy for everything I have planned for you tonight."

Clayton's lips formed a slow grin. "Well, what you waiting for then? Let's go get your coffee."

Special lucked out and found a parking spot right in front of the Jamba Juice, next door to the Starbucks. Before she could get out, Clayton jogged around and opened her door. He pulled her out and kissed her again.

Special had a dual purpose for this stop. She wanted to observe Clayton in the presence of other men. DL brothers, according to *On the Down Low*, had a discreet way of signaling each other.

This particular Starbucks, a popular neighborhood hangout, was always crawling with black men. As they approached, several men lounged in wrought iron chairs out front and more filled cushy chairs inside. Outside to the left, groups of men crowded around tables observing two chess matches.

Special joined a long line of customers. "You want something?"

Clayton kissed her on the side of the neck. "Just you."

A muscular black man in a red Lycra T-shirt entered from a side door and walked in Clayton's direction. The man gave Clayton a barely perceptible backward nod accompanied by a glance that was way too long for Special's taste. *Were they signaling each other with her standing right there?* She turned around and stared up at Clayton.

"Ma'am, may I help you?"

Clayton nudged her. "Your turn to order, babe."

"Oh . . . uh, a tall White Chocolate Mocha," Special said weakly.

"You okay?" Clayton apparently noticed her distress.

She tried to play it off. "I'm fine."

The clerk wrote Special's name on the side of a paper cup and they stepped away from the counter. More people entered the Starbucks. Every black man who approached eyed Clayton and nodded. *Dang! Is every black man in here gay?*

Special knew she had to calm down. The way one man greeted another was *not* a bona fide confirmation of his sexual orientation.

"Where's the restroom?" Clayton asked.

She pointed toward a short hallway at the back of the store. Special watched him as he walked away. *At least he didn't walk gay*. But neither did Eugene. And look where Maya ended up. Special gazed skyward and inhaled. *Girl, I miss you so much. Give me a sign, Maya. Please, help me figure this thing out.*

The clerk called her name and Special retrieved her drink. As she grabbed a napkin from a side counter, a smiling Clayton returned. "Drink up, baby, and let's go get this party started." He kissed her lightly on the lips.

Special's hand tightened around her drink. She would get the answer she needed soon enough. By tomorrow night, if Clayton was on the down low, he was about to get his ass outted big time.

# CHAPTER 26

Y ou look bushed, girl," Jefferson said when Vernetta trudged into the bedroom, still reeling from her discovery about Haley and O'Reilly.

She yawned and dropped her purse on the dresser. "That's certainly an understatement."

Jefferson was lying in bed, propped up on two pillows, one hand behind his head, watching basketball highlights.

Vernetta stood over the bed. "Guess what I just found out?"

"What?" His eyes did not leave the television screen.

"I think O'Reilly and Haley are messing around."

"Is that right?" He still didn't look her way.

"Is that all you have to say?"

Jefferson finally gave her his full attention. "What am I supposed to say? He's a man and she's a woman. And Haley ain't exactly bad on the eyes. She's kinda pale for my taste, but she's got a nice ass for a white girl."

"Since when did you have time to check out Haley's ass?"

"I wasn't checking out her ass. It was just there. Staring at me."

Vernetta pulled the pillow from behind Jefferson's head and started slugging him with it.

He laughed and blocked her blows with his forearm, then snatched the pillow back.

"Don't be mad at the girl. She's just using what she's got to get what she wants. That's the American way."

"Well, it makes me sick to my stomach." Vernetta stepped out of her heels and started to undress. "I'm really screwed now."

"I would have to agree. If Haley's banging the big boss, sounds like you better get on her good side."

"I would if she had one.

"Just stop trippin' and make friends with the girl."

"That's not going to happen." Vernetta slipped a nightgown over her head and plopped into the armchair next to the bed. "She's the one who needs to be nice to me. If I expose their little affair, she'll be the one out of the door, not O'Reilly."

Vernetta tried to watch television, but couldn't get Haley and O'Reilly off her mind.

"You, okay, babe?" Jefferson asked. "Ever since you got passed up for partnership, you've been in a constant funk."

*Passed up for partnership.* Vernetta hated the sound of the words. "Have I?"

Jefferson turned over on his side and faced her. "Lately, the first thing you do when you get home is start complaining about Haley or O'Reilly or the firm. You never talk about your cases anymore. Why don't you tell me what you're working on?"

She shrugged. "Nothing exciting."

"Babe, I don't understand what's going on with you. It's obvious that you don't like working at the firm as much as you used to. Why don't you just leave? It's not like you can't find another job. And we have enough cash saved that it wouldn't be a big deal if you didn't work for a while."

Vernetta didn't answer.

"Talk to me. All this moping around ain't good."

Her cheeks filled with air and she let it slowly seep out. "I don't feel like talking right now," she said softly.

"Even about adoption?"

Vernetta rose from the chair and sat down on the edge of the bed. "Now that's a shocker."

After finding out that they couldn't have kids of their own, Jefferson had flat out refused to consider adoption. She clicked on the lamp on the nightstand.

"So when did this change of heart occur?"

"I've been thinking about it for a while. I guess I just needed time to adjust to the idea."

She leaned down to kiss him. "That's the best news I've heard in weeks. But I need to figure out what's going on with my career before bringing a kid into this mess of a life I have."

Jefferson pulled her closer. "Your life is not a mess. You just need a nice long break from the law. When my project winds down, let's take some time off. Let's go to Hawaii for a week. Strike that. Let's splurge and take two weeks."

"Two weeks? Then I'd never make partner for sure. I need to show my total dedication to the firm right now. I'm expected to work until at least ten o'clock every night. Bill more hours than everybody else. Never take a vacation. Basically make the firm my life."

"And that's the way you want to live?" Jefferson asked.

"Nope."

"Then why are you doing it?"

She took a long time to answer. "Because that's what it takes to make partner."

"So, basically what you're telling me is you're going to stay at a job you hate and work yourself into the ground, even if it gives you a stroke?"

"I don't hate my job and I'm not going to have a stroke," Vernetta said, forcing a laugh. She pulled away to turn off the lamp, then stretched out next to him in bed. "I'm in excellent health."

"Physically, maybe. But not emotionally."

She didn't feel like trying to defend her career decision. She went mute and silently thanked her husband for not pushing the issue further. Nestling her face into the crook of Jefferson's neck, she enjoyed his scent. His body heat. The closeness.

Vernetta had almost dozed off when Jefferson's fingers crept underneath her satin nightgown. She felt exhausted. Too exhausted to make love, but she could not fight the rising swell of sexual excitement her husband could so easily arouse in her.

Jefferson rolled her onto her back, tugged her nightgown up and over her head and bent to kiss her breasts.

Vernetta moaned, barely loud enough for him to hear, then reached out for him, longing for more of him, all of him. And when he did finally come to her, she gripped him about the neck, arching her body to meet the rhythm of his.

Jefferson whispered gruff expressions of his own pleasure, while rocking and riding her body in long, penetrating waves. Going deeper and deeper, pulling away, then easing back to her.

As she came, just seconds before he did, she was grateful for the respite. Happy and satisfied to allow something besides work to totally consume her.

# CHAPTER 27

The Ida B. Wells Women's Center was the kind of place most people drove past without noticing. Sandwiched between a barbershop and a furniture store on L.A.'s southside, it looked like every other weathered storefront that lined Slauson Boulevard.

Nichelle entered the building and made her way to Wanda Richardson's office.

A petite woman in her early fifties with corn-rowed hair, Wanda greeted her with a motherly hug. "I'm glad you came early. Let me show you around before the women get here."

Wanda had arranged for Nichelle to talk with members of an HIV support group which met at the center twice a month. As part of her continuing research, Nichelle felt it was important to talk to women who were living with the disease.

"Here's where we conduct our classes." Wanda bubbled with pride as she guided Nichelle around the center. "This month we're doing interviewing skills and resume writing." The center also housed a day care center and sponsored after-school programs.

Wanda had spent years lobbying the city to donate the space, and once she had accomplished that goal, she kept it going through fundraising events and grants. "The group sessions are held in here." Wanda led Nichelle into a spacious room with soothing midnight blue walls.

"Wow!" Nichelle said.

"Pretty nice, huh? The wife of one of our board members is an interior decorator. She really hooked us up."

The room had the feel of an expensive day spa. Two eight-foot couches were surrounded by huge, leafy plants in colorful clay pots. Abstract art and lamps that resembled sculptures added a touch of elegance. Nichelle could smell the scent of eucalyptus. Mahogany folding chairs formed a circle in the center of the room.

Back in Wanda's office, Nichelle learned a bit about the background of the group members. "We usually have anywhere from ten to fifteen women. About half of them agreed to talk to you." She explained that

Nichelle would be meeting a Macy's salesperson, a college professor, two women who worked in health care, a software engineer, a rape crisis counselor, and a lawyer. All of the women had contracted HIV through heterosexual sex.

Just after seven, the women began to trickle in. Nichelle had not expected to meet such attractive, vibrant women who bore no visible signs of their illness. They laughed and mingled until Wanda called the session to order. She introduced everyone, then turned the floor over to Nichelle.

"The purpose of my visit," Nichelle began, "is to try to understand HIV from the perspective of women who are living with it." She checked her notes. "I guess I'll start with the most difficult question first. How did it happen to you?"

Darlene, the college professor, seemed eager to respond. "Sheer stupidity," she said with a gentle laugh. "I simply didn't think HIV was something that could touch me because I wasn't a gay man or an I-V drug user. I was in a monogamous relationship with someone who professed to be committed to God and to me. I had absolutely no reason to suspect that he was having sex with men."

"How long has it been since you were diagnosed?" Nichelle asked.

"Six years and I'm doing great." Darlene smiled big and high-fived the air.

The other women nodded encouragingly.

"But by no means is it easy," Darlene clarified, as if being too happy might backfire on her. "I don't have the energy level I used to have. I still have to take twelve pills a day and I battle with occasional nausea and dry mouth. And then there's the stigma of being HIV positive."

Lafaye, a dental assistant, concurred. "For the first year after I found out, I told everybody I got the disease from a patient. I was too ashamed to tell anybody. But I don't hide it anymore. If just one woman knows that it happened to me, she might just realize that it could also happen to her, too, and make the decision to protect herself."

"So you didn't practice safe sex?" Nichelle asked.

Lafaye, who appeared to be in her early thirties, blushed with embarrassment. "I thought the fact that my boyfriend didn't want to use a condom meant I was the only one in his life. In my mind, you only used protection with someone you didn't trust."

After that admission, the other women seemed to loosen up. "It sounds stupid," said Gloria, a registered nurse and the only Latina of the group, "but my boyfriend complained that he couldn't feel anything when he wore a condom. I guess I was afraid that if I didn't give in, he wouldn't want to be with me."

A visible chill went through Nichelle as she recalled the many times she had not insisted on using protection. She was astounded to learn that HIV was also devastating the Hispanic community. Gloria pointed out that HIV infection was the fourth leading cause of death for Hispanic women ages thirty-four to forty-four.

"I have to say I'm surprised that I don't get the sense that any of you are angry at the men who infected you."

There was a chortle of laughter from all six of the women. "That's because we've been coming here," said Teri. Nichelle had correctly pegged her as the lawyer because she was the only one wearing a suit. "You should've been within the vicinity during the first six months after I learned that I was HIV positive. I was ready to kill any man who had the nerve to look at me. I was shell-shocked for months. My fiancé was a successful stockbroker *and* a body builder. The thought that he was gay never crossed my mind."

"But these guys claim they aren't gay?"

"That's complete bull." Kiana, the Macy's sales assistant, crossed a pair of long, sleek legs. She was nineteen years old, but could easily pass for sixteen. "They're hiding behind this *I'm just a freak* crap. My boyfriend was in a rap group, if you can believe that, and tried to say *I* infected *him*. But I later confirmed that he had definitely been screwing other men."

Seneca rustled about in her seat. "Well, my husband wasn't gay," she said quietly. The software engineer had remained at her husband's side during his lengthy battle with the disease. "He was infected by a woman."

The other women collectively rolled their eyes.

"That's another big problem," said Brenda, the rape crisis counselor. "Even when the signs are staring us in the face, we refuse to believe that our wonderful, manly men are out there sleeping with other men."

Seneca was about to defend herself when Wanda intervened. "We do have rules here, ladies," she gently reminded them. "No matter what, we respect each other's views and feelings. People seem to forget that women are also infecting men. Men who are not gay *or* on the down low." She turned to Nichelle. "There's a big misconception that we can only contract HIV from a man who's sleeping with another man. That's just plain wrong. HIV is an equal opportunity disease."

Seneca sat more erect, as if Wanda had just proven her point.

"Do you have men in your lives now?" Nichelle asked no one in particular.

Everyone nodded except Seneca.

"And can you believe that I meet guys who know I'm HIV positive, but still don't want to wear a condom?" Kiana said.

The look on Nichelle's face conveyed that she couldn't.

"They think they're safe because I'm taking medication and because it's supposedly harder for men to get it from women. But it's possible to get reinfected and I'm not about to let that happen."

The door opened and another woman rushed in. "Sorry I'm late," she said as she breathlessly took a seat. "I'm Vickie."

Nichelle thanked her for coming and asked her to share her story.

"I don't have HIV," she said. "But I lost my father to AIDS six years ago. He told us he had pneumonia and we had no reason to think otherwise. You just don't think of your sixty-three-year-old father as being gay."

"I'm sorry," Nichelle said.

"That's just the beginning of the story," Vickie said with a stiff smile. "Because of the medical privacy laws, the doctors never told my mother that my father had HIV. If she'd known, she would've been tested and started taking medication. She just died of complications from AIDS two months ago. First there was the pain of losing my father, followed by a lot of anger and confusion after finally learning the truth when my mother became ill. Then my sisters and I had to watch her die only because she didn't get treatment."

Silence blanketed the room for a full minute. Nichelle scanned the circle of faces. "Is there anything you'd like to tell other women?" she asked of no one in particular.

"Use a condom," said Brenda, the counselor. "No matter what. Love yourself more than you love any man."

"Get tested," said Darlene, the college professor. "Even if you think you're not at risk. And demand that anyone you sleep with be tested, too. The disease isn't a death sentence anymore. Me and Magic Johnson are living proof of that."

Nichelle waited, but it appeared that the other women didn't have anything to add. Then Gloria, the nurse, spoke up.

"Don't be so judgmental of others." She toyed with the keys in her lap. "Some people assumed I got infected because I was promiscuous. And that's exactly what I used to think about people who got HIV. But I didn't do anything wrong but love my man. So be careful about judging others because you just might end up in their shoes."

# CHAPTER 28

J.C. drove westbound on the Century Freeway with a determined sense of purpose. Sometimes police work was all about instinct. J.C. was convinced that she was about to uncover evidence that would conclusively link the deaths of the three murdered men.

She now realized with frightening certainty that the deaths of the View Park doctor and that running back had nothing to do with a gang rivalry or white supremacists. Even before Special's revelation about Nathaniel Allen, her gut told her that the shootings were not random attacks. These killings were motivated by rage or revenge. Maybe both.

And now she had a very plausible theory to support what her gut was telling her. Both the doctor and the football player were dead because they were on the down low. J.C. was sure of it.

The excitement of her discovery made her want to run straight to the lieutenant with her theory. But good detectives were thorough. And J.C. was a good detective. She knew it was important to take her time, gather all the facts, and make sure that her theory was airtight. And at the moment, she had one more loose end to tie up: Marcus Patterson, the engineer killed at the Ramada Inn. If she could prove that the first victim was living a secret gay life, that would cinch her theory.

Patterson worked as a software engineer for Raycom. Interviews with his wife, sister, and two brothers led nowhere. There was no way J.C. could just come right out and ask his grieving family if Patterson had a secret, male lover. But there was someone else who might be able to lead her to the information she needed.

J.C. exited the freeway at Nash Street. Minutes later, she entered the Raycom lobby and asked for Shondra Simpson.

When Patterson's long-time secretary greeted her, J.C. was surprised to see a woman in her mid-forties. On the telephone, Shondra sounded much younger.

"I don't have a lot of time." She displayed none of the typical uneasiness most people exhibited when a cop showed up asking questions. "My new boss isn't going to cut me any slack when her work isn't done at the end of the day."

Shondra was professionally dressed in a simple black skirt and white blouse. Her hair was pulled back into a tight bun and her long bangs fell into her eyes.

"As I told you over the telephone, I'm investigating Mr. Patterson's death. I was hoping you might be able to fill in some blanks for me."

They walked to the farthest corner of the lobby and sat down on furniture that looked like huge toy blocks with cushions on top.

J.C. assumed that in a corporate environment like this, most bosses, particularly male bosses, had a special bond with their secretaries, sharing things they might not share with others, including their wives. Even if no such bond existed, secretaries often knew things about their superiors that no one else did.

"I'm not going to waste time beating around the bush," J.C. said. "I'm looking into an allegation that Mr. Patterson might've had a lover."

Shondra didn't react. "I didn't get into Marcus' personal life."

"I understand that you two were pretty close." Both Patterson's wife and brother had confirmed that.

"We were. But only professionally. He was a wonderful man to work for. He treated you like you mattered. Not like a lot of people around here."

J.C. waited for her to go on, but Shondra left it at that.

"So, did he have a lover?"

"I don't know, and I don't go around spreading rumors."

"I think you know more than you're saying."

Shondra shrugged. "You can think what you want."

"Don't you want to help the police find your boss' killer?"

Shondra's eyes refused to meet hers. "If I could, I would."

"I think you can," J.C. pushed. "So, we can talk here, or we can talk down at Parker Center."

Finally, J.C. saw a hint of a crack in the woman's tough exterior. Shondra pursed her lips and looked away. "I'll talk to you, but not here."

Shortly after five, Shondra walked through the door of a Denny's restaurant three blocks away and eased into the booth across from J.C. "I have acting classes at six-thirty. So we have to make this quick."

An actress, J.C. thought. That explained a lot.

"I think the shooting of your boss was personal. If he was having an affair with someone, that person could possibly have information that could be key to our investigation."

"Is this off the record?"

"It depends."

"On what?"

"On what you have to tell me."

"Look, Marcus' wife is a nice lady, and her husband hasn't even been dead a good two weeks. She doesn't need this."

J.C. felt a tingle of excitement. Shondra knew something. J.C. decided to try bluffing her. "Look, I know for a fact that Patterson was having an affair."

Shondra clucked her tongue. "So what's this? *Law & Order 101*? You act like you know something you don't and then I spill my guts and tell all. Get real." Her words were drenched in sarcasm.

"And I know," J.C. said, plowing ahead, "that he was having an affair with a man."

This time Shondra's acting talent failed her. Her mouth gaped open and her rigid posture turned limp. "I need you to talk to me, Shondra."

She was about to speak when the waitress appeared. Shondra ordered a vegetarian burger. J.C. asked for the real thing.

J.C. was surprised to see a lone tear roll down Shondra's left cheek.

"Marcus was so confused." Shondra wiped her face with her napkin. "I know he loved his wife, but he couldn't help himself. He was attracted to men. I can't condone what he did, but I know he really struggled with it."

Shondra ended up skipping her acting lesson and spent the next two hours telling J.C. everything she knew about Marcus Patterson and his secret life. He did not have a steady man as far as Shondra knew, and arranged most of his hookups over the Internet. He had planned to meet someone for breakfast at the Ramada Inn the day he was killed, but Shondra didn't know who. Marcus had confided in her to a degree, but he had never disclosed specifics.

After cheesecake and coffee, J.C. practically skipped back to her car. She couldn't wait to talk to Lieutenant Wilson. She was certain they had a serial killer on their hands.

A killer who was targeting men on the down low.

# CHAPTER 29

Vernetta sat in O'Reilly's office discussing her legal argument for a discovery motion she had to argue in a few days. She felt so relaxed it was almost like old times.

"Sounds like you have everything under control," O'Reilly said. "Just don't expect Judge Miller to know the facts because he never reads the briefs. Be prepared to recount all the hoops opposing counsel has put you through, even though it's in your papers."

For weeks, they had been trying to get some medical records and other documents from a plaintiff in an age discrimination case. The opposing counsel blocked them at every turn, even though he had no legitimate legal basis for withholding the records.

"I definitely will. At least Miller is one of the nicest judges on the bench. I argued my first motion before him and he cut me a lot of slack."

Haley stuck her head in the door. "What are you two up to?"

Vernetta had never seen a smile as big as the one that suddenly radiated across O'Reilly's face.

"C'mon in." He waved Haley inside. "We should've invited you to join us. You're on this case, too."

Haley pranced in and took a seat on the couch to the right of O'Reilly's desk. She crossed her legs, and her skirt, which was way too short for an office setting, inched up almost to her crotch. She tugged it down, but it slid right back up again.

"We're discussing the Jackson discovery motion," O'Reilly explained.

Vernetta could almost swear he was staring between her legs.

"Vernetta," Haley said teasingly, "I can't believe you didn't invite me to this meeting. After all, I *did* write the motion."

*No, you wrote a crappy draft of the motion that I spent two hours rewriting.* "You didn't miss much," Vernetta said.

"I think we've covered everything." O'Reilly directed his words to Vernetta, but his eyes were on Haley.

Now that his little tart had arrived, Vernetta was being dismissed.

"Thanks for the feedback." Vernetta was about to hoist herself out of the chair when Haley stopped her.

"Oh, don't leave, yet. I have a proposition for you." Haley turned to O'Reilly. "Well, really, it's for both of you."

"I was wondering if you guys would be willing to let me argue the motion. I know the case backward and forward and I've been itching for my first oral argument. The only court appearances I've made so far have been status conferences."

She turned her smile on Vernetta. "Please, Vernetta." .

"The plaintiff's counsel can be kind of difficult to handle," Vernetta said. "It's probably best if I argue this one."

Haley put a hand on her hip. "I handled him just fine when I defended the depositions of the two HR witnesses."

"Yes, but this—"

She cut Vernetta off and appealed to O'Reilly. "It would really be a good opportunity for me. Pretty, please." Haley clasped her hands in a prayer pose.

Vernetta knew the minute O'Reilly looked over at her that Haley's request would be granted.

"This *is* a pretty straightforward motion," he said. "And Haley knows the facts. On top of that, you just said Miller's the nicest judge on the bench. It would be good for Haley to argue her first motion before him. Just like you did, Vernetta."

She knew any further protests would be a waste of time. "Alright."

"You'll be there for back up, of course," O'Reilly said to her.

Haley hopped up from the couch and squeezed O'Reilly's arm. "Thanks!"

Vernetta wondered what body part she'd be squeezing later on tonight.

"I'm doing you a big favor, Vernetta." Haley actually winked at her. "Considering everything you've been going through lately, you should be glad to have the oral argument off your plate. The death of your friend Maya must've been difficult for you."

Vernetta did not trust Haley's feigned empathy. "I'm doing just fine. Thank you."

"That wrongful death lawsuit her family filed against that attorney at Ramsey & King has been getting a lot of media coverage."

"I read about that case," O'Reilly said. "What's your connection to it?"

Vernetta's eyes locked on Haley's. She did not want to discuss the lawsuit against Eugene with her or O'Reilly.

"You're helping litigate the case, aren't you?" Haley asked.

O'Reilly's face signaled disapproval. "I certainly hope not. You'd have to get the firm's permission to do that. And I'll tell you right now, I'm not in favor of it. When the Vista Electronics case heats up, none of us will have a spare moment."

"I'm not litigating that case," Vernetta said tightly. "Barnes, Ayers, and Howard is handling it."

"Oh," Haley said. "I saw one of the firm's partners here last night meeting with you about the case. That's why I thought you were involved."

*How in the hell would you know what we were meeting about?*

Haley seemed to read her mind. "Oh," she said again, looking flustered. "I recognized your friend Nichelle Ayers from a news report. I found a copy of a wrongful death case dealing with AIDS on the copier last night. You must've forgotten to take the original."

*You little bitch.* "Nichelle's a good friend. I'm only lending my moral support. She wanted to discuss her litigation strategy with me. I'm not involved in the litigation."

"Good," O'Reilly said. "Let's keep it that way."

Haley smirked at her, but Vernetta took the high road and looked away. As long as Haley was screwing the managing partner, Vernetta's high road would need to surpass Mt. Everest.

# CHAPTER 30

Nichelle knew she would regret going along with Special's outlandish plan, but her friend had pleaded for so long, she finally gave in. It wasn't exactly the craziest thing Special had ever talked her into. But it was pretty darn close.

She picked up the telephone and dialed Special's cell phone. "You sure you still want to go through with this?"

"I don't *want* to do anything," Special said. "I *have* to do this."

"No, you don't. You can have faith that Clayton is exactly who he appears to be. A wonderful *heterosexual* man who loves you."

"Are you forgetting something? Maya wasn't the only one who never suspected that Eugene was gay. We didn't either."

Nichelle pursed her lips. Just hearing Maya's name still created a lump in her throat. "I don't understand why you can't ask your cousin Thomas to do it."

"He's my boy and he'd definitely do it if I asked him, but he's way too flamboyant. Clayton would peg him as gay the minute he switched into the room. I need Jamal to do it because no one would ever know he's gay. He's still on board, right?"

"As far as I know."

"Just make sure you guys get here by eight," Special said.

Nichelle hung up the telephone and took the elevator to the third floor of her office building. She made a right off the elevator and entered the lobby of Russana & Rowles. She waited as the law firm's receptionist informed Jamal that Nichelle was on her way back to his office.

Jamal greeted her in the hallway with a hug. He leaned back to take in her outfit. "I see you're still stopping traffic."

"Doing my best." Nichelle's skirt suit was a red and black St. John Knit with gold accents.

Jamal, as always, was conservatively dressed in a dark suit and tie. He was clean shaven, with skin the color of melted caramel. He'd been a year ahead of her and Maya at Loyola Law School.

"I dropped by to make sure we're still on for tonight," Nichelle said, as Jamal showed her into his office.

"I guess so," he said, "but I'm only doing this for you." Jamal had never dated women, and had been out since high school. He was one of three openly gay associates in his firm.

"This down low stuff has really got you sisters on edge."

"Not me. This is all about Special. She's taking Maya's death so hard it's making her ultra paranoid. None of us suspected Eugene. So now she thinks every man she meets is perpetrating. Including her boyfriend."

"Well, some brothers are," Jamal said. "In my younger days, I had my share of married men." Jamal and his partner had been together for five years. They were one of the happiest couples Nichelle knew, gay or straight.

"I don't understand how they can get away with it. Aren't they afraid of getting caught?"

"Some women are way too accepting," Jamal said. "I could tell you some pretty wild stories, but I won't. The first married man I had sex with—my college professor—had been with his wife for fifteen years. He spent so much time at my place I had no reason to even suspect that he was married. His wife eventually found out about us, but last I heard, they're still married. And I doubt he's changed his ways."

"You're going to make me as paranoid as Special." Nichelle stood up. "I'll pick you up at seven-thirty."

"Now tell me one more time, exactly what am I supposed to do?"

"I don't know, just check Clayton out. Do whatever it is you guys do to figure out if another man is gay."

"I'll do my best. But I hope Special gets the answer she wants."

"Me, too," Nichelle said. "Because if she doesn't, I can only pray for Clayton."

# CHAPTER 31

Lieutenant Wilson was just finishing up an email when J.C. appeared in his open doorway. He waved her inside.

"What's so urgent?" He pushed the keyboard tray underneath his desk. "And why wouldn't you tell me over the phone? You're not transferring are you?"

J.C. beamed as she closed the door behind her. "No, Lieutenant, I'm not transferring."

"I know your partner's a real asshole. You won't have to put up with him much longer. I'll be making some reassignments in a few weeks. I wish I could ship him off to Siberia."

"After you hear what I have to say, you're going to love me." J.C. plopped down in the chair in front of his desk.

"I already love you. I offer you a Snickers every time I see you, don't I? You think I do that with everybody? That's the ultimate gesture of love in my book." He lifted the lid of a dark green candy dish shaped like a hand grenade. It was stuffed with the bite-size candy bars. "Have one?"

"No, thanks, Lieutenant."

"You look a little tense. So what's this all about?"

"This isn't tension on my face. It's excitement. I've discovered a link between the shootings of Marcus Patterson, Dr. Banks, and Nathaniel Allen that I think will lead us to their killer."

Lieutenant Wilson rolled his chair closer to his desk and planted his hairy forearms on his desk pad. "Lay it on me."

J.C. began with the information about Patterson, the Raycom engineer, explaining his secretary's confirmation of his affairs with men. She then shared the details of Dr. Banks' lunchtime romps, as confirmed by his sister-in-law and the Marriott desk clerk. By the time she passed on what Special had told her about the junior college running back, J.C.'s heart was pumping like an oil rig gone haywire.

"I think there's a serial killer out there who's gunning for men on the down low," J.C. said. "We need to meet with Media Affairs as soon as possible. Information about these guys' lives is going to hit the press sooner or later, and it's going to create a public relations nightmare for us."

Lieutenant Wilson's lips formed a stiff smile. J.C. had expected a much more enthusiastic response to her news.

"So you think this down low crap is for real?" The lieutenant rocked back in his chair. He laced his fingers, then rested his hands across his chest. "You think there are a lot of supposedly straight black men out there screwing other men?"

"I don't know if it's a lot, but I do think it's certainly happening."

"Wanna know what I think?" The lieutenant sat forward and gripped the edge of his desk. "I think it's all a bunch of bull. It's just another way to degrade African-American men. I wouldn't be surprised if that guy who wrote that book and started this whole down low mess is being funded by some right-wing religious group."

"Lieutenant, that's ridiculous. Why would—"

"Let me get this straight," he said, cutting her off. "Based on a bunch of rumors and hearsay, you want me to tell the whole world that three prominent, successful, African-American men—one of them a star athlete—are dead because they were out screwing other men. You want me to do this without a single piece of confirming evidence. Not a single eyewitness to any such activity and a bunch of witnesses who don't want you to disclose their names. Is that what you're telling me, Detective?"

The lieutenant's eyes blazed with fury. J.C. was about to respond, but he didn't let her.

"And after we hold the press conference calling these guys fags, who's going to defend the Department when their families sue us for defamation?"

J.C. felt like somebody had knocked her feet out from under her. She knew that a lot of cops were homophobic, but she had not anticipated this reaction from her mentor. "Using the word *fag* is like using the *N* word."

He guffawed, then rolled his eyes skyward. "Please forgive me. Can I call 'em homos then? Is that better? Or sissies? How about that?"

J.C. figured it would be useless to spend time trying to educate him. "I understand what you're saying regarding the impact of what I've discovered. I agree that the situation has to be handled delicately."

He chuckled. "That's certainly an understatement."

"It won't be easy for a lot of people to accept this, but we have a responsibility to warn the public. If these murders are the work of a serial killer, other men are in danger."

"I don't think you've gathered sufficient evidence yet." He snatched a Snickers from his candy dish and ripped it open. "In fact, I don't buy your theory at all."

J.C. sprang to her feet. "You can't be serious! You're blatantly discriminating against these victims because they're gay. You of all people know what it feels like to be discriminated against. I can't believe you're doing this."

"Don't you dare compare this to what black people have gone through. You and I can't change the color of our skin. Gays have a choice. We're talking apples and oranges here, Detective. Or perhaps I should say apples and fruitcakes."

"You can't just ignore this evidence because you think it'll make black men look bad."

"I can and I am. And if I were you, I wouldn't be mentioning this to anybody else. You got it? Not *anybody*."

"But we've got three dead men in a two-week period."

"People get shot in L.A. every day."

"But, Lieutenant!" J.C. was nearly shouting now. "What if I'm right? What if somebody *is* out there targeting men on the down low?"

Lieutenant Wilson took a bite from his Snickers. "If you're right, and there *is* a killer out there gunning down black fa—" He stopped chewing and raised his hand in the air. "Excuse me. If somebody is shooting black—he slowly enunciated every syllable—*ho-mo-sex-u-als*, then as far as I'm concerned, they're doing society one great big favor."

# CHAPTER 32

We really have to start doing this more often."

Jefferson leaned over and kissed Vernetta on the lips. They were snuggled up in a spacious corner booth at Chaya Venice restaurant, their first night out in weeks.

"Except I get to pick the movie next time," Jefferson said. "I'm sick of chick flicks."

"I saw you wiping away a tear at the end," Vernetta teased. "That movie was good, and you know it."

"I had something in my eye. The next movie we see, somebody's gotta throw some punches or blow up some stuff."

"I'll never understand why men get off on all that violent crap." She reached for one of the blackened shrimp on Jefferson's plate.

He put a hand over his plate, but wasn't fast enough. "If you wanted shrimp, that's what you should've ordered."

"I wanted what you ordered *and* what I ordered." She popped the shrimp into her mouth. "I think we should plan a date night at least once a week."

Jefferson gave her a look that said *get real*. "Don't even try it. Your ass would be standing me up every time."

"Okay, then. How about once a month?"

The skepticism on her husband's face deepened.

"Okay, let's not set a schedule. Let's just plan a date night when we can."

"Now you're talking."

Vernetta was just about to take in a forkful of halibut when a woman breezed past her and into the ladies' room.

"What's the matter?" Jefferson's eyes followed hers.

"I think I just saw Haley."

"Damn!" Jefferson dropped his fork. "I wanted to see her ass again."

Vernetta crumpled her napkin and threw it at him. "That's not funny."

"Yes, it is. You should see the look on your face."

She ignored him and started scanning the restaurant. "I wonder who she's here with."

"None of your business," Jefferson said.

"She might be on a date with O'Reilly."

"And so what if she is?" He sounded annoyed. "It's none of your business."

Vernetta tried to eat, but kept glancing toward the restroom. "Uh . . . I gotta go to the ladies' room."

"No, you don't. We came here to—"

Vernetta slid out of the booth before Jefferson could stop her. When she opened the restroom door and stepped inside, she found Haley standing in front of the mirror applying that too-red lipstick.

"Hi, Haley."

Haley actually jumped, dropping the lipstick tube on the countertop.

"I'm sorry." Vernetta picked up the tube and handed it back to her. "I didn't mean to startle you. How are you doing?"

"Oh . . . hi. I'm . . . fine." She snapped the cap on the lipstick tube and started digging around in her purse.

"You come here often?"

"Uh . . . no." It was clear Haley did not want to talk.

"Me neither. My husband picked it out of the Zagat's Guide. It's our first time here. What a coincidence running into you."

Haley ignored her, pulled a makeup bag from her purse and dabbed powder on her face. Her skin now had that bronzy tanning salon glow.

Vernetta took a paper towel from the metal container on the wall and dabbed at an oily spot on her forehead. She was determined to get a look at Haley's dinner date, so she wasn't leaving the restroom until Haley did. But Haley appeared to be in no hurry to go.

After brushing her hair, Haley pulled out her phone and pretended to make a call. Vernetta knew she was pretending because she had tried to check her voicemail when she first arrived, but couldn't get a signal. They both had the same O'Reilly & Finney-issued cell phone.

Vernetta thought about going into one of the stalls, but was afraid Haley would make a break for it. As Haley continued with her fake call, Vernetta conceded that she would have to leave first.

When Jefferson saw his wife whiz past their booth, he threw his napkin on the table in frustration.

Vernetta scanned the crowded restaurant again, convinced that she was going to spot O'Reilly. She was about to give up and return to her table when she saw him sitting at the bar. *I knew he was screwing that girl! What an idiot!*

Walking up behind him, she tapped him on the shoulder. "Funny seeing you here," she said playfully.

He had just taken a swallow of his drink. "Vernetta, uh . . . hey." He gave her a stiff hug. "How's it going?"

"Great," she said. "You won't believe who I just saw in the ladies' room. Haley."

He took a sip of his drink. "Is that right?"

Vernetta waited for O'Reilly to acknowledge that they were there together, but he didn't. Instead, he started telling her a funny story about a run-in he'd had with an obnoxious opposing counsel. Vernetta wasn't interested, but pretended to be. She was determined to stay planted until Haley rejoined him. She wondered what excuse they would use to explain why they were out together.

"You better get back to your husband," O'Reilly said, after he had finished his rather lengthy tale.

Vernetta wondered why Haley hadn't returned yet. When she turned to look for her, she realized her mistake. Her back was facing the entrance of the restaurant. O'Reilly had kept her talking so Haley could escape.

She left O'Reilly, then checked the bathroom. Haley wasn't there. She reluctantly returned to her table.

"I don't wanna hear it," Jefferson said, before Vernetta could open her mouth.

"Why?"

"'Cuz I don't care if O'Reilly is screwing that girl. We were in the middle of having a nice evening out for the first time since I don't know when and that's where I want to pick things up."

"But—"

"But nothing. If you say one more word to me about Haley or O'Reilly or that damn law firm, we're going home." He looked mad enough to march out of the restaurant and leave her sitting right there.

Vernetta took a bite of her now cold halibut and mulled over the situation. As an associate, she had an obligation to report inappropriate behavior that could potentially create liability for the firm. Most of the sexual harassment cases she had litigated over the years involved consensual relationships gone bad. When O'Reilly dumped Haley—and he surely would—she'd probably try to profit from O'Reilly's lapse in judgment by suing the firm for sexual harassment.

But there was no way Vernetta could breathe a word of this to anybody at the firm. They would both deny it anyway. O'Reilly would be furious, which would mean the end of her career.

Vernetta took another bite of her halibut and focused her energy on salvaging what was left of her date night.

# CHAPTER 33

A frown darkened Clayton's face the minute Special announced that they were having dinner guests. But when she mentioned that Nichelle had specifically requested his famous jambalaya, his ego kicked in. Suddenly, having dinner guests sounded like a great idea.

Clayton loved taking over her kitchen and was a far better cook than Special would ever be. While he prepared the jambalaya, Special whipped up a Caesar salad and garlic bread.

"You know," Clayton said, as he stood at the sink deveining the shrimp, "if I could have any job in the world, I'd be a chef in a five-star restaurant."

*Chef?* "I know you like to cook, but that's not exactly a very manly job."

"A job don't define me, baby, *I* define me. I happen to enjoy cooking, and I'm damn good at it."

Special turned back to chopping up the romaine lettuce. She knew a couple of chefs and she was pretty sure they were straight. She stopped chopping. *God, please don't let this man be gay.*

They finished preparing dinner with an hour to spare before Nichelle and Jamal were scheduled to arrive.

As Clayton stood shirtless in front of the bathroom mirror, shaving, Special sidled up behind him. "I like that sexy five o'clock shadow of yours. Gives you that George Michael look."

Almost instantly, she regretted the comparison. *Wasn't he the one arrested for lewd conduct in a public restroom?*

She pressed her face against his back and slid her hands below the waistband of his boxers.

"I love it," Clayton said.

"You know, it's not true what they say about old men," Special joked. "You got it worse than a twenty year old."

"Forty-one is not old, baby." He wiped the shaving cream from his face with a towel, then turned around to face her.

She stood on her tiptoes and kissed him. "Nichelle and Jamal will be here soon," she said between kisses. "So we better not start anything."

"You already started it so now *I* gotta finish it." He took her hand and pulled her into the bedroom.

Special had another test she planned to try out on Clayton later tonight. But now was as good a time as any. "I've got something new for us to try out," she said sheepishly.

Clayton smiled and reached for a condom from the bedside table.

"Hold on, cowboy. We'll get to that. First, let me show you what I read in *Cosmo*," she lied.

Clayton raised an eyebrow. "*Cosmo,* huh? I hope it's really freaky."

She instructed him to lay on his side and Special did the same, facing him. She began kissing his neck, slowly moving down his body. He moaned when her lips teasingly tugged his left nipple.

"I think I'm going to like this a *whole* lot."

As she licked and kissed her way down the rest of his body, she reached out with her left hand and began massaging his rear end. When she knew he was good and relaxed and really into it, she extended her arm a little further and tried to slip her middle finger between his butt cheeks.

"What the—" Clayton clutched her wrist in a grip tight enough to snap it in two. "What the hell are you doing?"

"Ow!" Special yelled. "Let go! You're hurting me."

Clayton apparently hadn't realized how tight he was grabbing her wrist. He released it and sat up. "What the hell was *that* about?"

"I told you," Special said, massaging her sore arm. "It was something I read in *Cosmo*. I thought it might turn you on."

"If that's what *Cosmo's* telling you to do, you need to cancel your damn subscription. You need to start reading *Essence*. I know they're not telling you to stick a finger up a brother's ass." He climbed out of bed. "I'm getting dressed. You've killed my mood."

As Clayton stormed out of the room, Special exhaled in relief. Her coworker claimed that gay men liked having a finger or a vibrator eased up their rear end. Clayton had passed that test with flying colors.

But then she remembered Chapter 11 of *On the Down Low* and her joy evaporated. According to the book, some DL men were tops, while others were bottoms. Tops only gave anal sex and never allowed themselves to be penetrated. *Maybe Clayton was a top.*

Special checked the time. Nichelle and Jamal would be arriving shortly. She anxiously mumbled a quick prayer that Clayton would pass her final test.

# CHAPTER 34

From the moment they were introduced, Jamal and Clayton bonded like long lost frat brothers.

"Man, you put your foot in that jambalaya," Jamal said. They had finished the main course and were enjoying a chocolate cake Nichelle had picked up.

"I would have to agree with you, my brother." Clayton extended his fist and Jamal did the same, bumping his against Clayton's.

Clayton turned to Special. "I wish I could've been here for Maya's services."

"Don't worry about it. I know you would've made it if you could have."

"I don't get that brother Eugene," Clayton said, shaking his head. "I never woulda thought he was a booty buster. I really don't understand the gay thing. With all the fine women in this city, it just don't make sense."

*Really?* Special knew from reading *On the Down Low* that a man's gay bashing didn't mean he wasn't gay. Clayton could just be perfecting his cover.

Nichelle nervously eyed Special. "So how long are you two going to continue doing this long-distance thing?" she asked Clayton.

"Funny you should bring that up." He reached over and took Special's hand in his. "I was going to save this for later, but I might as well tell you now. There's an opening in our L.A. office. I was thinking about asking for a transfer. But only if you're down with it."

Special nearly knocked her wineglass from the table. "Of course, I'm down with it!" She hugged and kissed him at the same time.

"Okay, then I guess I'll be packing up and moving to L.A. in a few weeks." He clinked his glass against hers.

Special couldn't be happier that Clayton was leaving D.C., the black gay capital of the world, next to Atlanta. "Why don't you two go into the living room while Nichelle and I clean up."

Nichelle cleared the table, while Special peered into the living room every few seconds.

Jamal was sitting next to Clayton on the couch, a respectable distance between them. The two men were laughing and joking, seemingly having a good time.

"He can't find out if Clayton is gay just by talking to him, can he?" Special whispered to Nichelle. "He needs to brush up against him or something."

Nichelle sighed. After putting the dishes away, the foursome spent the next hour playing Bid Whist.

"Okay, man, I'm out." Jamal threw down his cards. "If I didn't know better, I'd swear you marked the deck."

Clayton smiled. "A seven-no trump will do it every time, my brother. Sure you don't wanna go to Boston with me just one more time?"

Jamal laughed and held up his white napkin in surrender.

"Excuse me for a second." Clayton stood up, then stretched. "Gotta take a leak."

As soon as she heard the bathroom door close, Special pulled Jamal into the kitchen. "So what do you think?"

Jamal shrugged. "Well—"

Special gripped his arm. "Oh, my God! Well, what?"

"I think he's probably straight."

"*Probably?*" Special exclaimed. "I need to know for sure! Is he gay or not?"

Instead of answering, Jamal mumbled under his breath. "Damn."

At the same time, Nichelle hung her head. Special turned around and saw Clayton staring blankly at the three of them.

Nobody said a word.

Clayton finally broke the silence. "You think I'm gay?"

Special was usually good at lying on the fly, but her brain had quit on her. "No, Clayton . . . I . . . uh."

"You what? You brought this dude over here to try to hit on me or something?" He glared at Jamal. "So you're a punk like Eugene?"

Jamal's fingers balled into fists. "I'm outta here. I never should've let you two talk me into this." He started toward the door.

"No, hold up, man. Talk you into what?"

Jamal pointed at Special. "Your girl here thought you might be gay and asked me to check you out. But don't worry. I told her you were cool."

Clayton's eyes burned into Special like high-speed lasers.

She ran over and grabbed his hand. "Clayton, I'm sorry. Since Maya died, I've just been super paranoid."

Nichelle picked up her purse from the counter. "We're leaving." She gave Special an I-told-you-so look and led Jamal out of the apartment.

Clayton remained glued to the same spot, a dumbstruck expression etched on his face. "You think I'm gay?"

"No, I just—"

He stormed into the bedroom, slamming the door behind him.

"Wait," Special said, running after him. "Let me explain. I—"

"You don't have to explain a damn thing." He pulled his bag from the closet, tossed it onto the bed and unzipped it with such force it almost ripped.

Special couldn't believe everything had gotten out of control so fast. "No, Clayton, I don't want you to leave!"

"I don't see why not. You think I'm a punk! I'm getting the hell out of here. For your sake and mine."

Tears pooled in her eyes. "Clayton . . . I . . . you can't tell what's going on with men nowadays. Maya died because her fiancé was out there sleeping with other men. There was no other way for me to find out."

"You could've just asked me," Clayton shouted, then backtracked. "No, I take that back. That would've pissed me off, too. We've spent enough time together for you to know me a lot better than you apparently do."

"But that's just the point," she said, the tears freely flowing now. "Some of these guys are on the down low for years and their girlfriends and wives never know."

"That's bullshit! They don't know because they don't wanna know. And stop calling it *on the down low*. Like it's something legitimate. Those punks are gay, but just don't wanna admit it. And you bringing somebody up in here to hit on me is hella insulting."

Clayton charged into the bathroom, snatched his razor and toothbrush from the counter and jammed them into his toiletry bag.

"Clayton, I'm so sorry." She threw her arms around his neck. "Please don't leave."

After a long fit of crying, Special was finally able to get Clayton back into the living room. As she snuggled up next to him on the couch, she smiled inwardly. With her job kicking her ass and the torment over losing Maya, at least worrying about Clayton's sexual preference was one thing she could cross off her list.

She went to the bathroom to freshen up her makeup and when she returned, she found Clayton standing in the living room, his bag over his shoulder.

She rushed up to him, but he extended his hand, gently holding her at bay. "Part of me understands why you did what you did, but every time I think about it, it pisses me off all over again. I don't think I'm going to put in for that transfer. It's too crazy out here."

"So you're breaking up with me?" she whimpered.

Clayton didn't answer, but his heavy sigh told her he was at least thinking about it. "Just give me a little space and we'll talk."

"No, Clayton, don't leave! I'm sorry. Why don't you at least wait until tomorrow? It's going to cost a lot to change your flight." If she could convince him to stay, she planned to screw him until this evening was erased from his memory.

"I don't care about the money."

Clayton picked up his baseball cap from the end table, then stopped mid-stride. "Wait a minute. Is that why you were trying to play with my ass earlier? To see if I liked that shit?"

Special looked away.

"Well, I'm just glad I passed all your damn tests with flying colors."

Special looked around for her purse and keys. "I'll take you to the airport," she sniffed. She was determined to talk him into staying before they got there.

"I already called a cab." He sounded as if he were sapped of energy. "It's probably here by now." He pecked her on the forehead. "I'll call you."

Special stood there unable to see or think or move. The most incredible man who had ever walked into her life had just walked out of it.

# CHAPTER 35

When Special walked through the door of T.G.I. Friday's the following evening, Vernetta almost didn't recognize her.

Special wasn't wearing a lick of makeup and her hair needed a straightening comb. Her outfit—baggy jeans and an oversized sweatshirt—was the biggest barometer of her mental state. Skin-tight pants, too-short skirts and low-cut blouses were Special's normal wardrobe staples.

"Are you okay?" Vernetta asked, as Special took a seat across from her.

She nodded her head without opening her mouth.

Vernetta reached across the table and squeezed her hand. "It's going to be okay. Just give Clayton a few days."

Special had called Vernetta the second Clayton left. She had cried for a full five minutes before finally explaining what happened.

"I'm sure Clayton will call when he cools off," she said, though she wasn't really sure he would. Jefferson's reaction would have been much the same.

"I know it's over," Special said wearily. "He's not going to give me a second chance." Her voice cracked. "He won't even answer my calls."

When the waitress approached the table, Special didn't bother to wipe away the tears trailing down her cheeks.

"Give us a minute," Vernetta said. She was determined to boost her friend's spirits. "Just give him some time. He'll cool off."

Special's cell phone rang and she rushed to dig it out of her purse. She checked the caller ID display, frowned, then set it on the table without answering it. "I left Clayton four messages this morning. I thought that might be him."

Okay, so maybe cheering Special up wasn't going to be all that easy, Vernetta thought. She decided to change the subject and share her news about O'Reilly and Haley. "Want to hear some major law firm gossip?"

She took a sip of water. "Yeah, sure."

"Guess what little backstabbing blond at O'Reilly & Finney is screwing the managing partner?"

Special's face brightened slightly. "O'Reilly is messing around with that little witch, Haley?"

"You got it."

"Girl, you're lyin'!" The old Special was temporarily resuscitated. "How'd you find out?"

Vernetta told her about the two of them working late, then seeing Haley coming out of O'Reilly's office with her hair and lipstick a mess. She gave a blow-by-blow account of their chance meeting at Chaya Venice and how Haley would be arguing *her* motion next week.

"Girl, I bet she's giving that man blow jobs in the office," Special said.

"What I don't understand is why they didn't go to a hotel."

"Taking the risk of getting caught makes it more exciting," Special explained, smiling for the first time. "I dated this guy who got off on messing around in his office. Haley's about half O'Reilly's age, right?"

"Yep."

"I bet she's whipping some stuff on him the chick he's living with hasn't even read about." Special took a sip from her water glass and crunched on the ice. "Anyway, the big question is, what are *you* going to do about it?"

"And exactly what would you suggest?"

"No telling what she's whispering into his ear while they're snuggled up together doing the do. Start faking her out. She needs to become your new best friend."

"Like I already told Jefferson, I'm not doing that."

"You don't have a choice," Special said. "When something goes down between the two of you, who do you think O'Reilly's going to side with? You or the cute little blond who's making him come?"

"This is nuts. My job is to practice law, not to kiss up to that little wench."

"Until you make partner, you gotta do what you gotta do." Special aimed a finger at Vernetta from across the table. "If not, you can either pack your bags now or wait for Haley to do it for you."

# CHAPTER 36

James and Marcia Hill enjoyed entertaining friends at their spacious two-story home on Shenandoah Street in the Ladera Heights section of Los Angeles.

Their neighbors, Wallace and Juanita Sims, had moved across the street six months earlier and the two couples quickly established an easy friendship. The foursome sat around the dining room table feeling stuffed and relaxed.

"That was the best grilled salmon I've ever tasted," Wallace said to his hostess. He was an assistant pastor at one of the city's largest churches.

"Excuse me?" his wife gave him a sideways glance. "I cooked salmon two weeks ago. What about mine?"

Wallace leaned over and kissed his wife on the cheek. "I'm sorry, sweetheart. Yours was the best *baked* salmon I've ever had."

Easy laughter filled the room.

"My husband should've been a politician instead of a preacher," said Juanita. "He's faster on his feet with the bull than anybody I know."

The two couples made their way into the living room, where James put on a CD of Motown hits. "You know, you're alright for a man of the cloth." James took a seat next to his wife. "I always thought ministers were uptight."

"James, I can't believe you said that!" Marcia said, embarrassed.

Wallace laughed. "Everybody thinks that. But I wasn't always a minister."

"I've been holding off on approaching you about this," James said, "but I'd like to talk to you about some investments your church might find lucrative." James had been running his own investment banking firm for two decades.

"Anytime. The church could definitely use some help in that area."

James reached for the bottle of wine on the coffee table. "Anybody want a refill?"

Wallace and Juanita shook their heads. Marcia covered her glass with her hand. "I'm already a little tipsy."

Juanita looked at her watch, then at Wallace. "I told the sitter we'd be home by ten. We better get going."

"Hold up, man," James said to his neighbor. "You're not trying to run out on me, are you? You promised me a rematch."

Juanita picked up her purse from an end table. "I'm not hanging around for another one of your marathon chess matches. You can stay if you want, but I'm heading home."

Wallace escorted his wife safely across the street, then returned.

Marcia showed Wallace back into the living room. "You guys want me to make some coffee?"

Both men shook their heads.

"Then I'm off to bed. Don't stay up too late." She leaned down and kissed her husband.

James rubbed his hands together. "I hope you're ready, man. I got something special for you tonight."

Wallace followed James through the kitchen door and out to a back house that James had converted into a study. The comfy room was the size of a posh hotel suite. It was equipped with a separate bathroom, a small refrigerator and a microwave oven. A sleek, glass-top desk was framed by tall shelves stacked with books. A chess set—an expensive, hand-carved ivory model that cost over a grand—was already set up in the north corner of the room next to a six-foot couch.

James tuned in a jazz station, filling the room with a soft saxophone solo. After dimming the lights just a tad, the men stood over the chess set, facing each other.

James smiled. "Okay, preacher man, I'm about to make you beg for mercy."


When Marcia awoke the next morning and discovered that her husband's side of the bed had not been slept in, it did not concern her. James often fell asleep in the den while watching late night TV. He was probably already up, getting in an early workout.

Marcia swung her legs over the side of the bed and stepped into her house shoes. When she didn't find James in the den, she put on a pot of coffee, then peeked into the garage, expecting to find him on the treadmill. They had turned one section of their three-car garage into a workout area, equipping it with a high-tech treadmill and thousands of dollars worth of Nautilus equipment.

But he wasn't there either. The Lexus and the Escalade were parked side by side. Marcia searched the notepad near the refrigerator. James rarely left without leaving her a note. But the pad was blank. A slight panic began to set in. Maybe he had taken a walk. She went to the living room window and peered up the street.

She started for the back door, but decided to check the rest of the house before going outside to James' study. This house is too big, Marcia thought, as she made her way down the hallway. She checked the three guest bedrooms, looked in on her two daughters, then headed out back.

When she opened the study door, a scream loud enough to wake the entire neighborhood pierced the air. It took a second for Marcia to realize that the sound was coming from her mouth.

The study was a bloody, revolting mess and right in the middle of it, her beloved husband sat slumped on the couch, half his head blown away.

# CHAPTER 37

Nichelle left the office at four after calling in for a short interview on KABC radio. Interview requests were coming in nearly every day. To her surprise, she actually *was* becoming an authority on the subject of down low men. Maybe she would end up with her own TV show like Star Jones.

Instead of heading home, she decided to pay her parents a visit in Baldwin Vista. She found her father and brother in the driveway, tinkering under the hood of her father's newest toy, a 1965 Mustang.

"You still working on that old thing?" She gave her father a kiss on the cheek. He was a retired high school principal who now devoted most of his time to a long list of never-to-be finished household projects. Her mother still worked part-time as a nurse.

"You just wait," he said. "When I get it running, I'ma catch all the young women."

Nichelle laughed, then playfully punched her brother Marlon in the arm. At thirty-five, he was a big bear of a man with a baby face.

"Heard you on the radio, sis. Sounds like you're a celebrity."

She smiled. "I'm working on it. Where's Mama?"

Her father pulled out the car's oil stick and examined it. "The kitchen. Where else?"

Nichelle made her way inside and stepped into the kitchen just as her mother pulled a casserole dish from the oven.

"Your favorite," she said smiling. "Sausage Lasagna." The dish was sizzling with melted cheese.

Nichelle grunted. She was trying her hardest to stick to her third attempt at dieting this year. "Mama, you know I'm on a diet." Nichelle gave her a hug and marveled at how much of herself she saw in her mother's face.

"You don't need to be on a diet. A man wants a woman with some meat on her bones."

Nichelle glanced back over her shoulder and lowered her voice. "I'm surprised the warden let Marlon out of the house without her."

Shantel, her brother's long-time, live-in girlfriend, was not a family favorite. Her most annoying quality was the way she boldly professed to know everything about everything. For Marlon's sake, Nichelle and her mother kept their opinions to themselves. Her brother had always been attracted to bossy women, even back in junior high school.

Her mother tossed her head in the direction of the den. "She's in there," her mother whispered. "You know she's not letting that boy out of her sight."

Shantel floated into the kitchen amid a cloud of patuli oil. She was a wafer thin, Bohemian type, with short twists. She wore leather sandals and a thin, flowery cape over a pair of jeans. "Hey, sister-in-law."

*Not if I have anything to say about it.*

Shantel gave Nichelle a fake air kiss. "I'm glad you're here. We need to talk."

Nichelle cast a glance in her mother's direction. "About what?"

"I heard your interview this afternoon." Shantel was a social worker and also conducted sex education classes at a local youth facility.

Nichelle figured she was about to offer up a critique and really didn't want to hear it. She leaned back against the kitchen counter. "And?"

"I think you're doing black women a disservice."

Nichelle could feel the *be nice* look her mother was hurling her way. "And exactly how am I doing that?"

Shantel daintily held up two fingers. "Two things. First, you have a great platform to educate women about HIV, but you're blowing it. I've never once heard you mention in your interviews that HIV isn't a gay disease."

"Excuse me? It's a fact that African-American women are being infected primarily through heterosexual sex. No one disputes that. That tells me they're getting it from men on the down low."

Shantel blew out a breath and puckered her gloss-slathered lips. "No it doesn't. Your problem is you, like most people, think HIV is a gay disease. Well, it's not."

Nichelle opened her mouth to say something, but Shantel ignored her and kept talking.

"There's also a high rate of HIV infection among I-V drug users, *heterosexual* I-V drug users. And you're completely ignoring the fact that women are out there spreading the disease just like men. If a straight guy gets HIV from a woman and spreads it to five other women, being on the down low has nothing to do with it. And these days, a lot of women are just as promiscuous as men. During your interview today, you gave the impression that all women have to do to avoid being infected is not sleep with men on the down low. That's just not the case. You're giving women a false sense of security."

Nichelle started to argue the point, but then realized that Shantel was echoing exactly what Wanda had said during the support group meeting. Still, she couldn't bring herself to tell Shantel she was right.

The smell of the lasagna was getting to her. She needed to leave before her mother forced her to eat. "You mentioned that you had two points," Nichelle said, surprised at herself for encouraging the woman. "So what is your second point?"

"You also never once mentioned anything about black women's culpability in all of this."

Nichelle dropped her arms. "I know you're not trying to blame these women for getting infected?"

"Women need to start taking responsibility for their own bodies. Everybody knows HIV is out there running rampant. So why are women still sleeping with men they barely know and having unprotected sex? And why aren't they getting tested and demanding that their men get tested before spreading their legs. That's the first thing I made Marlon do."

The pan Nichelle's mother was washing slipped from her hands and rattled loudly in the stainless steel sink.

Nichelle knew this conversation made her mother uncomfortable. "Thanks for sharing, Shantel. I'll give what you said some thought."

"You really should. With all your education, I'm really surprised at your lack of insight on this."

Nichelle straightened up. "You know what, Shantel? Maybe you should—"

"Baby, help me set the table." Nichelle's mother shoved a plate into her hand. "Shantel, go get the guys and tell them it's time to eat."

# CHAPTER 38

Haley tried valiantly to play it off, but Vernetta could tell she was trembling like a leaf inside.

They were standing outside Department 5, waiting for the bailiff to open the courtroom. According to the docket posted on the door, their discovery motion would be the first matter heard by the judge.

"Everything okay?" Vernetta asked. "You're not nervous are you?"

"Of course not," Haley said with a huff. "This is only a simple discovery motion." She peered over her shoulder, as if she were searching for someone, then tucked a loose curl behind her ear.

"Looking for somebody?"

"O'Reilly said he would try to get by to watch my argument."

*And when did he make that promise? When you two were curled up in bed together last night?*

The bailiff unlocked the double doors leading into the courtroom and Vernetta and Haley, along with about a dozen other attorneys, filed inside. They handed business cards to the court clerk, who checked off their names. As Vernetta could have predicted, their opposing counsel had yet to show up. He was never on time.

Vernetta took a seat in the front row and Haley sat next to her. About ten minutes later, Vernetta heard a quiet murmur go through the rows of lawyers behind her. She turned around and spotted an attorney she recognized.

"What's all the commotion about?"

"Judge Miller won't be here today," the woman complained. "Judge Abernathy's taking his place."

Judge Alvinia Abernathy had the reputation of being one of the meanest judges in L.A. She got a kick out of embarrassing attorneys, and she seemed to have a particular dislike for female lawyers. The rumor was, the more attractive you were, the harder she grilled you.

Vernetta turned to Haley. "I think you better let me argue the motion. Judge Abernathy's not an easy judge to deal with. She's—"

"No way," Haley said defensively. "You're just mad that O'Reilly let me do the argument and not you."

"No, Haley, right now, all I'm thinking about is the client and how it's going to look if we lose this motion. This judge is—"

"We're not going to lose and you're not arguing the motion. I am."

Before Vernetta could convince her otherwise, she heard the bailiff's voice. "All rise, please come to order. The Honorable Alvinia Abernathy presiding."

Judge Abernathy entered the courtroom from a side door. She was in her late forties with dishwater blond hair which she wore in a short pageboy. She wasn't a bad looking woman, but could've used some help with her makeup. The dusty rose on her lips and the too-dark eye shadow on her lids looked atrocious.

She sat down and began shuffling papers.

Vernetta glanced over her shoulder. Joe Ross, their opposing counsel, still hadn't arrived and she was thankful for that. Due to his absence, their case would be moved to the end of the docket. By that time, Haley would have a chance to watch other oral arguments and see how vicious Abernathy could be. Then she would gladly hand over the reigns.

"Jackson versus Spectrum Services," the judge called out. Just then, Ross bolted into the courtroom. He followed Haley and Vernetta as they took their places before the judge. Haley looked at Vernetta as if she had expected her to remain seated in the gallery.

"Mr. Ross," the judge said, "do you own a watch?"

Ross shuffled his weight from one foot to the other. He knew what was coming. "Yes, Your Honor."

"Does it work?"

"Uh . . . yes it does."

"Then why did you come into my courtroom fifteen minutes late?"

"Your Honor, the traffic on—"

"I don't care about the traffic. Don't ever come into my courtroom late again. Now explain to me why you haven't turned over the documents requested by the defense."

Ross went into a rambling explanation that didn't make sense.

Haley smirked. "I have this in the bag," she whispered to Vernetta.

*Don't count on it.*

The judge chewed out Ross for a good ten minutes, then turned to defense counsel.

"Which one of you is arguing this motion?"

"I am," Haley said.

"Okay, then I want to hear from you and only you."

Vernetta slowly sat down.

"I see you cited *Pembroke*," the judge began. "What were the facts of that case?"

Haley's face went blank. They had cited *Pembroke* on procedural grounds, as part of a long string of citations. It had nothing to do with the substance of the motion. Few attorneys would know the facts of a case cited for that reason. The judge knew this.

"Did you hear my question, counselor?"

Haley's left leg started shaking. "Um . . . yes I did."

"Well, what's your answer? I don't have all day."

Haley was frantically searching through the brief, trying to figure out where they had cited *Pembroke*. Vernetta rose from her seat to rescue her colleague. "Your Honor, if I may address the court, *Pembr*oke—"

"No, you may not address the court," the judge retorted. "Ms. Prescott is arguing this motion and she's the only person I want to hear from."

The silence was deadly as Haley frantically flipped pages. Vernetta found the correct page and slid her copy of the brief in front of Haley. But Haley seemed to be stricken with stage fright and couldn't move.

Vernetta scribbled some words for Haley to recite and placed the legal pad in front of her. Still no response.

"Ms. Prescott, I see from your bar number that you've only been practicing law for a couple of years. But that's no excuse for your poor performance here today. If you submit a brief to this court, I expect you to know the cases you've cited. Each and every one of them. I figure your billing rate must be in the neighborhood of three or four hundred dollars an hour. When you leave here, call your client and offer them a refund."

There was shaky laughter from the gallery.

"I won't waste more time on this case," the judge said. "The clerk has my tentative ruling. I'm making it final. Next case."

The clerk handed them a copy of the ruling as they walked through the swinging gate leading back to the gallery. Vernetta scanned it and was relieved to see that the judge was ordering Ross to turn over the documents within five days and had also granted their request for monetary sanctions.

O'Reilly was sitting on the back row. He must have slipped in just in time to hear the judge berate Haley. He did not look happy. Haley was about to get her second grilling of the day.

They followed O'Reilly out of the courtroom, where he motioned them over to a deserted area near the escalator. "What happened in there was unacceptable!" His voice was low, but he was shouting just the same. "How did you let that happen?"

He was staring directly at Vernetta.

"Excuse me?"

"I'm holding you responsible for what just occurred in there." He pointed his finger in Vernetta's face. "You know what an asshole Abernathy is. Why did you let Haley argue that motion? You should have taken over."

"I tried to!" Vernetta shot back. "But Haley wouldn't let me. And when I tried to address the court, the judge wouldn't let me speak. Isn't that right, Haley?"

Haley's lips didn't move, then she shrugged. "I guess so."

"You guess so? I tried to—"

"Let's continue this discussion when we're back at the office."

He abruptly stormed off and Haley followed after him, leaving Vernetta standing there dumbfounded.

# CHAPTER 39

J.C. looked up from her desk and saw Detective Jessup headed her way. Since she didn't have time to hide, she picked up the telephone and pretended to be engaged in conversation.

"Yes, I'd like the information as soon as possible," J.C. said to the dial tone.

Detective Jessup pulled a chair up to her desk and sat down. He was apparently willing to wait.

"Hold on a minute." J.C. hit the hold button and hung the receiver over her shoulder. "May I help you?"

"Go ahead and finish your call. I can wait."

J.C. frowned, then said good-bye to the dial tone.

"I'm busy," she said, as she hung up the phone.

Detective Jessup scooted his chair closer to her desk. "Tell me something? Why do you find it so hard to be nice to me?"

"I told you, I'm busy."

"I just dropped by to find out what you did to upset the boss."

J.C. hadn't told a soul about her discussion with Lieutenant Wilson and she doubted he had either. "And who said I upset the boss?"

"Just a rumor floating around. You're usually in there shooting the breeze with him a couple times a day. I just noticed that you two seem to be avoiding each other. I'm very observant. That's why I'm such a good detective."

"I don't have time for this nonsense." She opened her desk drawer, pulled out a file and started reading it.

"You're the lieutenant's pet. It's really strange that he's keeping you out of the loop."

"You obviously have something you want to tell me. Why don't you just spit it out."

He was like a kid anxious to spill the beans. "Another big-shot black guy was found dead yesterday morning, but you were nowhere near the crime scene. I was just wondering why not."

J.C. could not hide her alarm. "There was another shooting?"

He nodded.

"Where?"

"Ladera. An investment banker with some major bucks. Shot in the head and chest just like the others. Looks like the weapon of choice was probably a twenty-two as well."

"I didn't hear any news reports about the shooting on my way in to work."

"They're trying to keep this one hush-hush for the moment. Direct order from the mayor's office. The election is only six months away. He's concerned about a backlash from the black community. Your people are starting to claim that we aren't doing enough to solve the murders. When they hear about a fourth shooting, they'll probably call in Al Sharpton *and* Jesse Jackson."

J.C. sat back in her chair. She couldn't believe there had been another shooting and the lieutenant was doing nothing about it.

"So why are you being kept out of the loop?" Detective Jessup asked.

"I'm about to find out." J.C. was out of her seat before he could ask any more questions.

The lieutenant was talking on the telephone when J.C. appeared in his doorway. After noticing her, he swiveled his chair around, turning his back to her. She folded her arms and waited.

Two minutes later, he cussed under his breath and slammed down the phone. "What do you want?" he asked gruffly.

They had both stayed clear of each other after the lieutenant rejected her theory about the murders being connected to the victims' possible homosexual liaisons.

J.C. stepped inside, but did not close the door or take a seat. "I heard there was another shooting. I was just wondering if you'd given any additional thought to my theory."

The lieutenant chuckled derisively. "I know for a fact that your little theory doesn't apply this time. James Hill is my fraternity brother. And he wasn't no fa— homosexual."

"You can't know that for sure. These men are good at putting up a front."

He guffawed. "Well, he must've been damn good to fool me."

J.C. put her hands on her hips. "I just need to know whether you're going to act on the information I gave you?"

"I'm looking into it. But for the time being, I'm not going public with an allegation that these men were . . ." He caught himself this time. ". . . were homosexuals. I care about my career. And you should start caring about yours."

Fuming, J.C. turned to leave.

"You know, Detective," the lieutenant said, before she reached the doorway, "I think I finally figured it out." He let his words linger.

J.C. started to leave, but turned back. "Figured out what, Lieutenant?"

"Why you're so concerned about these sissies, if they actually are sissies. Frankly, I'd think you'd share my feelings in light of what happened to that friend of yours."

J.C. said nothing.

"But then I got to thinking. You know, I've never once seen you with a man. And you've never been married. Do you even like men?"

His words left her speechless.

"Let's see. You didn't have a date at the Christmas party, you didn't have one at the Department picnic, and you brought a *girlfriend* to Lucinda's going away party. You're so concerned about these fa— excuse me, *ho-mo-sex-u-als,* because you're into that homo crap, too. I hear a lot of women cops are lesbians. But I never would've pegged you for one of 'em."

J.C. struggled for the right response as rage consumed her. "I expected a lot more from you, Lieutenant," she said tightly, then walked out.

Back at her desk, she grabbed her purse from the bottom drawer and hurried out of the building before she gave in to the urge to put her fist through a wall.

# CHAPTER 40

It was after eight by the time Vernetta pulled into her driveway. She was tired, hungry, and in a PMS funk. She remained in the car, listening to Luther Vandross' *Wait for Love* on the radio, which made her tear up. That was going to be Maya's wedding song.

She was still angry with O'Reilly for going off on her at the courthouse, though he later apologized. Haley had apparently come forward with an accurate accounting of the events that preceded her disastrous first oral argument. Vernetta realized that she should actually consider herself lucky. If Haley had decided to lie, O'Reilly would have surely taken her word over Vernetta's.

Jefferson was in the den, bent over a clipboard and a calculator. She dropped her purse on the coffee table and plopped down next to him on the couch.

"Good to see I'm not the only one working late."

He nodded without looking up and kept punching buttons on the calculator, then scribbled some numbers on the clipboard.

"How can you concentrate with the TV up so loud?" An episode of *Sex and the City* was on the screen. She reached for the remote and turned down the volume.

"The noise actually helps," Jefferson mumbled. "Makes me feel like I'm still out at the worksite."

Vernetta yawned. "Well, I had another awful day." She rested her head on her husband's shoulder. "First, O'Reilly had the nerve to—"

Jefferson held up his hand. "I don't wanna hear it."

She sat up. "That's certainly a crappy way to respond."

He ignored her and kept hitting buttons on the calculator.

"I try to tell you about my day and you just cut me off? What's up with that?"

"I'm just tired of hearing it."

A burst of heat inched up Vernetta's neck. "Tired of hearing what?"

"About how bad your day was and how much Haley gets on your nerves and how you have to work such long hours and how—"

Vernetta bounced off the couch. "Well, excuse me for thinking I had a husband I could talk to about my problems."

"I don't mind talking to you about your problems." Jefferson put his pencil down and gave her his full attention. "I'm just tired of you constantly complaining about your job and not doing anything to change the situation."

"Oh, I get it. This is turning into another conversation about you wanting me to leave the firm. Well, I'm not a quitter."

He turned off the TV even though it was already muted, then threw the remote down on the couch. "I don't want you to quit. I want you to be happy. And going to work at O'Reilly & Finney every day doesn't seem to make you happy. But you keep marching off to work like a good little soldier, then you come home every night and bitch to me for an hour about how miserable your job is. Well, I don't wanna hear it tonight."

"Fine! I had no idea that I was getting on your nerves." Vernetta snatched her purse and stomped off to the bedroom. "I won't bore you with my problems ever again," she hollered back at him from the hallway.

She had changed into her pajamas by the time Jefferson entered the bedroom ten minutes later.

He looked at her and laughed.

"I don't know what you think is so funny," she said.

"I guess I'm not getting any tonight, huh?" He chuckled. "Whenever you wear flannel to bed, that's usually what it means."

"Puh-leeze." Vernetta turned away and faced the mirror atop the dresser. "I wear flannel when I feel like wearing flannel. But you're right. You definitely ain't getting any tonight."

He tried to give her a hug, but she stepped around him and stalked into the bathroom. She doused a washcloth with warm water and pressed it to her face.

Jefferson stood in the doorway, arms folded, watching her. "I'm sorry for coming at you the way I did just now. But sometimes I get frustrated because there's nothing I can do to help you."

"I don't need any help," Vernetta snapped. "I'm just fine."

"That's the problem. You're not fine. You're not fine at all."

Vernetta dried her face and wished she could make him disappear.

"Leaving that firm wouldn't be the end of the world," Jefferson said gently. "And you don't have to be superwoman twenty-four/seven."

Vernetta chuckled sarcastically. "I'm not trying to be anybody's superwoman." She hung up the towel and tried to squeeze past him, but he blocked the doorway, threw his arms around her and wouldn't let go.

"Leave me alone!" She struggled to escape, but Jefferson overpowered her. When she realized that she couldn't escape, she finally stopped fighting. To her surprise, a gust of emotion seemed to appear from nowhere. She had absolutely nothing to cry about, so why was she crying?

"I love you," Jefferson said. "And it hurts me to see you unhappy."

Vernetta didn't respond because she couldn't. So, instead, she just cried into her husband's strong chest and wondered what in the hell she was doing with her life.

# CHAPTER 41

Special stared at her computer monitor and tried to concentrate on the report she'd been working on for the past hour. Every time a coherent thought entered her head, her mind wandered off and she forgot what point she was trying to make.

She knew she needed to get her act together and fast. But all she could think about was Clayton. It had been four days and he still wasn't returning her calls or answering her emails. She couldn't believe her stupid stunt was going to cost her the most incredible man she'd ever met.

Reaching for her coffee mug, she headed for the breakroom for her third cup of the morning. All the caffeine she'd been consuming had to be part of the reason she wasn't getting any sleep lately. She'd start cutting back. Tomorrow. When she entered the room, Radonna, one of her coworkers, snatched the television remote and hit the mute button.

"How you doing, girl?" Radonna asked.

Special figured her coworkers were talking about her. It surprised her that Radonna was up in the mix, since Special considered her a close friend. But she didn't have the energy to care.

Special reached for the coffee pot and filled her cup. "Why are you guys staring at me?"

Radonna smiled. "Nobody's staring at you, girl."

Special noticed that Radonna was intentionally blocking the television screen. Special stepped around her and read the crawl at the bottom of the screen. *Latest on local AIDS lawsuit on News at Noon.* Radonna hit the remote again, turning off the TV.

"Turn that back on," Special ordered.

"Girl, we need to get back to work." Radonna smiled nervously.

Special grabbed the remote from her hand and hit the power button. "They're about to do a story about the lawsuit we filed against Eugene. The noon broadcast should be on any minute."

Daisy, a sixtyish woman who worked the front desk, pursed her lips. "Baby, are you sure you should be watching this?"

"Yeah," Special said. "I'm glad the case is getting some publicity. I want that man to get everything he deserves." She sat her coffee cup on the table and pulled up a chair.

They waited in silence for the newscast to begin, watching a Gap commercial, followed by a Burger King spot, and Gary Coleman explaining how people in debt could get some quick cash. If Special had a pen handy, she would've written down the number for herself.

The familiar jingle for *News at Noon* came on and the lead anchor, a paunchy, conservative-looking white man with too-thick hair, quickly teased the top three stories. The AIDS lawsuit led the broadcast.

Special listened as the anchor did a quick intro, then tossed the story to a reporter standing outside the headquarters for the Gay and Lesbian Center.

> *Bill, I'm here in West Hollywood, where attorney and gay activist Barry Eagleman has announced that he will be defending attorney Eugene Nelson in one of the city's first wrongful death lawsuits alleging an intentional transmission of the AIDS virus.*

Special felt like she had taken a punch to the gut. The next scene showed a conference room with Eugene seated at a table next to Eagleman and two other men. The flashy attorney wore his hair slicked back in a long ponytail. He had small, piercing eyes and a handlebar mustache. Eagleman leaned over the microphone.

> *Unfortunately, discrimination, bigotry and ignorance are the foundation of this lawsuit. It's designed to disparage Mr. Nelson solely because of his sexual orientation. For that reason, I intend to use all of my resources to fight this malicious, homophobic attack. And I am more than confident that we will prevail at trial.*

Special reached out for her coffee, but her grasp was too unsteady and the cup clattered to the floor, splashing coffee everywhere. "That bastard! How dare he?"

Daisy grabbed some paper towels and started cleaning up the

mess, while Radonna put an arm around Special's shoulders and led her back to her office.

Margaret Hines knocked on the door just as Special sat down behind her desk. A middle-aged white woman who always wore a huge French bun and a hearty smile, Margaret was a manager in Human Resources. Special had always thought that anybody who smiled as much as Margaret did couldn't be trusted.

"I'd like to talk to Special. Alone."

Radonna gave Special's shoulder a squeeze, then left.

"I'll just get to the point," Margaret said. "Your coworkers are concerned about you, Special. I spoke with your supervisor. We both think it's a good idea for you to get some help."

"I don't need any help." Special reached for a tissue box on her desk and blew her nose. "I'm fine."

"I'd like you to see a counselor through our Employee Assistance Program," Margaret said gently.

Special waved off the suggestion. "I'm not about to lie down on a couch and tell my business to some stranger. That's why I have friends."

Margaret patted the back of her big bun. "Special, you've been in an extremely emotional state lately, and it's beginning to impact your job performance. I think it might be a good idea for you to talk a professional. "

"Thanks for your concern," Special said dryly. "But I'm fine."

Margaret eased an envelope from the pocket of her outdated plaid blazer. "This letter is for you. It's an EAP referral. A mandatory referral."

"I'm not going to no—"

"Perhaps you didn't hear me." Margaret's voice was much firmer this time. "This is a *mandatory* referral. You are required to see an EAP counselor and you can't come back to work until you do."

# CHAPTER 42

Haley pranced into Vernetta's office like she owned the place. She was carrying a thick stack of manila folders, which she dumped on the corner of the desk.

"Good morning, Haley." Vernetta stretched her lips into a big bogus smile. She had decided to make an effort to befriend Haley. No matter how much it pained her. "What case is this?"

"Hillman," Haley said. "The rest are being sent up from storage."

"Why are you giving them to me?"

Hillman was a dog of a case that had been passed around the firm at least twice before landing on Haley's desk. The lawsuit was filed by an unmanageable plaintiff who had gone through three attorneys and now represented himself. He submitted his briefs in handwriting and wrote long, rambling letters claiming that his firing was part of a CIA conspiracy. The case should have been dismissed a long time ago, but the assigned judge was almost as dippy as the plaintiff. The lawsuit was the biggest joke in the firm.

"I was told to deliver the files to your office."

"Why? I'm not on that case."

She swept her hair from her face with both hands. "Please don't tell me O'Reilly hasn't spoken to you about it."

"No, he hasn't."

"Well, give him a call. Hillman's your case now."

"Excuse me?"

Haley put both hands on her hips. "And I had nothing to do with it. If you have a problem with this, talk to O'Reilly." She turned on her heels and left.

Vernetta snatched the telephone to call O'Reilly, then slammed it back down. This discussion needed to be conducted face-to-face. She tore out for his office.

She knocked on the door and walked in at the same time. Towering over his desk, she peered down at him with a pair of irate eyes. "Haley tells me I'm handling the Hillman case now."

He looked up at her, frowned, then finished what he was writing.

"Sorry." He glanced up at her without making eye contact. "I meant to call you. I'd like you to take over the case. Haley's going to be much too busy with Vista Electronics."

"And so am I."

"Haley's made quite an impression with the execs at Vista. She's going to be handling many of the day-to-day responsibilities on the case."

A jolt of frustration surged through her body.

"It wasn't my decision," O'Reilly said quickly. He still hadn't looked her in the eye. "It was the client's request. And don't take it personally. The fact that Haley's billing rate is a lot cheaper than yours had a lot to do with it."

*Or maybe it's because she's screwing you.* "Are you telling me I'm no longer on the case?"

"No, I didn't say that."

"She's a second year associate, O'Reilly. Since when is she knowledgeable enough to play a lead role in a major case like this?"

"You and I will be keeping a close eye on her. Not that we'll have to do much of that. Haley's a very smart cookie."

*And you're apparently enjoying her cookies.*

This was total bull. O'Reilly was putting a plan in place to get her out of the way. She would need to show a solid record of strong performance on major cases when her name came up for partnership later in the year. She could not make partner handling a useless matter like the Hillman case.

"Where did things go wrong with us, O'Reilly?" Vernetta couldn't believe the words that had just slipped from her lips. But she had wanted to ask the question for some time. She used to be O'Reilly's favorite. Other associates even joked that she was the managing partner's pet. Now, he treated her like she was an afterthought.

"Vernetta, c'mon, don't be so sensitive." His eyes finally met hers, but not long enough for it to matter. "The client is calling the shots here. There'll be another great case coming through the door any day now. Don't overreact."

"I'm not overreacting. When the partnership vote comes up, I need to show that I've handled some key cases. Hillman won't cut it."

That was O'Reilly's cue to reassure her. To say that she already had a solid record of great work. That she didn't need to be overly concerned about the vote. That she was on track for partnership.

Instead, he scratched the back of his neck. "Vernetta, don't be so emotional. I bet you'll be the one associate who can wrap up the Hillman case once and for all."

The turtleneck sweater she was wearing felt like it was tightening around her throat. She was about to say something that she would surely regret later when O'Reilly's telephone rang.

"I have to take this call," he said dismissively. "Let's pick this up later."

Vernetta was so livid she could barely remember the way back to her office. She stepped inside, shut the door and dialed Jefferson's cell. It took way too long for him to pick up.

"Hey, babe, what's up?" Vernetta could hear what sounded like hammering in the background. She knew this wasn't a good time to call, but she needed him. Now.

She tried, but couldn't get any words out. Just a whimper.

"Babe, are you crying? What's the matter?"

"You're right," she finally sniffed. "I'm stupid for trying to stay here. They're not going to make me partner. I'm going to quit. Right now."

"Whooaaa," Jefferson said. "What's going on? I never heard you talk like this before. What happened?"

She recounted her conversation with O'Reilly.

"Babe, you know how I feel about your job. I felt you should've left a long time ago. But I think you should give it some more thought before quitting."

His words floored her. "I can't believe you're telling me *not* to quit."

"I can't believe it either," Jefferson said with a laugh. "And for the record, I'm not telling you not to quit. I'm just telling you not to quit right this second, when you're so emotional. I want you to think it through after you've calmed down so you don't wake up tomorrow regretting your decision. Why don't you just go home? We can talk about it tonight. And if you still feel the same way, you can quit in the morning."

As upset as she felt, Vernetta appreciated her husband's cautious wisdom. "Okay," she said, falling into the chair behind her desk. "But there's no way I'm going to change my mind."

# CHAPTER 43

Special's right knee anxiously bounced up and down as she sat in the waiting area of Dr. Shirley Blanchard's office on Santa Monica Boulevard in West L.A.

She didn't need to talk to a counselor, and she certainly didn't need to talk to some high-priced psychologist who probably didn't even know what being on the down low meant. But she couldn't afford to lose her job, so she was doing what she had to do. Anyway, she didn't expect it to take long to prove that she wasn't crazy. Then she could get her ass back to work.

Dr. Blanchard greeted Special in the reception area of her office. She had frilly black hair and a voice that sounded like a phone sex operator. Her makeup was way overdone, and her lips were fixed into a permanent pout. Bad botox job, Special thought.

"So tell me why you're here," Dr. Blanchard said, once they were seated in her office.

"I'm here because the people I work with think I have a problem, but I don't," Special huffed. "My cousin recently died because her fiancé infected her with HIV. I just broke up with my boyfriend. I'm behind on about every bill I've got and there's probably an eviction notice waiting for me when I get home." She grinned. "But I ain't crazy."

"That's quite a load to be carrying. You think people who go to counseling are crazy?"

"No. I'm sorry, I didn't mean it like that. I just meant . . . I know how to handle my problems."

Dr. Blanchard nodded. "Well, I'm here to see if I can offer some assistance in helping you do that."

"Okay, then, Doc, shoot your best shot. I can't go back to work until we go through this routine. So let's get to it."

Dr. Blanchard proceeded to ask her a series of questions about Maya. Before she knew it, Special had divulged the whole story about Maya's death as well as the events leading up to her breakup with Clayton.

"You've been through an extremely emotional period," Dr. Blanchard said. "Sometimes life's events can affect us in ways we don't see. So what are your feelings toward Mr. Nelson?"

"What are my feelings? That should be an easy guess for you, Doc. I wish he were dead. If I thought I could get away with it, I would kill him myself."

Dr. Blanchard reared her head back. "Those are some pretty strong emotions."

"Rightfully so, don't you think?"

"There are both proper and improper ways to express negative emotions."

"Yeah, I know. I'm cool. So how many sessions we gotta have, Doc?"

"It depends on your progress. Before our next meeting, I'd like you to write whatever words come to mind when you think of Mr. Nelson."

"Okay. That sounds easy enough. In fact, why don't I get started right now." She pulled an envelope from her purse, scribbled on it and held it up for Dr. Blanchard to see. She had written the word *hate* five times.

By the time Special left Dr. Blanchard's office, she felt ten times better. Talking about her hatred for Eugene turned out to be surprisingly cathartic.

Instead of going home, she went to the Jamba Juice in the Ladera Center and bought herself a large Caribbean Crush and a bag of onion bagel chips. She pulled up a chair at one of the wrought iron tables outside the Starbucks next door and took out the latest issue of *Star* magazine. The sun felt good. She couldn't remember the last time she'd felt so relaxed.

She had just finished reading an article about Brad Pitt and Janet Jackson's secret love child when a disturbing sight caused her to gag.

Eugene and a woman were walking out of the adjacent T.G.I. Friday's restaurant, smiling and laughing. She watched in stunned amazement as Eugene opened the door of his convertible BMW and helped the woman inside.

"Oh, hell nah! I can't believe that dog is back to his old tricks already!"

Special made a dash for her car two rows over, forgetting about her Caribbean Crush and *Star* magazine. She started the engine just as Eugene was backing out of the parking stall. When he drove past, she ducked, then followed.

Eugene kept straight out of the Ladera Center along Little Centinela and made a right onto Halm. She stayed a good distance behind as Eugene turned into a driveway on the left. Special pulled to a stop on the opposite side of the street, several houses back.

Eugene and his new woman strolled to the front porch. While the woman opened the door, Eugene bent over the porch railing, picked a yellow daffodil from the garden and handed it to the woman. She giggled and gave him a hug. Special wanted to vomit.

Turning off the engine, she rested her forehead against the steering wheel and tried to calm herself down. She didn't know when Eugene would be leaving the house, but she planned to wait. Even if it took all night.

And when he did, Special had an earful to tell his new girlfriend.

# CHAPTER 44

Special parked outside the woman's house for close to two hours, comforted by her collection of gospel CDs. After listening to the entire *Best of Yolanda Adams* CD, she switched to Fred Hammond. She had almost dozed off when she noticed Eugene exit the woman's front door.

It was almost dusk now, but she could see Eugene and the woman standing on the porch. They embraced, then Eugene kissed her on the cheek. At least the girl had the good sense not to tongue-kiss the man, Special thought.

The lawsuit they had filed against Eugene had been splashed all over the newspapers, TV, and radio. Had the woman been hiding under a rock? How could she not know the man was HIV positive?

As Eugene's car passed hers, Special ducked down in her seat and prayed he didn't recognize her Porsche. When he was out of sight, she drove closer to the woman's house, climbed out, and boldly knocked on the front door.

"Yes, may I help you?" The woman peered through the peephole.

Special tried not to sound confrontational. "Uh . . . I'd like to talk to you."

"Do I know you?"

"No, you don't. It's about your friend, Eugene. It's very important. It'll only take a minute. I'm not asking to come inside since you don't know me. But I do need to share some important information with you."

After a long moment, the woman opened the door, but did not remove the safety chain. "What about Eugene?"

"I don't know how to tell you this, but there's no other way to do it, so I'll just blurt it out. Eugene is gay."

The woman's face did not convey the alarm Special had anticipated. She actually looked rather nonchalant.

"I know this is a shock." Special tried to sound empathetic. "I saw the two of you come out of Friday's earlier today. I just felt you needed to know. And not only is he gay, he's—"

"HIV positive," the woman said. "I already know that."

Special's mouth flew open.

"You must be Special," the woman said. "Eugene told me all about how you've been harassing him. There's nothing you can tell me about Eugene that I don't already know. So I would suggest you just—"

"Did you know that he killed my cousin by intentionally infecting her? Did he tell you that?"

"He didn't *intentionally* do anything," the woman fired back. "He didn't even know he was HIV positive."

"Well, he knew he was screwing men!" Special shouted.

The woman bristled. "Eugene was very confused about his sexuality back then. He's saved now, and he's giving his life to God. God has forgiven him for his transgressions and so have I."

"His transgressions! Are you a fuckin' nut case? That man has a deadly disease. He killed my cousin. He could kill you, too!"

"I'm not going to stand here and discuss my personal relationship with a total stranger. Eugene told me you needed psychological help and I completely agree with him." She slammed the door.

"I don't need psychological help!" Special roared at the closed door. "You're the one who needs help!" She staggered to her car, nearly blind with rage.

There was no way she was going to sit back and watch Eugene continue with a happy, carefree life. The man had to pay for what he did. And suing his ass just wasn't going to cut it.

# CHAPTER 45

Seconds after Jefferson talked her out of quitting, Vernetta received an emergency call from a client. She ended up driving to San Pedro to deal with a union organizer who was demanding access to her client's facility. It was after seven by the time she made it home.

Vernetta had just put her key in the lock when Jefferson opened the door and pulled her into his arms.

"I was just about to get worried. But then I figured you'd ignored my advice like you always do and quit anyway."

"Nope, I didn't quit yet," she said.

"So where you been?"

She was about to answer, but he didn't give her a chance.

"I decided you needed some TLC tonight." He kissed her, then took her purse and briefcase. He picked up a wineglass filled with cranberry juice from a sofa table in the entryway and handed it to her.

"I knew you couldn't handle any Cognac and this was all we had in the fridge," he said with a big grin.

Vernetta smiled and took the glass. "I have the best husband in the whole wide world."

"Damn straight you do."

He took her hand and led her to the bedroom. After undressing her, he helped her into a terry cloth robe which he must have just pulled from the dryer, because it was nice and warm.

"Stay right here," Jefferson instructed, then disappeared into the bathroom. She could hear water running in the tub.

A few minutes later, he took her hand again and she obediently plodded along behind him like an exhausted puppy on a short leash. He stopped just inside the doorway of the bathroom, bowed and made a sweeping gesture with his hand.

"For you."

The Jacuzzi tub was filled to the rim with bubbles. Scented candles at the base of the tub provided the perfect mood lighting. The boom box in the corner softly played her favorite Alicia Keys CD. Vernetta squeezed Jefferson's hand, then kissed him on the cheek.

He helped her into the tub, then sat on the rim and lifted her right foot from the water. His big hands went to work, gently massaging her heel. Vernetta was thoroughly enjoying the pampering.

"So, I guess I must'a shocked you when I stopped you from running in there and quitting today, huh?"

"Yep, I would have to say that was quite a surprise." Vernetta leaned her head back and settled deeper into the tub. "All this time, I thought you wanted me to quit."

"I keep telling you that what I want is to see you happy. And if leaving that firm will do the trick, then I'm all for it. But I know how important making partner is to you. I didn't want you to do something you might regret. I wanted you to make the decision when you're calm and rational."

Vernetta closed her eyes. "Thank you. I'm actually glad you stopped me. I gave a lot of thought to what I wanted to do on the drive home."

She felt Jefferson's hands stiffen. "And?"

Vernetta was afraid to speak, but finally, she did. "Now that I've had some time to think about it, maybe you were right. Perhaps I was being too emotional."

The fingers that had been expertly stroking her foot slowed to a stop. Vernetta opened her eyes. The dim lighting in the room did not hide the disappointment on her husband's face.

Jefferson went back to massaging her foot, but the intimacy of his touch had lessened. "So you're staying?" he finally asked.

Vernetta timidly nodded, afraid to utter more words to disappoint him.

He gently laid her foot at the bottom of the tub, then crouched down on the floor facing her.

Vernetta looked over at him and noticed that his whole demeanor had changed. "I guess you're mad at me, huh?"

"Nah, I'm cool. But I don't get it. Some people stay in jobs they hate because they have to. They need the money. But you don't."

"I don't hate my job, Jefferson."

"As much as you complain about it, you could've fooled me."

Neither one of them said anything as a heavy tension saturated the room.

Jefferson got to his feet. "I stopped by Phillips on the way home and picked up some barbecue. I'll go heat up the food."

"I'm sorry. I just don't think the time is right for me to leave."

"That's cool," Jefferson replied with a shrug. "It's your life."

# CHAPTER 46

Nichelle spent most of the afternoon at the home of a client whose living trust needed updating. When she arrived back at her office later that evening, the first thing she noticed was a manila envelope with Barry Eagleman's return address.

She already knew what was inside, having caught his outrageous press conference, and did not bother to take a seat before removing several documents from the envelope.

The first was an *ex parte* motion, a tool attorneys use to ask a judge to resolve an issue on short notice. Eagleman was seeking a gag order and he wanted the judge to ban cameras from the courtroom. A declaration attached to the motion claimed that the excessive media attention focused on the case was tainting the jury pool and causing Eugene severe and undue hardship.

"What about Maya's hardship?" Nichelle said out loud.

As expected, Eagleman had filed an answer denying all of the allegations in the complaint. Nichelle scanned the remaining documents, then gasped. "Oh, my God!"

She read a declaration signed by Eugene and couldn't believe her eyes. Eagleman was filing a counterclaim against Maya's estate for negligence. Eugene was actually claiming that Maya had given *him* HIV. His countersuit stated that, to his knowledge, none of his male partners were HIV positive. Thus, Maya must have infected *him*. He was demanding ten million dollars in damages.

Nichelle did not notice Russell standing in the doorway. "You okay?" He rushed over.

She pressed her hand to her chest and sucked in air in uneven gulps.

Russell gripped her shoulder. "Are you having trouble breathing?"

Nichelle managed to eke out a "no," as tears began parallel tracks down her cheeks. Russell ran out and dashed back in with a cup of water, along with Sadie, their secretary.

"What's the matter? Do you need a doctor?" Sadie asked.

"I'm fine," Nichelle finally squeaked. "I just got these documents from Eugene's attorney. He's alleging that Maya infected *him*."

"You're kidding," Russell said.

Nichelle slumped into the chair behind her desk as Russell read the documents. "Special is really going to flip out when she hears this. In fact, I don't think I'm even going to tell her."

Sadie scowled in disgust. "That man is something else."

"Are you sure you have this case under control?" Russell asked.

"To be honest, no, I'm not. I didn't want to tell you, but Jamal's firm has decided that he shouldn't be involved. I thought I could handle it by myself, but now that Eugene's hired Barry Eagleman, I'm not so sure."

"Well, you know where you can find help," Russell said.

Excited, Nichelle sat up. "So you're going to help me?"

"Not me. You have another law partner who's one of the best litigators in this state."

She fell back into the chair. "Sam won't help me. He didn't even want me to take the case, remember?"

"Have you forgotten who we're talking about? This lawsuit is already making national headlines. Sam would love to be involved. He's just too cocky to admit it."

Fifteen minutes later, Nichelle knocked on the door of Sam's office. "How are you?" She walked in without waiting for his invitation. She hated groveling, but knew that was exactly what she would have to do.

He looked up from his computer. "I'm fine. What do you want?"

"I need your help."

Sam frowned. "With what?"

"The wrongful death lawsuit. Jamal isn't going to be able to help me after all."

"What did I tell you? I knew this would happen! You don't have enough civil litigation experience to handle a high-profile case like that. You just better be glad you know the family. Otherwise, we'd be looking at a malpractice suit."

Nichelle quietly inhaled. For Maya's sake, she would just have to take it. "I need your help, Sam. Eugene has hired Barry Eagleman.

He's seeking a gag order and wants the judge to bar cameras from the courtroom." She placed the documents in front of him.

Sam started reading the court papers. "This case is assigned to Judge Fuller. He despises the media. You can bet he's going to grant this motion."

Nichelle sat down. "That's what scares me."

"I told you taking on this case was going to be a mistake," Sam growled. "And now it looks like all that media attention you thought you were going to get is—"

He stopped reading and looked up at her. "Is this guy for real? He has the audacity to claim that your friend gave *him* HIV? He's actually countersuing her estate?"

Nichelle nodded.

"What a punk!" Sam threw the papers on his desk. "Yeah, I'll help you with the case. And I'm going to enjoy every minute of it."

# CHAPTER 47

Vernetta was thrilled to see a virtual zoo outside the Los Angeles Superior Courthouse when she and Special arrived for the hearing on Eugene's motion for a gag order. They couldn't have paid for this kind of publicity.

Television news vans topped with huge satellite dishes lined the street. Hundreds of people milled about on the courthouse steps while two cops were directing traffic and yelling at people to stay on the sidewalk. A Christian group carrying a huge *Homosexuality is a sin* banner squared off against a group of gay rights protestors flaunting rainbow armbands. Vernetta couldn't believe it when she saw CNN's legal analyst, Nancy Grace, hop out of a white news truck.

It took them nearly twenty minutes to make it through the metal detectors at the courthouse entrance. When they finally reached the courtroom, J.C. stood waiting. Luckily, the bailiff, a friend of J.C.'s, had saved seats for them. The small courtroom couldn't accommodate everyone who wanted to attend the hearing, so the three women received quite a few nasty looks as they strolled past a line of spectators who had been turned away.

The judge had yet to take the bench. They sat near the first row, directly behind the plaintiff's table where Nichelle and Sam were already seated inside the well of the courtroom. Eugene sat at an adjacent table, surrounded by Eagleman and two other men. Eagleman was perched on the edge of the table, his arms locked across his chest, facing the gallery. He was smiling and laughing and looked like the character that he was. He sported a tiny rainbow pin on the lapel of his jacket.

"Eugene is just trying to sweep this case under the rug," Special moaned. "That judge better not grant no gag order. The whole world needs to know what he did."

"Just be cool," Vernetta cautioned. Special was already way too wound up. Nobody had been brave enough to tell her about Eugene's countersuit. Vernetta just prayed Special didn't go off in the courtroom if the subject came up.

It was another fifteen minutes before the bailiff announced, "All rise," and Judge Fuller entered from a side door. Woodrow J. Fuller was a senior judge who looked like he'd been around since the building went up. His bushy grey eyebrows were thicker than the hair on his head and he spoke as if he needed to spit. Once the judge was seated, the bailiff instructed everyone to sit down.

"I've taken a look at your papers, counselor," the judge said in the direction of Eagleman. "You may address the court."

Eagleman stood. "Your Honor, I only have a brief statement." He was almost yelling, and talking very, very slowly. "I believe the basis for this motion is clearly set forth in our papers. As you well know, the court has the authority to issue a gag order on three grounds: to protect a defendant's right to a fair trial, to protect the fair administration of justice, and to preserve the sanctity of jury deliberations. All of those factors are present here.

"That fiasco out front," he dramatically pointed east, toward Hill Street, "demonstrates that it will be very difficult for my client to get a fair trial. Even in the short timeframe since we filed this motion, Ms. Ayers has continued to conduct more interviews falsely maligning my client. It is my request that she be barred from granting further interviews with the media and that cameras be barred from all phases of the proceeding. My brief contains a long list of supporting case law." He sat back down.

The judge turned to the plaintiff's table. "Counselor, tell me why you feel it's necessary to try this case in the press rather than here in this courtroom?"

Special's knee started to bounce. "Because women need to know about men like Eugene."

Sam started to rise, but the judge motioned him back down. "I want to hear from Ms. Ayers. She's the one doing all the talking outside the courtroom."

Nichelle stood up and Vernetta could tell that she was nervous by the way she tugged at the sleeve of her blouse three times. They had planned for Sam to argue the motion. "Your Honor, I don't feel that I've been trying this case in the media. I've been—"

"What?" The judge took off his bi-focals and pointed them at her. "I can't hear you. Don't come in my courtroom mumbling. If you have an argument to make, say it so I can hear you."

Sam lowered his head. Nichelle had apparently forgotten that the judge was nearly deaf.

She cleared her throat and spoke in a louder, slower voice. "Our opposition brief cites numerous cases which support our position that media coverage of this case would in no way prejudice the defendant, impede the fair administration of justice or influence the jury. Mr. Eagleman has cited a long list of cases, but none of them are directly on point. I also would like the court to note that Mr. Eagleman has made quite a few media appearances himself."

"Only in response to yours," Eagleman interrupted.

Nichelle inhaled and rolled her eyes at him. "This motion for a gag order is nothing but a publicity stunt on Mr. Eagleman's part. Just like his ten-million-dollar counterclaim alleging that Ms. Washington was actually the one who infected Mr. Nelson."

Special whipped her head in Vernetta's direction.

"Yes," Vernetta whispered, "he's claiming Maya infected him. Just don't wig out in here. If you do, you're going to jail."

Special closed her eyes, wrapped her arms around her upper body and started rocking back and forth. Vernetta leaned forward and silently signaled J.C. to be on the look out for any sudden moves from Special. The likelihood of her diving across the railing and strangling Eugene was a very real possibility.

"Your Honor," Nichelle went on, "the rules governing the fair administration of justice apply to both the plaintiff and the defendant. The real plaintiff in this case, Maya Washington, is not here to speak for herself. The heart of this lawsuit is about deceit. Barring the media from covering this case would be as big a travesty as Ms. Washington's death."

"Oh, come on," Eagleman muttered, then dramatically threw his pen on the table. The judge wasn't only deaf, he must have been blind, too. Any other judge would have warned Eagleman to cut the theatrics.

When Nichelle finished, the judge turned back to Eagleman, who did some more grandstanding. Judge Fuller finally cut him off and asked a few questions of both attorneys that gave no inkling as to how he might rule. He then announced that he was taking the case under submission and would issue a ruling within a week.

Vernetta and J.C. ushered Special out of the courtroom as soon as the judge banged his gavel. Special didn't utter a word until they arrived at the parking lot.

"Eugene is such a dog!" Special snarled as she hopped into the front seat of Vernetta's Land Cruiser. "How dare he claim Maya infected *him*!"

"Let's just have faith that the legal system is going to work," Vernetta said.

"Screw the legal system. We should just kill his ass ourselves. You're a cop, J.C. Don't you know any criminals who can do the job for us?"

"Just get in the car," J.C. ordered. She looked across the passenger seat at Vernetta. "Please take her home. Tie her up if you have to."

"Did you know he has another girlfriend?" Special said to J.C. "Can you believe that?"

"How would you know?"

"Because I followed—" Special stopped, realizing that she was about to confess to stalking in the presence of a cop. A cop who was a close friend, but a cop just the same.

"Please tell me you're not still harassing that man," J.C. said. "If he files a complaint against you, you're going to jail and there won't be a thing anybody can do about it."

"It's not right," Special said, settling into the car and snapping on her seatbelt. "Everybody's treating Eugene like *he's* the victim."

# CHAPTER 48

Eugene awoke before five the next morning to the loud shrill of an alarm. In his drowsy state it took several seconds for him to realize that the sound was *his* car alarm and was coming from *his* driveway.

He snatched his robe from the foot of the bed and ran barefoot down the stairs and out of the house. When he saw his BMW—his precious ninety-thousand-dollar BMW—he wanted to cry. The shiny black exterior had been splashed with red paint. The front windshield looked as if it had been bashed in with a tire iron.

He didn't understand how he could have slept through this.

"Ow!" He lifted his foot and removed a thick shard of glass. Blood slowly dripped from the wound, but Eugene was so enraged he barely felt the pain.

Eugene knew who was responsible for the vandalism and this time he was pressing charges. Somebody had to do something about the crazy bitch even if she was Maya's cousin. He was about to head back into the house when he saw the word *fag* spray painted across his garage door. He walked around to the side of his house, careful to avoid stepping on another piece of glass. He stared up at more homophobic epithets.

He hurried back inside, bandaged his foot, then snatched the telephone from the kitchen counter. First he called the police, then the *L.A. Times* City Desk. He told the woman who answered that he was the victim of a hate crime and that the vandalism would make good pictures for the evening paper. Then he made similar calls to all five of the local TV stations and at least four radio stations.

After calling his lawyer, he jumped in and out of the shower, dressed, and prepared to be the center of another news story. If Special wanted a war, he was more than ready to do battle.

As he waited for the onslaught, he decided to call J.C. It wasn't even six yet, but he didn't care. She picked up on the second ring.

"This is Eugene," he said, not waiting for a hello. "Special vandalized my car and spray painted my house. I'm tired of her harassing me. This time she's going to pay."

"So when was this?" J.C. asked.

"Earlier this morning."

"Did you see her do it?"

Eugene chuckled. "I didn't have to see her do it. I know she's behind it. She even had the nerve to follow me on a date and confront my friend after I left."

"Nice to know you're back out there, Eugene."

"What I do is my business. I know you guys think I'm responsible for Maya's death, but—"

"*Think* you're responsible? *Think?* We don't *think* you're responsible, we *know* you're responsible and you know it, too. Despite that crap your attorneys said in court yesterday."

Eugene closed his eyes. Yes, he knew he had caused Maya's death and he knew his lawyer's arguments were nothing but legal maneuvering. If Maya's family won the lawsuit, his attorneys said the verdict could be in the millions. He wasn't about to lose every dime he had ever worked for. He had to do what he had to do.

"I know you don't believe that I loved Maya, but I did. If I could give my life for hers, I would. But I can't and I will not sit back and let your psycho friend continue to harass me."

Eugene slammed down the phone just as he heard a knock at the door. Two cops, an African-American and a Latino, stood on his front porch. He opened the door and invited them in. He could tell from their expressions that they recognized him.

The black cop pulled out a small notepad. "You called about the car outside, right?"

Right away, Eugene knew that he would not get the help he needed. The look on both men's faces conveyed that they believed he had gotten exactly what he deserved. Their indifference infuriated him. He was a goddamn taxpayer and he deserved protection.

"I know who did this," he said.

"We're listening," the Hispanic cop replied. He was barely five-seven and looked like he'd been stuffed into his black uniform.

"Her name is Special Moore and—"

Though he had taken out his notepad, the black cop had yet to write anything down. "Did you see her do it?" he asked

"No. But she's been harassing me."

The Hispanic cop was busy checking out the plush surroundings. The living room walls were painted a soft brick color and were bordered with stark white baseboards and crown molding. An L-shaped couch with African-print fabric took up one corner of the room. The officer gawked unabashedly at the baby grand in the corner.

"She lives in Fox Hills on Buckingham Drive." He picked up a note from the coffee table that he had written before their arrival. "Here's her address and telephone number."

"And what makes you think she's behind this?" the black cop asked.

"Like I just said, she's been harassing me."

"I think I heard about your case. You're the guy whose fiancée died of AIDS and you're suing *her* for ten mil, right?" He chuckled sarcastically. "I suspect there are a lot of people who could've done this."

Eugene felt a tightening in his chest. They couldn't care less about his car and home being vandalized.

"Unless you have some hard evidence, we can't just go around arresting people." The black cop finally scribbled something on his notepad. "We'll take some pictures and collect some evidence, but vandalism's not an easy crime to solve."

The Hispanic cop was still inspecting the living room. He took a few steps and peered into the kitchen. "You've got two refrigerators?"

"One's a deep freezer," Eugene said irritably.

He nodded. "Anyway, like my partner said, vandals aren't easy to catch. Hopefully, you've got insurance."

When they stepped outside, an *L.A. Times* photographer and a news truck from the local Fox station were snapping pictures of the damaged car and the spray-painted epithets. Two other news crews were pulling up. In seconds Eugene had microphones and cameras in his face.

"This is without a doubt a hate crime," Eugene proclaimed. "And I'm asking anyone who may have witnessed this attack to please come forward."

After interviewing Eugene, a reporter stuck a microphone in the black cop's face and his demeanor completely changed. He gave a short sound bite that made it sound like this was the crime of the century and he was determined to solve it.

Two hours later, when all the commotion had died down, Eugene sat on his living room couch and tried to decompress. He felt such a sense of hopelessness that he didn't trust himself to be alone. He picked up his keys and opened the front door, then realized that he didn't have a car to drive.

Pulling his cell phone from his pocket, he dialed Belynda's number. Her voice instantly soothed him.

"It's Eugene," he said, his voice cracking. He didn't know where to begin, so he said what he felt. "I need you."

# CHAPTER 49

It had taken a while, but Belynda had finally convinced Eugene to seek counseling at the church. He pulled Belynda's Honda Civic into the parking lot of Ever Faithful and turned off the engine.

At nearly every stoplight, Eugene considered making a U-turn and heading home. But he knew he needed help. For the first time in his life, he felt like he was nearing the breaking point.

Despite Belynda's assurances, Eugene had no idea how sympathetic Bishop Berry would be. He'd never heard the bishop deliver one of those fire and brimstone sermons condemning homosexuality, but with most ministers he knew, Christianity and homosexuality didn't mix.

Eugene steeled himself and made his way into the church. The empty vestibule had a serene feeling that welcomed him. He had never been inside Ever Faithful when the church wasn't packed with people. He looked around, not sure which hallway led to the bishop's office.

An older woman greeted him. "Good afternoon and welcome to Ever Faithful. I'm Bettie."

"Hello," Eugene said. "I'm looking for Bishop Berry."

Bettie pursed her lips. "Did you have an appointment?"

"No, but I was hoping to speak with him. I was told he held office hours today."

"Normally he does," she said apologetically. "But one of our members had a death in the family, so he's out dealing with that. Reverend Sims is available, though. He's one of the assistant pastors. Just follow me."

Eugene hesitated.

"I guarantee you'll like Reverend Sims." Bettie patted him on the back. "I'll show you to his office."

Without waiting for Eugene to make up his mind, she escorted him down a corridor toward the south side of the church. She tapped lightly on the door and waited for permission before entering.

Reverend Sims stood.

"I have a gentleman here who wanted to meet with Bishop Berry for counseling, but he's out," Bettie explained. "I told him he could talk to you."

"Of course." The reverend extended his hand, then offered Eugene a seat.

Eugene had expected to see someone in a white collar. Reverend Sims was casually dressed in slacks and a turtleneck. He was a handsome, bearded man who looked to be in his early forties.

"Give me just a second to finish up here," Reverend Sims said, returning to his desk. "I was working on a sermon."

"Sorry to interrupt."

"It's no interruption at all." He stacked the papers and set them off to the side. "How can I help you?"

Eugene sat back in the chair. He didn't know how to begin. He wasn't one to talk much about his problems, particularly to strangers. "I'm not sure where to start," he finally admitted.

"Let *me* start then," the reverend said. "I can't say that I don't recognize your face. You've been all over the news lately. I can only imagine how tough it's been for you. But you're on the right path because you've turned to God."

Eugene stared down at his hands as tears blurred his vision.

"I can't imagine that there are many people who have a kind word for you these days," Reverend Sims continued. "But none of us are perfect, though many of us profess to be. We've all made mistakes, but the good Lord is all about forgiveness. Just put everything in His hands, and I guarantee you, your burdens *will* be lifted."

Eugene nodded through his tears. They talked for a long time and Eugene found it easy to share his thoughts and feelings.

"You'll be amazed at what prayer can do, brother," Reverend Sims said. "Why don't we pray right now." He walked around his desk and stood over Eugene, placing a hand on his shoulder.

"It's going to be fine, brother. You're going to get through this."

Eugene stood and the reverend embraced him.

"I want you to immerse yourself in the Word. I'm going to recommend some verses I'd like you to read."

Eugene felt such a sense of well-being in the man's presence, he almost didn't notice the arousal creep up on him. He winced. He did not want to have these feelings.

Reverend Sims offered to escort him out. "So what do you do for fun?" the reverend asked, as they made their way to the church parking lot.

"I can't remember the last time I even had any fun. I used to enjoy playing racquetball. But it's been a while."

"That's my game, too," Reverend Sims said. "I don't get many invitations to play, though. People don't think ministers do normal things like play sports. Maybe we can play some time?"

*Tell him no.* In light of everything Eugene had been struggling with, he knew he couldn't handle being around a man to whom he felt even remotely attracted. But who was he kidding? He wasn't going to turn out a minister of all people. This was the safest male relationship he could have.

Eugene stopped and faced the reverend. "A game of racquetball might be just the thing I need."

# CHAPTER 50

It was after six and Vernetta and Haley had been cooped up in a conference room for nearly two hours. Hundreds of computerized payroll records from Vista Electronics covered the table.

When her cell phone rang and displayed Special's number, Vernetta had a bad feeling even before she picked up.

"The police are here," Special cried into the telephone. "I think they're going to arrest me!"

Vernetta stood. "Arrest you? For what?"

Haley's head sprang upward. Her baby blues were wide with curiosity.

Vernetta silently berated herself. She should've had the foresight to leave the conference room the minute Special's number popped up. She opened the door and stepped into the hallway.

Special still hadn't answered her question. "Arrest you for what, Special?"

Vernetta hurried past a long row of secretaries' cubicles and didn't stop until she reached the bank of elevators in the twelfth floor lobby.

"They wanna talk to me about Eugene." Special spoke in shallow breaths, as if she had just run up a flight of stairs. "Somebody vandalized his car this morning."

Vernetta hung her head and closed her eyes. She was almost afraid to ask Special if she'd had a hand in the crime. "So did you do it?"

"I can't believe you even asked me that. Do you know how many women in this city hate Eugene for what he did to Maya? There's a girl at my job who despises him almost as much as I do."

Vernetta recalled a conversation she'd heard at the beauty shop. Eugene definitely had a growing list of haters.

"They're waiting downstairs." The panic in Special's voice escalated with each syllable. "They want me to buzz them inside." Vernetta could practically see her friend pacing back and forth across her living room, one hand on the phone, the other glued to her tiny waist. "I told 'em I knew my rights and needed to call my lawyer first."

"Good," Vernetta said. "Just tell them—"

"No," Special whined. "I want *you* to talk to them. Please, come over."

Vernetta thought about all the payroll records waiting to be reviewed. Technically, she needed the firm's permission before running off to act as Special's attorney. But she didn't want to go to O'Reilly or any other partner to explain. Anyway, it was highly unlikely that anyone at the firm would find out. Special was her best friend. She had to take the risk.

"I'm on my way," she said, exasperated. "Call Nichelle and ask her to meet me at your place. Tell the police your lawyers are on the way. And whatever you do, don't let them upstairs. Make them wait in the lobby."

Vernetta practically sprinted back to the conference room and snatched the jacket of her pantsuit from the back of her chair. "I have a family emergency." She wiggled into her coat. "I'll be back in a couple of hours." She could tell that Haley was dying to know more.

"So who was that?"

"My cousin."

"Anything I can do to help?"

*Yeah, keep your big mouth shut.* But Vernetta knew that in a matter of minutes, Haley would start blabbing that Vernetta had run off to save some family member from being dragged to jail.

"Just finish reviewing those last two stacks of records from the Norwalk plant. We can finish the rest tomorrow."

Vernetta pulled up in front of Special's apartment just as Nichelle was getting out of her car.

"Special claims she didn't have anything to do with it," Nichelle said. "But I'm not sure I believe her. She still hasn't admitted sending that vile email to Eugene's law firm or throwing nails in his driveway."

"Let's just hope she's telling the truth this time."

Vernetta had a key to Special's apartment and used it to open the double glass doors that led into the lobby. She looked around, expecting to see the two officers, but the lobby was empty. "The elevator in this building takes forever. Let's take the stairs."

When they reached the third floor landing, they heard a commotion coming from the vicinity of Special's apartment.

"What in the world is going on in there?" Nichelle said, verbalizing the same uneasiness that Vernetta felt.

She had a vision of Special pinned to the floor, wrestling with the two officers as they struggled to slap handcuffs on her wrists. They rushed to the door and just as Vernetta was about to knock, her hand froze in mid-air. The sound emanating from inside sounded like laughter. Vernetta tossed Nichelle a confused look. Nichelle tossed the same look right back at her.

She gave the door three quick raps. When nothing happened, she knocked again, harder this time. It still took a while before they heard the approach of footsteps.

Special opened the door with a devious grin stretched across her pretty face. She was wearing cutoff jeans with a tank top tied into a knot just above her belly button. The straps of her three-inch, high-heel sandals were wrapped around her long, muscular legs, almost to the knee. Her hair was fanned out across her shoulders, with her bangs swept seductively across her right eye.

When they stepped inside, they saw two cops—one black, one Hispanic—relaxing on Special's sofa, eating from two small saucers. The officers looked up, but never stopped stuffing their faces.

Special introduced Vernetta and Nichelle as if they were uninvited guests, then gave the two cops a much perkier introduction. "This is Officer Fred Donovan." Special extended her arm and pointed her index finger in the direction of the black cop. "And this is Officer Manny Gomez." She actually giggled. "And don't worry, I followed your instructions. I haven't answered any questions. But I decided to feed my two new buddies while we waited for you guys to get here."

The black cop reached for the glass of milk sitting on the coffee table in front of him. "This sweet potato cheesecake is incredible," he said, guzzling down his milk. "I had no idea they even made this kind of cheesecake. You don't find too many women in your age bracket who can throw down in the kitchen like this." When he smiled up at Special, his eyes zeroed in on her cleavage.

Vernetta looked from the cops to her scantily clad friend. The dessert they were chowing down on came from Harriett's Cheesecakes Unlimited. Not Special's kitchen.

Officer Gomez wiped his mouth with the back of his hand and set his empty saucer on the coffee table. "It's time for us to get down to business." His black uniform had a snug fit, especially around the biceps, which Vernetta estimated to be a good twenty inches in diameter. He pulled a notepad from his shirt pocket and flipped it open.

"First—"

Vernetta cut him off. "Instead of starting with your questions, Officer," she said with an appropriate level of deference, "I have a few questions of my own."

Special waved her off. "Girl, that ain't even necessary." She perched herself on the arm of the couch next to a smiling Officer Donovan, then smiled up at the other cop. "Go ahead, Manny. Ask away."

Vernetta was ready to wring Special's neck. "You called us over here to represent you," she said testily. "I think you should let us do that."

"That was before I had a chance to get to know Fred and Manny." She winked at Gomez.

"Special, I don't think you should—"

Officer Gomez followed Special's lead and ignored Vernetta's protests. "This shouldn't take too long." He scanned his notepad. "An individual by the name of Eugene Nelson claims that you spray-painted graffiti on his house and vandalized his car sometime before five a.m. this morning. Did you?"

"Of course not," Special said.

"Okay, good." Gomez scanned his notepad again. "He also claims that you tossed nails in his driveway a couple of weeks ago."

"Not guilty." Special held up her hand like she was taking an oath, which made her tank top rise up, revealing more of her flat stomach.

"Okay. And did you hack into his law firm's computer system and send a defamatory email to everybody in the firm two days before that?"

"C'mon, Manny," Special purred. "Do I look like a computer hacker to you?"

Officer Donovan devoured a huge forkful of cheesecake. "Not to me."

"Okay, then." Officer Gomez shoved his notepad back into his front pocket. "Case closed. Can I have some more sweet potato cheesecake now?"

The two cops broke into hearty laughter. Special picked up Manny's saucer and scampered away to fetch his second serving.

Before Vernetta could say anything, Nichelle took the lead. "So . . . uh, you're done with your questioning?" she asked, amazed.

"Pretty much," Officer Donovan said. "This Nelson guy didn't see any of this stuff happen. Like we told him, vandalism is a very difficult crime to solve. Without an eyewitness, he's screwed."

"Let's face it," Gomez added, "as much as his name has been dragged through the mud lately, a lot of people are probably gunning for him. He didn't do himself any favors by filing that countersuit."

"You got that right," Officer Donovan agreed. "Guys like him make me embarrassed to be a black man."

Special pranced back into the living room carrying another saucer of cheesecake. She bent over to hand it to Officer Gomez, at the same time, treating Officer Donovan to a view of way too much of her tight little tush.

"Here you are, Manny," Special cooed. "Would you like another piece too, Fred?"

# CHAPTER 51

"What do we want? *Justice*! When do we want it? *Now*!"
J.C. was a block away from Parker Center, but heard the chants before she even caught sight of the haphazard crowd marching in front of police headquarters in a ragged procession.

"There's no justice for African-American men in this city!" A middle-aged black man with dreadlocks bellowed into a bullhorn. "Four prominent African-American men are gunned down in a matter of days and the LAPD couldn't give a damn!"

J.C. rolled down her window and turned off the radio, slowing to a crawl as she passed the protesters.

"Somebody's killing African-American men—our best and our brightest—and the police don't even bother to warn the black community that we're at risk."

Even before J.C. got a good look, she knew the ringleader was Leon Webber, a community activist who was always Johnny-on-the-spot when any issue arose involving L.A.'s African-American community. A reporter motioned him off to the side for an interview and he readily followed.

J.C. made a U-turn, parked, and jogged across the street. She stayed clear of the TV cameras, not wanting to be mistaken for a protester. She listened as Webber spouted off to not one, but three reporters.

"We have the murders of four African-American men—an engineer, a doctor, a star football player and an investment banker—in less than two weeks and the LAPD is treating them like they were gangbangers. If four white men had been killed under the same circumstances, somebody would've called in the F.B.I *and* the C.I.A. The LAPD simply does not value the life of its African-American citizens. Not the poorest African-American in Watts or the wealthiest one up in View Park."

"Exactly what would you like the police to do?" one of the reporters asked.

"To care!" Webber fired back. "They haven't even warned us that there's a killer on the loose gunning for us. How irresponsible is that?

The word I'm hearing is that there's some white supremacist group who's vowed to kill every professional African-American man in this city. If *I've* heard that, I know the police have, too. But they've chosen to do nothing about it because they want us all dead."

J.C. couldn't stomach any more. She returned to her car and drove around back to the lot where employees parked their personal vehicles. She had just removed her knapsack from the backseat when Detective Jessup snuck up behind her. She flinched.

"Wow, you're a little jumpy there, Detective. That's not good for a cop."

She pulled her bag over her shoulder and stepped around him.

"Did you see that excuse for a protest out front?" Detective Jessup followed her into the station. "Those people have too much free time on their hands."

"They're absolutely right about our failure to warn the public. That should've been done a long time ago."

"That's not our call. We don't know for sure yet that the murders are even connected."

*Yes, we do.*

J.C. wasn't able to shake Jessup until she escaped into the women's locker room. Two patrol women waved as she walked in. J.C. was one of only three female detectives, and the women patrol officers looked up to her. Whenever they had problems with a sexist male partner or wanted advice about a promotional path, they consulted her.

Katrina, a single mother who'd been on the force for only two years, took a seat on a bench near J.C.'s locker.

"Did you see that story about the shootings in the *Sentinel*?" Katrina asked.

"No," J.C. replied. "But I heard Larry Elder's radio show yesterday."

"So, what do you think?"

She shrugged. "I don't buy the theory about white supremacists or gang retribution."

A female desk sergeant hollered into the locker room. "Detective Sparks, the lieutenant wants to see you."

More than a week had passed since J.C. stormed out of Lieutenant Wilson's office. They now spoke to each other only when absolutely necessary. When she reached the lieutenant's doorway, he was just finishing up a call.

"We'll get to it right away," he said into the receiver. "I'm about to assign an officer to the job right now."

Lieutenant Wilson hung up the telephone. "Have a seat."

J.C. slowly sat down, wary about what was in store for her.

"I have a job for you," the lieutenant began. "The mayor's office is getting a lot of calls about these shootings, and that poor excuse for a protest out front isn't helping. When there's heat on the mayor, there's heat on us. We need to do what we can to diffuse it."

"And just how do we do that?"

"The mayor's putting together a team to handle communications between the Department and his office. I'm designating you as our liaison."

"Why me? Detective Jessup would love this opportunity."

"You're a lot smarter," he said. "And cuter."

J.C. didn't smile. The lieutenant wanted to pretend as if their run-in had never occurred. She didn't.

"Mayor Caranza is also planning to hold a press conference. The chief is trying to talk him out of it. It doesn't do any good to talk to the press when you don't have anything concrete to tell 'em. But there's an election just around the corner and you know how politicians are. Always trying to get their mugs in front of the cameras. Anyway, you'll need to be there."

J.C. moved to the edge of her seat. "Why do I need to be there?"

"The mayor feels safer when he's surrounded by cops."

J.C. wanted no part of this. Lieutenant Wilson was intentionally withholding information that could lead to catching the killer solely because of his homophobia and fear of stigmatizing black men.

"And before you say anything about that homosexual crap," he said, "we're looking into it. I still don't believe it, but that angle is being quietly investigated. But we can't go public with it until we have solid, irrefutable evidence to support it."

J.C. welcomed the news and her face showed it. "Why aren't you taking advantage of this photo op yourself, Lieutenant?"

He chuckled and swiveled in his chair. "I thought it would be a great opportunity for you, Detective. Give you some visibility. I'll let you know the date and time once everything's scheduled."

J.C. almost laughed in his face. The lieutenant wasn't doing her any favors. He was protecting himself. When any controversial issue had even the slightest potential of hitting the fan, Wilson stayed far enough away so that not even a speck of crap landed on him. That was the primary reason he had survived three mayors.

"Is that it?" J.C. asked.

There was an awkward moment of silence.

"I ... uh ... I was out of line during our last conversation." Lieutenant Wilson gazed at his candy dish, not her.

J.C. nodded, surprised, but pleased by his attempt at an apology. She wouldn't push the issue. "I hope I'm not expected to say anything at this press conference."

"You'll get some talking points from Media Affairs telling you what to say." He reached for a Snickers from his hand grenade candy dish, but did not offer her one. "What's most important is that you know what *not* to say."

# CHAPTER 52

On the morning Judge Fuller was set to announce his decision on the gag order, the crowd outside the courthouse had ballooned at least threefold. Pro and anti-gay groups hurled insults at each other through bullhorns, while TV cameramen stood at the ready, hoping that a full-fledged melee broke out. Vernetta and Special had to practically fight their way to the courtroom.

Just as Vernetta was about to step inside, she noticed Eugene and Eagleman at the opposite end of the corridor being interviewed by a reporter from the *L.A. Times*. She hurriedly nudged Special inside, fearing that if she spotted Eugene's impromptu press conference, she might pop a blood vessel.

"I'm so hot I don't know what to do," Special said, as they took seats near the back of the courtroom. "This case needs to be publicized."

Vernetta agreed with her, but if the judge did ban cameras from the courtroom, it wouldn't be the end of the world. "Even if the trial isn't televised, reporters will still be in the courtroom covering the case."

"That's not good enough. I want cameras in here broadcasting every word."

J.C. joined them just before Sam and Nichelle walked down the center aisle and into the well of the courtroom. They handed business cards to the court clerk and took seats at the plaintiff's table. Nichelle turned around and smiled back at them. Special flashed her two thumbs-up.

Eugene, Eagleman, and three other men entered the courtroom to murmurs of recognition.

"That don't make no sense." Special's voice was both louder and nastier than it needed to be. "So now his ass has four attorneys?"

"Shhhhh," Vernetta said.

But Special ignored her. "Every time I see that asshole he looks healthier than he did the last time."

"You better cool it," J.C. warned. "If you go off in here, I guarantee you'll be spending the night in jail."

Special smacked her lips and clutched her purse to her chest.

The bailiff called the court to order and everyone rose as Judge Fuller took the bench. Instead of focusing on the judge, Special was glaring at a petite woman sitting directly behind Eugene and his attorneys.

"That's Church Girl over there." Special rudely pointed in the woman's direction.

Vernetta grabbed her hand and forced it back into her lap. "Didn't your mama teach you not to point?"

Belynda, or Church Girl, as Special liked to call her, appeared to be in her early thirties. She was an attractive woman despite her somber expression. Eugene turned around and winked at her. Special was about to say something when J.C. gave her a silencing look.

"When addressing the issue of a protective order," Judge Fuller began, "it's important for the court to balance the rights of the parties against the public's right to know."

Vernetta grabbed Special's hand, ostensibly to comfort her friend, but also to calm her own fractured nerves.

"I find that the weight here lies with the defendant, Mr. Nelson. The plaintiff's counsel, Ms. Ayers, has made it her business to use every possible opportunity to personally attack him. Her conduct will no doubt make it more difficult for this court to seat an unbiased jury. For that reason, I'm issuing a limited protective order."

"This ain't right!" Special seethed. A few people glanced back at her. Thank God the judge was almost deaf.

"Cut it out," J.C. warned her.

The judge went on to issue an order prohibiting the attorneys from discussing the evidence in the case, the merits of their opponent's case, or the expected testimony of witnesses. He also ordered the attorneys, as well as the parties, to refrain from disparaging each other in the media. Then he announced that television cameras would be barred from the courtroom.

Special's knee started bouncing and Vernetta could hear her foot tapping the floor. "This ain't right. What ever happened to freedom of speech?"

The judge closed a folder, took off his spectacles, and shuffled off the bench. Reporters pulled out cell phones, BlackBerries and laptops and dashed into the hallway. Eugene, smiling from ear to ear, hugged each of his attorneys, then gave them congratulatory slaps on the back.

Still holding Special's hand, Vernetta finally looked over at her. "You okay?"

"He probably paid off the judge," she said quietly.

"Don't worry about it. Two local television stations said they'd file amicus briefs supporting our appeal if the judge banned the cameras." That news didn't appear to cheer her up. Special stared across the courtroom at Eugene.

When he reached over the railing to hug Church Girl, Vernetta felt Special twitch.

Special made a move to rise. "Let's go."

J.C. extended her arm across Special's chest. "Wait. Let Eugene and his attorneys leave first."

Even after the victorious defense team and their client strolled past them, the three women just sat there, motionless. Vernetta felt like *she* had just lost a big case.

Nichelle and Sam finally joined them. "Well, we tried," Nichelle said.

"You're going to appeal, right?" Special asked anxiously.

"It's not worth it," Sam declared. "Fuller will take it personally and I don't want him taking it out on us at trial. Let's just move on."

J.C. stood and Nichelle took the seat next to Special. "You okay, girl?"

"I'm fine," Special said.

Nichelle took Special's other hand. "We just have to have faith in the system."

Special laughed sullenly. "Yeah, right."

# CHAPTER 53

Vernetta pushed open the courtroom door and was relieved to find the hallway nearly deserted. They trudged in defeated silence toward the bank of elevators.

Special looked totally dejected. She lagged behind, forcing Vernetta to slow her pace. Her own emotions were a muddle of anger and confusion. While she didn't believe Eugene had intentionally infected Maya, his infidelity and deceit put her life at risk and ultimately ended it. The public needed to witness every second of this trial. Vernetta hoped Nichelle and Sam did appeal the judge's ruling.

J.C. suggested that they exit the courthouse on Grand, opposite the way they had entered. She didn't say it, but Vernetta knew J.C. wanted to avoid the throng of media camped out at the Hill Street entrance.

When they reached the exit, there wasn't a reporter in sight. Vernetta figured they had successfully dodged the press until they turned the corner onto First Street and saw a circle of reporters surrounded by a bigger crowd of bystanders. Eugene and his attorneys stood in the middle of the mob.

"No comment," Vernetta heard Eagleman say. "We're not permitted to talk to the press."

"Let's cross the street." J.C. was already heading for the cross-walk.

"Good idea," Nichelle said. "I can't handle some reporter sticking a microphone in my face."

"No," Sam protested. "We can't talk to the press, but we can at least get our faces in a few camera shots. That's exactly what Eagleman is doing. This'll be good publicity for the firm." He took off in the direction of the reporters.

Vernetta looked over at Special, fearing that she might blow any second. She'd seen her friend go from zero to sixty in a snap. At the moment, Special appeared semi-catatonic.

They watched Sam walk past a line of cameras, ignoring their questions. "That gag order doesn't apply to me," Special said. "And since Maya isn't here to speak for herself, I'm going to do it for her."

Special was about to head for the horde of reporters, when a reporter from KCBS approached Nichelle.

"What are your thoughts about today's ruling?" The man aimed his microphone inches from her lips. An accompanying cameraman took a wide shot, then zoomed in on Nichelle.

"Pursuant to the judge's gag order, I'm not permitted to talk to the press about this case." Nichelle tried to move past them.

"Well, I can talk," Special said. "I—"

Vernetta stepped in front of her, fearing that Special might say something they would all regret. "We were all very close to Maya Washington and we feel the judge's decision to ban cameras from the courtroom interferes with the public's right to know," Vernetta said. "The problem of men on the down low is a crucial issue in the African-American community. This case should be televised not just for Maya, but for every woman out there who's being deceived by a man engaging in this type of fraud."

"Do you know if there are any plans to appeal the ruling?"

Vernetta looked at Sam, then Nichelle. "It's my hope that they will. This case is too important to keep from the public."

A few of the reporters who'd been trying to get Eugene to talk joined the growing crowd that had gathered around Vernetta. Another reporter asked a question and in no time, dozens of people seemed to appear from nowhere. Vernetta looked to her right to check out Special's reaction. Special wasn't there. She turned to her left, then did a half circle to search to the rear. Special had been standing right next to her a second ago. Vernetta frantically scanned the area as panic began to mount. She spotted Nichelle and Sam a few feet away, but didn't see Special or J.C.

More reporters were firing questions at her now, but Vernetta ignored them. Maybe Special couldn't stand to hear any more talk about the case and had gone back to the car. Vernetta brushed past the reporters, who continued to call out to her, while shoving microphones in her face. There were pockets of people everywhere, and she had to maneuver around them to continue her search for Special.

When she finally did locate her friend, Special was several yards away, marching toward the spot where Eugene was standing. His back faced Special and he did not see her coming.

Vernetta's body wanted to react, but her brain was momentarily paralyzed. She tried to run, but her feet felt like they were plodding through quicksand. Special was just a few feet away from Eugene when Vernetta saw her stop and reach inside her purse. Special's hand came out and Vernetta caught the glint of something shiny in the blinding, midday sun. Her mind refused to believe what her eyes clearly saw.

A look of utter terror on the face of one of Eugene's attorneys caused Eugene to abruptly swing around.

The moment he did Special extended her right arm and pointed a weapon in his face.

"Oh, my God!" Vernetta screamed. "Special, don't!"

# CHAPTER 54

I hate you!" Special shrieked as she charged at Eugene. "How dare you claim Maya infected you!"

Eugene's attorneys dashed behind a parked car. Two reporters who had been trying to interview him nearly tripped over each other as they fled in opposite directions. Several bystanders hit the ground.

Eugene held out both hands, his eyes glued to the object Special was pointing at him. "What are you doing?" His voice was rattled with fear. "Are you crazy?"

"You're the crazy one!" Special roared. "You need to pay for what you did. You're nothing but scum!"

The whole scene erupted in chaos as people ran for cover. A cameraman, using a big oak tree for cover, captured the melee on videotape. Vernetta finally gathered her bearings and took off toward Special, but her feet got tangled up with someone who was running in the opposite direction and they both fell to the ground.

Eugene suddenly howled in pain as Special ranted at him.

"You're the one who should be dead!"

*What had Special just done?* Vernetta hustled to her feet. She hadn't heard a gunshot. *Had she missed it?*

Eugene was screaming at the top of his lungs now. He dropped to his knees and covered his face with both hands. Belynda ran to his side, pulled a bottle of water from her purse and began dousing his eyes. Only then did Vernetta realize that the weapon in Special's hand wasn't a gun, but the copper-colored, plastic pepper spray canister she always carried in her purse.

Vernetta ran toward her, but J.C. managed to get there first. She snatched the canister from Special's hand and grabbed her from behind, pinning Special's arms to her sides. Special continued to shout obscenities at Eugene, all the while kicking like a bucking bronco.

"You're the one who should be dead! You asshole!" Special was sobbing now, struggling with all her might to break free from J.C.'s grasp.

Now that Special was no longer a threat, the cameramen and

photographers reemerged, zooming in with their lenses.

"Back up!" J.C. ordered, as she struggled to gain control of an out-of-control Special. "I'm a police officer!" she yelled. "Back up! Now!"

It was close to ten that night before Special walked out of the Inmate Reception Center. Sam called a friend in the D.A.'s office and managed to get her released from jail on her own recognizance.

J.C. escorted Special into a crowded room where Vernetta and Nichelle had been waiting for more than two hours. They all just stood there. Vernetta couldn't ever remember being this mad at her best friend. But she would save her tirade for later.

Vernetta, Special and Nichelle made their way to Vernetta's SUV which was parked in a lot across the street. As they pulled onto the street, Special finally broke the lethal silence. "I couldn't help it," she said.

"Is that what you're going to tell the jury when they sentence you to prison for ten years?" Vernetta asked.

"Ten years?" Special replied in alarm. "You can't get ten years just for spraying somebody with pepper spray, can you?"

"What you did constitutes a hate crime. You certainly aren't getting out of this with a slap on the wrist. Attacking the man like that was just plain stupid."

Special grunted. "I didn't hurt his ass."

"No, you didn't," Nichelle said. "The only person you hurt was yourself. But look at the bright side. At least J.C. can have some of the prison guards look out for you when you're doing your time."

"That ain't funny," Special grumbled, which made them all laugh. "I'm hungry. I was not about to eat that slop they served in jail."

Vernetta wanted to tell her that she deserved to starve, but she was hungry, too. Other than Denny's, the selection of late-night eateries in L.A. wasn't nearly as plentiful as one would think. Then she remembered the perfect place.

Twenty minutes later, they lucked up on a prime parking spot in the main lot of Tommy's on Rampart. The 24-hour burger stand was always packed, day or night, weekday or weekend. Its saucer-sized chiliburgers were Vernetta's personal favorite.

"I'll order." Vernetta threw open the door of her Land Cruiser. There was no need to ask what anyone wanted. They always ordered the same thing: double-doubles—double meat, double cheese—with a Diet Coke for Vernetta and orange sodas for Special and Nichelle.

As she waited for their order, Vernetta wondered if anyone else remembered that Maya had been with them on their last trip here. It was long before her illness. A time when their lives seemed carefree.

She returned to the car carrying the food in two cardboard containers. They ate without a word, listening to Stevie Wonder's *Ribbon in the Sky* on the radio.

Vernetta stole a glimpse at Special in the rearview mirror. Her pink blouse was dingy and wrinkled, and her hair was a complete mess. She looked haggard and defeated. Vernetta almost wanted to climb into the backseat and give her a hug. She would never admit it to Special, but she envied her friend's ability to give in to her rage.

"I'm sorry," Special said, setting her burger in her lap. "I just couldn't stand looking at Eugene smiling like he'd won the lottery. If I have to spend some time in jail for what I did, then so be it." She turned to look out the window. "He'll probably end up getting the lawsuit dismissed, too."

"Not if I can help it," Nichelle said. "And even if that does happen, he'll pay. Eventually. What goes around, comes around. I truly believe that."

"Well, I want him to pay now! The way Maya paid!" Special's jail stint had not diminished her anger. "And when he's ready to die, I'm going to plant myself by his bedside as a reminder of what he did to her."

Special's level of rage was clearly over the top. Vernetta just prayed her anger would soon subside. She collected everyone's trash and hopped out to dump it in a nearby bin. Just as she settled back into the driver's seat, she heard the sultry voice of one of KJLH's late-night DJs.

*DJ: Our phone lines are open so call in and tell us what you think. Did our legal system do right by Maya Washington? We have a caller from Carson on the line. How are you doing tonight?*

*Caller: How am I doing? Not good at all. A man gets to deceive you by telling you he's straight when he's really gay and give you HIV and just walk away? With no repercussions? That's crazy.*

*D.J.: But brothers on the D-L claim they're not gay.*

*Caller: That's bull, they're just—*

Vernetta leaned forward and clicked off the radio. "I can't take this tonight. Let's go home."

"I don't wanna go home," Special said weakly. "This might sound weird, but I'd like to hang out at Maya's place for a while. I need to feel her spirit tonight."

Special still had the keys to Maya's place. It would be a few more weeks before her affairs were settled.

"I don't think that's weird at all," Vernetta said. "In fact, it's the best idea I've heard all day."

# CHAPTER 55

Eugene was turning into a virtual recluse. The video of Special attacking him outside the courthouse had been played and replayed on television stations nationwide and had attracted more than a million hits on YouTube. No matter where he went, the gas station, the grocery store, the doctor's office, people stared, pointed, and whispered.

He realized now that there was no way he could resume his legal career. He spent most of the day watching pay-per-view movies, going deeper and deeper into a state of depression. Belynda tried her best to cheer him up, but it wasn't working. Four days after Special assaulted him, Belynda finally convinced him to visit Reverend Sims for another counseling session.

"I still need your prayers." Eugene took a seat in front of the reverend's desk. "I've been reading those verses you gave me, but I'm still feeling pretty low."

Reverend Sims nodded. "Just stay prayerful, brother. Leave that lawsuit to your lawyers and to God. I've seen Him do some amazing things in my day."

They prayed together, then Eugene shared his growing fears that Special might attack him again. "I don't think she's mentally stable. I'm going to ask my attorneys to file a restraining order against her."

"Do what you have to do to protect yourself. But let's put that situation in God's hands, too."

A couple of hours after their counseling session ended, Eugene and the reverend were battling each other on the racquetball court at the Spectrum Club in Manhattan Beach.

"Don't tell me you're going to let an old man whip you," Reverend Sims taunted him.

The reverend breathed easily, while Eugene gasped for air. "You talk a lot of smack for a man of the cloth."

Reverend Sims grinned. "I wasn't born with a collar, you know."

Eugene slammed the ball with his racquet, hurling it into the wall in front of them. The reverend quickly moved into position, hitting it a split second after it bounced off the floor. Their rally went on for a couple of minutes, then Eugene missed an easy shot.

"Uncle!" Eugene dropped his racquet. "I really gotta get back in shape."

"So, dinner's on you, right?"

Eugene was so winded, all he could do was nod.

They gathered their gym bags and made their way to the locker room. As Eugene stepped into the showers, another man coming out of a stall obviously recognized him and rushed off like he was afraid of catching something. Eugene hated the loss of his anonymity.

He dressed and found the reverend waiting for him in the lobby.

"So where are we eating?" the reverend asked as they approached their cars.

"How about a rain check?" Eugene said uneasily. He was tired of fending off scornful looks every place he went. "I know you have a wife and kids to get home to."

"My family's out of town visiting my in-laws. I hate going home to an empty house. I'm not about to let you become a hermit."

Eugene thought about suggesting that they pick up some carry-out and go back to his place to eat.

But Reverend Sims insisted on going out. "Let's head over to the Howard Hughes Promenade. We can get a table at Marie Callender's Grill without much of a wait."

A short time later, the men were seated at a table for two near the front of the restaurant. They had a full view of the street outside.

Eugene studied the menu. He didn't have much of an appetite.

"I usually get the chili," Reverend Sims said. "And I could eat a whole pan of their cornbread by myself."

"I want to thank you again for all your support," Eugene said, closing his menu. "You've gone above and beyond the call of duty. It's been cool having you to talk to."

"Frankly, it was good for me to get out tonight, too. I recently lost a friend. So this was a nice diversion for me."

"I'm sorry to hear that. What happened?"

"You probably read about it in the papers. He was shot to death at his home in Ladera. Nobody seems to know why."

They spent the first few minutes talking about the late James Hill, then the conversation turned to politics. In the midst of a discussion about Barack Obama, Eugene's head jerked to the left and he gazed down the street.

"What's the matter?" Reverend Sims seemed to sense Eugene's distress.

Eugene rubbed his eyes with his thumb and index finger. "I could've sworn I just saw the woman who attacked me. Special Moore." He continued to stare out of the window. "I just hope I'm hallucinating, but I wouldn't put it past her to start stalking me."

The reverend chuckled. "You've been through a lot. The mind can sometimes play funny tricks on us."

The waiter brought their food and Reverend Sims began talking about his wife and two daughters.

"Sounds like you have a wonderful family."

"I do," he said. "And you will, too, one day."

Eugene half-listened as he struggled to fight his growing attraction to the man. He knew plenty of men who professed a deep commitment to their wives, but were sleeping with men on a regular basis. Eugene doubted the reverend spent this much time with other members of his congregation. So how should he interpret that? Eugene had also known his share of ministers who lived a Godly life by day and a very sinful one by night. Was Reverend Sims one of them?

He tried to think about something else. "I just finished remodeling my kitchen. It took forever, but it turned out pretty nice."

"Redoing our kitchen is at the top of my list of honey do's," the reverend said. "Can you recommend a good granite guy?"

"I've got the best. When you get some time, you should drop by and check out his work."

"Why don't we run by there right now? I would love to surprise my wife by telling her I found a contractor."

Eugene paused just long enough to shut out the inner voice cautioning him to retreat. "I'm game if you are."

# CHAPTER 56

You guys are being too emotional," Sam said testily.

Vernetta sat across from Sam in the main conference room at Barnes, Ayers, and Howard. It was after eight o'clock, and she was wiped out. Nichelle and Vernetta had been going to war with Sam over his recommendation to approach Eugene about settling the case.

"You guys can win this case at trial," Vernetta insisted.

"That's not a sure bet," Sam replied. "Why rack up deposition fees and attorney time when Eugene might easily fork over several thousand dollars?" He pointed at them from across the table. "You guys aren't acting like attorneys. You're acting like scorned women."

Vernetta resented the comment, but she couldn't deny that this case was indeed personal for them.

"We didn't file this case solely for the money," Nichelle said. "This is about warning other women. Even with the ban on cameras in the courtroom, the media is still going to heavily cover the case. The longer it goes on, the more women we can reach."

"This case has gotten so much publicity there can't be a woman alive who doesn't know about this down low stuff. And you're still getting calls from the media despite that gag order. You guys have made your point."

"Think about the publicity for your firm," Vernetta said, hoping that an appeal to Sam's wallet might make a difference. "The longer it goes on, the more clients you'll attract."

"We've got plenty clients already." There was an air of arrogance in his delivery.

Vernetta continued to push. "This is an important issue. We need to use the case to make a statement."

"*We*?" Sam snarled. "That's certainly easy for you to say. You're sitting over there in your big office in the hallowed halls of O'Reilly & Finney making the big bucks while all of our time and resources are being sunk into this case. You have nothing at stake here."

"Nichelle and I are paying all of the costs," Vernetta reminded him. "This case isn't costing your firm a dime."

"Oh, yes it is. Every second Nichelle and I spend on this case rather than other billable work reduces our firm's income. So don't try to tell me it's not costing us."

Vernetta couldn't refute that, so she just frowned at him. Some people enjoyed being a grouch. Sam was one of them.

"I can't believe you," he bellowed at Vernetta. "You've tried enough cases to know that anything can happen in litigation. And even if we did win at trial, Eugene would appeal. It could be years before Maya's mother sees a dime." He tapped the table with his index finger. "We have an ethical obligation to raise the issue of settlement with Maya's mother. I don't know why I'm even sitting here talking to you. You have no say in this case."

"You don't have to be rude," Nichelle said. "Vernetta's here to help."

"I'm not trying to be rude. I'm trying to get you two to look at reality."

Vernetta was surprised that someone so unlikable outside the courtroom had been so successful with juries. She was glad Nichelle's relationship with him had not gone anywhere. She was way too good for him.

Sam stood up and collected the papers in front of him. "Let's continue this conversation after we talk to Maya's mother."

No one said a word as Sam tore out of the conference room. "I guess this case is over," Vernetta conceded, "because I doubt Maya's mother will want to keep reliving Maya's death in the media. She hasn't been happy about all the reporters bugging her for interviews. This has to be hard for her."

Nichelle wasn't ready to give up. "I'm sure Special could convince her to keep fighting."

"Yeah, but is that really the best thing to do? I hate agreeing with Sam, but he's probably right. Eugene would be glad to settle. A trial only means he'll have to take the witness stand and talk about all the men he slept with. We need to approach this case with the same objectivity we would any other case."

Nichelle's eyes started to water. Vernetta hoped she didn't start crying.

"Well, at least once the case is over, I can go back to accepting interviews. I turned down three requests yesterday, including one from Larry King's producer. People are actually looking to *me* as an expert on down low men. Can you believe it?"

"Good for you. Just remember me when you start raking in thousands of dollars in speaking fees." Vernetta stretched her arms, then started gathering her things.

"So what are you doing tonight?"

Vernetta gave her an odd look, then pointed to her watch. "It's already late. I'm going straight home to snuggle up with my husband before he forgets who I am."

Nichelle had a sheepish look on her face. "I've been doing a lot of research on my new area of expertise," she said. "As a matter of fact, I'm doing some more tonight. Why don't you come with us?"

"What kind of research and who's us?"

"Me and Jamal."

Vernetta held up her hands in a stay-away posture. "No way. I heard all about that stunt you guys pulled that ended Special's relationship with Clayton. Leave me out of your antics."

"That wasn't my idea. I tried to talk her out of it."

"I wish you had. I really thought Clayton was the one."

"Anyway, I'm picking Jamal up at nine-thirty and we're going to this gay club."

"What for?"

"These guys on the down low spend their lives pretending to be something they aren't. I just wanted to hang out with them in an atmosphere where they can be themselves. I think one of the reasons they lead double lives is because they can't be who they are in the black community."

"Yes, they can," Vernetta disagreed. "I know plenty of black guys who are out of the closet. One of my first cousins is gay. And he's never been on the down low."

"Really? I've been to two of your family reunions and had Thanksgiving dinner at your parents' house more times than I can count. How come I've never met him?"

Vernetta shrugged. Her family had not welcomed her cousin with open arms.

"Your family's no different than mine," Nichelle said. "We whisper about our gay family members behind their backs and basically act like they don't exist. Jamal told me that when his mother found out he was gay, she brought their minister to the house to pray the demons out of him."

"I understand how they're treated. And it's not right. But that doesn't give these guys the right to deceive us."

"I'm not saying it does. Just come out with us tonight," she prodded. "You might just learn something."

# CHAPTER 57

Eugene and Reverend Sims ordered apple pie to go and headed over to Eugene's place in Baldwin Hills.

When Eugene opened the front door and led the way inside, the reverend stopped just inside the doorway and whistled. "Wow! This place belongs on HGTV."

Pride showed on Eugene's face. "I put a lot of blood, sweat, and tears into hookin' it up."

The reverend admired the baby grand to the left of the doorway. "You play?"

"Yeah, but it's been a while. I keep it here to add a little class to the place."

"Well, you've certainly accomplished that." The reverend ran his hand along the piano keys. "Who was your interior decorator?"

Eugene proudly tapped his chest. "You're looking at him. Excuse me while I put the pie in the kitchen. Then I'll show you the rest of the house."

He returned within seconds. "Let's start upstairs."

As Eugene ascended the staircase, he felt the presence of Reverend Sims close behind him. Too close. *Was he imagining things or was the reverend about to make a move?* Eugene could almost hear the heavy pounding of his own heart.

"I think of the top floor as my personal retreat," Eugene said, distracted. "The master bedroom and bath take up the entire level."

Eugene stopped at the second-floor landing and flipped on a light switch. He opened two double doors that led into a bedroom with slate green walls and grey carpet. A window that ran the length of the room looked out over a sea of lights.

"Wow, again!" The reverend scratched his head. "This is really something."

Eugene smiled proudly. There was an enormous circular bed positioned in the center of the room and a 60-inch flat-screen TV on the wall opposite the window. The adjacent wall contained three rows of built-in cabinets. The only other items in the room were two small nightstands and a king palm that stretched to the ceiling.

Eugene led the way to the bathroom which was equipped with a fireplace, another flat screen TV, and a built-in stereo system with in-wall speakers. The Jacuzzi tub was big enough for four.

"I've only seen stuff like this on TV," the reverend said.

Eugene switched off the light and returned to the bedroom. If he was indeed feeling a vibe from the reverend, this was the place where he would find out for sure. As he lingered near the bed, Eugene felt his pulse quicken.

"Brother, you're in the wrong business." Reverend Sims walked up beside him and peered down at the circular bed. "This place is fantastic. You ought to go into interior decorating."

Eugene stood stock still, waiting for the reverend to make his intentions clear.

"Can't say I've ever slept in a round bed before. I wonder how Juanita would feel about one of these."

The mention of *Mrs*. Sims rocked Eugene back to reality. He was way off base with the reverend. The man was apparently exactly what he appeared to be. A smart, caring minister who was as straight as an arrow.

"Let's go downstairs," Eugene suggested.

He gave the reverend a quick tour of the den, his office, the two downstairs bedrooms, another full bathroom and a powder room. He saved the kitchen for last.

The reverend headed straight for the granite topped island in the center of the room. "Your contractor did some high quality work here." The reverend ran his hand across the smooth surface. "Tell me something? Why does a single man need two refrigerators?"

Eugene chuckled. "That always trips people out. Actually one of them is a deep freezer. I like to buy in bulk. I entertain a lot. Or I used to."

Reverend Sims circled the island, then pulled out a bar stool and sat down. "Your real friends will still be there for you," he said. "You'll see."

Eugene swung open a cabinet over the dishwasher. "How about some coffee with our dessert?" Eugene perused the shelves. "I have a very expensive espresso machine that I don't get to show off too often."

The reverend held up a hand. "I'm afraid that stuff is a little too strong for my constitution."

"Regular it is, then. So will it be Hawaiian Mocha, Hazelnut, Dark Peruvian or—"

"You choose," the reverend said with a grin. "I'm not much of a coffee connoisseur. And I take it black. No cream, no sugar."

"Okay, let's go with the Dark Peruvian."

Eugene took the canister of coffee from the middle shelf and was about to turn around, when he felt Reverend Sims standing behind him. So close that he could feel the reverend's breath on the back of his neck. Eugene stiffened, then relaxed in anticipation.

*So he wasn't imagining things.*

# CHAPTER 58

Special stood in Eugene's backyard peering through his kitchen window, trying to muzzle her emotions. She couldn't believe that she was about to watch Eugene make out with some man!

Her knees buckled and she gripped the windowsill with both hands to keep from collapsing.

The day had started out well for Special. Though she'd been released to return to work by Dr. Blanchard, she was finding it more and more difficult to stay focused. So when her alarm clock rang that morning, she called in sick and slept in until noon. Then she put on her cutest workout clothes and did a grueling three miles up and down the steep hills on Green Valley Circle.

At five-thirty, she had another session with Dr. Blanchard. The psychologist was finally helping her see what everybody else saw, that her anger at Eugene was turning into a dangerous obsession that had to end.

Her court date on the assault charge was six weeks away and she prayed every night that she would not have to go to jail. In the meantime, she had promised herself that she was going to put Eugene Nelson completely out of her mind.

After her therapy session, she stopped by the Howard Hughes Promenade for a manicure and pedicure. Her final treat for the day was the new Samuel L. Jackson movie. Now that was a *real* man.

Special had not felt this good in weeks. She only wished Vernetta could have shared the day with her. She had just eased her Porsche out of the parking structure and turned right onto Center Drive toward Sepulveda when she thought she saw Eugene and another man sitting at a table in the window of Marie Callender's Grill.

She was so startled that her foot hit the gas instead of the brake and she darted into the intersection at Park Terrace. She had to run the red light to keep another car from ramming her from behind. She couldn't believe the man was already back to his old tricks! Church Girl had to be a stone fool for dating that asshole.

Making a left rather than a right onto Sepulveda, she circled back just to make sure her eyes weren't deceiving her. When she drove past the restaurant a second time, she slowed to a crawl as she approached the window, then sped up. It was definitely Eugene! He was sitting there in full view, looking happy and relaxed with some man whose face she couldn't see.

A voice in Special's head told her to forget what she had just seen. But another, louder more insistent voice drowned out that advice. She parked illegally in front of the office building across from the Promenade's north parking structure and waited for Eugene to leave. There were three different exits, and Special had no idea which one he would use. From her vantage point, she had a clear view of the cars leaving the two exits on Center Street.

Almost a half hour later, just when she was about to give up, she spotted Eugene pulling out of the garage in what she assumed was a rental car. It was dark now, but she could see that no one else was in the car with him.

"Dang, I wanted to see his date!" Special said out loud as she started up her car. "I bet he has a wife or girlfriend at home."

Only after turning right onto Centinela did Special realize that another car was following closely behind Eugene. It was no doubt his dinner date. Special tried to speed up to get a look at the man, but she soon dropped back for fear that Eugene would recognize her car.

Eugene turned north onto La Brea and Special assumed he was heading home. "They're going back to his place to do their deceitful dirt."

She dropped back even further, since she knew the way to Eugene's house. When the Honda turned right onto Don Lorenzo and left on Don Felipe, the man in the second car did the same. This confirmed that they were headed to Eugene's house. Special kept straight down Don Lorenzo and headed back west up Stocker toward Fox Hills.

If Eugene was still running around sleeping with men, Church Girl needed to know about it. This time Special planned to deliver the news to her in living color.

She sped the four miles back to her apartment, grabbed her digital camera, and made it back to Eugene's in exactly twenty-two minutes. She thought about taking a picture with her cell phone, but wanted to make sure the photo was crystal clear.

Special parked two doors away and hurried toward Eugene's house, looking over her shoulder every few seconds. The living room curtains were drawn and she had no idea what part of the house they were in. She wasn't even sure she could actually get a picture of Eugene and his lover, but she was going to give it her best shot. When she was certain that the coast was clear, she tiptoed as quietly as she could through the side gate that led into his backyard.

The minute she stepped onto the deck and peered into his kitchen window, she saw the man and Eugene in the kitchen, talking. The man was sitting on a stool facing Eugene, so Special couldn't see his face. She prayed that she could get a shot of them hugging or kissing, since just sitting there talking wasn't likely to convince Church Girl of the obvious.

Special pulled a wallet-sized camera from the pocket of her jeans, and prepared to snap a picture the second the moment presented itself. She looked through the camera lens, satisfied that the porch lamp provided sufficient lighting. Special couldn't risk using the camera's flash and drawing attention to herself.

Eugene's lover stood up and something told Special that she was about to get lucky. Too bad she couldn't see his face so she could out his ass, too. It seemed to take forever for the man to walk over to Eugene. When he finally did, Special's nerves were so frayed she could barely hold onto the camera.

She watched as the man stood directly behind Eugene, way too close for any doubt about what was going to happen next. Just as Eugene turned around and moved in to kiss the man, Special snapped a single picture and hightailed it back to her car.

# CHAPTER 59

Hey!" Reverend Sims yelled when Eugene turned and leaned in to kiss him. "What are you doing?" The reverend stepped back, both palms extended in front of him.

Eugene froze with embarrassment. "I thought you were—"

"You thought I was what?!" The reverend sounded as angry as he was amazed.

Eugene tried to swallow, but his throat wouldn't open. "You came up behind me so . . . I thought you were coming on to me."

Reverend Sims took another step back. "Coming on to you? I was trying to get a look at that light fixture over there." He pointed to a purple light hanging by a thin black cord to the left of where Eugene was standing.

"Reverend, I'm so sorry. I—"

"Son, you have to get your life in order. God has granted you His favor. Don't you dare spit in His face like this."

Reverend Sims stared at him with a harshness that Eugene did not want to acknowledge.

The reverend scratched his chin. "We need to have a serious talk, brother. Why don't you finish making that coffee. I'll be in the living room."

Eugene joined him a few minutes later with two steaming coffee mugs and set them down on coasters on the coffee table. He realized he had forgotten to bring the pie, but he didn't have an appetite for it anyway. He took a seat on the couch across from the reverend, still too embarrassed to look him in the eye.

"Brother, I have to confess that I truly don't understand what's going on here. It was my understanding that you had made a decision to turn away from this behavior."

"I did . . . but I . . . I thought you were about to—"

"You're not the first man I've counseled in this situation. It doesn't matter what you thought *I* was about to do." Reverend Sims pointed a stern finger at him. "You need to know where *you* stand."

Eugene looked down at his hands, too embarrassed to respond.

The reverend asked him several pointed questions, then Eugene's story poured out of him.

Even as a young kid, he'd always known his attraction to other boys, not girls, wasn't acceptable. A voracious reader, he enjoyed accompanying his father to a neighborhood convenience store and browsing through the magazines. He loved the colorful pictures of beautiful black people on the covers. One particular day, when he was around eleven or twelve, instead of picking up an *Ebony* or *Jet*, he noticed a *Playgirl*. When he opened the magazine and saw all the attractive nude men, he felt a tingle of arousal like nothing he'd ever felt before. Soon, he started stealing the magazines by stuffing them down the back of his pants.

"Your parents never found them?" Reverend Sims asked.

"No," Eugene said, his weary face drawn back to his youth. "I kept them in a big Corn Flakes box in the attic. My father would have skinned me alive if he'd known his only son got off on looking at naked men. I think my mother suspected I might be gay, but hoped I would grow out of it. Thank God they're both gone now. I couldn't handle having them exposed to everything I've been going through."

"Okay," the Reverend said. "So you considered yourself gay back then?"

"I didn't know what I was. But I knew I couldn't let anybody know I was attracted to boys."

"Wasn't there anybody in your family you could talk to?"

He laughed. "Absolutely not. Everything I'd ever heard about gays was evil. My family was Pentecostal. Since the time I was a kid, our minister preached that homosexuals were an abomination and would burn in hell forever. I didn't want that to happen to me. So I hid what I was feeling."

"You obviously stopped hiding it at some point," Reverend Sims said.

Eugene took a sip of coffee. "I didn't have my first sexual experience with a man until my sophomore year of college. I'd dated women up until that time. Sex with women was okay, but I still enjoyed looking at my magazines and, by this time, I had a pretty extensive collection of gay porn."

Eugene felt embarrassed and only continued after the reverend's nod of encouragement.

"I hung out with a lot of jocks at UCLA and even joined a fraternity. One night my roommate and I staggered back to the dorm after a party. We were so blasted I have no idea how we found our way back to our room. We were too drunk to even find the light switch. I dived onto my bed and Curtis fell on top of me. We didn't even say a word. It just happened."

Eugene didn't think it was necessary to provide more details. "We were together until we graduated. Then he returned to Atlanta and married his high school sweetheart. I was his best man. The last time we were together was the night before his wedding."

The reverend frowned. "So if Maya had not become ill, you planned to marry her and continue this type of behavior?" The reverend's tone was an equal dose of amazement and condemnation.

Eugene lowered his head. "I wanted to be faithful to Maya and I planned to try. But I realize now that I would've failed. But I just couldn't come out. My family would've disowned me. Maya's cousin told my sister and aunt about how she became ill. They barely speak to me now."

"I'm pretty liberal in my religious teachings and I don't agree with the fundamentalist views on homosexuality," Reverend Sims said. "But I do believe in honesty and integrity. And your behavior toward that young woman you were engaged to can't be excused."

Eugene looked down at his hands.

"And there's something else I need to say. I know you've been seeing the head of our new members group, Belynda Davis. She talks about you constantly. And until tonight, I thought that was a good thing." His eyes burned with disapproval. "I pray it's not your intent to continue this type of behavior. Because if it is, I won't sit by and let you destroy another young woman's life."

# CHAPTER 60

Vernetta had no idea what to expect when they parked outside what looked like an abandoned building on Hawthorne Boulevard. On the way over, Jamal had given them the 4-1-1 on the best gay hangouts in L.A. Most of them were underground clubs only insiders knew about.

Jamal led the way into the building, having promised Vernetta and Nichelle an entertaining night on the town. Once inside, the place looked like nearly every other nightclub Vernetta had visited. Loud music, low lights, nicely dressed people. Here, though, most of the couples on the dance floor were of the same sex. The crowd was about seventy-five percent black.

Vernetta slowed near the bar, struck by the droves of handsome, masculine-looking black men everywhere she turned. There were also a good number of lesbian couples. Two men were kissing near the bar. A few guys were flamboyantly dressed in leather and chains, but most wore stylish clothes suitable for an office setting. What Vernetta was seeing took her stereotypical image of *gay* and turned it upside down and sideways. If she had met half of these guys on the street, she would have assumed they were straight.

Jamal nudged her. "You okay?"

Vernetta smiled and nodded, embarrassed that she was standing there with her eyes bugged out.

Nichelle did a three-sixty turn. She was just as confounded as Vernetta. "This is something, isn't it?"

"Follow me." Jamal led them through a pack of men toward the back of the club. There was a high energy level in the place that didn't just come from the music and dancing couples. Everybody looked carefree and happy.

"You haven't really partied until you've partied at a gay club," Jamal shouted over the music. He stopped in front of a booth that had a reserved label on it and slid in. "I know the owner," he bragged.

Just as they sat down, Nichelle pointed at a man in drag. "Now that's something I don't get. Why would a gay man want to be with a man dressed up like a woman?"

Jamal spread his hands, palms up. "To each his own. But that isn't my thing."

A young white guy walked up and Jamal introduced him as his stockbroker. When he found out Nichelle and Vernetta were attorneys, he asked for their business cards and started offering them investment advice.

Two muscular men in doo rags, white tank tops and baggy jeans moved past their table holding hands. They looked like gangbangers, Vernetta thought. A popular rap song with some hard-core anti-gay lyrics drew a rush of men to the dance floor.

"I can't believe they'd play that in here," Vernetta said to Jamal, as she tried to square her image of gay with the two men who had just walked by.

"Nobody's listening to the words," he said. "The beat is slammin'. Lots of rap songs refer to women as bitches and ho's, but women still dance to it. Same difference."

As Vernetta continued to take in the scene, she could feel an air of abandon. She gathered that this was one of the few places where these men could be exactly who they wanted to be without fear of being hassled or condemned.

Vernetta watched a gay couple hugged up in the booth next to them out of the corner of her eye. Nichelle took a quick look and turned away. She seemed a lot less unnerved by this whole experience.

"So," Vernetta asked, after Jamal left to flag down a waiter and order drinks, "is your research going well?"

"Yep. Look at these guys. You'd have no idea that most of them were gay." She pointed to the right at a man who looked like a bouncer. "If I had run into that hunk of beef over there on the street, I would've been dying to take him home."

She elbowed Vernetta, just as Jamal returned. "Check out the guy at ten o'clock."

Vernetta turned and spotted a very well-known and wealthy rapper.

"He's gay?" Vernetta asked.

"I hear he's bisexual," Jamal clarified.

"Isn't he afraid of being seen here?"

Jamal laughed. "No. Men aren't like women. We don't run and tell. What goes on here, stays here."

The rapper's tight Lycra T-shirt enhanced his rippled muscles. He had a shaved head, a shiny gold chain around his neck, and huge—grossly huge—diamond earrings in both ears.

"Wanna dance?" Jamal extended his hand to Vernetta.

"Uh . . . I'll pass." Vernetta wasn't proud of the way she was reacting, but she couldn't help it. Nichelle gladly sauntered off to the dance floor with him. Jamal had a smooth, sexy dance style. They step-danced as if they had been partners for years.

Nichelle returned to the table, leaving Jamal with a male dance partner. "Stop frowning," Nichelle said.

"It's just so . . ." Vernetta hated to say it, but it was the only word that came to mind, "weird."

"To you. But not to them. We're stuck on this image of gay women as masculine and gay men as feminine, and we refuse to recognize that they look just like you and me. The black community is going to have to recognize that condemning these guys because they're gay is wrong."

She took a sip from her drink, then gave Vernetta a look that was dead serious. "Once we do, maybe they won't feel the need to hide who they are."

# CHAPTER 61

For more than an hour after Reverend Sims departed, Eugene sat alone in his darkened living room, the minister's words echoing in his head. Eugene was tired. Tired of denying who he was. Tired of living a lie.

Without giving it further thought, he did something he'd promised both God and Belynda that he'd never do again. He picked up the telephone and made the most important call of his life.

When Lamont, his ex-lover, rang the doorbell forty-five minutes later, Eugene had changed into a pair of sweats and a T-shirt. After an awkward greeting, Lamont followed him to the living room couch. Eugene had cleared the mugs from the coffee table and replaced them with wineglasses. A bottle of Chardonnay sat cooling in a sterling silver ice bucket.

"I was surprised as hell to get your call, man," Lamont said. They sat on opposite ends of the couch facing each other.

"Kind of surprised me, too. How've you been?"

"I'm cool. The gig at the new firm is working out. They don't work us half as hard as Ramsey & King."

Lamont was sporting a new look, a closely shaven beard. "The facial hair looks good on you."

"Thanks." Lamont absently shifted on the couch. "I heard you left the firm."

"Yeah," was the only response Eugene could think of. Lamont obviously knew all about the lawsuit. Who didn't? He reached for the wine bottle and poured himself a glass. Without inquiring first, he poured one for Lamont, too.

"I heard about your girl. I'm sorry."

Eugene nodded.

"And of course, I've been watching the news. I guess you've been through a lot lately."

Eugene tried to smile, but his lips felt stiff. "You can say that again." They sipped wine and engaged in small talk for another ten minutes.

"Let's cut to the chase," Lamont said finally. "Why am I here?"

"'Cause I needed to see you."

"About what?"

Eugene took another sip of his wine before answering. "About us." He wanted to pull Lamont to him and bury himself in his arms, but he held back.

"So what about us?"

"I think we should give it another try."

Lamont looked away. "Man, I'm getting too old for running the streets. I'm looking for a serious relationship. And I'm not trying to hook up with a guy who's out there running women."

"I'm done with that. I'm ready to commit . . . and to come out."

Lamont responded with a skeptical look.

"Besides," Eugene said, "my story's been told from here to Timbuktu. I'd have a hard time staying on the D-L now. I can't even go grocery shopping without some sister shooting me a nasty look." He laughed.

Lamont did not. "So is that why I'm here? Because you can't pull women anymore?"

"No," Eugene replied. "You're here because I miss you and because I want to be with you."

"What about your family?"

"What about 'em?"

"I always figured they were one of the main reasons you never came out."

"They were, but now they know. Anyway, it's time for me to start living my life for me. Not them. So, I guess I'm asking whether you're still down with me." The desire rising inside Eugene was so strong it hurt.

Lamont set his wineglass on the table. His silence lasted so long that Eugene knew what was coming. Lamont was about to tell him it was too late. When he couldn't take the silence any longer, Eugene decided to give him a break. "I understand, man. There's no reason for you to take the risk of—"

Lamont held up his hand. "No, that's not it. I wanna kick it with you, too. But uh—"

He paused. "There's somebody else."

"It's cool. I understand." Eugene tried to smile. "They always say it's all about timing. I'm glad you found somebody who—"

"No," Lamont interrupted, "it's not that serious. At least not as serious as you and I were. Excuse me, as I *thought* we were. I'm just going to need some time to tie up some loose ends. The dude I'm with is kinda possessive. He's into me way more than I'm into him. We've been living together for the last three months."

Eugene nodded, relieved. He still saw concern on Lamont's face. "Is that all?"

Lamont twirled the ring on his baby finger. "There's something else I gotta tell you."

Eugene braced himself.

"I'm HIV positive, too. Looks like that test I took when your girl first got sick was wrong. The lab contacted me a while back. Told me my results had gotten mixed up with somebody else's. Then I found out the guy I'd been with before we hooked up was positive, too."

Eugene took a big gulp of wine, which went down the wrong pipe. So he *had* been the one who had infected Maya. Not that he'd ever doubted it despite what his attorneys were arguing in court. He would call Eagleman Monday morning and tell him to drop the counterclaim.

His heart went out to Lamont. Eugene understood exactly what he was going through. He recalled his own fears upon first learning the news that he was HIV positive.

Eugene put his glass down and reached out to comfort Lamont. The two men embraced, then kissed like the long lost lovers they were.

# CHAPTER 62

Early Saturday morning, Special drove down Halm Street and parked half a block from Belynda's house. If she knocked on the door, she figured Church Girl would run for the phone to call the police. She would have to play it cool and somehow convince the woman to hear her out.

Surveying the houses, she wondered how Church Girl could afford to live in this neighborhood. The cheapest place on the block had to cost close to a million. "She's probably stealing money from the church," Special muttered.

Since Church Girl practically lived at Ever Faithful, Special assumed she'd be leaving to go there soon. Saturday mornings were always busy days at a black church. Bake sales, usher board practice, youth events. Special had heard that Church Girl basically ran the place.

She was about to take a sip of the coffee that she had picked up on the way when she saw Belynda's front door open. Church Girl walked out dressed in tennis shoes and a jogging suit. Special prepared to exit the car. She needed to reach Belynda before she drove off.

Before Special could make it out of her Porsche, Belynda disappeared through a side gate leading to her backyard. She came out a minute later holding a German Shepherd on a worn leather leash. The dog was almost waist high. Church Girl and the dog then headed downhill toward Centinela. Special hadn't figured the dog into her plan. She wouldn't put it past Church Girl to order the mutt to attack her.

Special let Church Girl walk several yards before following after her on foot. She was glad she'd worn tennis shoes. Belynda was almost at the end of the block when she spotted Special behind her. Alarm spread like a windshield wiper across the woman's face.

"I'm calling the police!" Belynda cried out, swinging around to face Special, then taking several steps backward. She pulled a cell phone from the pocket of her windbreaker, but couldn't dial and hold onto the dog at the same time.

Sensing its owner's distress, the dog growled and lunged at Special, who darted behind a truck.

"You don't need to call the police. I'm not going to hurt you. I just want to talk to you for a minute."

"Well, I don't want to talk to you!" Belynda exclaimed. "Get away from me!"

The dog was barking now and baring a set of large, sharp canine teeth.

"I'm not going to hurt you," Special said again, leaving the protection of the truck. "I just need a few minutes of your time. Not even minutes really. Just a few seconds."

"I said get away from me!"

"I think you should know what Eugene is up to," Special said hurriedly. "I don't know what lie he's been telling you, but the man is still out there screwing around with men. And I have proof."

When Special reached into her pocket, the woman yelped, which made the dog lunge at Special again.

"Hold onto that monster!" Special demanded. She realized that Church Girl probably thought she was reaching for her pepper spray. "The only thing I have in my hand is this camera. See?" She held the camera out in front of her. "I just want to show you a picture I took."

Belynda gave the leash some slack and the dog charged toward her again. Special was barely able to jump out of the way. Belynda had to use both hands to restrain the dog.

"It's okay, Princess." Belynda gave the dog a pat on her side. "It's okay, baby." She sneered at Special. "If you don't leave me alone, I'm letting her loose."

"I *will* leave you alone," Special said, "as soon as you take a look at this picture." She had thought about leaving a copy of it in Church Girl's mailbox. But she wasn't that stupid. She was already facing assault charges. Eugene would've taken the picture straight to the D.A. and filed trespassing charges

"This won't take long. Just tie that dog up for a second so I can show you this picture."

"Whatever it is you have, I don't want to see it. Now get away from me!" Belynda backed away and started reciting Bible verses. "The Lord is my light and my salvation; whom shall I fear? The Lord is the strength of my life; of whom shall I be afraid?"

*You are sho nuf one crazy ass heffa.* "I'm telling you, you need to see this." Special held the camera toward her. "Here take it. I took the picture last night through Eugene's kitchen window. It shows him and another man."

Belynda repeated the verses louder now, as if she were trying to drown out Special's words.

"It shows them kissing."

That stopped Belynda mid-verse. "I don't believe you." She loosened her grip on the dog's leash again. "You're mentally ill just like Eugene said you were. Now get away from me." The dog growled and snapped at Special.

"You don't have to believe me," she said, backing up. "Just look at this picture."

An elderly woman stepped onto the porch of a neighboring house. "Ms. Belynda? What's going on out there?"

Belynda looked from the woman to Special. "Either you get away from me right now," she hissed, "or I'm telling her to call the police. Now which way do you want it?"

# CHAPTER 63

Babe, you need to wake up."

Jefferson stood over the bed, gently shaking Vernetta by the shoulder.

"It can't be six o'clock already," she said groggily, not bothering to open her eyes. Vernetta hated Mondays. "Wake me up in fifteen minutes."

"No," Jefferson said firmly. "Wake up. Now. This is important."

Vernetta finally sat up. "Why do you have the TV up so loud?"

"Because I know you'll want to hear this." He pressed a button on the remote control, turning it up even louder.

*The body of local attorney Eugene Nelson was found this morning at his home in Baldwin Hills. He was reportedly shot three times. Nelson was the subject of one of the city's first wrongful death lawsuits based on the transmission of the AIDS virus."*

Vernetta stumbled to her feet, covering her mouth with both hands. "Oh, my God! Eugene is dead?"

"Sure looks that way," Jefferson said.

*Just last week, attorney and gay activist Barry Eagleman convinced a local judge to issue a gag order in the case and to ban television cameras from the proceedings. The mother of Maya Washington claimed that Nelson caused her death by infecting her with HIV. The lawsuit alleged that Nelson hid the fact that he was gay and HIV positive. Nelson's body was discovered early this morning by his long-time housekeeper . . ."*

"If I were you," Jefferson said, "I'd call your girl and ask her if she has an alibi."

Vernetta fumbled with the telephone on the nightstand next to the bed, almost knocking it to the floor. Her hands trembled as she dialed.

"Special," she said, the second she heard her friend's voice, "did you hear about Eugene?"

"What about him?" Special sounded as groggy as Vernetta had just seconds ago.

Vernetta waited a beat. "He's dead."

"What? You're lying! When? How?"

"Turn on Channel 11."

Vernetta waited as she did. They both listened as the news anchor went live to a reporter camped in front of Eugene's house. The camera panned to Eugene's distraught housekeeper, a thin Hispanic woman, who was being comforted by two police officers. Yellow crime scene tape roped off Eugene's front yard. There were a handful of people from the neighborhood gathered across the street.

"I guess what they say is really true," Special said when the report ended.

"And what's that?"

"The Lord really does work in mysterious ways. That dog got what he deserved!"

"Special!"

"I know you can't possibly expect me to feel an ounce of sympathy for his ass, 'cause I don't."

Vernetta closed her eyes. "Special, I'm only asking you this because I'm a lawyer, okay?"

"Asking me what?"

"Please tell me you didn't have anything to do with Eugene's murder."

Special laughed easily. "I wish I had. But, girl, you know I'm too afraid to shoot somebody."

"Yeah, but you weren't too afraid to hack into his law firm's computer system, throw nails in his driveway, bash in his car, and assault him with pepper spray."

"I'll admit to the pepper spray since they got that on tape," she said, "but as for everything else, I'm taking the Fifth. And anyway, I should be offended that you think I could've done something like that. You know I didn't kill that man."

"Jefferson thinks you were angry enough to have done it."

"Jefferson ain't my best friend. You are."

There was hurt in Special's voice and Vernetta felt guilty for her uncertainty. She just prayed Special was telling the truth.

"Because of your tirade outside the courthouse, you're going to be the first person the police look at. Do you have an alibi?"

"An alibi?"

"Yes, an alibi. According to that news report, Eugene died either late Saturday night or early Sunday morning. Can you account for your whereabouts during that time?"

It took Special several seconds to respond. "I was at home by myself Saturday evening and all day on Sunday."

"Well, that may not be good enough."

"It has to be. I didn't kill that man," she said, alarmed.

"Babe," Jefferson tapped Vernetta on the shoulder and pointed to the television screen. "Take a look at this."

The screen flashed footage of Special attacking Eugene outside the courthouse.

Vernetta dropped the telephone receiver on the bed. "Oh, no."

*Just a week ago, Nelson was attacked with pepper spray by Special Moore, the cousin of Maya Washington. Sources tell us that Moore was extremely distraught over her cousin's death. One source even claims that she took to the pulpit at Ms. Washington's funeral and vowed revenge against Nelson.*

Vernetta picked the receiver back up. "Did you see that?"

"I'm suing them for defamation!" Special shouted. "They can't be using my name like that!"

"You can't sue them," Vernetta said sadly. "What they just reported was the truth."

# CHAPTER 64

$\mathbf{J}$.C.'s Range Rover rolled to a stop in front of Eugene's house within minutes of receiving the call from dispatch. The front lawn was already crawling with cops. An antsy group of looky-loos and reporters were herded into a tight circle directly across the street.

She hopped out, flashed her badge, and slid underneath the yellow crime scene tape. Her eyes scanned the area. To her surprise, Lieutenant Wilson was standing near Eugene's front door, no coffee or Snickers in hand. That was a first. He met her halfway up the driveway.

"Well," J.C. said, "*now* are you finally willing to accept my theory? There's no disputing that *this* victim was on the down low." There was too much *I told you so* in her voice, but she didn't care.

Lieutenant Wilson gave her a harsh look, but said nothing.

"Exactly how many men have to die before we warn the public that somebody is out here gunning for these guys?"

"We don't know for sure that this murder is connected to the others," the Lieutenant said stubbornly. "The M.O. here is different. This guy wasn't capped in a public place. Looks like someone entered through an unlocked window in his kitchen."

"That investment banker was killed in his home, too, Lieutenant."

He guffawed. "Anyway, somebody had a definite motive for wanting this guy dead. And I think you know exactly who I'm talking about."

"What are you talking—" When J.C. realized the lieutenant was referring to Special, the tiny hairs on the back of her neck jumped to attention.

"I know that woman's a friend of yours. I just hope she has a solid alibi for her whereabouts when this guy was knocked off."

"I know my friend. She was devastated about her cousin's death and still is. But I don't think she's capable of murder."

The lieutenant made a face. "You don't sound much like a cop right now. You've been in this game long enough to know that anybody's capable of murder. And if she does become a suspect, you're off the case."

J.C. was well aware of Department policy. She wanted to get back to the real issue. The one the lieutenant was trying to avoid. "Lieutenant, we can't dismiss the possibility that the same person who killed those other men committed this murder as well."

The lieutenant ran a hand across his bald head. "So far, only three of the four murders have a link to this homosexual thing, so—"

"No, Lieutenant," J.C. said, correcting him, "counting Eugene, it's now five of five. I've been reluctant to tell you what we discovered yesterday about your friend, James Hill."

"Aw crap! Please don't tell me some guy's come forward claiming he was Hill's friggin' gay lover."

"No, not that, but we did find some information that raises some questions about his sexual orientation."

He scratched the stubble on his chin and looked down at the ground. "Go ahead. Let's hear it."

"Hill's computer showed that he was a frequent visitor to several gay websites. And he had a pretty extensive collection of gay porn hidden in a safe beneath a floorboard in his home office."

"Son of a bitch!"

"Sorry, Lieutenant." J.C. remained silent as Lieutenant Wilson paced about in a small circle on the grass, cursing. "Are you okay?"

"Yeah," he said, but didn't look it. "You'll be happy to know that I've discussed your theory with the captain. He agrees with me. The repercussions of going public about these men being homos isn't a risk the Department is willing to take right now."

J.C. was ready to explode. "*Isn't a risk the Department is willing to take?* Somebody's out there targeting these guys. They need to know so they can take precautions to protect themselves."

"Lower your voice," he ordered, even though his own decibel level had increased.

"Lieutenant, we cannot ignore the fact that—"

A Honda Civic plowed past the police barricade and screeched to a stop near Eugene's driveway. Belynda threw open the door and tried to get past an officer who stood in her path.

"Ma'am, I can't let you go in there." The officer was struggling to be gentle with Belynda, knowing his actions might be broadcast on the evening news.

"I know who did this," Belynda cried. "I know who killed Eugene!"

A reporter from KABC, in the midst of interviewing a neighbor, dashed across the street and ran up to Belynda. "Are you getting this?" the reporter excitedly called over her shoulder to her cameraman.

Belynda crumpled into a heap of tears on the grass near the curb. "I'm telling you I know who did this!"

The officer helped her to her feet and gently tried to stuff her into the car, but Belynda kept resisting. The cop finally pushed her into the backseat and tried to close the car door, but Belynda reared back and pressed both feet against the door, preventing him from closing it.

"You're standing here wasting time while Eugene's murderer is walking around free!"

The KABC reporter bent down and peered into the car. She extended her microphone toward Belynda. The cop, still struggling with Belynda, almost knocked it out of her hand.

"So who do you think killed Mr. Nelson?" the reporter asked.

"Special Moore killed Eugene!"

J.C. wanted to run over and clamp a muzzle on the woman. Her hysterical allegation was nothing short of slander. There was no way any responsible news station would risk a defamation lawsuit by airing her accusation.

A couple of officers were about to assist their comrade, but the lieutenant waved them off. "That woman can't weigh more than a buck twenty-five. He ought to be able to handle her." The lieutenant apparently didn't want any news footage of a gang of LAPD officers taking down a lone, wisp of a woman.

Somehow Belynda managed to push her way past the much larger cop and propel herself out of the car. More reporters swooped out of nowhere, forming a tight circle around her, anxious to hear what she had to say.

"You saw her attack Eugene outside the courthouse," Belynda declared. Now that a herd of cameras were focused on her, she magically composed herself. She tugged at the hem of her sweater. "And I have proof that she killed Eugene."

"What kind of proof?" asked a reporter whose microphone bore a KNBC emblem.

Belynda ran her fingers through her tussled hair. "Special Moore confronted me outside my house early Saturday morning. I was scared to death because I knew she was mentally unstable. She tried to get me to look at a picture on her digital camera, but I refused. She claimed it showed Eugene and another man . . . kissing. But it was all part of her delusional psychosis. She even admitted trespassing on his property and peeping into his kitchen window Friday night to take the picture."

The lieutenant gave J.C. a somber look. J.C. prayed the woman was making this all up. But what Belynda had just described didn't sound too farfetched for Special.

"She was stalking him and she wasn't going to stop until he was dead." Belynda turned away from the reporter who had asked the last question and stared directly into the lens of a camera to her right.

"If the police want Eugene's killer," she said with the confidence of an attorney delivering a closing argument, "all they need to do is go arrest Special Moore."

# CHAPTER 65

Deputy D.A. Ray Martinez sat across the desk from Melvin Hathaway and tried to hide his discomfort. Being summoned by the District Attorney himself could mean only one of two things. Good news or really, really bad news. Ray just wished Hathaway would cut the chit chat and get to the point.

"You've had an incredible career here," Hathaway said. "Your win-loss record is one of the best. A lot of prosecutors have high success rates because they're afraid to try difficult cases. You've tried some real dogs and won."

Ray started to respond with a thank you, but decided to let it pass. Hathaway had been blowing smoke up his ass for the past ten minutes. *Why in the hell am I here?*

"I guess you're wondering why I wanted to see you," Hathaway said.

"Yes," Ray admitted, "I am a little curious."

Martinez had been a Deputy D.A. for more than seven years and had never even been in the office of his boss' boss. A product of East Oakland, Ray attended NYU Law School and spent three years in the Alameda County D.A.'s office before making the move to L.A. He had wavy, dark hair and a thick mustache that gave him the distinguished air of a much older man, though he had just hit thirty-five. Copper-colored skin advertised his Mexican heritage.

"Well, today's your lucky day, Martinez." Hathaway smiled and leaned back in his leather chair. His teeth glistened from repeated laser treatments. "I'm about to drop one of those career-making cases into your lap."

Some of the anxiety left and Ray finally smiled. "Tell me more."

"You're the lucky D.A. who's going to prosecute the Eugene Nelson murder case," Hathaway said. "I'm sure you've been reading about it."

This time, Ray sat up.

It was rare to get an assignment directly from the District Attorney himself and now he knew why. Hathaway was a politician, a very savvy politician. He'd been campaigning hard for the mayor's job, and the election was right around the corner. Hathaway had much to gain by getting a quick conviction in the Nelson murder case.

In the days following the attack outside the courthouse, Eugene Nelson had become a cause célèbre in the gay community. The media coverage after his murder intensified and gay activists were now demanding that someone pay for what they viewed as a vicious hate crime.

Putting Nelson's killer behind bars would brand Hathaway a true friend of the gay community, a nice constituency to have on your side. Having a Latino D.A. deliver the conviction would also help when it came to the Hispanic vote. Ray would probably be asked to accompany Hathaway on his campaign appearances in East L.A. Ray was being used. Still, he liked being the chosen one.

He played it cool, even though he knew Hathaway would have preferred to see him jumping for joy over this opportunity to prosecute a murder case that had already garnered national attention. But Ray wasn't one of those *Sí, Señor,* media-chasing kind of prosecutors. He was good at what he did because he focused all of his attention on proving guilt. Not on trying to become a celebrity lawyer.

"As I understand it, no one's been arrested yet," Ray said.

"An arrest is imminent."

"The woman who attacked him outside the courthouse?"

Hathaway nodded.

"We got any hard evidence linking her to his murder?"

"Not yet. But I personally made a call to the chief. So trust me, if there's some evidence to be found, they'll find it. That's why I wanted you involved early on."

Ray knew the D.A. had one final issue he needed to raise before dismissing him. But Ray wasn't going to cut Hathaway any slack. He would have to broach the subject on his own.

Ray made a show of glancing at his watch. He was anxious for Hathaway to get to the point. "Thanks for this opportunity. Is there anything else we need to discuss?"

Hathaway steepled his fingers and rested his hands on his desk. "As a matter of fact, there is."

Ray waited, leaving no readable expression on his face.

"The media can be real barracudas," Hathaway said. "And nowadays, nothing is off limits. When I was in your shoes, all the attention was focused on the victim and the defendant. Rarely on the attorneys. Now, it's a different ball game. The media is likely to dig around in your personal life, if you know what I mean."

Ray chuckled inside. What Hathaway wanted to know was whether Ray could handle the pressure when the media put his personal life on front street. Ray had never hidden who he was. He wasn't in the closet, but he wasn't exactly out either. If the subject came up, he didn't run from it. If no one raised it, he saw no reason to. Heterosexuals didn't walk around professing their sexual orientation, and Ray didn't feel the need to do so either. He was what he was.

Luckily, he'd been raised by a loving mother who would have accepted him no matter what. His relationship with his father remained strained and always would be. Ray had been living with his partner Antonio since moving to L.A. He wondered, though, if Antonio could stand the public scrutiny.

Ray could only imagine the headlines: *D.A. Selects Fag Prosecutor to Try Down Low Murder Case.* He'd have no trouble handling the media or dealing with criticism from the generally homophobic public. He'd been called a fag before and he'd no doubt be called one again. He decided to let Hathaway off the hook.

"I understand what you're getting at," Ray said. "The media's going to make a big deal of the fact that I'm gay. I can handle it."

"Great." The tension eased from Hathaway's face. "Now get outta here and get me a conviction."

# CHAPTER 66

Two days after Belynda's emotional television debut, Special sat between Vernetta and Nichelle in a dingy, windowless interrogation room at Parker Center. The police had asked Special to voluntarily come in for questioning on less than an hour's notice.

"So how long we gotta sit here?" Special nervously rocked back and forth.

Vernetta was glad to see fear on her friend's face. Special was finally beginning to comprehend that her antics toward Eugene had landed her in very big trouble.

"As long as it takes," Vernetta said snidely. "We wouldn't even be here if you hadn't attacked Eugene with that pepper spray. You just better be glad none of those TV stations ran all of that interview with Belynda. J.C. said she fingered you as Eugene's killer."

Special twisted her lips. "And if they had aired it, I would've sued her and every single one of 'em for defamation. Church Girl has some nerve calling me mentally ill. She's the one who knowingly dated a man who was on the down low."

Nichelle chided Special with her eyes. "And after assaulting the man, I can't believe you had the nerve to trespass on Eugene's property and take a picture through his kitchen window."

"And to make matters worse," Vernetta added, "you actually admitted what you did to Belynda. She's not the sick one. You are."

"I was just trying to help her ass. Anyway, that picture is long gone. I erased the entire disk the minute J.C. told me what Belynda said to those reporters. So it's my word against hers."

Vernetta checked the clock on the wall. She had to get back to the office for an afternoon meeting and prayed that she would be able to make it on time. Appearing at this interrogation on behalf of Special without the firm's permission was, once again, crossing the line. But she had to be here. Vernetta realized now that if Special did end up being charged with Eugene's murder, she very much wanted to be part of the defense team. She refused to even think about what that would mean for her partnership chances.

Special kept fidgeting in her chair. "This is ridiculous. They know I didn't kill that man. They're just messing with me 'cause they can."

"No, they're messing with you because you made it known to the world how much you hated Eugene, which gives you a clear motive for killing him."

"And don't give them any more ammunition." Nichelle was just as perturbed.

Special slouched further down in her chair. "I thought you told them I had nothing to say."

"I did," Vernetta replied. "But they're still going to try to bully you or perhaps trick you into talking. And like we told you, don't say a word unless we tell you to."

"Okay, okay." She turned to Nichelle. "I've been meaning to ask you something. Just because Eugene's dead doesn't mean we have to drop the lawsuit, does it?"

"Nope, but it's a lot more complicated. We're going after his estate. But right now, the only legal case you should be worried about is your own."

The door opened and J.C., followed by two men, walked in.

"I'm Detective Jessup," said a white man with macho written all over him. Vernetta noticed his swagger even though he'd only taken a couple of steps into the room. "This is Ray Martinez from the D.A.'s office," he pointed to an attractive, well-dressed Hispanic who was on the short side. "I understand you already know Detective Sparks."

Vernetta nodded at J.C.

"We'd like to ask Ms. Moore a few questions," Detective Jessup announced. "But before we begin, I want to make sure you're comfortable with Detective Sparks being here." J.C. looked as if she wanted to slug him.

"Why wouldn't we be?" Vernetta asked.

"I understand you all are pretty close. I just thought—"

"The lieutenant gave me the okay to be here," J.C. said to Jessup. "Just start the interview." She folded her arms and leaned against the wall.

Detective Jessup pulled out a chair from the table and straddled it backwards. He slapped a notepad down on the table. Vernetta tried to read it upside down, but his handwriting looked like a three year old's.

"I'd like to begin with your whereabouts last Saturday morning," Detective Jessup said.

Vernetta smiled in a way that communicated that she was about to get nasty. "I've already told you, Detective, based on our legal advice, Special isn't saying a word. You gave us very little notice. We'd like to cooperate with you, but we need time to conduct our own investigation first. Perhaps you can share with us the specific charges against Ms. Moore."

"There aren't any charges at the moment. For the time being, your client is a person of interest in the murder of Eugene Nelson."

"I didn't kill that man," Special said. "This is crazy. The only person I know guilty of murder is Eugene."

"Special, please don't say another word." Vernetta sounded like an impatient parent scolding a naughty child.

"I'm not going to just sit here and not defend myself," she fired back. "I didn't shoot anybody."

"The way I hear it," Detective Jessup said, egging her on, "you stood up at your cousin's funeral and told the entire church that that was exactly what you planned to do."

"I never said anything about shooting the man. I only said—"

"Shut up!" Vernetta grabbed Special by the upper arm, then turned to Detective Jessup. "We need a few seconds alone with our client."

Vernetta caught J.C.'s eye on the way out. Her unspoken message advised Vernetta to get a grip on their friend.

As soon as the door closed, Vernetta let Special have it. "When I said you weren't supposed to talk, that's what I meant."

"But they're trying to—"

"Do you understand that you could be facing a murder charge?" Vernetta said. "We're not talking about you attacking Eugene with pepper spray. They're trying to pin his murder on you."

"But—"

"But nothing! You asked us to represent you and that's what we're trying to do. But if you say one more word, we're out of here and you're on your own."

Special looked to Nichelle for support.

"And I'm leaving with her," Nichelle said.

Special stuck out her lips. "That man gets to kill Maya, and everybody treats *me* like I'm the criminal. I was just—"

"Special," Vernetta said, "all I want you to do is be quiet. Do you understand?"

"Fine."

Nichelle went to the door and signaled for them to return.

Detective Jessup led the procession back into the room. "I see you're having some client control problems." He chuckled. "Anyway, where were we?" He remained standing and flipped open his notepad. "Let's see . . . oh, yeah, last Saturday morning I understand you admitted to a Ms. Belynda Davis that you had been stalking Mr. Nelson."

Special flinched, but otherwise obeyed orders.

Vernetta could tell that J.C. was dying to interject. But Vernetta knew she couldn't. Too bad she had to work with such a jerk.

"Detective," Vernetta said, "I think we've made it clear that Ms. Moore isn't answering any questions at this time."

He acted as if he hadn't heard her. "Perhaps I should treat you all to a little preview of what we have so far." He flipped past a few pages in his notepad. "We know for a fact that Ms. Moore physically assaulted the victim with pepper spray. Luckily, we have that on tape." He winked at Special. "Let's see here. We're also close to figuring out how she hacked into his law firm's computer system. And if that wasn't enough, she vandalized his house and threw nails in his driveway. We happen to have an eyewitness to that last incident."

Special's eyes blinked in a way that spelled guilt more clearly than any words could have.

"I think you're bluffing," Vernetta said. "Exactly who's your witness?"

"We aren't at liberty to disclose that information at this time."

Martinez moved from his position near the door. He pulled up a chair and sat down at the table, directly in front of Special. "You'll find out the evidence we have at the appropriate time." He directed his words to Vernetta. "You know how this game is played. It would behoove you to let your client answer our questions. If we're going after the wrong suspect, her responses will tell us that."

Vernetta simply could not allow Special to talk. In a case where she knew her client was innocent, she would've been far more cooperative.

But she couldn't do that here. Even though Special denied any role in the other attacks against Eugene, she didn't believe her. Having committed those crimes, however, didn't mean she was also guilty of murder.

"We'll answer your questions," Vernetta said, "but at the *appropriate* time for us. For now, our client has nothing to say."

"It's always the guilty people who're afraid to talk," Detective Jessup muttered.

"We don't have time for these little head games." Vernetta stood up. Nichelle and Special followed her lead. "It's obvious that you don't have any basis for charging Ms. Moore with Eugene's murder. And since you don't, we're out of here."

# CHAPTER 67

Vernetta made it back to the office with twenty minutes to spare before her meeting with Haley and O'Reilly. The Vista Electronics case was finally heating up. This was the worst possible time for her best friend to be charged with murder. She prayed that didn't happen.

Sheila, her secretary, stuck her head in the door as Vernetta scanned her incoming emails. "I hate to deliver bad news, but Haley was nosing around here looking for you."

"When?"

"About thirty minutes ago. I told her you had a meeting out of the office. She tried to pump me for more information, but I played dumb. So how'd it go with Special?"

"Not good." After Sheila closed the door, Vernetta gave her a quick recap.

"I know Special was hella mad at that guy. I would've been, too. But do you think she was angry enough to go gunning for him?"

Vernetta didn't like the fact that Sheila was even asking that question. "I know my friend," Vernetta said. "She didn't kill Eugene."

"I hope she knows how lucky she is to have you in her corner. If she gets charged, is the firm going to let you defend her?"

"I'm not sure," she said, though O'Reilly had already made his feelings quite plain. "Just keep everything I told you under your hat."

"You got it," Sheila said, then left.

Vernetta was already waiting in the conference room when Haley and O'Reilly strolled in together. Perhaps she was imagining things, but both of them looked as if they were in their own little world of bliss. Vernetta had been trying her darnedest to get along with Haley, but it wasn't going well. She decided to get in some more practice.

"I love that suit you're wearing, Haley."

"Thanks," she replied. "I bought it at Neiman Marcus."

Which meant it cost a grip. Haley sat down across from her, on the same side of the table as O'Reilly.

"Give me a minute before we get started." O'Reilly scrolled through his BlackBerry.

Haley grinned at Vernetta from across the table. "So how was your morning?"

Vernetta's internal antenna shot straight up. "Fine."

"This case is going to be quite challenging. I've been analyzing that report from our expert. Looks like the employees haven't been taking meal breaks, and on top of that the company isn't computing overtime correctly. I've been here since seven o'clock this morning going through the records."

*Good for you.*

"So how'd your friend's interrogation go this morning?"

Vernetta felt her brain short-circuit. "What?"

"A friend of mine is a deputy D.A. He saw you down at Parker Center this morning. He said you're representing Special Moore. The police apparently believe she murdered that guy, Eugene Nelson."

O'Reilly looked up from his BlackBerry. "I thought we already had this conversation," he said sternly. "You're not permitted to be involved in any outside legal work without the firm's permission. If you make some misstep, the firm could be on the hook for a malpractice claim."

Vernetta folded her hands to keep from reaching across the table and strangling Haley. "I'm not doing any outside legal work," she lied. "As Haley just explained, Special is a very close friend. I was only there this morning for moral support. She's being represented by attorneys from Barnes, Ayers, and Howard. Nichelle Ayers, another close friend of mine and one of the firm's name partners, was also present at the interrogation." No need to explain that Vernetta was the one running the show.

"Okay," O'Reilly groaned, "let's just keep it that way. But I have to say I'm concerned about your using firm time to do this."

"I wasn't using firm time," Vernetta said, her voice taut. "I charged my time out of the office this morning to personal time."

That didn't seem to satisfy him because he continued to lecture her. "The Vista Electronics case is going to take up all of your time and then some. From this point forward, I'd like you to clear *any* involvement in your friend's case—or any other outside case—with me. In advance."

"Fine. But I only—"

"Let's get started." He handed a document to both of them.

Haley smiled at Vernetta. She smiled back. O'Reilly was about to say something when his cell phone rang. "I need to take this," he said, then stepped outside.

Vernetta tried to read the document O'Reilly had given them, but she was too steamed to concentrate. She knew she should just ignore Haley, but the girl deserved a piece of her mind. "Thanks for bringing up my friend's case in front of O'Reilly."

"I'm sorry. Was it a problem for me to mention it?"

"What do you think?"

"I have no idea why you're so upset." Haley ran her fingers through her hair. "Maybe I shouldn't say this, but you have a very big chip on your shoulder."

Vernetta was just about to tell Haley to kiss her ass when O'Reilly came back in. "I need to finish taking this call in my office. We'll have to postpone our meeting for about an hour." He picked up his folder and left.

Haley stood up to leave, but Vernetta stopped her.

"We weren't through yet," she said. "If you want to sleep your way to partnership, that's your business. Just stay out of mine."

The deep red that settled along Haley's cheekbones told Vernetta that she was dead right about their affair.

"Exactly what do you mean by that?"

"You know exactly what I mean." Vernetta gathered her belongings from the table. "You can fuck O'Reilly or anybody else around here. I don't care. Just stop trying to screw me."

# CHAPTER 68

Special thought about going home after leaving Parker Center, but she couldn't afford to be docked for missing another day's work. As much as she'd been absent lately, they were probably on the verge of firing her anyway.

From the moment she stepped into the lobby of her office building, she felt stares from every direction. The guard at the main desk usually waved at her, but averted his eyes when she sauntered past. A woman on her way out of the building was staring so hard she almost plowed into the glass doors. When Special stepped into an elevator car that was about to close, three women who'd been chatting away suddenly stopped.

Special kept her focus on the elevator light as it ascended from floor to floor. This whole thing was one big nightmare that she prayed would hurry up and blow over. All the police had on her was the pepper spray attack. Despite what Vernetta and Nichelle told her, she refused to believe she would actually be charged with Eugene's murder. Her friends were just trying to scare her into keeping her mouth closed. Lawyers were always so pessimistic.

When she finally made it to her office, Special turned on her computer and pulled up her unopened emails. She quickly scrolled down and was surprised to see a long list of new emails from people whose email addresses she didn't recognize. The subject lines for all of the messages were blank. She assumed they were spam and was about to delete them, but decided to open the first one.

*You homophobic bitch! I hope you get the death penalty!*

"Oh, my God!" Special opened a few more of the emails and the messages were equally malicious.

She picked up her phone to call Vernetta, but noticed that her message light was lit. She punched in her voicemail password and heard the automated voice advise her that she had sixteen new messages.

"Oh, my God!" she said again. She figured that the same nut or nuts who had emailed her had also called her office. She timidly listened to the first message.

*You vicious cunt. You think you can go around—*

Special slammed the phone down and clutched her chest. Fear caused her to peer over her shoulder, down at the street four stories below. Who was harassing her? For all she knew it could have even been someone she worked with. There were two guys who worked in the mail room that Special always thought were suspect. She wondered if one or both of them were behind the threats. They would have access to both her email address and office number.

She got up and marched to Human Resources.

"Margaret, I need to speak with you," she said, walking into the HR manager's office.

Margaret smiled her trademark infomercial smile. "I'm glad you're here. I was about to head down to your office."

"Okay," Special said, "you go first."

As usual, she was dressed like a 1960's sitcom mom. Long skirt, frilly blouse, pearl necklace and matching earrings. "No, it can wait. Tell me why you're here."

"I received some harassing emails and voicemail messages this morning," Special began. "I'm hoping we can turn them over to security so they can find out who sent them."

"We can do that." Margaret did not show the level of concern Special had expected. "Is there anything else?"

"No, that was basically it. So what's the first step? Maybe we should call somebody in security right now."

"Sure, but first . . ." Margaret moved her coffee mug from one side of the desk to the other. "What I wanted to discuss with you is somewhat related to those messages you received. Of course, you know everyone's aware of the problems you've been having. It's been all over the news."

Special stiffened. "Yeah, and . . ."

"We don't think it's a good idea for you to be in the workplace until this whole matter regarding the murder of that gentleman blows over."

Special locked her arms across her chest. "First, he wasn't a gentleman. And second, I didn't kill anybody. Nor have I been charged with killing anybody."

"Yes, but you did assault the man. I gather you'll be facing criminal charges in connection with that."

"Maybe, maybe not. He's dead now."

Margaret refused to look at her. "You're a supervisor here. You know how disruptive something like this can be. We think you should take a leave of absence until this matter's been cleared up. This explains everything." She extended an envelope across the desk.

Special did not reach for it.

"Your medical benefits will remain in effect as long as you continue to pay the employee portion of the premium."

Special glowered at the woman. "So is this a paid leave?"

"No, I'm sorry. We aren't able to pay you under these circumstances. That wouldn't be consistent with how we've treated other employees who've been in trouble with the law."

"I've seen this company bend the rules for other employees."

Margaret absently patted the pearls around her neck. "There's nothing I can do. I'm sorry." She was still holding out the envelope, waiting for Special to take it.

Special wanted to slap the envelope out of her hand and the smile off her face.

"You know what?" She rose from her chair, still ignoring the envelope. "You're absolutely right. Considering everything I've been through lately, it's probably not a good idea for me to be at work. I'm happy to take a leave of absence . . . for stress. You'll have the workers' comp forms from my doctor by the end of the day."

# CHAPTER 69

$W$hat in the world did you do wrong?"

Sheila was standing in the doorway of Vernetta's office with a worried look on her face. "I just got a call from O'Reilly. He wants to see you ASAP and he sounded really pissed off."

It hadn't even been twenty minutes since Vernetta had squared off with Haley. She must have run straight to O'Reilly to tattle. As far as Vernetta was concerned, *she* was holding all the trump cards. They were the ones screwing around. If the firm's management committee found out about their affair, O'Reilly would be in a whole lot of hot water. He needed to be nice to her so she would continue to keep his little secret.

Vernetta boldly made her way to O'Reilly's office.

"You wanted to see me?" The second she stepped across the threshold her bravado evaporated. Vernetta saw nothing but anger chiseled into O'Reilly's face.

"Close the door," he said stiffly.

Before she could even take a seat, he lit into her.

"As a senior associate in this firm, your position with respect to a junior associate is the same as a manager to a subordinate. And as a manager, you represent the firm and, therefore, your actions can create liability for the firm."

*Liability for the firm? What about your actions?* His words came at her at a rapid-fire pace. The only thing missing was the smoke rising from his nostrils.

"When you act inappropriately toward a subordinate you—"

"I wasn't aware that I had acted inappropriately toward an associate," Vernetta said, trying to sound calm, though anger swirled inside her.

"I'm talking about your inappropriate insinuation to Haley just a while ago."

Vernetta thought about playing dumb, but figured it might make matters worse. But she wasn't exactly sure how to play it. "Perhaps you should start by asking for my side of the story."

O'Reilly twirled a gold pen between two fingers. "Okay, then why don't *you* tell me what happened?"

Vernetta was at a complete loss for words. She had accused Haley of screwing O'Reilly and she could not come up with a story that would alter that reality.

"I guess your silence means I got it right."

Vernetta just stared back at him.

"So, as I was saying," he continued, "it's highly inappropriate to accuse an associate of improper behavior with absolutely no evidence to support it. If you had such a concern, you should have come to me or someone else in the firm. I'm very disappointed in you."

*You have to be kidding.* Vernetta found it interesting that O'Reilly conveniently left himself out of this conversation.

"Since you two have to work together, you're going to have to develop a much better working relationship."

Vernetta realized now that without a picture of the two of them naked in bed together, her suppositions were just that. She didn't hold any trump cards. O'Reilly held them all. There was no way she could go up against somebody like him and win.

"I want you to walk down to Haley's office and apologize to her," he ordered. "And another thing, I just made some calls. I guess you didn't hear me when I said you were not to be involved in any outside legal matters without the firm's permission. You weren't completely honest with me earlier. It's my understanding that you were the one representing your friend when she was questioned by the police this morning. I also understand that you talked to the media after some hearing a few days ago."

"I spoke to the media as a family friend, not as a lawyer."

"It doesn't make a difference. As long as you're an attorney in this firm, anything you say or do could have consequences for the firm." O'Reilly stopped and pointed his pen at her. "This is the last time I'm going to say this. You are not to do any outside legal work without my knowing about it. That includes talking to the media about your friend's case."

"My friend hasn't been charged, but if that happens, I was thinking about requesting a leave of absence to assist in her defense."

"Don't bother." His eyes bore angrily into hers. "I don't think it's a good idea for the firm to be associated with that kind of case."

"What kind of case? This firm has taken on murder cases before."

"Your friend's case involves a very malicious hate crime. It wouldn't be good for the firm's image."

As long as a client could fork over enough money, O'Reilly & Finney had never been worried about its image before. Vernetta was dizzy with rage.

O'Reilly turned to his computer screen. "Unless you have something else to say, you can leave."

Vernetta stood up, intending to leave, but her feet felt rooted to the floor. "I don't know where things between you and me went awry, but they obviously have. And in light of that fact, I don't think it makes much sense for me to remain with the firm. Consider this my two-weeks' notice."

She saw a spark of relief on O'Reilly's face. He was obviously thrilled that she was leaving before having a chance to expose his affair with Haley. Vernetta's departure also let him off the hook since he probably didn't plan to recommend her for partnership.

"The firm would obviously hate to lose you." O'Reilly was barely able to hide his delight. "But if that's your decision, I'll have to accept it."

Vernetta wanted to say something snippy, but chose to remain professional. "I'd like to request a severance package to help me with my transition," she said. "Six months, including medical, should do it."

She saw a hint of protest in his eyes, but it disappeared the minute he noticed the defiance in hers. Six months' salary was a pittance to the firm, but it was more than sufficient hush money to give Vernetta time to contemplate her career plans.

O'Reilly leaned back in his chair and fiddled with his pen. "I don't think that will be a problem."

"Thanks, I really appreciate it," Vernetta said, then calmly walked out.

# CHAPTER 70

Not long after leaving O'Reilly's office, Vernetta was waiting inside the trailer at Jefferson's worksite while one of his workers went to look for him. It was late afternoon and the place was in full swing.

Jefferson charged through the trailer door in a near panic. The first thing he did was take in his wife's attire: jeans, cowboy boots, and a tank top. "What's the matter? Why aren't you at work? What happened?"

Vernetta laughed. "Calm down. Nothing's wrong. I just decided to bring you an early dinner since I know you rarely take a lunch break." She held up a heavy picnic basket with both hands. "Grilled catfish, mashed potatoes, macaroni salad, and cornbread. Plus, my hand-squeezed lemonade."

He blinked.

"And it's all homemade." Of course, it was homemade by M & M's Soul Food, but she figured he didn't need to know that. "I almost forgot." She dug deep inside the basket and pulled out a pint of ice cream. "I brought you an extra special treat. Your favorite, Ben & Jerry's Coffee Heath Bar Crunch. You gotta eat it quick before it melts."

Jefferson smiled, but he was too confused to otherwise react. "How come you're not at work? What's going on?"

"I made two very important decisions today."

"Okay," Jefferson said cautiously.

"First, I quit my job."

Jefferson's lips transformed into a goofy grin, then reverted. "Hold up. You've *already* quit your job or you're *thinking* about quitting your job?"

"It's a done deal."

"You serious?"

"As a heart attack."

He gave her a hug that lifted her off her feet. "So what happened? Are you okay about it?"

"Do I look okay?"

"Yeah, you do. As a matter of fact, you actually look pretty damn happy."

"Not happy," Vernetta said. "Ecstatic. If I'd known it would feel this good, I'd have left months ago. Anyway, until I figure out exactly what I'm going to do with my life, I plan to spend all of my time pampering my wonderful husband. That's the second decision I made today."

Vernetta began taking plastic containers from the picnic basket. "Pull up a chair so I can feed you."

As they ate, Vernetta gave him an extended play-by-play of her run-in with Haley and her subsequent conversation with O'Reilly.

Jefferson took a big bite of cornbread. "I'm sure glad they pissed you off."

"Me, too."

They laughed and joked for the next thirty minutes. It felt great spending this unscheduled time with her husband. When they were done eating, Vernetta started packing up. "I guess I should let you get back to work."

Jefferson approached from behind and threw his arms around her waist. "So, you bringing me dinner tomorrow?"

"I might," Vernetta said, turning around to face him. "But I have to be careful not to spoil you. Just hurry up and get home." She raised her eyebrows seductively. "I'll be waiting at the door in my birthday suit."

"Why I gotta wait?" He eased his hand underneath her tank top. "We can do it right here."

Vernetta laughed and tried to squirm away. "What if one of your guys walks in?"

"Then he'll probably end up learning something." Jefferson cupped one of her breasts and nuzzled his lips down into her top which sent a shiver straight to her toes.

"Anyway, I'm the boss, remember? I can do whatever I want."

"Boy, I am not having sex with you in here."

"How you gonna come up in here talkin' about being butt naked when I get home and expect me to get any work done? I'm so happy you're leaving that firm, I want to celebrate. Here. Now."

He lifted her top higher, exposing her bare breasts. "See, you ain't even wearing a bra." His lips gently tugged on her nipples, then grazed her breasts in slow, wide circles. "You intentionally came down here to mess with me."

Vernetta laughed and pulled her top back down. "We can't do it in here. Somebody might walk in on us."

He grabbed her hand, then took several steps backward, pulling her along with him. He stopped when he was within arm's reach of the trailer door. Never taking his eyes off of her, he reached back and turned the lock on the doorknob.

"Okay, now it's safe. Now can I have some?" He started dotting her neck with kisses. "I've always had a fantasy about having sex at work."

"Jefferson, you'll be home in a couple of hours. I promise to make it worth your wait."

"Nah, baby, I want you here. Now." He ignored his wife's protests, unsnapped the button of her jeans and slid his hand inside.

"I bet Haley was giving O'Reilly blow jobs in his office every night," he mumbled. "Black women are way too uptight. That's why all the freaky white girls are getting the brothers."

Vernetta playfully socked him in the chest. "I can't believe you said that!"

He laughed. "You know I'm telling the truth." His fingers quickly found a welcoming place between her thighs, which quieted the fierce protests from her brain. When their eyes met, she saw his hunger for her.

All of a sudden, the locked door, her husband's dare, and a desire she could no longer fight, caused all of her inhibitions to slip away. Vernetta pulled off her top, looped it around the back of Jefferson's neck and pulled him even closer.

"C'mere," she said, smiling big, "and let me show you how freaky a sister can get."

# CHAPTER 71

I hate to be the one to bring this up," Special said, glancing around the table, "but this is one sad ass celebration."

Vernetta, Special and, Nichelle were sitting at their regular booth at T.G.I. Friday's. Special had called the impromptu gathering to celebrate Vernetta's new career move, though she had no idea exactly what that move might be.

Within twenty-four hours of resigning, the reality of her situation finally hit her. Vernetta didn't regret quitting, but leaving O'Reilly & Finney before making partner was admittedly a big disappointment.

"I guess I'm just not used to being unemployed," Vernetta said.

"Girl, please," Special chided her. "We ain't having no pity party up in here. You don't have nothing to be down in the dumps about. You walked away with six months' pay. I'm the one who can't pay my bills and who might be facing prison time. I'm glad you left that firm. They were working you like a slave. You'll have another job just like that." She snapped her fingers. "So pick your lips up off the table."

It had been three days since Vernetta resigned. The firm decided that there was no need for her to work another two weeks. O'Reilly was probably afraid that she'd steal some client files or worse, run off to HR and report that he was screwing an associate. She had returned to work the next day, wrote a lengthy memo summarizing the status of her cases, packed up, and left.

A waitress set a big plate of nachos in the middle of the table. Everybody dug in except Nichelle. She was determined to stick to her new diet, even if it killed her. And it just might. She was nibbling on a small salad that barely had enough dressing to fill a thimble.

"Any idea what you'd like to do next?" Nichelle asked.

"Actually," Vernetta said, brightening for the first time, "me and Jefferson are talking about adopting."

Nichelle affectionately squeezed Vernetta's hand. "Congratulations!"

"I thought Jefferson didn't want to adopt," Special said.

"He didn't at first. I guess it just took some time for him to warm up to the idea."

"Just be careful who you bring home," Special warned. "I'm not babysitting no bad ass kids."

"I didn't say anything about kids with an *s*. Just one will do for now."

"So you're going to be a full-time mommy?" Nichelle asked.

Special acted as if the question had been addressed to her. "Ain't no way Ms. Workaholic can stay at home every day. She'll be at another firm by the end of the month."

"For your information, I promised Jefferson I was going to take at least three months off before looking for another job."

Special took a loud sip of her Long Island iced tea. "You can make all the promises you want. That'll happen right after I win the Miss America Pageant."

"What's that supposed to mean?"

"It means you couldn't take three months off if somebody tied you up and glued your butt to a chair."

"I think you're going to be surprised."

"If *you* take three months off," Special said, "I *will* be surprised."

Nichelle laid down her fork. "Well, there goes my big plan."

Vernetta reached for another nacho, spilling guacamole on the table in the process. "What big plan?" she asked.

Nichelle grinned playfully. "Never mind. You probably wouldn't be interested anyway."

"Interested in what?"

Nichelle let a few more beats pass before she finally spilled it. "What would you think about joining our firm? We need an attorney with employment law expertise. A lot of the companies that Sam and Russell represent have labor issues. You'd have a built-in client base."

Nichelle's offer surprised her. "Wow."

"Wow, nothing." Special wagged her finger in Vernetta's face. "Didn't you just tell us you promised Jefferson you'd take three months off?"

"Yeah, but—"

"But nothing. That man has been hanging with you through thick and thin. You need to use this time off to give him some TLC. You know how needy men are."

Vernetta was only half listening. She had actually been thinking about starting her own law practice, but she was concerned about the hefty start-up costs. Joining Nichelle's firm would be the perfect solution. She could set her own hours, so she would still be able to devote time to Jefferson and a new baby."

"Dang," Special said. "I can see the gleam in your eyes already. Poor Jefferson."

"That might not be a bad idea," Vernetta said to Nichelle. "I don't want to commit to joining as a partner or even as an associate. I just need a place to practice for a while. I could be an independent contractor until I figure out my next move."

"However you want it," Nichelle said.

Then Vernetta remembered her rocky relationship with Sam. "I know Russell would be an easy sell. But I'm not so sure Sam would go for it."

"He will," Nichelle assured her. "He's not as much of a brute as he comes off sometimes. His bottom line is green. I'm sure we could figure out a fee arrangement that will work out for you and the firm. That's all Sam will need to hear."

"Thanks for the offer. I think it's something I'd seriously like to consider. But before you discuss it with Russell and Sam, I need to talk to Jefferson."

"Great." Nichelle eyed the plate of nachos, then bravely dug into her salad.

Special wagged her finger in Vernetta's face. "Jefferson's going to be hella mad at you."

Nichelle gave Special a pointed scowl. "If I were you, I'd be trying to encourage Vernetta to come to our firm. If they end up charging you with Eugene's murder, you're going to need all the legal help you can get."

Vernetta could almost see the light bulb flash in Special's head.

"On second thought," she said, cozying up to Vernetta, "I think Nichelle's firm would be the perfect place for you. How soon can you start?"

# CHAPTER 72

Ray Martinez walked into the conference room where his trial team sat waiting and slapped a thick manila folder on the battered, rectangular table.

"Okay, everybody, let's get started. What do you have for me, Denny?"

Denny Marconi was an investigator with the D.A.'s Felony Unit. Ray had never worked with him before, but he was considered one of the unit's shining stars. The rest of the prosecution team assigned to the Eugene Nelson murder case included Deputy D.A. Colleen Carraway Higgs, who was serving as second chair, and their long-time paralegal, Carolyn Gildersleeve Jones.

"Unfortunately, we don't have much," Denny said. He was a bearded, pear-shaped man in his fifties who enjoyed getting paid to dig up dirt on people. In his younger days, he had longed to be a cop, but couldn't meet the physical requirements, even after they lowered the height requirement.

"The law firm where Nelson worked still hasn't been able to link Special Moore to that email," Denny said, "and we don't have anything that conclusively proves she threw those nails in his driveway or vandalized his house and car."

"As far as I'm concerned that video of her attacking Nelson with pepper spray is some pretty good evidence as far as motive is concerned," said Carolyn, the paralegal. "We also have three witnesses who can attest to the comments she made at her cousin's funeral. She told the whole church she wanted revenge."

Carolyn had found six witnesses and obtained written statements from each of them. She was a quiet introvert who blushed at off-color jokes. But when it came time to dig into a case, she transformed into super sleuth.

"Motive alone isn't going to get us a conviction," Colleen said. She was as cautious as they came. A tall, cream-colored black woman with sexy hips, her no-nonsense personality suited Ray. Colleen's assignment to the case was no huge surprise. Hathaway was playing to the public.

The Latino/African-American duo would be pitched to the press as a model of diversity, which would in turn translate into a few extra votes for the man who teamed them up. The D.A. was destined to go far.

"We need something solid to link her to his death, and so far, we have nothing," Colleen said.

"It's still early," Ray reminded them. "But I agree. We have a strong motive, but without some solid evidence to support it, we can't move forward with an indictment. Unfortunately, the D.A. is on my butt for a quick conviction."

"Did we get confirmation of the time of death yet?"

Denny opened a folder and pulled out a page. "The coroner puts it sometime between midnight Saturday and six Sunday morning. I read your notes from Moore's interrogation. The fact that her attorneys refused to let her answer any questions tells me she has something to hide."

"I agree," Ray said. "We just need to find out what it is."

"Finding the murder weapon sure would be nice," Colleen said wistfully.

"If she's smart," Denny said, "she's already dumped it."

"Do we know what we're looking for?" Martinez asked.

"Yeah." Denny riffled through more pages in his folder. "Definitely a small-caliber gun. I'd bank on a twenty-two. The perfect weapon for close-range shooting. Also the weapon of choice for female killers. Fits nicely in a small purse."

"Belynda Davis, a close friend of Nelson, claimed Moore approached her the day before and tried to show her a picture of him kissing some man," Colleen said. "Moore supposedly took the picture on her digital camera the night before. We need to get a search warrant ASAP."

"That's in the works," Denny said.

"Won't do us much good now," Carolyn, the paralegal added. "She probably erased that picture a long time ago."

"Yeah," Denny said, "but there's a good chance we can restore it. So the sooner we get our hands on that camera, the better."

Ray got up and took a seat on the edge of the table. "What I'm about to say can't leave this room." He waited until he was certain that he had everyone's full attention. "I received a heads up this morning about a news story that's going to break tomorrow. And it's going to make this case much bigger than it already is."

Everyone was piqued with interest. "Nelson was the fifth African-American man—professional African-American man—to be murdered in a three-week period. The *L.A. Times* thinks the cases are linked. That one killer is responsible for all of the murders."

"You're pulling my leg," Denny said.

"No, I'm serious. The *Times* story isn't going to say this, but Special Moore is considered a person of interest in each of those murders."

Colleen blinked. "The police think this woman is a serial killer?"

Ray nodded.

"If this story is breaking in the *Times* tomorrow," Carolyn said, "then it can't be much of a secret."

"I haven't told you the confidential part yet," Ray said. "And I want to make it clear, one more time, this information can't leave this room."

They all nodded.

"It appears that each of the victims led heterosexual lives, but were involved in covert gay relationships," Ray continued.

Denny slammed his folder on the table. "So these guys were a bunch of fruitcakes?"

Ray flinched, but didn't otherwise react. "It appears that they were gay or perhaps bisexual."

"What's this either or stuff?" Denny said. "If a guy's banging another guy, he's a fruitcake."

Ray knew he was going to hear a lot worse during the course of this case, so he needed to get used to letting comments like that roll off his back. Both Colleen and Carolyn knew he was gay, though they had never discussed it. Carolyn looked away when Ray glanced in her direction.

"These guys claim they're not gay, just adventurous," Colleen explained. "They call it being on the down low. Oprah did a whole show on it."

Denny snorted. "What in the hell is the world coming to?"

Ray quietly sighed. He knew that as soon as the meeting ended, Colleen would pull Denny aside to tell him Ray was gay and warn him to watch his mouth. Ray just hoped Denny would still want to remain on the team. He needed his expertise.

"Anyway," Ray said, "the police believe Special Moore murdered the other men for the same reason she targeted Nelson. Because of their double lives."

# CHAPTER 73

The hostile look on Lieutenant Wilson's face made J.C. want to run for cover. She had just pulled out of a McDonald's drive-up when she received an urgent call from dispatch summoning her to his office.

"You wanted to see me?" She stepped inside.

"Have a seat." Instead of asking her to close the door, he got up and did it himself, then perched on the corner of his desk, inches away from her.

J.C. braced herself.

"Is there anything you want to tell me?" The lieutenant was extremely ticked off about something.

"Excuse me?"

"I said, is there anything you want to tell me?"

"No, not that I can think of." J.C. wondered what was going on.

The lieutenant snatched a copy of the *Times* from his desk and tossed it into her lap. "What's this crap?"

J.C. picked up the newspaper and read the bold headline splattered across page one. *Serial Killer Targets African-American Men.*

Scanning the story, J.C. quickly ascertained that the reporter's account was fairly accurate. It reported that the police believed each of the victims were killed by a single gunman. The story, however, made no mention of the Department's theory about the men's sex lives.

"This story quotes *sources close to the investigation*," the lieutenant said with more than mild sarcasm. "Is that you?"

J.C. placed the newspaper on the corner of the lieutenant's desk. "No," she said, "I had nothing to do with that story. But what's the big deal? It doesn't mention anything about the victims being gay."

"As I understand it, the *Times* reporter is well aware of your theory. His editors were just too afraid of being sued, so they left that angle out of the story. For now."

The lieutenant narrowed his eyes and scowled as if he were trying to scare her into confessing.

She defiantly scowled back. "I'm not stupid, Lieutenant. There's no way I'd run to the media with that information. I had nothing to do with that story."

"So where's the leak coming from?"

"I don't know. You said you discussed my theory with the captain. It's possible he mentioned it to others. There's no telling who leaked that information."

After a long stretch of silence, the lieutenant's anger seemed to thaw. He took a seat behind his desk. "Since the cat's about to be out of the bag, what's the latest on your investigation?"

"There were wineglasses on a coffee table in Eugene's living room. One glass had prints belonging to Eugene. The other one didn't. The prints definitely belong to a man. He could be our killer."

"Any idea who he might be?"

"Not yet. The prints on the wineglass don't match the ones found on the window, which is how we think the killer entered Eugene's house."

"Just remember," he said, "if your friend is charged, you're off the case. I'm already cutting it close."

"I understand."

"The mayor's ready to proceed with that press conference I mentioned a while back. This story has put even more fire under his ass. It's tomorrow morning at ten in the City Hall Press Room. Media Affairs has some talking points for you just in case some jackass reporter shoves a mike in your face."

J.C. nodded.

"I have no idea how extensive this leak is," the lieutenant continued. "So, if someone happens to ask you about this down low crap tomorrow, fudge your answer."

"Fudge? What exactly does that mean?"

"It means lie, Detective. Nobody can find out that you suspected weeks ago that all the vics were—" he caught himself, "homosexuals."

# CHAPTER 74

After a few days of pampering her husband, Vernetta moved into her new office at Barnes, Ayers, and Howard.

"So what did Jefferson say when you told him?" Nichelle was helping her unpack. She couldn't stop gushing about how much fun they were going to have practicing law together.

"He wasn't happy that I reneged on my promise to spend a few months as a stay-at-home wife," Vernetta said. "But let's just say I've been using my womanly ways to make him forget."

Nichelle laughed. "No wonder you've been looking so tired lately."

"You've got that right. Being a top-notch wife is hard work."

Nichelle hung Vernetta's UC Berkeley law degree on the wall behind her desk, then stood back to take a look. "Does this look straight to you?"

"Perfect."

Russell stuck his head in the door. "Welcome, counselor."

Vernetta gave him a hug. "I was just telling Nichelle that if I'd known how great having my own practice would feel, I would've left O'Reilly & Finney months ago."

"Yeah, it is pretty nice. Except for all the administrative hassles and never actually knowing when the next case is going to come through the door. But don't knock the big firm experience. I picked up some excellent skills there. O'Reilly & Finney will always look great on your resume."

"True."

Sam stomped past the open doorway and into his office across the hall.

Vernetta raised an eyebrow. "I thought you two said Sam was okay with my being here."

"He is," Russell assured her. "Don't mind him. He's a big, harmless grouch. We just give him his space. Do the same and everything'll be fine."

As they left, Vernetta decided to make the first overture toward her new colleague. She knocked on Sam's closed door.

"Come in," he barked.

Sam's office was a sight. There were papers, folders, clothes and gadgets everywhere. Vernetta counted six empty paper cups on his desk and two mugs that were growing mold. The blinds were drawn, which gave the room a cave-like feel, and the smell of something foul irritated her nostrils. Vernetta hoped he never brought any clients in here.

"I just wanted to say hello. I'm looking forward to working with you."

He tried to smile, but she could tell his lips weren't used to moving in that direction. "So did you bring any O'Reilly & Finney clients with you?"

"That remains to be seen. I just mailed letters letting my clients know that I've left the firm. I know there are a few who'll probably throw me some work. The lower rates will be a real incentive."

Vernetta was still standing, and since it didn't look like Sam was going to offer her a seat, she took one on her own. The expression on Sam's face told her that was a bad move.

"Uh . . . it looks like you're pretty busy." Vernetta slowly stood up. "So I guess I'll let you get back to work."

She had almost made it to the doorway before Sam spoke again. "I still have a lot of friends at the D.A.'s office. It doesn't look too good for Special."

Vernetta shot back to his desk. "What do you mean?"

"They're hell bent on proving that Special killed Eugene. They're digging deep and they're not going to stop until they pin it on her."

"They can dig as much as they want. She didn't kill him."

"You better hope not."

They would need Sam's expertise, not to mention his connections in the D.A.'s office, if charges were filed against Special. As much as the man got on her nerves, she needed to start buttering him up.

"If Special is charged," Vernetta said, "we'd really like your help at trial."

"You've tried your share of cases."

"Yeah, but only one murder case. You've tried dozens. And on top of that, you're a former prosecutor. You know how prosecutors think. Having you on the defense team would be an incredible advantage. So if this nightmare comes true, I hope you'll help us."

"I'm not used to playing second chair. Or third for that matter."

*Asshole*. He knew the amount of media attention this case was going to attract, and he wanted it all for himself. But if his help meant getting Special out of this mess, Vernetta would just have to deal with the jerk.

"That's fine with me." She decided to massage his ego even more. "I'm sure there's a lot I could learn from you."

# CHAPTER 75

I really must applaud you," said Professor Curtis Michaels as he led Nichelle down a narrow hallway at Haines Hall on the UCLA campus. "Few women have much of a desire to understand any of this."

Nichelle's former sociology professor had recently gained a national reputation as a commentator on gay issues. Since she was continuing to receive interview requests to discuss men on the down low, Nichelle thought the professor's insight would be beneficial.

"So where should we begin?" Professor Michaels took a seat behind his desk. He was a broad-shouldered man with an equally broad smile. He wore a gold hoop in his left ear and was most comfortable in khakis and golf shirts.

Nichelle pulled a legal pad from her bag. "I guess my first question is why this down low phenomenon seems to only be associated with African-American men?"

"White men are engaging in this activity, too," the professor clarified. "In fact, you might remember a string of white politicians who made headlines a while back. There was McGreevey, the former New Jersey Governor who resigned after confessing to an affair with a gay staffer. There was that Idaho Senator arrested in that foot-tapping bathroom sting, a Florida state representative picked up for soliciting gay sex at a park, and a Washington state legislator who allegedly had sex with a guy who ran off with his wallet." He chuckled. "All of these men were married and white."

Nichelle stole a glimpse of a picture on his credenza. The professor was on the slopes, standing next to another African-American man, both of them decked out in ski garb. Nichelle assumed the man was his partner.

"Then how come I've never heard anybody refer to white men being on the down low?" she asked.

"I think that label's been exclusively associated with African-American men primarily because of J.L. King's book, *On the Down Low,* and his appearance on *Oprah*. But this definitely isn't unique to the black community."

Nichelle folded her arms. "What concerns me is how these guys admit to having sex with other men, but claim that they're not gay."

The professor arched a brow and spread his hands. "In their minds, all they're doing is engaging in a sex act. African-American men—gay or straight—take pride in their masculinity. Since many people consider homosexuality the antithesis of manliness, they aren't willing to label themselves as gay. The Center for Disease Control uses the term MSM—Men Who Sleep with Men—in their surveys for this very reason. For these guys, the questions *Are you homosexual?* and *Do you engage in sex with men?* don't result in the same answer."

Nichelle scribbled a note on her legal pad.

"Before we continue," the professor said, "I'd like to clarify something." He planted his forearms on the desk. "When I refer to men on the down low, I'm not talking about the gay guy who might be in the closet. It's easy to understand why many gay men, black, white or otherwise, don't come out. Just so we're on the same page, I'm talking about the guy who's having sex on a regular basis with another man, but doesn't think of himself as gay or even bisexual."

"Got it," Nichelle said. "So is he the reason HIV is impacting African-American women at such a high rate?"

"He's part of it, but I don't think the down low problem is nearly as widespread as black women fear. We know there's a high incarceration rate among African-American men, and that they're contracting HIV through homosexual sex in prison, then spreading it to women upon their release. Intravenous drug use is another factor. And straight men are also spreading it to straight women and vice versa."

Nichelle crossed, then uncrossed her legs. "I suspect most women believe they can only contract HIV from a gay man."

"That's unfortunate. Many women also believe that all gay men are effeminate. That's why they never suspect that their strong, virile boyfriends and husbands are on the down low. The so-called homo thug certainly contradicts that stereotype."

Nichelle's face contorted. "Excuse me, but what's a homo thug?"

He pulled a thick book from the shelf to his left. "This is an urban dictionary," he said, as he flipped the pages. "I'll read the definition."

"*Homo thug* is actually in the dictionary?"

"Right here in black and white." The professor tapped his finger on the page. "*A black or Latino homosexual who dresses hip-hop and does not act 'gay'. Sometimes a homo thug has relationships with women and keeps his gay sex on the D-L.*"

"You're kidding me." Nichelle rose from her seat to take a look for herself. She read the definition, then slumped back into her chair.

"Sounds to me like you're saying black women are in this situation, at least in part, because we're being fooled by macho-looking men on the down low?"

The professor fervently shook his head. "That's certainly not the entire message I meant to convey." He picked up the remote from his desk and pointed it at the small TV in the corner of his office. He flipped past three channels, then stopped at a burger commercial which showed enough cleavage to garner an *R* rating. Then he switched to a music video. Three bone thin, semi-nude girls were grinding and humping the air.

"What's happening to black women with regard to HIV is a by-product of what you see on that screen. Our kids grow up with these images. Yet, we're surprised that they're having sex at the age of twelve and thirteen."

"So you're blaming television for the HIV epidemic?" Nichelle asked.

"In part, yes. I also blame the lack of sex education in schools, poor parenting, an absence of proper moral teachings, and of course, the Internet." He turned away and began punching keys on his computer. "Come take a look at this."

Nichelle stood over the professor's shoulder as he pulled up the *Casual Encounters* listings on the Craig's List website.

"These days a man or woman looking for sex can find a willing partner without ever leaving the comforts of home. You can search by city, state and even country. Let's try L.A. He slowly scrolled down the screen. Nichelle stared at the listings, dumfounded.

*Athletic white male looking for a threesome.*

*In town for a few days and need some company.*

*Nice girl needs a bad guy to blow.*

When a photo of a penis popped up, Nichelle yelped and covered her mouth with both hands. "Oh, my God."

"Sorry about that. It can get pretty graphic. And this isn't just happening in the major metropolitan areas." He switched over to Indiana and clicked on Muncie. The listings were much the same. "And you can find any kind of sex you want."

He moved over to *Men Seeking Men* and scrolled down the Atlanta listings.

*DL guy looking for sex with other buddies.*

*Married man needs a quick release.*

*Any DL guys need head tonight?*

He clicked open a listing entitled *Married, but wanna play while the wife's away.*

> *I'm a good-looking, muscular, successful, 42-year-old black male from Buckhead. Looking for a married guy like myself who wants M2M sex when the mood hits. Weekend afternoons are the best time for a hookup. Must be in good shape, masculine and very discreet.*

Nichelle frowned. "What's *M2M sex*?"

"Man to man," the professor explained.

"This is frightening."

"Hold on, I'm not done yet." He switched over to *Women Seeking Men*. Nichelle was relieved to find that the listings weren't nearly as sexually explicit. The professor opened a New York listing with the title *Single white female looking for a sugar daddy*.

> *Attractive, 30-ish, single woman looking for some discreet sex on the side. You must be married, well-endowed and able to help me out financially. Race not important. I won't respond without a picture.*

Nichelle shuddered. "What in the hell is going on with our society?"

The professor smiled up at her. "Great. That's exactly the point I was trying to make. The guy on the down low is just one small part of a much bigger problem. We live in a culture of sexual promiscuity and HIV is happily thriving in it. The biggest problem for the black community is that we're the perfect hiding place for the disease."

Nichelle returned to her seat. "What do you mean?"

"We're less likely to get tested so we unknowingly spread the disease to others. We have less access to medical care, so we don't get the early treatment that could save our lives. Many of our young black men view themselves as invincible, so they don't feel the need to use protection. And our women don't feel empowered enough to demand that they do. And just like everybody else, we're out there engaging in casual sex simply because it feels good."

Professor Michaels paused and when he spoke again, Nichelle saw a spark of anger in her eyes. "And the most influential body in our community, the black church, has its head buried in the sand while the disease ravages our community."

Nichelle inhaled. The professor was causing her to see a much bigger and much scarier picture.

"If you really want to make a difference when you speak about this subject," the professor said, "help women understand that HIV doesn't pick you because you're gay or because you're a bad person. It picks you because you're available."

# CHAPTER 76

The news conference in the City Hall Press Room was about to start and J.C. was nervous enough to barf. Thank God she had skipped breakfast.

She stood near the podium, next to Los Angeles Mayor Pete Caranza. The mayor's chief of staff and press aide were on the opposite side.

"I'm here to discuss the rumors of a serial killer at work on the streets of our great city." The mayor gripped both sides of the podium. "At this point, we have no conclusive evidence of that, but because of a spate of recent shootings, the LAPD felt that we needed to take the extra precaution of advising the public about these murders."

"A little late for that, isn't it?" The voice came from the back of the room. "Five men, five African-American men, are already dead." It was Leon Webber, the community activist and publisher of a community newspaper. "Why didn't you hold this press conference sooner? Before all these men were murdered."

"It was only recently determined that these murders might have even a tenuous connection."

"I knew weeks ago," Webber challenged. "Exactly when did you find out?"

Mayor Caranza turned to J.C. "Maybe the LAPD can answer that question."

In a classic politician-like move, Caranza placed J.C. directly in the hot seat. "This is Detective J.C. Sparks with the LAPD. She's one of many law enforcement officers who've been investigating these shootings. Detective, perhaps you'd like to address Mr. Webber's question." He stepped away from the podium.

*No, thanks, Mr. Mayor.* J.C. took her time taking the mayor's place at the podium. The talking points prepared for her by Media Affairs did not specifically address this particular question. But they did include a standard line that would be appropriate for almost any question she was asked.

J.C. leaned closer to the microphone. "I'm not at liberty to give you many specifics," she said. "Not with a dangerous killer on the loose. We can't risk doing anything that might jeopardize our investigation."

"So what *can* you tell us?" asked a radio reporter who was standing along the wall.

"I can only tell you that we're looking into each of these shootings and our investigation is ongoing."

"The *L.A. Times* claims the Department has some pretty clear evidence that the murders are the work of a single killer. Is that true?"

J.C. swallowed. "We aren't at liberty to disclose any information about our investigation at this time. As for that *L.A. Times* story, you have to discuss that with the *Times*."

A few heads turned toward the *Times* reporter at the back of the room. He knew about the homosexual connection, but wasn't about to announce it and lose his exclusive, not to mention get his paper sued.

J.C. was poised to repeat her line about not jeopardizing the investigation when a reporter friendly to the Department stepped in to save the day. The Department often used a handful of long-time reporters as public relations tools. In exchange, they were given tips that other reporters weren't.

"We've heard rumors of white supremacists targeting black men," said John Stole, a reporter from a small paper in the Inland Empire. "Is that true?"

"No, not to our knowledge." J.C. felt good telling the truth.

Another question came from the far right. "So, what's the purpose of this press conference? You want black men to stay off the streets until the killer's caught?"

The mayor stepped forward again. "What we want is for all citizens of L.A., but especially African-American men, to be extremely cautious and careful of their surroundings. If you see anything suspicious, you should call the police right away."

For the next ten minutes, J.C. listened to the mayor straight-out lie. She wished she could put an end to this farce and shout out the truth.

"Is Special Moore going to be charged with the murder of Eugene Nelson, and is she a suspect in the other shootings?" asked a reporter from KNBC.

The mayor started to speak, but before he could, J.C. leaned over the mike. "As I've already said, the Nelson murder is still under investigation. Just like the others. We don't have a suspect in his death yet and—"

"Is she at least a person of interest?" the reporter challenged. "You have the woman on tape screaming that the man deserved to die. And she clearly had a motive because of her cousin's death. What else do you need?"

"Something we don't have," J.C. said. "Solid evidence linking her to Mr. Nelson's murder. And as to your other question, we also don't have any evidence that she had anything to do with the other shootings."

The mayor fielded the last few questions, then his chief of staff stepped forward and ended the press conference. Reporters yelled out more questions, but they ignored them and exited through a private entrance that led to a meeting room reserved only for the mayor.

"Nice job, Detective," the mayor said before being whisked away. J.C. thanked him and made her way into a private hallway. She was surprised to find Lieutenant Wilson waiting for her.

"You did good."

J.C. didn't respond. If this is what being part of the big brass required, she would prefer to remain with the peons. They walked silently to the mayor's private elevator, which would take them directly to the underground parking garage, bypassing the reporters. The lieutenant pushed the button for the garage.

"I know you don't agree with our approach here, but I think it's the right thing to do."

"You made your point very clear. You don't care how many gay men are killed."

"I do care," the lieutenant said defensively. "But I also care about maligning these men and further destroying their families by announcing that they were gay. And you should, too."

"So you finally believe it?"

He lowered his head. "I took a closer look at all the evidence, including your case file. Yeah, I think you're right."

As they exited the elevator, Lieutenant Wilson put a hand on her shoulder. "This press conference wasn't the only reason I came over here. I wanted to give you a heads up about something. Your friend's going to be arrested for the murder of Eugene Nelson."

"When?"

"They're on the way to her place now. So, this means you're off the case."

J.C. wanted to protest, but knew it wouldn't do any good. "Lieutenant, I want to be there when they arrest her."

She saw the reluctance in his eyes.

"I won't get in the way," J.C. pleaded. "I just want to be there. Please, Lieutenant."

He took a while before answering. "Okay, but stay out of the way. She's your friend, but she's also a suspect. Don't forget who you work for."

"I won't," she said, darting off.

He called after her. "Hold on a minute."

J.C. stopped, anxious to get going. It seemed to take forever for the lieutenant to catch up to her.

"You need to know that both the mayor and the D.A. want somebody behind bars for Nelson's murder as of yesterday. The word I'm hearing is that they're both hoping to gain some political leverage with the gay community by getting a conviction before the election. And right now, your friend is the only suspect they've got."

"What are you saying, Lieutenant? That they're going to railroad her?"

The lieutenant shrugged. "Let's just say I've seen it happen."

# CHAPTER 77

Special had been receiving so many crank calls lately that her nerves were shattered. So, when she heard a knock at the door of her apartment, her heart leapt to her throat. Had one of the crazies come after her?

She tiptoed to the door and peered through the peephole. She let out a loud yelp when she saw four uniformed officers.

"Open up! LAPD!" they shouted.

"Oh, my God! What do you want?"

"We have a warrant for the arrest of Special Sharlene Moore as well as a warrant to search the premises. Please open the door."

"Oh, my God!" Special scurried into the bedroom, dug her cell phone out of her purse and dialed Vernetta's number.

She wanted to scream when Vernetta's voicemail came on. She hung up and called Nichelle. "The police are here to arrest me!" she blubbered when Nichelle picked up. "I don't wanna go to jail. I didn't kill nobody!"

The officers were pounding on the door now.

"First," Nichelle said, "I want you to calm down."

"I can't. I'm scared!"

"Special, you'll have to open the door and let them in."

"Why? I don't want them to come in!"

"If you don't open the door, they can lawfully break it down."

"Oh, my God!"

"Special, I'm only a few minutes away. I'll call Vernetta and J.C. on my way over. If you don't open the door, they'll think you're in there destroying evidence. Let them in, then tell them your attorneys are on the way. And don't say *anything* else. You got that?"

"Yeah," Special whined. "But what if they ask me—"

"*What if* nothing," Nichelle said forcefully. "I don't care what they ask you. Just tell them you don't want to talk without an attorney present."

Special hung up and tiptoed to the front door. Just as she was about to unlock it, she heard a voice that cut her stress level in half.

"Special, this is J.C. Open the door. Right now."

When she finally did, the police officers charged into her living room. A young white cop with a crew cut roughly snatched Special's arms behind her back and locked her wrists in plastic handcuffs.

"Owww! You're hurting me!"

"When the police tell you to do something, that's what you're supposed to do," he snorted. "You're going to be facing additional charges for obstruction of justice."

"Not so rough," J.C. said to the cop. He ignored her, dragged Special over to the living room couch and forced her into a sitting position.

Two officers barged into her bedroom. "What the hell are you doing? You can't go in there!"

"They can go wherever they want and do whatever they want," Crew Cut said. "You're under arrest for the murder of Eugene Nelson."

"You're crazy! I didn't kill that man!"

Nichelle stepped into the room and ran over to Special. Crew Cut blocked her path. "Get outta here!"

"I'm Ms. Moore's attorney. I'd like to see the warrants, please."

Crew Cut pulled some papers from his back pocket and slapped them into Nichelle's hand.

"You don't need to handcuff her."

"Get real. This woman is a murder suspect," Crew Cut growled.

Special was crying and sniveling and wiping her cheeks with her upper shoulder. "I don't wanna go to jail! "

An officer who was ransacking the kitchen pulled out a drawer and dumped utensils onto the floor with a loud crash. He opened the cabinets and tossed plates and saucers around like Frisbees.

"Those are Calvin Klein dishes!" Special yelled. "You can't be destroying my stuff like that!" She tried to get up, but the officer gripped her shoulder and held her down.

"Let's be reasonable," Nichelle said to Crew Cut. "I'd be glad to bring her down to the station."

He gave her an astonished look, then laughed. "What in the hell have you been smoking? This woman is a cold-blooded killer. She's not getting any special treatment."

Nichelle whirled around to face J.C., who stood back, observing. "Can't you do anything?"

"Sorry, Nichelle. This is standard procedure."

"Please, please, please, do something," Special begged. "I can't go to jail. Somebody might attack me."

Nichelle kneeled down before Special. "Sam and Vernetta are going to meet us downtown. I need you to get it together for me. You're going to get through this, but you can't start wigging out."

She leaned in to give Special a hug when Crew Cut snatched her up from the couch and dragged her toward the door.

"Promise me I won't have to spend the night in jail," Special cried as Crew Cut dragged her toward the door.

Tears began to roll down Nichelle's cheeks. "I wish I could make that promise," she said. "But I can't."

# CHAPTER 78

By the time Vernetta made it over to the jail, Special had already been booked. Thanks to Sam and his connections at the D.A.'s office, within a matter of hours, Special had been processed and released on a million dollars bond.

Sam successfully argued that Special deserved bail because she wasn't a flight risk, had close ties to the community and no prior convictions. Her parents put up their two rental units in Carson as a property bond. The terms of her bail required Special to stay within a three-mile radius of her home, to call the court on a daily basis and to show up in two weeks for her arraignment.

While Nichelle saw to it that Special got home safely, Vernetta and Sam set up a meeting to talk to Ray Martinez, the Deputy D.A. assigned to prosecute the case.

"What do you know about Martinez?" Vernetta asked Sam as they waited in the lobby of the D.A.'s office.

"I've had a couple of cases against him. He's basically a straight shooter. Not as much of an egomaniac as most prosecutors. If the evidence says the defendant might be innocent, he won't ignore it and plunge ahead like a lot of D.A.s. He also doesn't play hide-the-ball with the evidence. In the cases I've had against him, he put his cards on the table pretty early."

"That's certainly good news."

"I heard he was assigned to the case because he's gay," Sam added.

"He's gay?" Vernetta said, taken aback.

"That's what they tell me."

Vernetta was still mulling over that tidbit when Martinez walked into the waiting area.

"Good afternoon." He shook both their hands. "There's a conference room we can use down the hall."

When they were all seated, Sam spoke first. "We just wanted to get a few formalities out of the way. When can we get a copy of the initial police report?"

"You'll have it tomorrow," he said. Martinez appeared just as laid back as he'd been when they'd tried to question Special at Parker Center.

"As I understand it, your entire case seems to be circumstantial," Vernetta said.

"For now. But it's a very strong circumstantial case. Ms. Moore publicly vowed revenge against Mr. Nelson at her cousin's funeral and, of course, half the country's seen that videotape of her attacking him with pepper spray. She also told her therapist that she wanted Mr. Nelson dead."

His last comment threw her. "I don't know how you could possibly have information about what Special supposedly told her therapist. But even if you do, you can't use it. Those conversations are protected by the therapist-patient privilege."

"Not here. If a therapist has reason to believe that a patient is a threat to herself or others, she has an obligation to report it to the authorities. And that's exactly what she did. The therapist contacted the police because she feared your client was a very real threat to Mr. Nelson. Turns out she was right."

"You can't possibly be basing your entire case on what you've just told us." Vernetta tried to keep her voice level. She didn't want Martinez to think she was running scared, though she was.

"There's more, but I'm sure you're well aware of it. She hacked into the computer system at Mr. Nelson's law firm and outted him. She ruined a set of perfectly good tires by leaving nails in his driveway and also vandalized his home and car."

Vernetta grumbled. "You have no evidence that she did any of that. And even if you did, it doesn't mean she killed Eugene."

"We understand that she was also stalking him. She admitted to Belynda Davis, a friend of Mr. Nelson's, that she had trespassed on his property and took a photograph of him with another man through his kitchen window. Police believe the killer entered Mr. Nelson's house through that same window. It's my hunch that we'll find your client's fingerprints somewhere in the vicinity." He paused for effect. "I'd say most juries would convict based on the facts I've just recounted even without a smoking gun."

Vernetta's blood pressure edged skyward, making it hard to keep her cool. "Eugene and Maya entertained at his place all the time. So

Special's prints are probably all over that house, including the window on his back deck. I suspect my prints are *somewhere in the vicinity* of that window, too. And as far as that stuff about Special taking a picture of Eugene and some man, for all we know, Belynda made that up."

"We'll find out soon enough," Martinez said calmly. "We confiscated your client's camera during the search of her home earlier today. If that photograph turns up, it only strengthens our case."

"Or, perhaps, our case." Vernetta smiled.

"How so?" Martinez asked.

"Assuming there is a picture of Eugene and some man, he could well be the killer. Eugene could've been murdered by a jealous lover for all we know. And I don't think you're likely to garner much sympathy for your victim. The jury will feel a lot more compassion for Special, who lost her cousin because her fiancé deceived her in the cruelest way."

Ray smiled, then nodded. "Interesting approach, but jury nullification is rare. Jurors look at the facts and the law. If they think Ms. Moore committed murder, it won't matter what they think about Mr. Nelson's conduct. They're going to convict her."

Vernetta could tell the man was shrewd. It would be quite a challenge going up against him. Sam interrupted their stare-down.

"Eugene was the fifth professional African-American man to be shot to death in L.A. in only a five-week period," Sam added. "According to the *Times*, there's a serial killer on the loose. It's more likely that Eugene was also one of the killer's victims."

"Frankly," Martinez said, "I don't think it's too farfetched to assume that your client killed those other men, too."

Vernetta felt an icy chill shoot through her. "You can't possibly believe that!"

"As a matter of fact, Ms. Henderson, I do. We have evidence that links Ms. Moore to four of the five victims. And we're working on a link to the fifth."

"Evidence like what?" Sam asked.

"The first victim was killed at the Ramada Inn on Bristol Parkway. That hotel is walking distance from Ms. Moore's apartment and we found out that it's part of her regular jogging route."

"Is that what you call evidence?" Vernetta said facetiously. "That doesn't prove she killed him."

"Not by itself. But it does present opportunity. Your client was also the patient of an ear, nose, and throat doctor who just happens to have an office in the Horton Medical Plaza on the same floor as the second victim, Dr. Quentin Banks. He was shot to death getting out of his car in the parking garage."

"So, what are you saying?" Vernetta asked. "Every woman who saw a doctor in that building is a suspect in that doctor's death?"

Martinez ignored her question. "Your client was also seen near the Trojan Arms apartments across from USC on the night Nathaniel Allen was shot."

That surprised her. Special had absolutely no reason to be in that area. "You can't be serious."

"The police have a very solid witness who can place her near the crime scene at the time of Allen's shooting."

"What witness?" Sam asked. Vernetta admired his cool demeanor.

"A clerk at Starbucks says he served Ms. Moore about twenty minutes before Allen was gunned down. He even remembers what she ordered. A Java Chip Frappuccino. That Starbucks is in the shopping center across from the apartment complex. Twenty minutes was more than enough time for her to shoot Allen and drive home."

The stuff about Special being near USC had to be a case of mistaken identity. Vernetta had accompanied Special to Starbucks a million times. Day or night, rain or sunshine, she'd never ordered anything other than a White Chocolate Mocha.

"I'm sorry, guys," Martinez said, "my experience tells me that when there are this many coincidences, they're not."

"But what motive would Special have for killing these men?" Vernetta said, still reeling from his revelations.

Martinez smiled ruefully. "Oh, she had a motive. One which I'm not at liberty to reveal to you at this time. But you'll find out soon enough."

Vernetta and Sam couldn't help staring at each other.

"I'm waiting for our investigator to get back to me regarding a few other loose ends," Martinez said. "And when they're all tied up, Ms. Moore is going to be facing multiple murder charges."

# CHAPTER 79

The traffic on the Santa Monica freeway moved at a crawl and it took Vernetta close to an hour to get to Special's apartment.

She found Nichelle and Special sitting in the living room with TV trays, eating Golden Bird fried chicken and watching a rerun of *Girlfriends*. Nichelle had completely abandoned her diet. Food had always been her stress buster.

It was good to hear Special laugh again, but the news Vernetta was about to deliver would surely put a stop to that.

Special tossed a sweet pickle wedge into her mouth, then noticed Vernetta's troubled expression. "What's the matter?" The alarm in Special's eyes was a mirror image of Vernetta's. "Please don't tell me I have to go back to jail!"

Vernetta sat down on the couch next to her. "Sam and I just met with Ray Martinez. He's the deputy D.A. who's going to be prosecuting your case. He shared some of the evidence he has against you."

Nichelle picked up the remote control from the coffee table and muted the television.

"What evidence?" Special said worriedly. "They ain't got no evidence 'cause I didn't kill that man."

"*I* know that and *you* know that, but sometimes the facts can make an innocent person appear guilty. The killer entered Eugene's house through the kitchen window. They'll be comparing your fingerprints to the ones they found at the scene." Vernetta inhaled then slowly exhaled. "Please tell me you didn't touch that window when you were over there playing peeping Tom?"

The chicken leg in Special's hand fell to her plate with a loud thud and she pressed her palm to her chest. "I almost fainted when I saw that man walk up behind Eugene. I had to hold on to the windowsill to keep from passing out."

Vernetta took in a breath. "We'll just deal with that when we have to."

Special gave Nichelle a wide-eyed look, then faced Vernetta again. "Sounds like they're going to railroad me," she said in a shaky voice.

"We're not going to let that happen." Vernetta pulled a legal pad from her bag. "I need to ask you some other questions. And I don't want you to overreact, okay?"

Special pushed her plate away. Vernetta saw the muscles along Special's jawline tense and she heard the gritting of her teeth.

"First, do you have a regular jogging path?"

Special's entire face crumpled in confusion. "What? What's that got to do with—"

"I've had an extremely long day. Can you please just answer my question?"

"Okay, okay. Yeah, I guess so."

"Tell me where you run."

"Um... I usually go left out of my apartment on Buckingham Drive, then left onto Green Valley Circle. After that, I run north along Centinela past the Ramada Inn, then I backtrack."

Vernetta tried to remain stone-faced. "Do you have an ear, nose, and throat doctor?"

Special looked even more puzzled. "Yeah . . ."

"What's his name?"

"It's not a him, it's a her. Dr. Fletcher. Dr. Flaxie Fletcher."

"How long has she been your doctor?"

"I don't know. About six years."

"Special," Nichelle interrupted, "can I have your pickles?"

"Take 'em." Special dumped the small paper cup of pickles onto Nichelle's plate.

"Where's her office?" Vernetta held her breath as she waited for Special's answer. The questions were clearly baffling her. Vernetta would explain later.

"In the Horton Medical Plaza. In Inglewood."

"When was the last time you were there?"

"I don't know. I only see her when my sinuses flare up."

"Special, this is important. I need you to tell me, to the best of your recollection, the last time you went to that medical building."

She stopped to think about the question. "About six months ago, I guess."

"Were you anywhere near her office on Saturday, March third?"

"How am I supposed to remember where I was weeks ago?" Still, Special stopped to think. "That was the day of Maya's funeral. No, I didn't go there that day."

Vernetta cupped her forehead in her hand.

"What? What's the matter?" Special grabbed Vernetta's arm. "Girl, you're scaring me. What's going on?"

"You were late getting to the church. Where were you before that?"

"I was right here. Crying my eyes out."

"Did anybody see you?"

"Did anybody see me? I don't know."

"Special, I need you to think. Did you talk to anybody in your building that morning? Go to the store? To the gas station? Anywhere? It's very important that we pinpoint your exact whereabouts before you got to the church."

Special stared off into space. "I don't know if anybody saw me, and I don't recall talking to anybody. I was so messed up that day I wouldn't even remember if I *had* talked to anybody."

"What about telephone calls? Did you call anybody from your home phone or cell phone that morning?"

"Um . . . I don't know. I don't think so. I got dressed for Maya's funeral and just sat here crying and staring at the walls. Then I realized that I was late and ran over to the church. Vernetta, please tell me what's going on."

"I'm sure you heard about it on the news. There was a shooting in the Horton Medical Plaza. A doctor who worked there. That's where J.C. went when she left Maya's repast. His name was Dr. Quentin Banks. His shooting happened around the same time that you don't seem to have an alibi for."

It took less than a second for Special to comprehend the meaning of what Vernetta was telling her. "Why in the hell would I need an alibi for that?"

"Oh, no!" Nichelle's eyes welled with tears. "Please don't tell us they're trying to say Special murdered that man, too."

Vernetta nodded.

Special pulled her knees to her chest, looped her arms around them and started rocking back and forth the way she had in court. "Somebody needs to wake me up right now because I don't think I can take any more of this."

"Please, Special, just keep it together," Vernetta said. "I only have a few more questions."

Special stared straight ahead.

"Two days after Maya's funeral—that would've been a Monday—where were you between nine and ten o'clock that night?"

"You have to be kidding. I don't know. My memory's not that good."

"This is important. I need you to think."

"I can hardly remember what I did last night."

Nichelle interjected. "Maybe this'll help jog your memory. That was the same week we watched my first television interview at T.G.I. Friday's on Wednesday evening, remember? Right before I got there, Eugene called me accusing you of hacking into his firm's email system and leaving nails in his driveway. You weren't there, Vernetta, because you were working late."

"Okay, Special," Vernetta said, "does that help you remember?

"Yeah." She cringed. "I'm gonna have to take the Fifth on that one."

"What?"

"I'm sorry but I can't tell you or anybody else where I was Monday night."

"Why?"

"Duh?" Special said. "Because it might incriminate me."

"Special, I don't have time for this. We're your attorneys. Whatever you tell us is protected by the attorney-client privilege."

Special started rocking again. "Uh . . . well . . . Don't be mad at me, but I lied when I said I didn't send that email to Eugene's law firm."

"Tell us something we don't know," Vernetta said. "So where were you?"

"That's what I was doing that night."

"You barely know how to turn on a computer," Nichelle said. "Exactly when did you become a computer hacker?"

"I had some help."

"From who?" Vernetta demanded.

"I can't tell you. I don't wanna get him into any trouble."

Vernetta felt her temples throb. "Eugene's law firm has a whole team of computer experts trying to track down the source of that email. When they finally do, do you really think your friend's not going to give you up? Who was it?"

Special abruptly stopped rocking. "It was one of the guys who works part-time in the IT Department at my office, Eddie Chin. I went to his apartment that night and we did it there."

"What time did you get there?"

"Now *that* I remember. We had an eight o'clock appointment. I got there about five minutes early."

"And where does Eddie live?"

"Across from USC. In the Trojan Arms apartment complex."

Vernetta lowered her head over her legal pad.

"What? What?" Special asked. "Please tell me what's going on?"

"Remember Nathaniel Allen? That football player who was murdered?"

"Yeah?"

"He was shot outside the Trojan Arms apartments."

"So. What's that got to do with me?"

Again, Vernetta gave her a moment to connect the dots. The incredulous expression on Special's face showed the exact moment that she made the connection.

"Yes," Vernetta said, "they're trying to pin his death on you, too."

"What reason would I have for wanting to kill him? Or that doctor? I don't know them."

Vernetta decided not to bring up the engineer. "I don't know, but the prosecutor believes you had a motive. He just hasn't told us what it is yet."

Special and Nichelle appeared ready to keel over. Then Special's left hand flew to her mouth. "Oh, my God. He was on the down low, too!"

"What?" Vernetta asked. "Who are you talking about?"

"That football player. He was messing around with this dude Donte. Shawnta, my braider, saw a picture of the two of them together naked. Maybe that doctor was gay, too. The police think I'm running around killing men on the down low!"

Vernetta thought about what Special had just said. That had to be the motive Martinez refused to reveal. Now, Vernetta was about to have trouble holding it together.

She was afraid to ask her next question, but somehow found the courage to proceed. "Special, what time did you leave Eddie's place?"

"I don't know. It didn't take us that long," she whimpered. "I think I left about ten minutes before nine."

"Where did you go after you left?"

"Home."

"Special, I want you to think real hard. Are you sure you went straight home? This is very, very important."

She stared up at the ceiling. "Oh, I remember, now. After I left Eddie's, I drove over to the Starbucks in the shopping center across the street."

Nichelle looked at Vernetta. "What time was that football player shot?"

"Nine-forty-seven," Vernetta replied. "Several students heard the gunshots." Her eyes met Special's. "Don't tell me. You don't have an alibi for your whereabouts after you left the Starbucks."

"I don't need an alibi." Special's fear had converted to anger. "I was probably in my car driving home. Anyway, there's no way that Starbucks clerk would remember me considering how many people go in and out of that place."

Vernetta recalled what the Starbucks clerk told the police. "What kind of drink did you buy at Starbucks?"

"What? What do you wanna know that for?"

Vernetta had less than an ounce of patience left. "I just do. So tell me."

"I don't understand what this has to do with anything," Special complained. "I usually get a hot drink, but I decided to try something new. So I bought one of those cold ones. A Java Chip Frappuccino."

# CHAPTER 80

Reverend Sims stood near the window of his office, staring out into the empty church parking lot. He was still coping with the death of his neighbor and friend James Hill when he learned of Eugene's murder. As a minister, he was usually the one offering comfort to others. Now, *he* needed a shoulder to lean on. But he didn't have a soul he could confide in. Not about this.

The reverend knew he should go to the police and tell them that he had been with Eugene the night before his murder. The police needed to know about Eugene's suspicions that Special Moore was stalking him and that he planned to get a restraining order.

But going to the police would require him to do a whole lot of explaining. For one, why was he, a respected minister, having dinner with and visiting the home of a gay man? No, he could not allow himself to get tangled up in this mess.

According to Belynda, Special Moore claimed she had a picture of Eugene with another man in his kitchen Friday night. *He* was the other man in that picture. He prayed that picture never surfaced.

The reverend returned to his desk and checked his leather datebook. He had three counseling sessions, but the first one wasn't for another hour. Just as he was about to open his email, he heard a knock.

"Reverend," said Bettie, the church secretary, "there's a very troubled woman outside who would like to speak with a minister. She wanted to see Bishop Berry, but he's not here. Do you have time to meet with her?"

He nodded. Handling someone else's problems might help him forget his own.

Moments later, when Bettie escorted Special Moore into his office, the reverend became so flustered, he knocked over his coffee.

Bettie rushed over to help him clean up the spill.

"Excuse my clumsiness." Reverend Sims pulled a wad of napkins from his desk and blotted the coffee. He extended his hand to the woman.

Special reached out to shake it. "I'm Special Moore. I'm not a member here, but my friend Nichelle Ayers urged me to come." She studied the reverend's face. "You look very familiar. Have we met before?"

Reverend Sims hid his growing angst behind a smile. "I preach here every few weeks."

"No," Special said. "I'm pretty sure it wasn't here. But I know I've seen you someplace."

"I also preach at other churches from time to time. Why don't you have a seat and tell me why you're here."

Special took a chair in front of the reverend's desk and set her purse in her lap. He could tell that the woman was a mere shell of what she used to be. Stress had a way of wearing the body down. That videotape of her running up to Eugene and attacking him with pepper spray played over and over again in the reverend's mind.

"Well, I can't put my finger on where I've seen you before, but I'm sure you recognize *me*." She fumbled with the strap of her purse. "My face has been plastered on TV stations and newspapers from here to the moon. And for the record, most of what you've been reading about me isn't true. I've been falsely accused of killing a man." She stifled a whimper.

"I'm here because I need prayer. Lots of it. I don't have a church home right now. Nichelle told me Bishop Berry counseled her a couple years ago. She said it was very helpful." She broke down into a full sob. "I feel like I'm falling apart."

Reverend Sims reached for the tissue box on the corner of his desk and offered it to her. He waited as she dried her eyes.

"I'm glad you came," he said. "God's never failed me yet, and he's not going to fail you either."

Reverend Sims began by asking her several questions about her spiritual life.

"I'm embarrassed to say that I haven't attended church in quite a while," Special said. "After Maya became ill, I was so mad at God, I refused to set foot in a church."

"Sometimes difficult things happen, and we don't understand their purpose," Reverend Sims said empathetically. "But God's power is tremendous. All you have to do is call on Him and He'll see you through."

"My predicament might be even more than God can handle," Special said with a sad chuckle. "As my daddy would say, I'm in a whole heap of trouble."

"I don't need to know all the specifics," Reverend Sims said. "God knows." He pulled open a side drawer of his desk, took out a brown leather Bible and handed it to her.

A larger Bible lay open on his desk and he pulled it closer to him and put on his reading glasses. "I'd like us to read a few verses together."

Reverend Sims recited a short prayer, then directed Special to the Twenty-Third Psalm. When they were done reading together, he took off his glasses. "I've turned to that verse over and over again during my own difficulties. And when you're feeling at wit's end, that's exactly what I want you to do."

Special nodded as she dabbed at the steady stream of tears falling from her eyes.

They read a few more verses together and when they were done, Reverend Sims wrote down some additional verses for her to read at home and handed her two pamphlets.

After another short prayer, Reverend Sims escorted her out.

"Thank you so much," Special said. "I do feel a lot better."

"Good. Spending time in prayer can do that for you."

She started to leave, then turned back to him. "I'm probably going to remember where I know you from as soon I get home."

Reverend Sims scratched his cheek. "When you do, you be sure to let me know."

He remained in the doorway of the church until Special drove off. The reverend was now in a state of complete panic.

Special apparently hadn't gotten a good look at him when she took that picture. He just prayed that she never made the connection. No one would ever believe his story about pushing Eugene away. His family would be devastated and he would be disgraced.

The reverend rushed back to his office. He only had fifteen minutes before his next counseling session. Now, it was *his* turn to ask God not to forsake him.

# CHAPTER 81

Vernetta tiptoed into their darkened bedroom and tried to undress without waking Jefferson. She was almost out of her clothes when she heard him stir.

"Sorry I'm so late," she whispered as she hung up her clothes. "I was with Special."

Jefferson yawned, then sat up and turned on the lamp on the nightstand. "How's she doing?"

"Better. She spoke with a minister today, and I think it helped. Too bad he couldn't work a miracle on her legal problems."

"What's going on with the case?"

"As it turns out, the prosecutor has some pretty damaging circumstantial evidence against her."

"Enough to convict her of killing Eugene?"

"Him and possibly four other guys, too."

Jefferson's brow furrowed. "What other guys?"

Vernetta slipped into a nightgown, then stood in front of the mirror brushing her hair. "I know you've heard all the talk about a killer who's been gunning down prominent African-American men."

"Yeah," Jefferson said. "One of 'em was that running back at Fox Hills Junior College"

"Well, believe it or not, the prosecutor thinks Special is the serial killer who shot every one of them."

Jefferson's silence caused Vernetta to glance over her shoulder. She couldn't remember her husband ever being speechless.

"I understand why Special might've wanted to off Eugene," he said finally, "but what motive could she possibly have for killing those other guys?"

"I'm not sure you're ready for this, but I think they were on the down low, too."

Jefferson smacked his lips and slid back under the covers. "Ain't no way in hell I'd believe that running back was gay."

"That's the word on the street."

Jefferson fluffed up his pillow, then plopped back down. "That's some bullshit. If they're not calling us criminals, then they're saying we're lazy and irresponsible. And now they're pinning this homo crap on us. A brother can't get a break."

"Sounds like you think this down low stuff is some kind of conspiracy against black men."

"That's what it feels like. I don't even get the whole gay thing."

"What's there to get? Some people are gay, some people are straight."

"I will never, in a million years, understand how a brother couldn't like pussy."

Vernetta shook her head in dismay. "I can always count on you to break down any issue to the crudest possible level."

"I'm serious." He rested his back against the headboard. "Why would a brother wanna be rubbing up against some ashy, hard ass dude, when he could be with a nice, soft woman? It just don't make sense to me."

"So you don't believe people are born gay?"

"Hell, nah! They're making a choice to do that shit. And anyway, these dudes claim they're not gay, just freaks. If I wanted to be a freak, there's a whole lot of freaky shit I could think of doing before getting with a dude *ever* crossed my mind."

"Being gay is not about sex. And it's certainly not easy being gay. So I doubt anyone would make that choice considering the way our society treats them."

"Why in the hell are you defending 'em?" Jefferson asked. "Black women are the ones they're hurting. I was in the drugstore yesterday and overheard two women discussing this crap. They were intentionally talking loud enough for me to hear. One of 'em was saying there's no way for a woman to tell if a brother is straight or gay anymore. She had the nerve to roll her eyes at me. I was about to tell her to kiss my ass, but she looked like a real ghetto girl. I didn't wanna have to call you from the county jail."

"Thanks for showing such restraint."

"Well, I ain't got too much of it left. Everybody's trying to act like half the brothers in America are punks."

"What a lot of people refuse to accept," Vernetta said, "is that being homosexual is as natural for some people as being heterosexual is for you and me."

"I don't care if it is natural for them, that don't make it right. It ain't natural for a man to be monogamous, but we still do it. They need to just suck that shit up and act like a man."

This time Vernetta put down her brush and gave Jefferson her full attention. "What do you mean it's not natural for a man to be monogamous? What kind of sexist crap is that? So you want another wife now?"

"Hold on, don't start trippin'. I wasn't talkin' about *me*. I'm talking about most men. We . . . I mean they . . . see women every day who they're attracted to and wanna get with. But if you're a man, a real man, you have to ignore those feelings because you made a commitment to your girlfriend or your wife, or whatever. These dudes are with women but claim they're attracted to men. They need to man up just like we . . . just like other men do and handle their responsibilities."

Vernetta thought about responding, but it was useless to get into a debate with him on this issue. Jefferson, however, refused to let it go.

"A big part of the reason these dudes are the way they are is because they were raised by single women. A woman can't teach no boy to be a man."

Vernetta picked up the brush from the dresser and threw it at him. Jefferson ducked just before it clacked against the headboard.

"Hey! You coulda put my eye out."

"Sorry," she said. "I was aiming for your forehead, not your eye. Sometimes the most ridiculous things come out of your mouth. So now you're saying these guys are on the down low because they were raised by single mothers?"

"I'm saying it's part of the problem," Jefferson insisted. "I know a dude whose mama taught him to take a piss sitting down. That's crazy. Black women are teaching their sons to be too soft. They do everything for 'em and give 'em everything and then wonder why they can't stand up and be men. Black mothers need to stop raising their sons to be punks and force 'em to man up."

"You're actually serious?"

"Yeah, I am. Nobody wants to speak the truth because it's not politically correct. Well, I ain't with the gay thing. Johnny ain't supposed to have two fathers."

Jefferson was growing more and more animated as he spoke, stabbing the air with his finger for emphasis. "And a lot of these dudes have major self-esteem issues. Their mamas chose men who were no good, and all they heard growing up was how much of an asshole their daddy was. So when they look in the mirror, that's exactly what they see. An asshole."

Vernetta was surprised at how impassioned Jefferson was about this topic. She tied her hair with a scarf, then went to the bathroom and turned on the faucet, partly to drown out her husband's ranting. Jefferson was still in the midst of his tirade when she reentered the bedroom.

"I had no idea you were so homophobic," she said.

"I'm not homophobic," he said defensively. "As long as those dudes ain't trying to rock my way or undress near me at the gym, I couldn't care less what they do." He grinned. "Now, I'm cool with the lesbian thing. I could watch two fine lesbians do their thing all day long."

Vernetta picked up a paperback book from the corner of the dresser and hurled it across the room. This time she hit her mark.

"Ow!" Jefferson rubbed the side of his head. "I'm reporting you for spousal abuse."

"You're a man, aren't you?" Vernetta laughed and slid next to him in bed. "Just suck it up and act like a man."

# CHAPTER 82

Detective Jessup inspected Lamont Wiley's roomy, West Hollywood apartment as if he were Alice and had just stepped into Wonderland. "So this guy is actually gay?"

"Could you please lower your voice," J.C. warned through clenched teeth.

They were standing just inside the doorway, waiting for Eugene's ex-lover to conclude a telephone call.

When J.C. learned that Detective Jessup planned to interview Lamont, she begged him to let her tag along. He consented, knowing it was against the lieutenant's order. J.C. figured he wanted something to hold over her head. She would deal with that when it came up.

Detective Jessup's eyes scanned the apartment. "This place looks macho enough for me to be living here."

The living room was decorated in basic bachelor. Black leather couch, off-white walls, a couple of abstract paintings, a 42-inch flat screen and end tables that didn't match.

"What did you expect," J.C. said, "pink walls?" Before she could caution Jessup to stop acting like an idiot, Lamont walked back into the room. He had answered the door shirtless. Now his muscular upper torso was covered by a wrinkled white T-shirt.

Lamont motioned toward the couch. "Have a seat." He took the armchair on the other side of a glass coffee table, facing them.

"I'm sure you heard about Eugene Nelson's murder," Detective Jessup began.

Lamont nodded.

"I understand you were . . . involved with Eugene."

Lamont nodded again, but didn't follow up with an explanation.

J.C. saw the pain of loss in the man's eyes. "When was the last time you saw or talked to Eugene?"

Detective Jessup gave her an annoyed look. She knew what he was thinking. This was *his* interview. She wasn't even supposed to be there.

"It's been a while," Lamont said.

Detective Jessup took the lead back. "What's a while?"

Lamont peered to his right, down a long hallway. J.C. and Detective Jessup looked in the same direction.

"Are we alone?" Detective Jessup asked.

"No, my . . ." he glanced down the hallway again. "My roommate's here."

"Would you prefer that we talk someplace else?"

The bedroom door opened before Lamont could respond and a young Tom Hanks look-a-like joined them.

"I'm Ken." The man extended his hand to J.C., then to Detective Jessup. "Lamont's partner." Ken announced that fact as if he were daring them to challenge it. He sat on the arm of Lamont's chair, closer than necessary.

"We were just asking Lamont some questions," J.C. said, taking control again. There was something going on here, she thought. Lamont looked even more uncomfortable now that Ken had joined them. "It's probably best for us to talk to Lamont alone."

"He can stay," Lamont said. "So where were we?"

"We were asking about the last time you saw or heard from Eugene," Detective Jessup said again.

"Like I just said, it's been a while. We talked a couple of times after I left the firm, but that was it. It's been several months since I've seen him."

"Okay, so you haven't seen him. What about *talking* to him?" Detective Jessup said. "On the telephone?"

Lamont's eyes darted about evasively. "I haven't."

J.C. felt Detective Jessup's eyes on her. Lamont was lying. They were only there because Eugene's cell phone records showed that the last call he made was to Lamont.

"When was the last time he called you?" J.C. asked.

He half shrugged. "Months ago."

"Lamont hasn't been with Eugene since we got together," Ken said possessively. "I hope you're not here because you think Lamont had anything to do with Eugene's murder." He did not try to hide his indignation.

J.C. ignored Ken and continued to direct her questions to Lamont. "Where were you between the hours of midnight Saturday and six Sunday morning the weekend Eugene was killed?"

Ken was quick to answer. "He was here with me."

It had been a bad idea to allow Ken to stay. She turned to Lamont. "Were you?"

"Yeah," Lamont said.

Detective Jessup moved to the edge of the couch. "Would you mind giving us a set of your fingerprints?"

Lamont visibly tensed. "For what?"

"To see if they match the prints we found at Eugene's place."

"Of course, he wouldn't mind," Ken said, hand on hip. "But since he's not a suspect and because he didn't kill the man, he's not going to."

They waited for a response from Lamont. He seemed tongue-tied. "If I'm not a suspect, I see no reason why I should give you my fingerprints."

Detective Jessup turned to Ken. "What about you? Can we get your prints?"

"Don't try to intimidate me, Officer," Ken snorted. "I didn't even know the man. But I do know my rights."

"So I guess that means no."

"You got it, big boy." Ken winked. The detective winced.

They spent the next twenty minutes asking a bunch of innocuous questions designed to give them an opportunity to observe Lamont's demeanor and perhaps catch him in more lies.

When Lamont showed them to the door, he stepped out into the hallway along with them. J.C. gave him a puzzled look.

"I need to check my mail," he explained.

Lamont hurried down the stairs ahead of them. They watched from the top of the stairs as he opened his mailbox slot and thumbed through the mail. He tossed several pieces of junk mail into a small trashcan near the lobby door, then brushed past them back to his apartment.

"Looks like we may have a new suspect," Detective Jessup said, after he heard the apartment door close.

"Or suspects," J.C. said.

Lamont could very well be the man Special photographed that night at Eugene's place. But something was also going on with Ken. He was way too defensive. If Lamont and Eugene were sneaking around, that would have given Ken a motive for murder.

Detective Jessup pulled open the lobby door. He had already stepped outside when he realized J.C. wasn't behind him. He stuck his head back inside the lobby.

J.C. had a big grin on her face.

"Why do you look so happy?"

She reached into the trashcan and gingerly pulled out three pieces of junk mail that Lamont had just discarded, carefully holding them along the edges. "I bet we could get a decent set of Lamont's prints from one of these."

An even bigger grin formed on Detective Jessup's lips. "That's pretty good, Detective," he said. "Too bad I didn't think of it."

# CHAPTER 83

Special sat down on the edge of her bed, slipped on a pair of thick, white ankle socks and laced up her running shoes. Exercise always made her feel better. She had spent much of the morning meditating and praying and had just finished reading some of the Bible verses Reverend Sims had recommended. She was amazed at how much better she felt.

She took the elevator down to the lobby of her apartment building and crossed Buckingham Drive to the small park across the street. When she had first moved to Fox Hills, she was thrilled to have a park so close. But in recent months, she hadn't gotten over there much.

Fox Hills Park had a jogging track, tennis courts, picnic tables, and several exercise contraptions. The park was a popular hangout spot for young singles. Special had picked up a date or two there herself.

She was debating whether to jog or walk, then opted for the latter since she didn't want to sweat out her press 'n curl. She was avoiding the beauty shop until all of this stuff with Eugene blew over. There was no way she was about to face all those gossiping women.

The worst part of the whole ordeal was that her face was now as recognizable as Paris Hilton's. Almost every place she went people were doing a double take.

Except for an elderly Asian couple and a few people letting their dogs roam about on the grass, the park was deserted. It was after ten o'clock, so most people in her neighborhood were at work.

She passed the Asian couple who did a half bow and smiled at her. At least two people in L.A. didn't watch TV news, she thought.

Special settled into a speed walk, pumping her arms for forward momentum. On her second lap around the track, she came upon two twenty-something African-American women, jabbering and strolling along the track at a leisurely pace. She stepped around them and hurried past.

On her third lap, when she was several feet behind the two women, one of them peered over her shoulder, then nudged the other one with her elbow. "Girl, that *is* her! I told you!"

The other woman turned to see for herself.

Special looked straight ahead and tried to ignore the women. She was only a few feet behind them when the taller one stopped and blocked her path.

"We just wanna say, we're with you." The woman had dark skin and her thick hair was corn-rowed into a long braid. "If a brother had done that to my cousin, I woulda killed his ass, too."

Special was about to set the woman straight, but before she could, the other one offered her two cents.

"Don't worry, girlfriend, you're gonna get off. All you have to do is make sure your lawyer gets at least one black woman on that jury. There ain't a sister in this city who would send you to jail for killing that man. As far as I'm concerned, he got what he deserved."

"Sho did," the other woman echoed.

Special managed a weak smile, then plowed past them.

The realization that everybody in L.A. thought she was a cold-blooded killer made her want to throw up. Special picked up her speed and tried to fight back tears. She passed the Asian couple again and hoped they mistook her moist cheeks for sweat.

If everybody in L.A. thought she was guilty, that meant there was a good chance that she *would* be convicted. What in the hell happened to innocent until proven guilty? Vernetta was trying to be upbeat about her case, but every time they met, Special saw more distress on her friend's face than the time before.

She decided not to do another lap for fear of running into the two women again. So she descended the short flight of steps at Green Valley Circle and walked downhill to Centinela Boulevard. The steep, uphill climb on the way back would give her a good workout.

Special knew that she had to keep it together. Mentally, physically, and spiritually. Her faith in God was going to get her through this. One of the verses Reverend Sims had given her came to mind. She repeated it out loud as she marched down Green Valley Circle, not caring if passersby thought she was talking to herself.

"Do not be afraid or dismayed," she said in a strong, confident voice, "for the Lord God, my God, is with you."

# CHAPTER 84

Following her workout, Special showered, put on a pair of jeans and a T-shirt and decided to pick up a few snacks from the grocery store.

She drove to the Ralph's supermarket in the Ladera Center and hopped out of her car. Before she had even made it to the entrance, she could feel the curious gazes pressing down on her. Judging her. She did an abrupt about face and hurried back to her car. She'd do her shopping at Ralph's on Lincoln Boulevard in the Marina, where she wouldn't run into that many blacks. White people didn't seem to recognize her as much. Or if they did, they didn't gawk at her the way black folks did.

She made the short drive up the 90 Freeway, parked, and put on sunglasses to hide her face. Next time, she would wear a hat. She had less than forty bucks in her checking account so her shopping options were limited. She picked up a frozen pepperoni pizza, four oranges, a party-size bag of Nacho Cheese Doritos, and a two-liter bottle of fruit punch. Telecredit was contesting her workers' comp claim and she had yet to receive a dime. She was already a month behind in her rent before her leave started.

She placed her groceries on the conveyor belt then moved over to the keypad in front of the clerk, swiped her ATM card, and held her breath. After a few long seconds, it cleared and she relaxed.

The clerk looked her up and down. She was a middle-aged bleached blond with cold, green eyes.

Special noticed that the woman had not greeted her with a cheery hello the way she had other customers. She must have recognized her.

*Do not be afraid or dismayed*, Special repeated to herself, *for the Lord God, my God, is with you.*

The clerk slapped her receipt on the counter without saying a word. Special waited for the woman to bag her groceries. There was no one else in line behind her. The woman put her hands on her hips and just stood there.

Special knew she should just pack up her stuff and get the hell out of the store, but her stubborn streak wouldn't let her. "Are you gonna bag up my groceries?"

The woman grunted, then pulled out a white plastic bag and hurled Special's frozen pizza inside.

"I have a twenty-year-old son," the woman said snidely. She slammed the oranges into the bag. "Last year, somebody bashed his head in just because he's gay. It scares me to think that there's some homicidal, homophobic maniac running around killing people because of their sexual orientation."

Special sucked in a breath. *Do not be afraid or dismayed, for the Lord, my God, is with you.*

Still taking her sweet time, the woman picked up the Doritos bag and shoved it inside. Special heard a pop when the Doritos bag punctured. "I don't know why they let you out on bail. After you're convicted, I hope they put you *under* the jail."

Special tried to call on God for strength. She wanted to turn the other cheek, but the devil was tugging at her soul.

"I didn't kill anybody," she said through tightly clamped teeth. "And I'm not homophobic." She yanked the bag from the woman's hand and grabbed the fruit punch bottle.

"I'm sorry somebody hurt your son. I just hope he wasn't out there deceiving women by professing to be straight," she hissed at the woman. "When something bad happens to gay men who do that, I just figure they got what they deserved."

The woman gasped and her face paled in horror.

Special tore out of the store. She was in tears by the time she reached her car. She started up the engine and tried to collect herself before pulling out of the parking spot.

She drove back to her apartment coughing and sniveling all the way. When she turned the corner onto Buckingham Drive, she saw four police cars parked near her apartment building. In seconds, she broke out in a sweat. The park across the street was crawling with cops. *Were they here to arrest her again?* It wasn't until she was just a few yards from the entrance of her building's underground garage that she noticed a police car blocking the entrance.

She pulled her car into an open space on the street. As soon as she opened her car door, the same cop who had arrested her the first time ran up with his gun drawn. Two other cops also had their guns pointed directly at her.

"Put your hands up!" Crew Cut yelled.

Special was so terrified she couldn't will her hands or any other part of her body to move. She was frozen solid with fear.

He repeated the order. "I said put your hands up!"

Sobbing and trembling, she finally raised her hands high above her head.

"Where have you been?"

"I went grocery shopping," Special cried.

"Where?"

"At Ralph's."

"Which one?"

"Off the 90 freeway . . . on Lincoln. In the Marina. Why do you care?"

Crew Cut holstered his gun and charged forward. He whirled Special around, slammed her against the car and slapped handcuffs on her wrists. "You're under arrest."

"For what?" Special cried. "This is police brutality! I'm out on bail."

"Not anymore. You just admitted violating the judge's bail order."

"What the hell are you talking about?"

"You were supposed to stay within a three-mile radius of your apartment. That store is more than three miles away. I'm taking you in."

"You can't do this to me!" She was crying now and struggling with the officer as he tugged her toward a patrol car.

She noticed Martinez, dressed in a dark suit, standing off to the side, quietly watching. He was trying to send her to prison for the rest of her life. Their eyes met. Special's registered fear and resentment. His communicated nothing.

The street was growing crowded with people. She could see the elderly man in apartment 104 peeking through his curtains. A white TV news van pulled up and a cameraman jumped out.

Crew Cut was about to toss her into the backseat of his patrol car, but waited for the cameraman to shoot some footage.

"This is a setup!" Special screamed. "Why are you doing this to me?"

"I predict you're going to be looking at another murder charge pretty soon," Crew Cut said, smiling at her. He stuffed her inside the patrol car and climbed into the front seat.

"What the hell are you talking about?" she whimpered through her tears.

"What I'm talking about is Gerald Dunn," he said, his voice filled with glee. "The guy you whacked this morning."

"I have no idea what you're talking about! Why are you doing this to me?"

"Dunn is the man we just found shot to death in the men's room over there." He pointed across the street to the park. "The sixth man you murdered."

# CHAPTER 85

I thought you said Martinez was a straight shooter!" Vernetta yelled into her cell phone.

"What the hell are you talking about?" Sam replied. "And why are you screaming at me?"

"They just arrested Special! Martinez should've called us." She was near tears. "The police ambushed her on the street with their guns drawn."

"Ambushed her? What happened? Did they revoke her bail?"

"There's been another murder and they're trying to pin that one on her, too. She just called me from jail. I'm on my way down there now. Can you meet me?"

"I'm on my way."

Vernetta and Sam arrived at the jail only minutes apart. They tried to get in to see Special, but were told it would be a while. Vernetta contacted J.C. to see what she might know, then asked Nichelle to meet them at a nearby sandwich shop. Vernetta, followed by Sam, had just stepped out of an elevator car when Martinez exited an adjacent one.

Vernetta hurried over to him. "Do you have a minute?" She had apparently invaded his personal space because he took a step backward.

"Sure," he said.

There was never a trace of emotion, of any kind, on the man's face.

Martinez hit the elevator button. "We can use one of the offices upstairs."

The elevator ride was long and tense. Vernetta's heart was filled with worry for her best friend. Her primary concern was getting Special out of jail as soon as possible.

Martinez escorted them to a room barely big enough for three people. He sat on the edge of a small table, facing them. "Have a seat."

"I'm fine standing up," Vernetta replied. "What's going on? Why didn't you give us a heads up that the police were planning to arrest Special?"

"We needed to get your client off the streets as soon as possible. She was already a prime suspect in five murders. Then another man is found dead just a few yards from where she lives. We don't give *heads up* under those circumstances."

"You can't possibly believe Special had anything to do with killing that man." There was too much anxiety in her voice, but she couldn't restrain herself. "Her arrest has to be some kind of media ploy to appease the public because the police are too incompetent to figure out who really killed those men."

"Ms. Henderson—" He paused. "May I call you Vernetta?"

"Sure," she said, though she felt like telling him no. He must have read that on her face.

"As I've shared with you before, I have a very strong circumstantial case against your client. If you were to calm down and look at the facts, you'd probably agree. This is exactly why they say it's not a good idea for lawyers to represent people close to them. I think your friendship with Ms. Moore may be clouding your legal judgment."

Vernetta didn't like the condescending way Martinez was talking to her. "You let me worry about my legal judgment. I suspect this case must be pretty personal for you, too."

When she heard Sam jostle in his chair, Vernetta knew he felt her last comment was below the belt.

For the first time, Vernetta saw a flash of emotion in Martinez's normally empty eyes, but she couldn't tell what that emotion was.

"Every case I handle is personal for me, Ms. Henderson. My job is to put criminals behind bars and I take great pleasure in doing that. I believe your client is a dangerous serial killer and I'm glad we got her off the street before she could claim a seventh victim."

"This is unbelievable. All you've got is a bunch of circumstantial evidence. Nothing else. What could possibly make you think Special killed the man they found this morning?"

"The guy was practically shot on her doorstep. Two women reported seeing her in the park earlier that morning."

"So in other words, you have nothing. For all you know, somebody could be setting her up."

Martinez lifted his shoulders and spread his arms. "If you've got evidence of a setup, I'm willing to listen."

The room fell silent.

"How soon can we schedule the arraignment?" Sam asked.

"We're not ready to charge her yet in today's murder," Martinez said. "She was picked up for violating the terms of her bail. I'm requesting a bail revocation hearing."

"I guess that confirms that you don't have enough evidence to charge her."

Martinez smiled. "Not yet. But we will."

Sam folded his arms. "We'd like to get that hearing scheduled as soon as possible."

"I'll see what I can do. But if you're planning to oppose it, you're wasting your time. She's not getting bail. She's too big of a threat to the community. I took some heat for not fighting bail harder after her initial arrest for Nelson's murder. That decision apparently cost another man his life. Anyway, I have to run. I have a press conference in ten minutes."

"Sounds like you're running for office or something," Vernetta said.

Martinez started to respond, then stalked out of the room.

# CHAPTER 86

$V$ernetta and Sam watched Martinez's live press conference on a 13-inch television in a room that J.C. secured for them at the jail.

Vernetta wanted to bash in the screen when Martinez branded Special "a deadly threat to the citizens of L.A." and "an example of homophobia at its worst."

She thought it was interesting how both the police and the D.A.'s office were skating around the issue of the sexual orientation of the other victims. They identified Eugene as a gay man, but steered clear of pinning the same label on the others.

"Well," Vernetta said when it was over, "there's one good thing about Special being in jail. She didn't have to watch that crap." She stood up and leaned against the wall. "We're going to have to fight this case in the courtroom *and* in the media."

Sam rested his arm on the back of his chair. "I agree. But first we need to establish a few ground rules. It doesn't gain us or our client anything by antagonizing the prosecutor. That's not how I like to work."

"I wasn't trying to antagonize him."

"Whether you were trying or not, you did." Sam was on his feet now. "I couldn't believe it when you made that remark about the case being personal for him, too. Martinez's sexual orientation is off limits. You're going to end up being branded as homophobic as Special."

"I'm not homophobic and neither is Special."

"Looks that way to me."

"Maybe you shouldn't be defending this case if you think we're all homophobic."

"What I think is that you—"

Nichelle stepped into the room. "Stop it! Both of you! I could hear you all the way down the hallway. You should both be ashamed of yourselves. Special needs us. All three of us. So you two are going to have to find a way to get along. All this energy you're spending bickering with each other needs to be used trying to figure out a way to get our friend out of jail."

Vernetta rubbed her eyes. "You're right."

Sam fidgeted with an ink pen, then sat down.

"We should be able to see Special now," Nichelle said. "Let's go."

While they were waiting in the visitor's area of the jail, J.C. came out to greet them.

"I know you're the enemy," Vernetta said jokingly, "but is there anything you can tell us?"

J.C. led them over to a corner, then lowered her voice. "The camera they took from Special's apartment is going to be sent out for analysis. I know she erased the disk, but it may be possible to retrieve the images."

"That picture will prove Special was stalking Eugene," Sam said. "That could really bury her."

"Maybe not," Vernetta said. "It's possible the man in that picture could be Eugene's killer. The fact that he hasn't gone to the police means he has something to hide."

"Maybe he's on the D-L, too," Nichelle said, "and is just afraid to come forward. Anyway, Special said she couldn't see his face."

"With all the technology they have these days, I wouldn't be surprised if they couldn't enhance the picture in some way so that his face is visible," Sam said. "I think she's going down."

"Why do you have to be so negative?" Vernetta sniped. "If you can't have a more positive attitude, maybe you shouldn't be involved in this case."

J.C. ushered all of them into a small office off the waiting area. "You two need to— "

"I'm a lawyer, not a cheerleader," Sam retorted. "And I call 'em as I see 'em. You may not want to believe it, but it *is* possible that Special killed Eugene and those other guys, too."

"That's it! If that's your attitude, you don't need to be on this case. We can try it without your help!"

"No, we can't!" Nichelle exclaimed. "We need him. Everybody just calm down."

"We don't need him!" Vernetta insisted. "He's too damn negative. With his attitude, we might as well take a guilty plea now. I refuse to work with somebody like that."

"Fine." Sam grabbed the door and hurled it open. "You two are on your own."

# CHAPTER 87

"Looks like your secret is finally out."

Ray Martinez sat up in bed and stretched as his partner approached.

Antonio tossed the *Long Beach Press-Telegram* onto his lap. "I hope you're ready for this."

Martinez picked up the paper. At first, the page one headline startled him: *Gay D.A. Goes on Attack in Down Low Murder Case.* There was a picture of Martinez outside the courthouse at yesterday's news conference. He scanned the article and slowed halfway through it.

> *The Stanford Law grad, who has resided with his partner for the past seven years, has been an active member of many local gay and civic organizations.*
>
> *"Ray is definitely the right pick to prosecute this case," said Mel Armstrong, a local gay activist. "You couldn't find a man with more integrity. He's a smart, sensitive attorney who understands the complexities of being gay in America. Having that knowledge will be extremely important in prosecuting this case."*

Antonio sat down on the edge of the bed. "You okay with this?"

A graphic artist with warm coffee-brown skin, he had thick, curly hair and was both taller and thicker than Martinez. Though he was Puerto Rican, Antonio was often mistaken for African-American.

"It's not like I didn't know it was coming." Martinez tossed the paper aside. "I haven't exactly been in the closet. Many of my coworkers know that I'm gay."

"The operative word being *many*, not *all*. For the majority of the people you work with, it would never cross their mind that you might be gay. So some people are definitely going to be surprised."

"I can handle it. The question is, can you?"

Except for a younger sister, Antonio had no communication with his family. They were deeply religious and refused to accept what they called his "alternative lifestyle." Martinez's mother made up for the rejection by treating Antonio like one of her own.

"I'll be fine," Antonio assured him. "I just want *you* to be careful. There are still a lot of people out there who think we should all be burned at the stake. As a matter of fact, you're prosecuting one of them right now."

Martinez laughed.

"When you get to work," Antonio warned, "you're going to find that some of the people who were fine with you yesterday won't be today."

"I'm cool," Martinez said. "Thanks for worrying about me."

Antonio embraced him affectionately. "Just be careful."

Martinez arrived at the office ninety minutes later. He was surprised when a tremor of nervousness hit him as he exited the elevator in the Criminal Courts building. Maybe having his sexual orientation displayed to the world wouldn't be as easy as he thought.

"Nice story," his secretary said, when he passed her desk.

He smiled at her. "Thanks, Connie."

Martinez placed his briefcase on his desk and made his way to the men's room. He stepped up to one of the urinals just as the door opened. John Marshall, another Deputy D.A., walked in.

Martinez glanced over his shoulder at his coworker. "What's up?"

Marshall stopped in his tracks. "Uh . . . Hey, I . . . I . . . uh . . . I just remembered a call I need to make." He turned around and dashed out.

Martinez shook his head. He never would have pegged John as a homophobe. They had been standing side by side at these urinals on a daily basis for the last three years. But now, that would never happen again.

Chuckling to himself, Martinez bent over the sink to wash his hands. He couldn't wait to get home to share this incident with Antonio. Straight men always acted as if every gay guy who crossed their path wanted to screw them. There's no way Martinez would have ever given the time of day to a fat, out-of-shape slob like John.

"Only in your dreams," Martinez muttered as he headed back to his office. "Only in your friggin' dreams."

# CHAPTER 88

Sitting at her desk, Vernetta tried to psyche herself up for Special's bail revocation hearing. There was no way they'd be able to spring her from jail. They would just be going through the motions.

Special now faced the possibility of multiple murder charges, though it was a good sign that Martinez had not actually filed any additional counts against her. That was basically an admission that he didn't have the evidence. Yet.

Vernetta had always believed lawyers should not represent people close to them. When an attorney is too emotionally involved in a case, objectivity can be compromised. But she could not see trusting her best friend's defense to anyone else. She would get it together. She had to.

Nichelle walked in and took a seat. "So are we ready?"

"As ready as we're going to be." The hearing was scheduled for later that afternoon.

"Have you given any thought to what I said?"

Nichelle had been pestering Vernetta to make up with Sam. Vernetta hated admitting that she needed his help. Despite the hassle he would be, she had to swallow her pride and do what was best for Special.

"I'll call him after the hearing."

"Good." Nichelle looked relieved. "And if you don't, I will."

They had read nearly two dozen cases and stayed up late the night before rehearsing their legal arguments. Nichelle played the role of prosecutor, throwing curve balls at her and seeing if she could hit them. At the end of the night, Vernetta knew they were only fooling themselves. Even though all the evidence against Special was circumstantial, there was no way the judge was going to let her back out on bail.

"Too bad we don't know anybody who can slip the judge some cash to let her out," Nichelle joked.

"That's wishful thinking. And even if we could, neither one of us would ever do anything like that."

"That's our problem," Nichelle said. She turned to look out of the window. "We always play by the rules, but the bad guys have no problem pulling whatever dirty trick it takes to win. By the way, are you still on good terms with O'Reilly?"

"We're not nearly as close as we used to be, but we're still more than cordial." Just a couple of days ago O'Reilly had recommended Vernetta to a company in need of help with an employment case that wasn't big enough for O'Reilly & Finney to handle. "I think he's being nice to me so I won't blab that he's screwing Haley."

"Can't he do anything to help us?"

"Like what?"

"I don't know. He's one of the most connected attorneys in this city. He must know people who know people who know the judge."

"As a matter of fact, O'Reilly is a pretty close friend of Judge Winston. I think their fathers were law school classmates or something."

"You should give him a call," Nichelle urged.

"And ask him to do what? Bribe the judge?"

"I don't know." Nichelle's face turned sullen. "I guess I'm just thinking out loud. I know Special's innocent, but I'm not sure we can prove it. If she has to go to prison for killing Eugene or anybody else, you might as well lock me up in the same cell because I won't be able to handle it."

Vernetta was about to tell her she felt the same way, but kept that thought to herself. They had to be optimistic. No matter what.

This conversation reminded Vernetta that there *was* something O'Reilly could do to help Special. She picked up the phone.

"Who're you calling?"

"O'Reilly."

Nichelle's eyes widened.

When O'Reilly came on the line, he greeted Vernetta like the old mentor who adored her. "Hey, kiddo. You're all over the TV lately. You've got yourself a pretty big case. I'm jealous."

*Sure you are.* "I'm calling to ask for a favor." Vernetta could almost hear him tense up over the telephone. "We have a bail revocation hearing before Judge Winston later this afternoon. I know that you know him pretty well."

"I'm afraid I have to stop you right here," O'Reilly said. "I hope you're not about to ask me to use my influence with the judge to—"

"No," Vernetta said, cutting him off. "That would be both illegal and unethical. I was about to say that I don't think Judge Winston's going to let her out on bail. And since I also know you're pretty good friends with Sheriff Robinson, I was wondering if you could ask the sheriff to have somebody look out for Special in jail. Make sure she's safe."

"I think I can make that happen."

"Thanks. I'd appreciate it."

"Did you hear that Haley left the firm?"

"Really?" Actually, Vernetta had learned from Sheila that the pair had become more and more brazen with their affair. The rumors finally made their way to the management committee. Obviously one of them had to leave and it certainly wasn't going to be the rainmaker.

"Her father's ill, so she needs a job that's not so demanding of her time. She's been offered an in-house position with Vista Electronics. It's a big loss for the firm."

*And your gain.* Now they were free to carry on their affair without violating any firm rules.

"That's wonderful for Haley," Vernetta said. "She'll do great in-house. Knowing her, she'll be general counsel in no time."

# CHAPTER 89

Vernetta was not prepared for what she saw when a sheriff's deputy brought Special into one of the attorney-client meeting rooms at the jail.

She had chains around her waist and wrists and was wearing an oversized orange jumpsuit. Her skin had paled and there were dark circles under her eyes. Her sunken cheeks made her look like something out of a horror movie.

Nichelle quietly gasped. J.C. looked down at the floor.

"Hey, y'all," was all Special could manage to mumble.

Just as Vernetta reached out to touch her, a deputy poked his head into the room. "No contact with the inmates," he growled.

The room wasn't much bigger than a broom closet and had peeling paint and a tiny, metal table. A claustrophobic's nightmare. There was a long row of identical client meeting rooms which had front and side walls made of glass. A deputy strolled the corridor, monitoring everything going on inside.

"I asked a couple of the deputies to look out for you," J.C. said. "Have they?"

Special raised, then lowered her shoulders, causing the chains to rattle. "I guess so. Nobody's forced me to join a female gang yet." She laughed, but her three friends didn't join her.

J.C. ignored the deputy's warning and gave Special's shoulder a quick squeeze. "I'll leave so you guys can talk shop."

Vernetta started to reach for Special's hand, then remembered that she couldn't. "We're going to do everything we can to get you out of here."

"Okay." Special had yet to look her in the eyes and Vernetta could tell that she didn't believe her.

"The bail revocation hearing is going to start in just a little while," Nichelle explained. "It's going to be an uphill battle."

The hearing was only a formality. There was no way Special would be released since she violated the conditions of her bail. Another murder happening just an arm's throw from her apartment further complicated things. But neither Nichelle nor Vernetta could bring themselves to tell Special the truth.

Special looked at Nichelle, then turned to Vernetta. "I know I won't get out," she said with a frail smile. "Anyway, it's not so bad. Orange is a good color for me."

Again, nobody laughed.

"Special," Vernetta said, "when they bring you in, I want you to follow our lead. Don't say anything unless we tell you to."

She nodded.

O'Reilly had called back and reported that the sheriff promised to make sure Special was well treated behind bars. With his pull and J.C.'s, Vernetta felt Special was as safe as she could be under the circumstances.

"Is there anything you need us to handle?" Nichelle asked. "Do you have any bills you need us to take care of?"

That question generated a genuine chuckle. "Be careful what you offer. I've got a mountain of unpaid bills and no money to pay 'em. At least the bill collectors can't hassle me up in here."

"Do you want us to bring you anything?" Vernetta wasn't sure what she was allowed to have in jail, but maybe they could bend the rules a bit where that was concerned.

"Can you drop by and check on my parents and make sure they're okay? All this trouble I'm in is killing them. And please talk them out of coming down here again. I hate having them see me like this. They came earlier today and my mother cried the whole time."

"Anything else?" Vernetta asked.

"Yeah. Reverend Sims gave me some Bible verses to read. I left them on the nightstand in my bedroom. Could you bring them over along with my Bible?" She repositioned herself in the chair, which caused the chains to rattle. "I need them really, really bad."

# CHAPTER 90

As they stood facing the judge, Vernetta could sense the inevitable with every syllable uttered from Martinez's lips.

"Your Honor, The People strongly urge the court to revoke the defendant's bail. She violated the court's restrictions by going outside the three-mile radius that you imposed. The charge at issue here is an extremely vicious murder."

He picked up his legal pad from the table.

"We have irrefutable evidence that the defendant stalked and assaulted Eugene Nelson. Her fingerprints were found on the windowsill where the crime scene investigators believe the killer entered his home, and there is strong circumstantial evidence linking her to the murder of several other men who—"

Vernetta jumped to her feet. "Objection, Your Honor!" Her voice was much too loud. She mentally chastised herself, then proceeded. "My client has only been charged with *one* murder. We're here to address bail associated with that case and only that case."

"The defendant hasn't been charged with the other murders *yet*," Martinez said, "but she will be."

She didn't like the smug look on Martinez's face. "It's my understanding that the state has no credible evidence linking my client to any of those murders. Hence, they're irrelevant to this hearing."

Vernetta hated the way Special was sneering at Martinez. She had specifically warned her not to do that. At trial, the jury would convict her on that basis alone.

The bantering between Martinez and Vernetta went back and forth for another couple of minutes. Then, as expected, Judge Winston granted Martinez's motion, revoking Special's bail. It took an hour before Special was escorted into the meeting room to see them again.

As soon as the deputy left the room, Special lashed out at them. "What in the hell did you call that?"

The sharpness of her tone could have sliced Vernetta in half. "What's the matter?"

*"What's the matter?* That man stood there and talked about me like I had a tail and you barely opened your damn mouth! I know I'm not paying y'all, but if this is the kind of defense I'm getting, I need to find me some new attorneys."

Vernetta couldn't believe Special was attacking them. "You have to be kidding! If you hadn't been harassing Eugene, your ass wouldn't be in here. We're not magicians. We can't—"

"Cut it out, you two," Nichelle pleaded. "This isn't helping." She checked to see if the deputy was coming, then patted Special's shoulder in a gesture of calm. "The judge wasn't going to let you out on bail," she said gently. "We had no valid legal basis for putting up much of a fight."

Special flung Nichelle's hand from her shoulder like it was a flake of dandruff. "I don't care about a legal basis," she shouted. "There were a bunch of cameras rolling in there. When people watch the news tonight, they're going to think I'm guilty. Just like y'all apparently do." She burst into tears.

The deputy appeared from nowhere and popped his head into the room. "Is everything okay in here?"

"Yes," Vernetta and Nichelle said in unison.

"We're fine," Vernetta said.

The deputy stepped outside, but planted himself near the door, watching them.

Vernetta looked at the tears rolling down her friend's cheeks and her anger dissipated. Special was scared. And Vernetta was just as scared for her.

"We don't think you're guilty," she said softly. "We did our best." Vernetta felt a big, sad lump in her throat.

"I can't stay in here," Special sobbed. "I just can't. You have to get me out of here!"

It took them a while to get Special calmed down. Vernetta was emotionally drained by the time they left thirty minutes later. When the elevator car opened, they came face-to-face with Martinez.

"Hello, ladies," he said.

Nichelle nodded. Vernetta couldn't stand to look at him.

They rode in silence for several seconds, then Martinez broke it. "Must be nice to have friends in high places."

Vernetta refused to take his bait.

"What is that supposed to mean?" Nichelle asked.

"I heard from a couple of deputies at the jail that your client is getting some very special treatment."

"Really?" Nichelle asked. "How so?"

"She's been moved to a nicer area of the jail and gets more telephone time than other inmates."

"Really?" she said again. "That's nice to hear."

"I wonder what the public would think of that?" Martinez said. "Might make an interesting story. *Serial Killer Gets Special Treatment.*"

The elevator came to a stop in the lobby and they all walked off.

"Are you threatening us?" Vernetta asked.

"Nope," Martinez said. "Just thinking out loud."

# CHAPTER 91

So how'd it go?"

Sam barged into Nichelle's closed office without knocking. She had just returned from the bail hearing. Sam was the last person she wanted to see right now.

"Special didn't get bail."

There was a look of satisfaction on his face. "I'm not surprised."

"Neither were we." Nichelle did not have the energy for Sam's pessimistic attitude. She knew he was dying to be back on the case. Nichelle and Vernetta had appeared on several local newscasts and Sam longed to be in the spotlight with them. She started to tell him to expect a call from Vernetta, but decided against it.

"I saw your press conference. Too bad Vernetta hogged it all for herself."

"She didn't hog anything. I didn't want to talk."

"She wouldn't have let you if you wanted to."

"Sam, I don't need this right now. Unless you have something helpful to say, you should leave."

"So, you think Special really killed that latest guy?"

"No, Sam. I don't."

"That's exactly what I thought you'd say," Sam groused. "You're too close to this case. Just like Vernetta. I don't think it's a coincidence that the murder happened right across the street from her apartment building. And she was seen in the park that morning. Your emotions are clouding your judgment. That's not good for your client."

"My judgment is fine." She couldn't resist taking a dig. "Vernetta's one of the best trial lawyers I've ever seen. You haven't had the pleasure of seeing her in action. If you had, you'd agree."

Sam bristled. "Yeah, but she's not a criminal attorney. Criminal law is a whole different ball game. There's a lot more on the line. You have to—"

Sadie, their secretary, stepped into the office with a big smirk on her face. "Nichelle, there's a woman waiting in the reception area for you. She saw one of your interviews and wants to talk to you about the wrongful death case you filed against Eugene Nelson." Sadie brought her hand to her mouth, stifling a giggle.

"What's so funny?" Nichelle asked.

"You'll see."

"Well, who is she?"

"Says her name is Rhonda Whitehead. She's organizing a conference. I think she wants you to be a guest speaker."

"Is she legit? I don't have time right now to deal with any kooks."

"Oh, she's legit. I'll go get her."

"I'm outta here," Sam said.

A minute or so later, Sadie showed an attractive, African-American woman into Nichelle's office. There was nothing funny or unusual about her. She looked to be in her mid-thirties and was dressed in an expensive knit suit.

Rhonda introduced herself and extended her hand to Nichelle. The woman smiled like she had just been introduced to a celebrity. "Please forgive me for barging in like this. I work across the street. I'm an analyst for Bear Stearns. I had a meeting in this building and I saw your name on the directory downstairs. I had no idea your office was so close by."

Nichelle motioned toward the empty chair in front of her desk. "My secretary said this has something to do with the lawsuit we filed against Eugene Nelson."

"Yes, it does," Rhonda said. "I'm the president of a new women's organization. We'd like you to be the keynote speaker at our first luncheon. We want to hear about the lawsuit and your research on down low men. The luncheon is Thursday at the Proud Bird. Sorry for the short notice."

Nichelle was enjoying her growing celebrity status and this sounded like another great opportunity to get her name out there. But with everything going on with Special's case, she wasn't sure she had time to work on a speech. "Tell me a little about your group."

"We have about one hundred and fifty women who have officially joined so far, which is pretty good considering we've only been in existence about eleven months. This will be our very first luncheon. I formed this organization because this issue needs attention. African-American women are being infected with HIV left and right and it's ridiculous that nobody's doing a damn thing about it. If this were happening to white women, the President would've formed a special task force by now."

The woman had a point. "Exactly what does your organization do?"

"Right now, our focus is on education and awareness. We're also in the process of adding a page on our website outing brothers who are out there sleeping with men and putting us at risk."

"Hold on a minute." Nichelle held up a hand. "I don't know if that's a smart thing to do. You could end up being sued for defamation."

"You're the fourth attorney to tell me that. But I've done my homework. You're not guilty of libel or slander if you're telling the truth. We plan to be very, very careful. No one will go up on the website unless they are in a confirmed relationship with a woman *and* we have solid evidence of their homosexual conduct."

"And just what do you consider solid evidence?"

"You heard of *Cheaters?*"

Nichelle was familiar with the TV show that used undercover cameras to catch cheating spouses and mates in the act. "Yes," she said, growing more and more uneasy.

"Well, let's just say we're doing something similar."

"That's still a pretty dangerous thing to do."

"We realize that." Rhonda dismissed Nichelle's concern with a mindless wave of her hand. "Anyway, will you be our keynote?"

Rhonda obviously sensed Nichelle's hesitation. "This could be great publicity for you," she prodded. "There are lots of women out there being deceived and I'm sure others will want to sue, too. You'll probably end up with some new clients. We can pay you an honorarium of five hundred dollars."

The more she thought about it, the more Nichelle realized that she had an important message that the group very much needed to hear. She opened her datebook and flipped to Thursday. "I'm open, so I guess there's no reason I couldn't do it." She picked up a pen to write down the appointment. "Does your organization have a name?"

"Sure does." Rhonda's eyes sparkled with pride. "And you're going to love it. My cousin, Raynetha, came up with it. We call it SADDDL, but we spell it with an extra D and no E."

"Okay," Nichelle said, curious. "Exactly what does SADDDL stand for?"

Rhonda smiled like someone had just asked her to say *cheese*. "It stands for Sisters Against Dirty Dogs on the Down Low. You like it?"

# CHAPTER 92

Belynda looked around Eugene's empty bedroom one last time, making sure she had packed up all of his belongings.

She had spent part of the day helping Eugene's sister collect his insurance policies, bank statements, and other important documents. Most of his personal possessions and furniture would be shipped to his aunt in Chicago. The items that Belynda had just stuffed into large garbage bags were being donated to the church.

As she was about to leave the room, A shiny, silver object imbedded in the carpet caught Belynda's eye. She bent down to pick it up, instantly realizing what it was. She smiled sadly, then slipped the lapel pin she'd given Eugene into the pocket of her jean skirt.

She was on her way downstairs, but stumbled to a stop.

"Wait a minute," she said out loud. She pulled the pin from her pocket and examined it more closely.

This wasn't the pin that she had given to Eugene. She had purchased two of them, one in gold and the other in sterling silver. She had given the gold one to Eugene and the silver one to Reverend Sims. So what was the reverend's pin doing in Eugene's bedroom?

She stood there for a moment, trying to make sense of this discovery when a disturbing possibility flooded her brain, causing her knees to buckle.

Reverend Sims had worn the pin everyday since she'd given it to him. Finding it in Eugene's bedroom could only mean that the reverend had been here. What reason would Reverend Sims have to visit Eugene's home? And if he had, why would he have been in Eugene's bedroom?

A perverse realization shook up her senses, causing her to slump to the floor. Her mind went back to that Saturday morning when Special had accosted her on her walk with Princess and tried to force her to look at a picture that she claimed showed Eugene kissing some man. Now, Belynda regretted not looking at the camera. *Could Reverend Sims have been the man in the picture?* No. It was ridiculous for her to even think such a thing. The reverend was a dedicated man of God.

She picked up the last of the garbage bags she had stuffed with Eugene's clothes and tried to put the wicked images out of her mind. She headed downstairs and dumped the bags near the door next to several boxes that she also planned to drop off at the church.

Her mind would not shake the ungodly thoughts. *Had she gotten the gifts mixed up?* Maybe she had given the silver pin to Eugene and the gold one to the reverend. Belynda loaded the bags and boxes into the trunk of her car and drove to the church. She pulled into the parking lot and went straight to Reverend Sims' office.

He was sitting at his desk, typing on the computer.

"Good afternoon," the reverend looked up and spotted her standing in the doorway.

For a long moment, she just stood there, staring at him. The lapel pin he normally wore on his right collar wasn't there. She couldn't remember the last time he had worn it.

Reverend Sims' attention was focused on his computer monitor. "So what can I do for you?"

Belynda cleared her throat. "I didn't want anything, Reverend." She struggled to appear upbeat. "I just dropped by to say hello." She scanned his desktop, desperately hoping to spot the pin.

"Are you okay?" He was looking up at her now.

"Yes, I'm fine. I see you're not wearing that lapel pin I gave you." She tried to sound playful.

Reverend Sims lowered his head like a child in trouble. "I didn't want to tell you this, but it seems I've misplaced it. I think I may have lost it when I went to the gym a couple of weeks ago. It was a wonderful gift and I regret being so careless with it."

His admission prompted visions that made her skin crawl. "Don't . . . don't worry about it. It wasn't very expensive. I'd be glad to get you another one."

"No, you don't have to do that."

She said a short, silent prayer. There was still another possibility. Maybe she had been mistaken. "Reverend, was the pin I gave you silver or gold?"

He smiled and pointed to his wrist. "It was silver," he said. "It matched my watch perfectly."

# CHAPTER 93

Special's apartment was dark and musty. After hauling her off to jail for the bail violation, the police had ransacked her apartment a second time and the place was still in shambles. They would have to clean up before Special came home. Assuming she ever did come home.

The absence of Special's presence made the room seem so desolate. Vernetta pulled back the curtains to let in some light and opened the windows to air out the place.

Before going into the bedroom to look for Special's Bible and the list of verses, Vernetta sat down on the living room couch and had a good cry. Then she prayed long and hard for God to take care of her best friend.

The bedroom was a bigger mess than the rest of the apartment. Dresser drawers hung open, its contents strewn about the room. The mattress was askew on the box spring and the comforter was on the other side of the room. Papers littered the floor. Vernetta found Special's Bible and the list of verses on the floor near the nightstand, buried underneath a pile of shoes. She went to the closet in search of a conservative outfit for Special to wear for her next court appearance and found a black skirt and white blouse with tiny ruffles along the neck.

Vernetta picked up the Bible and the list of verses and was about to leave, but instead sat down and opened the Bible in hopes of lifting her own spirits.

When she plopped down on the bed, she felt something hard underneath her. She stood up and looked down at the bed. There was no visible lump to indicate that she had sat on anything, so she figured it must have been a loose spring. She sat down again and felt the same hard lump.

Vernetta eased off the bed and ran her hand across the bare mattress. It felt smooth. But when she pressed down, she felt the hard lump again. She bent down to get a closer look at the mattress and her eyes zeroed in on an almost invisible line where the mattress had apparently been carefully sewn together with thread.

Vernetta looked around and spotted a pair of manicure scissors on the floor near the foot of the bed. Ripping open the seam, she shoved her hand inside the mattress and hit something hard and cold.

She gingerly retrieved a small silver handgun. It couldn't have weighed more than a couple of pounds, but it felt as heavy as a brick. Vernetta finally had to set it down on the mattress because her hand was too unsteady.

According to the *Times,* each of the murder victims had been killed with a small caliber handgun, probably a twenty-two. Vernetta knew nothing about guns, but it was hard to imagine one much smaller than this.

Trembling, she pulled her cell phone from her purse and hit the speed dial button for Nichelle. After the phone rang just once, she changed her mind, hung up, and pushed a different button.

"I need you to meet me at Special's place," Vernetta whimpered when Jefferson picked up. "Right away."

# CHAPTER 94

Belynda left Reverend Sims' office, hopped in her car and drove downtown to the jail. She prayed over and over and over again that Reverend Sims was not the man Special claimed she saw kissing Eugene. That would be a disgrace to God.

A short time later, she was sitting in the jail's reception area. A deputy had told her it would be at least forty minutes before Special would be brought down. Belynda had no problem waiting.

She knew that Special was not likely to greet her with open arms. But she desperately needed to talk to the woman about what she claimed to have seen at Eugene's house that night. If the man with Eugene was Reverend Sims, Belynda needed to know that. The entire congregation of Ever Faithful Missionary Baptist Church needed to know.

When a deputy finally brought Special down, Belynda was already seated on a stool in front of one of the scarred Plexiglas windows that separated the inmates from their visitors.

"Booth number three," the guard said, pointing Special toward Belynda.

Special's eyes squinted in disbelief. She sat down and snatched the two-way phone. Belynda was already holding the telephone on her side of the window.

"What are you doing here?" Special asked, seething.

"I'd like to speak with you."

"About what?"

"About that morning when you tried to show me that camera with Eugene's picture. Do you still have it? If you do, I'd like to see it."

"Do I look that stupid to you? You think I'm going to sit here and let you set me up. I never came to your house, and I have no idea what camera or picture you're talking about."

"I'm sorry about everything that's happened to you." Belynda was hoping she could calm down the obviously psychotic woman. "This is extremely important. I think it's possible that I might know the man in that picture."

"What picture? Anyway, I thought you told me Eugene had gone straight. What would he be doing in some picture with a man?"

"Perhaps I was mistaken about that." She had to play along with the woman. "Eugene had his problems. Many people have sexual identity issues. But with God's help, he was trying to work through them."

"*Sexual identity issues*? Are you really that naïve or are you just stuck on stupid? Eugene was gay, and he lied about it. How could you even want to be with a man who'd done what he did to my cousin?" Special choked back a sob.

"I'm a Christian," Belynda said. "There's no sin God won't forgive. I also forgave Eugene for his sins."

"But he was still out there sinning! And if he hadn't been killed, he was going to end up doing the same thing to you that he did to Maya."

"I came here to ask you about that photograph. Not to discuss Eugene. God will handle him." Belynda opened her purse and pulled out a piece of paper. "This is one of the church bulletins from Ever Faithful." She held it up to the window. "Is this the man you saw him with?"

Special refused to even look at the paper. "Maybe you didn't hear me. I just told you I was never at Eugene's place, I never took a picture, and I never saw him with anybody." Special stood up, but the short phone cord forced her into a slight stoop. "I only have one more thing to say to you. I don't know how far you went with that man, but if I were you, I'd go get tested."

She slammed down the phone and signaled for the deputy to take her back to lockup.

# CHAPTER 95

It took Jefferson about thirty minutes to make the drive from Torrance over to Special's apartment. Vernetta had refused to explain the reason for her urgent request over the telephone. She knew he must have been worried to death.

When Vernetta opened the door, he looked at her swollen red eyes and could obviously tell that she had been crying.

"What happened?" Jefferson asked, embracing her. "Is Special okay?"

"She's fine." Vernetta handed him a piece of paper that she had written before he arrived.

Jefferson gave her a puzzled look, then unfolded the note and read it to himself.

> *I know I'm being paranoid, but I don't feel comfortable talking in here. I'm going to show you something I just found in Special's bedroom and then let's go outside to talk.*

He followed her into the bedroom without comment. Vernetta walked over to the bed, pulled back a blanket and pointed to the gun resting in the center of the mattress.

"Whoaaa! Where'd you find this? I didn't know Special even owned a—"

Vernetta put her index finger to her mouth. "Shsssssh!"

Jefferson pulled a pen from his shirt, stuck it through the trigger guard and raised it in the air. He brought it close to his face and examined it.

After he set it back down, Vernetta took his hand and led him outside. Neither of them said a word until they were seated inside his truck.

Jefferson waited for her to speak, but she didn't. "Okay?" he said.

"Okay what?" Vernetta replied.

"Did you know Special owned a gun?"

"Nope."

"Where'd you find it?"

When she told him, Jefferson rubbed his chin. "That says she was definitely trying to hide it. I'm surprised the cops didn't find it when they tore up her place. But they miss stuff all the time. She's damn lucky. So tell me what you're thinking."

Vernetta didn't want to share what she was thinking. "I still don't think she killed anybody, Jefferson. I swear I don't."

"The newspapers said all of those guys, including Eugene, were killed with a small caliber gun, probably a twenty-two. That gun is a twenty-two."

Vernetta started to cry and Jefferson squeezed her hand. "Nobody has to know about that gun except you, me and Special."

"What are you talking about?"

"Let me get rid of it."

Vernetta eased her hand from his. "Jefferson, we can't do that. We'd be destroying evidence. That's not why I asked you to come over."

"Do I think Special killed all those dudes? Hell, nah. Do I think she killed Eugene?" Jefferson rubbed the back of his neck. "Yeah. I do."

"Jefferson!"

"Just hear me out. You're a lawyer, Vernetta. Put your emotions aside for a second and look at the facts. If Special wasn't your best friend, you'd be thinking the same thing everybody else in this city is thinking. That she shot Eugene because of what he did to Maya."

Vernetta turned away and stared down the street.

"Special is like a sister to you. To me, too. And if one of my sisters were in her shoes, I would do everything I could to prevent her from spending the rest of her life in prison. Sometimes taking care of family means doing what you have to do."

"But what you're proposing is illegal."

"So are a lot of things." Jefferson pressed his head back against the headrest. "Let me tell you a story. When I was sixteen, I worked for this electrical subcontractor who had an office over on Western. He was the one who got me interested in being an electrician. I remember him coming in one day mad as hell after this general contractor refused to pay him. With me sitting right there, he picked up the phone, explained what had gone down, and asked somebody to *handle* things for him. By the end of the day, that contractor walked into my boss' office looking like somebody had beat him down with a crowbar. He threw an envelope full of cash on the desk and left."

Jefferson paused, then continued. "I'll never forget what my boss said to me after the guy walked out. He said, *Jefferson, I want you to remember something. There's right and there's wrong and there's business. This was business.* I view this situation exactly the same way. Getting rid of that gun would just be taking care of business."

Vernetta closed her eyes. She had seen people do the wrong thing too many times and end up in even more trouble. That wasn't the way she liked to operate. She was used to playing everything by the book.

"If I let you dispose of that gun, it would be just our luck that you'd get caught with it or the police would find it or who knows what."

Jefferson chuckled. "Babe, I know you've spent a lot of time trying to smooth out my rough edges, but have you forgotten who you're married to? I got cousins, lots of 'em, who grew up in the Rolling Sixties off Sixty-first and Crenshaw. They taught me a few things. So, I know how to take care of business."

Vernetta wiped her eyes. She was a lawyer. She understood right and wrong, guilt and innocence better than anybody. But she had also watched innocent people go to jail.

"This ain't the movies," Jefferson said. "This is the real deal. You just give me the word and I'll make sure that gun disappears. Permanently."

# CHAPTER 96

An air of apprehension swept over Nichelle as she stared out into a sea of African-American faces in the largest ballroom at the Proud Bird Banquet Center near LAX.

If the measuring tool were sheer numbers, the first luncheon hosted by Sisters Against Dirty Dogs on the Down Low was an overwhelming success. Nichelle listened as Rhonda solicited entries for "Dirty Dogs of the Week," the newest feature on the SADDDL website.

"So if you know any men on the D-L," Rhonda said, "let us know so we can pass on their information to our investigator. We're going to out these brothers on our website so they can't prey on us anymore."

Nichelle pressed her hand to her cheek and felt her stomach flutter. Rhonda was playing with fire.

"And don't send me photographs of men you *think* might be on the D-L, you have to *know* for sure 'cause this investigator is costing us a bundle."

"I have three names for you right now," shouted a fair-skinned woman with a short blond Afro. Other women in the audience waved their hands and shouted *me too*.

Nichelle didn't like what she was hearing. This type of hate would send these guys even deeper into the closet. Her conversation with Professor Michaels had opened her eyes. She hoped to have the same effect on the SADDDL members.

"Now, ladies," Rhonda said, looking across the dais at Nichelle, "we are honored to have with us a woman who is on the forefront of the battle against these trifling men. Ms. Nichelle Ayers is a partner with the law firm of Barnes, Ayers and Howard, but most important, she filed that lawsuit against Eugene Nelson. He's the man who gave HIV to Nichelle's dear friend, Maya Washington. But the dirty dog got what he deserved because he's no longer with us."

Rhonda's last statement set off a chorus of hand clapping.

"But hold on," Rhonda said, trying to curb the applause. "Ms. Ayers is also defending Special Moore, our fellow sister accused of murdering that dirty dog. I just pray she's able to get her off. Please welcome our special guest."

Nichelle made her way to the podium dressed in a burnt orange pants suit with a cream blouse. By the time she had taken her place, the cheering had increased. One woman stood, then another, and another, until they were all giving her a standing ovation. Nichelle hoped she didn't look as jittery as she felt. She wondered if there would be any applause *after* she finished her speech.

"Good afternoon." Nichelle's voice trembled with anxiety. "Please forgive me if I'm a little nervous. I've never had a standing ovation before, and I haven't even said a word."

The room vibrated with laughter. "Go on sistah-girl, you're among friends," a woman sitting a few feet from the dais said encouragingly.

Nichelle glanced down at her notes. "As you all know, the AIDS epidemic remains at a crisis level, particularly for African-American women. But what no one's discussing is how to stop the tide."

"I know how to stop it," yelled a petite woman in a pink hat. "Round up all the men on the down low and shoot 'em!"

More laughter rocked the room.

Nichelle patiently waited for the laughing to cease. "I think the answer lies more with understanding these men and examining our own culpability."

An uneasy hush washed over the room like a tidal wave. Nichelle reached for the glass of water near the edge of the podium and took a sip.

"We should start by examining why these men feel the need to be on the down low in the first place. I believe one of the reasons they do is because they're subjected to such scorn from the black community."

This time an angry buzz seemed to spring up from the floor. At nearly every table women were muttering to their neighbors and eyeing Nichelle with disapproval.

"In the black community, gays are despised as—"

"They should be despised," someone interrupted.

Nichelle paused momentarily, then scanned the audience. With such hostility in the room, there was no way she was going to get through her prepared speech. Nichelle pushed her notes to the side. She would just have to wing it.

"Should they be despised?" she challenged, looking past a woman who was the spitting image of Church Girl.

"I'm sure there are women in this room who have friends, brothers, sons, and maybe even fathers, who are in the closet. They wouldn't need to lie to us if we accepted them for who they are."

Rhonda leapt to her feet, Bible in hand. "Sister Ayers, homosexuality is a sin. We didn't invite you here to encourage us to accept this perversion." She flipped open her Bible. "Leviticus 20:13 says, and I quote: *If a man lies with a man as one lies with a woman, both of them have done what is detestable. They must be put to death; their blood will be on their own heads.*" She dramatically slammed the Bible shut.

The entire room cheered. Nichelle took another sip of water. She had anticipated this response.

"You know," Nichelle said, turning briefly to face Rhonda who was still standing, hand on hip, "I'm a Christian just like you. I also remember the Bible saying something about love and forgiveness and not judging others. And with regard to the verse you just read, what about the other admonitions in Leviticus?" Nichelle reached for her notes. "Leviticus 20:10 says, and this, too, is a quote: *If a man commits adultery with another man's wife—with the wife of his neighbor—both the adulterer and the adulteress must be put to death.*" She faced the audience again. "But, of course, I'm sure nobody in this room has *ever* committed adultery."

This time there was a loud rustling of bodies in chairs, but no outward sentiments of support.

"I think it's important that we start taking responsibility for our own lives. I suspect that there are women in this room who don't even want to ask their man to wear a condom, much less get tested. But it's your body, therefore, it's *your* job to protect it." Nichelle gripped both sides of the podium. "And you're mistaken if you believe you're going to protect yourself from HIV simply by outing gay men. You're completely ignoring the fact that women who've been infected are also spreading the disease to men . . . straight men."

The warm eyes that had welcomed her were now full of contempt.

"I think this group's efforts would be better spent teaching women to protect themselves. We should all get tested and demand that anybody we sleep with be tested, as well.

"More than anything else," Nichelle continued, her confidence level suddenly heightened, "I fear for our daughters, our granddaughters and our nieces. They're growing up in a climate of sexual promiscuity.

Many of them don't even view oral sex as sex. We need to talk openly to them about the danger of HIV and teach them to honor their bodies. And if they're not going to abstain from sex, at least encourage them to use a condom."

One woman frowned as if she had just uttered a dirty word.

"There's a lot of pain in this room. I'm in pain." Nichelle felt her eyes get misty. "I lost one of my best friends. Maya Washington was an incredible woman who had a lot to give this world and I miss her like I've never missed anybody in my life." She could almost feel Maya place an encouraging hand on her shoulder.

"But in addition to the pain, there's also a lot of hatred. Hatred that is coming from people who profess to know God, to love Him and to follow His Word. I don't think hate is consistent with God's message, and I don't think it's the answer to solving this crisis. In fact, I think this kind of hate created it."

Now the murmuring was back. Nobody could shoot a mean look like an irate black woman. Nichelle wondered if she would need a security guard to escort her to her car.

"You're a hypocrite!" someone called out. "You're the one who sued Eugene Nelson. Why didn't you just love and forgive him for killing your friend?"

"You know," Nichelle said, "at the time, I thought suing Eugene *was* the right thing to do. But I don't anymore."

"So we're just supposed to accept this abomination?" Rhonda asked, her tone just as threatening as her body language.

"I don't have all the answers," Nichelle said. "I just know all this hate isn't one of them."

# CHAPTER 97

Vernetta pushed a half-eaten bran muffin to the corner of her desk. As much as she tried, she could not shake the thoughts running through her head. *Could Special actually have killed Eugene?* She refused to even consider the possibility that her best friend had murdered the other men.

It was time for Vernetta to start thinking like a lawyer, not a friend. She had to weigh the evidence as if Special were a paying client, not her friend.

She reached for a legal pad, then drew a line down the middle of the page. She was about to prepare a list of the evidence for and against Special when the telephone rang.

Vernetta checked the caller ID display. She did not recognize the number. Having an assistant who had time to screen her calls was one of the big-firm luxuries she missed most.

The voice on the other end of the line was only vaguely familiar.

"I'm calling from Vista Electronics," the caller said. "We met a few weeks ago. I'm Sheryl Milton, the HR Director."

Vernetta quickly remembered the woman who had escorted them to the conference room. She was surprised that Milton had tracked her down at her new firm and wondered why she was calling.

"How can I help you?"

"We've extended a job offer to your colleague, Haley Prescott. I wanted to ask you a few questions about her."

Vernetta felt her skin prickle. Could Haley really have been arrogant enough to think Vernetta would give her a glowing recommendation? "Haley listed me as a reference?"

"No," Sheryl said. "But I know the two of you worked together. No one ever lists references who might say anything bad about them. I always do a little extra digging. The HR and legal groups here work hand in hand. I wanted to double check to make sure Haley's the right personality fit for our team. So may I ask you a few questions?"

Vernetta would have loved to screw over Haley, knowing Haley wouldn't have passed up the same opportunity. But she couldn't bring herself to do it. "I'm not sure I'm the best person for this. We didn't work on that many cases together."

"Let me be frank," Sheryl said, "I sensed some tension between the two of you during your visit here. I just want to make sure we're bringing on a real team player."

*Then you definitely don't need to hire Haley.* "I thought you already made Haley an offer?"

"Yes, but it's contingent upon passing a background check, a drug test, and a reference check."

Vernetta inhaled. "Haley's really bright. Even though she's pretty junior, she's a real go-getter."

"Most people who graduate from the top of their class at Yale Law School tend to be smart. That's not what I'm asking you. How is she in terms of working with others? We don't need another egomaniac lawyer around here. I need you to level with me."

Vernetta knew that if she told the truth, Haley wouldn't get the job. As she was weighing her options, Sheryl read between the lines.

"I guess your silence tells me everything I need to know."

"Haley's a good attorney," Vernetta said finally, "but if you're looking for a team player, that might be a bit of a stretch for her. She likes being the shining star. Haley's young. So she may learn to be more of a collaborator in time, but that's a skill she hasn't picked up yet."

Sheryl asked a few more questions, then hung up. Vernetta was trying to convince herself that she had nothing to feel guilty about when the telephone rang again. This time it was O'Reilly.

"Hey, kiddo. I just wanted to give you advance warning that you might be getting a call from someone at Vista Electronics asking about Haley. Put in a good word for her, okay?"

Vernetta quietly sighed. "I just got off the phone with the HR Director."

O'Reilly let a long beat pass. "And you said glowing things about her . . . right?"

"I told them she was very bright."

"And what else did you say?"

"I told the truth, O'Reilly."

He grunted. "And exactly what was the truth?"

"That Haley isn't much of a team player."

"Was that really necessary?"

"It was necessary for me to give my honest opinion."

She could feel O'Reilly's fury through the telephone line.

"You seem awfully invested in Haley getting that job," Vernetta said boldly.

"Having a person on the inside would mean more work for the firm."

"Is that all?"

"Exactly what are you getting at?"

Vernetta was tired of holding her tongue. "I'm sure you've heard all the rumors. I heard Haley was asked to leave the firm because she was involved in a personal relationship with you."

"Since when do you put stock in the law firm rumor mill?"

*Since I saw Haley coming out of your office with her hair mussed and her lipstick smeared and since you kept me occupied so she could sneak out of that restaurant.* "Are they true?"

"I'm not going to waste my time confirming or denying ridiculous law firm gossip."

"Well, I'm sure if Haley doesn't get the job, she'll still land on her feet. You'll probably see to that."

"Actually," O'Reilly said, "you can bet on it."

# CHAPTER 98

The next day, Nichelle invited Vernetta and J.C. to lunch at T.G.I. Friday's.

"It feels strange not having Special here," J.C. said. "Maybe we should order a Long Island iced tea and set it on her side of the table." They all smiled.

Vernetta told them about her conversation with O'Reilly.

"Sounds to me like he was definitely screwing her," Nichelle said.

"There's no way the firm would have asked her to leave if he hadn't been," Vernetta replied.

J.C. opened her menu. "Powerful men feel they can do whatever they please. And basically they can."

A waitress brought their drinks and took their orders.

"Well, I might as well get started," Nichelle said. "I had a specific reason for asking you guys to join me for lunch." She looked over her shoulder to confirm that the booth behind them was empty. "I'm worried about Special's case. Particularly that camera. I'm scared to death that they're going to be able to restore that picture Special took at Eugene's place."

"You should be," J.C. said, "but there's nothing we can do about it now."

"Do you know whether the camera has already gone out for testing?" Nichelle asked.

"Not yet. Contrary to what you see on *CSI*, it could take weeks or months to get something like that done."

"That's what I figured. If it hasn't been done yet, I think there's something we *can* do to help Special. But it's going to fall on you, J.C."

Vernetta eyed Nichelle. Whatever she was about to suggest, she had neglected to share with her. "Nichelle, what are you talking about?"

"I'm talking about doing everything in our power to make sure Special doesn't end up in jail for the rest of her life."

Vernetta grew nervous. "Everything like what?"

Nichelle glanced over her shoulder again. "Like switching the camera the police have with another one just like it," she whispered.

"Nichelle!" both Vernetta and J.C. sputtered at the same time.

Vernetta turned sideways to face her. "I can't believe what you just said. You of all people."

"Don't give me that," Nichelle shot back. "I get tired of people always acting like I'm Miss Goody Two Shoes. We all know the system isn't fair. There's no way Special should be facing a murder charge, but she is. And it's up to us to do whatever we have to do to make sure she isn't convicted of murder when all she's really guilty of is harassment."

"Do you understand what you're asking J.C. to do?" Vernetta said. "You're not just asking her to put her job on the line, you're asking her to commit a crime and risk going to jail herself. We shouldn't even be discussing this. So let's just change the subject."

"It won't be a crime if she doesn't get caught. And she won't."

"How can you say that?" J.C. demanded. "Even if I could make a switch, where in the hell would I get another camera like that."

Nichelle looked at both of them, then opened her purse, and pulled out a small rectangular object wrapped in a brown paper bag. She pushed it over to J.C.'s side of the table.

"The camera inside that bag is the same model as Special's. I bought both of them on the same day. I gave one to Special last year for her birthday, and kept the other one for myself. They're exactly alike."

J.C. glanced at the bag, then at Nichelle. "There's no way I or anybody else could get away with something like that. First, I've been taken off the case. And second, they would know the cameras had been switched because they don't have the same serial numbers. They usually record them when they log evidence into the property room."

"*Usually* is right. Half the time the guys who run the property rooms are so lazy, they don't even bother to take down the serial numbers. I've had cases where they couldn't even find the evidence once they *had* logged it in."

Vernetta couldn't believe that Nichelle was actually serious.

"You know why criminals get caught?" J.C. said. "Because they don't cover every angle. Have you thought about the fact that Special's prints won't be on your camera?"

"Her prints *are* on my camera," Nichelle said. "So are yours and Vernetta's and Maya's, because you all took pictures with it at one

time or another. Special borrowed it whenever she couldn't find hers. I
would bet more of her prints are on it than mine. And there are pictures
of all of us stored on this camera. So no one would question that it's
Special's."

Nichelle groaned. "Stop looking at me like that. Desperate times
call for desperate measures."

"You're a former prosecutor," Vernetta said. "I can't believe you
would even suggest such a thing."

"That's exactly why I am suggesting it. I saw far too many poor
people being convicted while people with money walked. Everybody
thinks I left the City Attorney's office because I got tired of prosecuting
cases. What I got tired of was all the unfair treatment of black and
brown people. We'd have to send some black crack addict to jail for
being caught with three rocks, while the white guy on the west side
who got picked up with three times as much powder cocaine, never did
a day behind bars. It's not fair. And you know it isn't, J.C. You see so-
called justice from a different angle than we do."

Neither woman could dispute what Nichelle had just said.

"What I'm asking you to do may be illegal, but it's not wrong."

J.C. slowly swung her head from side to side. "The reason Special
is in trouble is because she took the law into her own hands and started
harassing Eugene rather than waiting for the legal system to deal with
him. Now you're proposing that we—no, that *I*—do the same thing.
You're the one always talking about putting things in God's hands.
Where's your faith?"

"It's still there. But sometimes you have to rely on a little more than
faith."

Vernetta thought about Special's gun. She had initially told Jefferson
she needed time to think about his proposal, but ultimately decided to
put it back where she found it. Since the police had already searched
Special's place, it was unlikely that they would discover it. She had
not mentioned the gun to Nichelle and now she was glad she hadn't.
Nichelle would have urged her to let Jefferson get rid of it.

"Nichelle, this is wrong," Vernetta said. "You can't ask J.C. to put
her career on the line like this."

"At least think about it," Nichelle replied calmly. "If you don't think
you can get away with it, fine." She ignored the stunned expressions on

their faces. "But there's no doubt in my mind that if Maya were sitting at this table and one of us were in the same trouble Special is in, she'd agree with me one hundred percent."

Nichelle circled the rim of her glass with her index finger. "So, if you can't do this for Special," she said, staring at J.C. with a defiance Vernetta had never seen before, "then do it for Maya."

# CHAPTER 99

Vernetta sat in the client meeting room of the county jail, waiting for Special to be brought in.

Jefferson had warned her not to tell Special about the discovery of the gun, but after Nichelle's outrageous proposal earlier that day, she had decided that it was best to confront her.

Special sat down across from Vernetta and waited for the guard to close the door before speaking. "What's the matter?" she asked. "You look worse than me, and I'm the one about to go down for a murder I didn't commit."

Vernetta tried to laugh. It was so unnerving to see her friend all chained up in the faded orange jumpsuit.

"You're scaring me. Please don't say you're here to tell me I'm going to be convicted!"

"I have something important I need to ask you."

"Okay," she said uneasily. "Go ahead."

"Why didn't you tell me you owned a gun?"

Special opened her mouth, then slowly closed it. "I . . . I didn't want you to know."

"Where'd you get it?" Vernetta asked, then raised her hand. "Never mind. I don't want to know."

"I got it from my cousin," she said. "And I know what you're thinking, but I swear I didn't kill Eugene."

Vernetta stared solemnly across the table, uncertain of what to believe. "Did you throw those nails in his driveway?"

Special looked down at the table. "Yeah."

"And what about bashing in his car and vandalizing his house?"

She looked up. "Nope . . . but I had it done."

"How?"

"How?" Special laughed softly. "Girl, puh-leeze. Do you know how many crazy, ghetto-ass people I have in my family? It didn't cost me but fifty bucks."

When Vernetta didn't laugh, Special turned serious.

"But that stuff and the email was all I did. I did *not* shoot Eugene. Or anybody else."

"When did you buy the gun?"

"A few days before Maya died. The day the doctor told us she probably wouldn't survive another week." She looked down at the table again. "I'll admit that when I bought the gun killing Eugene was exactly what I wanted to do. But I couldn't. So I decided to start harassing him instead."

"Eugene was killed with a small-caliber gun. Probably a twenty-two. So were all those other men. Your gun is a twenty-two."

"That's just a coincidence."

"So if I hand that gun over to the police and they conduct ballistics testing on it, it won't match?"

"It absolutely won't match. Not unless somebody stole it from my apartment then put it back."

"Are you saying that's what happened?"

"No. I'm saying that as far as I know, that gun didn't kill Eugene or anybody else. I'll swear to that on a stack of Bibles."

Vernetta desperately wanted to believe her friend. "Jefferson asked me to let him get rid of it."

Special chuckled again. "What did you say?"

"I told him I needed time to think about it."

"Well, at least there's one good thing that's come out of all this."

"And what's that?"

"At least I know you really got my back." Special started to tear up. "I'm shocked that you, Ms. Law and Order, would even consider doing something illegal like getting rid of a gun." Her chains rattled when she wiped her eyes with the back of her hand. "That's nothin' but love."

This time Vernetta smiled.

Special looked over her shoulder to make sure the guard wasn't watching, then reached across the table and squeezed Vernetta's hand. She remained silent until Vernetta's eyes met hers.

"I swear on Maya's grave," Special said, "I did not shoot Eugene. So, please, don't let them convict me."

# CHAPTER 100

J.C. tossed and turned for most of the night. She finally climbed out of bed at four, showered and arrived at the station an hour before the start of her shift.

Nichelle's request continued to weigh on her even though she knew switching the cameras was something she could never do. So why was she still wrestling with the thought?

It was her job to enforce the law, not break it. Being an upstanding, by-the-book cop wasn't easy when others chose to abandon right and wrong anytime it suited them. Lieutenant Wilson's refusal to notify the public that a serial killer was gunning down gay black men was a prime example of that. But two wrongs did not make a right.

Other than Special, no serious suspects had surfaced. They were still waiting for the analysis of Lamont's mail to confirm whether his prints matched the ones found on the wineglass and kitchen window at Eugene's house. Though Detective Jessup was convinced that Lamont could be their guy, J.C. thought his partner, Ken, might have more of a motive. The police were keeping both men under surveillance.

Despite rejecting Nichelle's request, J.C. had confiscated the camera, concerned that Nichelle might try to find another way to make the switch. Right now, it was locked in J.C.'s desk drawer.

Later that afternoon, a thought came to her. She wondered if she actually *could* make the switch without getting caught. She wouldn't even have to switch the cameras, just the disks. Not that she *would* do it. She was just curious to see whether she *could*.

J.C. waited until the end of the day, ten minutes before the shift change when she knew the regular property desk guy, Nick O'Connell, would be anxious to leave.

"Hey, Nick," she said, stepping up to the counter. "I need to take a look at the evidence log in the Nelson murder case. Here's the case number."

Nick did exactly what she had expected him to do. Check his watch. "I was just about to leave. Marty'll be on duty in a few minutes."

"C'mon, you have another ten minutes before quitting time. I won't be long. I promise."

He grudgingly reached under the counter and handed J.C. the log. She ran her finger down the list of items, searching for the camera. *What a surprise.* No one had bothered to record the serial number.

J.C. handed the logbook back to him. "Just one more thing. I need to go in the back and take a look at some of the evidence. I only need a couple of minutes."

Nick frowned. "I told you Marty'll—"

"C'mon, Nick. I have to get out of here, too," J.C. begged. "Tell you what? I'll go get it myself."

It was against procedure for J.C. to retrieve an evidence bag herself, or to even go in the property room without an escort. But all Nick cared about was going home on time. He spread his arms out. "Go for it."

He hit a buzzer and opened a metal gate that gave J.C. access to the area behind the counter. J.C. had to hurry before Marty showed up. He never would've allowed this.

*What the hell am I doing?* She passed shelf after shelf of items bagged in plastic and marked with red tags. *I'm not going to switch the disks. I just want to see if I could.*

J.C. could hear the pounding of her heart as her eyes quickly scanned the case numbers on the shelves. She found the bag she was looking for and tugged it loose. She set it on a nearby counter, pulled out the camera and removed the disk. J.C. then slipped her hand into her pocket and retrieved the disk she had taken from Nichelle's camera and held them side by side. They were identical.

J.C. stood there for a long tense moment. As much as she wanted to do this, she couldn't. She was about to slip the disk back into Special's camera when someone shouted from the front.

"Hey, what are you doing back there?" Marty was marching straight toward her.

Just as she picked up the bag, a slip of paper floated away. She grabbed it from the floor and shoved it back into the bag, then jammed the disk back into the camera. She had already put the evidence bag back on the shelf when she realized she had put the wrong disk inside the camera. *Or had she?*

"You're not supposed to be back here by yourself," Marty admonished her.

"I just needed to check out some evidence." J.C. slipped the remaining disk into her pocket. "You know how Nick is around quitting time." She stepped around him and headed for the ladies' room.

Locking herself in the last stall, J.C. pulled the tiny disk from her pocket. She'd been so nervous she had no idea whether it was Nichelle's disk or Special's she was now holding. She pressed her forehead against the stall door. *How stupid!*

Deep inside, she had actually *wanted* to switch the disks, even though doing so was against everything she professed to stand for.

J.C. knew what she had to do. She would go get Nichelle's camera and check the disk. If it were blank, she would know that it came from Special's camera. And if she had indeed switched them, she would just have to figure out a way to switch them back.

# CHAPTER 101

When Vernetta learned about Special's jailhouse visitor, she began to wonder why Belynda was suddenly curious about that photograph Special took. So, with Nichelle in tow, she decided to attend Sunday services at Ever Faithful in the hope of talking to the woman.

On the ride over, Vernetta suggested the possibility that the man Special saw kissing Eugene was someone from Ever Faithful, perhaps a member of the church leadership. Nichelle, however, refused to consider the possibility that a minister from her esteemed church was on the down low.

"Think about it," Vernetta reasoned, "Belynda tried to show Special a picture of someone in the church bulletin. You just said the only pictures in the bulletin are of Bishop Berry and the three assistant pastors. That means she obviously thinks Eugene was seeing one of the ministers."

Nichelle wasn't hearing it. "I don't care. It's not possible."

"I hope you're right, but this is an angle we have to investigate."

Even though they arrived twenty minutes before the start of the service, the church parking lot was already full. They ended up parking a block away. When they finally made it inside the church, the only available seats were near the back.

Nichelle scanned the pulpit, then opened her program. "It looks like Reverend Sims is preaching today."

Vernetta looked around for Belynda, but didn't see her.

"Welcome to the Ever Faithful family," Reverend Sims said after a selection from the choir. "Our esteemed leader Bishop Berry has been in Houston all week at the National Baptist Convention. So you have to contend with the B team today."

The congregation laughed good-naturedly.

Following the church announcements, the offering, altar prayer, and two more selections from the choir, Reverend Sims took to the pulpit.

"Today, brothers and sisters, I want to talk about forgiveness. The Bible teaches us to be kind, tenderhearted, and forgiving toward one another. Just as God has forgiven us. But that's hard for many people to do." His voice rose and fell in a melodic rhythm as the animated congregation shouted, *preach, Reverend* and *amen, Reverend*.

"If you've been reading the newspapers or watching the news these past few weeks, then you know that there's a lot of wickedness going on out here in this crazy world we live in. People don't even think twice about taking a life. We even lost one of our own flock, Eugene Nelson. Before his death, Mr. Nelson was the subject of a pretty nasty lawsuit. And I've heard some hateful things said about Mr. Nelson." He stopped to wipe his face with a handkerchief. "Well, let me tell you that the God I worship loves all of his children."

There were no calls of *amen* or *preach, Reverend* in response to this comment. Vernetta saw disapproval on the faces of many people in the audience. Young and old.

"The ugly things I've been hearing about our gay brothers and sisters as of late truly trouble me because I don't think it's God's way."

Reverend Sims continued on the topic of tolerance and forgiveness for the next fifteen minutes. As he reached the end of his sermon, emotion seemed to overwhelm him.

"I, myself, am a man of God who is in no way perfect," he said, his voice quivering. "I pray every day for God's guidance because sometimes I fall short. But one thing I know for sure is that the good Lord will always be there to pick me back up and dust me off." His face was wracked with pain. "And I tell you today, church, that I'm a living testimony. No matter what you're going through, there's nothing that God's grace can't fix."

As the pianist played, he wiped his face again and nearly collapsed into a throne-like chair behind the podium.

Nichelle nudged Vernetta with her elbow and pointed across the aisle. Belynda was heading out of a side door.

"Let's try to talk to her," Nichelle whispered.

By the time they made it out to the vestibule, Belynda was nowhere in sight. They searched the hallways, but no luck.

Nichelle peered into an open doorway. "Maybe she went to the restroom."

They stepped inside the ladies' room and found Belynda standing at the mirror combing her hair.

"Hello," Vernetta began, hoping Belynda didn't recognize her from any of the news reports.

Her scornful look told Vernetta that was wishful thinking.

"I don't have anything to say to either of you," Belynda spat, before Vernetta could even get her spiel out.

Vernetta positioned herself near the door, hoping to block the exit in case Belynda tried to leave. "I'm sure you don't want to see the wrong person convicted. Special told us about your visit to the jail. I'd like to know why you think Eugene was seeing someone from this church."

"I never said that."

"But you tried to show her a picture of someone in the church bulletin. The only pictures in there are of the ministers at this church. You must think Eugene was involved with one of them."

"That's ridiculous." Belynda tried to push past her, but Vernetta stepped in front of the door. "I don't have to talk to you. Now please move."

"Don't you want to see the real killer caught?"

"The real killer's already been caught."

"Who are you protecting?" Nichelle interjected.

"I'm not protecting anyone. Now get out of my way." Belynda was stronger than she looked. She bowled past Vernetta and jerked the door open. It would have slammed into Vernetta's back if she hadn't jumped out of the way in time.

The two lawyers left before the service ended and headed to brunch at Dulan's on Crenshaw.

"What do you know about the ministers at Ever Faithful?" Vernetta rolled to a stop at a traffic light at Stocker.

"Not that much," Nichelle replied. "There's Bishop Berry, Reverend Sims, and two part-time ministers, Reverend Charles and Reverend Hooks. All of them are married. Bishop Berry is an institution in L.A. He's been at Ever Faithful for nearly thirty years. Reverend Sims is the newest minister. They ran a profile on him in the church bulletin a few months ago. Before his appointment six months ago, he was an assistant pastor at a church in Carson. His wife is a nurse and I think he has two children. I don't know much about the other two."

"Why in the world would Belynda want to protect a minister she thought might be gay?" Vernetta wondered aloud.

"Don't ask me. I still can't understand why she started seeing Eugene."

"Well, she obviously doesn't know for sure if one of the ministers was the man Special saw with Eugene. Otherwise, she wouldn't have needed Special to identify him."

Nichelle gazed out of the passenger window. "If somebody in that pulpit does turn out to be gay, I just hope it's one of the assistant pastors." There was an unmistakable note of dread in her voice. "Because if sixty-one-year-old Bishop Berry is on the down low, I'm too through."

# CHAPTER 102

J.C.'s cell phone rang and she pulled it from her pocket. She answered it despite the anxiety she felt at seeing Nichelle's number in the display panel.

"I don't want to make a habit of asking you to do illegal stuff," Nichelle said, "but you're our last hope."

J.C. grimaced. What in the world did Nichelle want her to do now? Nichelle had not mentioned switching the camera again and J.C. hoped she wasn't about to bring it up now. Her stomach had been tied up in knots since confirming that she had indeed switched the disks. The next day, she had dropped by the property room, planning to switch them back, but this time Nick insisted on playing it by the book. He escorted her into the back and watched as she examined the evidence bag. There was no way she could make the switch under those conditions.

"I'm listening," J.C. said into the telephone.

"I know you're off the case, but I was hoping you might be able to interview Belynda Davis. We tried to talk to her yesterday at church, but didn't have any luck. The man Special caught on camera with Eugene may have been one of the ministers at Ever Faithful. We think Belynda may know which one."

"Are you kidding?"

Nichelle told her about Belynda's visit to the jail.

"Please tell me Special didn't talk to that woman."

"Thank God, no. She even refused to look at the picture Belynda tried to show her. So we don't know which minister Belynda suspects was with Eugene."

J.C. was curious about Belynda's visit. The odds of the lieutenant finding out about her interview would be slim. "For whatever it's worth, I'll give it a try."

Later that afternoon, J.C. knocked on Belynda's front door and flashed her badge. "Good afternoon. I'm sorry to disturb you. I'm a detective with the LAPD. I was one of the investigators looking into Eugene Nelson's murder."

"I remember you." Belynda gave her a warm smile. "You were at the courthouse the day that psychotic woman attacked Eugene. Thank God you were there to take her away. Come on in."

Belynda's home was a shrine to her faith. Religious symbols lined the hallway and were positioned all around the living room. There were crosses on the walls next to portraits of Jesus and his disciples. Two huge leather-bound Bibles sat on matching coffee tables. J.C. also counted at least a dozen framed photographs of an older woman who resembled Belynda.

"Your mother?" J.C. asked.

"Yes," Belynda said with a longing in her voice. "She died three years ago. I still miss her so much."

J.C. continued taking in the room. The view through an oval picture window extended for miles. The house had to be a good three thousand square feet. "You have a very nice place."

J.C. wondered how Belynda could afford a house like this on a meager church salary.

Belynda seemed to read her mind. "This was my mother's home," she explained. "Why don't you join me in the kitchen?" Belynda led the way.

"I was in the middle of cooking for a meeting at the church tonight," she said proudly. "You mind if we talk while I cook?"

"No, go right ahead." J.C. took a seat at the breakfast nook. She watched as Belynda combined milk and eggs in a large bowl.

"You told reporters and the police that Special Moore tried to show you a picture of Eugene Nelson kissing another man."

Belynda nodded. "That is one troubled woman. I pray for her every night."

"I know you've talked to the police already, but I need you to go over it one more time with me."

Belynda dipped a chicken breast into the egg-and-milk mixture, coated it with flour, then dropped it into a deep fryer filled with hot cooking oil. J.C. waited as Belynda filled the fryer with chicken. She rinsed her hands in the sink and joined J.C. at the table.

"I was walking my dog and she came out of nowhere. The woman scared me to death. This wasn't the first time she had ambushed me like that. Several weeks ago she showed up on my doorstep ranting and raving, telling me I had no business seeing Eugene. Like I said, she is a very disturbed woman."

Belynda went on to describe in greater detail both of Special's visits.

"So you never actually saw the picture Ms. Moore claimed to have of Eugene and another man."

"No. When she tried to show it to me, I refused to look."

"I understand that you visited Ms. Moore at the jail a couple of days ago."

Belynda seemed surprised that J.C. was aware of her visit. "Well, yes. I began to wonder about who was in that picture with Eugene. If she even had a picture, that is."

"Why?"

She hunched her shoulders. "I don't know. I know that woman is ill. It was a waste of my time to even go down there."

"I understand that you tried to show Ms. Moore a picture of someone in one of Ever Faithful's church bulletins. Did you think one of the church's ministers was seeing Eugene?"

"That's absurd." She looked away. "I'm not about to damage anyone's reputation unnecessarily. I have a responsibility to the church. I mean—" she abruptly stopped.

*Responsibility to the church?* "It's very possible that the man in that picture may have been the last person to see Eugene alive."

"That psycho Special Moore was the last person to see Eugene alive. When she killed him."

"That hasn't been proven in a court of law yet."

"Don't worry," she said smugly. "I've prayed about it. So it will be."

# CHAPTER 103

J.C. left Belynda's house and raced to the station to begin delving into the background of the four ministers at Ever Faithful. Based on Belynda's slip of the tongue about having *a responsibility to the church*, J.C. was certain that the woman was protecting one of her beloved pastors.

Whatever J.C. found, she knew she would have to pass on to Detective Jessup. That meant he would get credit for solving the case. That didn't please her, but if it meant Special's freedom, she could live with it.

She had just printed out three articles about Bishop Berry from the Internet when Detective Jessup sat down on the corner of her desk. "Lieutenant Wilson wants to see you," he said. "And he's pretty irate."

*So what else is new?* "What's wrong now?"

"I don't know and frankly, I don't want to know. I don't think I've *ever* seen him this hot before."

Apprehensively, J.C. made her way to the lieutenant's office.

She slowed as she reached the door, then ventured inside. "You wanted to see me?"

"Close the door," he said sternly.

She did, then sat down without waiting for an invitation to do so.

"I consider myself pretty much a law-and-order, by-the-book kind of guy, wouldn't you agree, Detective?"

"I would." *Except where gay men are concerned.*

"So it disturbs me when someone under my command does something really stupid."

J.C.'s jaw tensed, but she didn't say a word. *The disk!* He had found out that she had switched the disks. *But how?* Her mind frantically searched for a valid defense to the accusation that was about to be leveled at her.

"I just got off the phone with a hysterical woman who claims that you showed up at her house and tried to intimidate her into saying that one of the ministers at the most respected black church in this city is a fa—" He cracked his knuckles. "Excuse me. A homosexual."

The tension that had tightened every muscle in J.C.'s body slowly eased away. "I didn't try to intimidate her. And I had a very good reason for questioning Belynda Davis about the ministers at Ever Faithful." She was about to explain but the lieutenant cut her off.

"If I recall correctly, I told you that you were off the case, didn't I, Detective?"

She nodded, but hoped that the end justified the means. She proceeded to tell him about Belynda's visit to the jail and her slip about protecting someone at the church.

"Son of a bitch!" His face contorted. "I don't believe this shit. You tellin' me one of the ministers at Ever Faithful is a sissy?"

She started to correct him, but let it go. "It could be, Lieutenant."

"Son of a bitch!" He reached for a Snickers from his candy dish. "The fact that you had a good reason for talking to that woman doesn't get you off the hook," he admonished. "You should've given that information to Jessup to follow up on. It wouldn't look good if the press knew that an LAPD detective was investigating a case in which one of her friends was the chief suspect. That could cost both of us our jobs."

J.C. nodded again.

"But I have another problem with you, Detective." His eyes hardened. "A much, much bigger one."

J.C. swallowed, not knowing what was coming next.

"I understand you made a visit to the property room a few days ago."

J.C. tried not to move. Cops were trained to pick up visual cues from suspects. She didn't want to give off any.

"Yeah," J.C. said slowly. Most guilty people talked too much. She wasn't about to do that.

"Did you happen to remove any evidence pertaining to the Nelson case?"

J.C. knew she'd been caught. *But how could he know?* Her only impulse at the moment was to deny, just like a common criminal. "What are you talking about, Lieutenant?"

"You were very, very sloppy, Detective. Even though that lazy fuck, Nick, let you in the property room unescorted, you weren't quite as slick as you thought you were. You forgot to do a visual check before you switched those disks. The one that was originally in the camera we confiscated from your buddy's apartment had a tiny nick on the side. The disk you replaced it with was in mint condition."

J.C. didn't bother to stop her hands from fidgeting, nor did she try to offer up another denial. She was about to lose her job. Her life.

"If I were a different kind of guy, I'd have Internal Affairs in here right now. But you're a good cop. Too good to have done such a stupid thing."

J.C. just wanted him to lower the boom. She had been stupid. She wondered if she could convince him to let her quietly resign.

"I examined that camera and the disk last week before a meeting I had with the captain. And I distinctly remember that nick. When I asked who'd checked out the evidence bag since then, lo and behold, it was you."

J.C. flexed her fingers. She just wanted him to get it over with.

"I would've expected something like this from Jessup, not you." Lieutenant Wilson didn't speak for a long time. His way of extending the punishment. "Here's what we're going to do. You're going to give me the other disk and I'm going to switch them back. I should be telling you to clean out your desk, but I'm going to do you a big favor. I'm going to let you keep your job."

J.C. exhaled audibly. "Thank you, Lieutenant. I really appreciate—"

"I don't want to hear it. All I want from you is a promise that you won't risk your career by doing any more stupid shit. You're not the first cop to do something foolish to save somebody you care about and you're not the first one to get caught. But don't let it happen again. And by the way, they won't be able to restore the pictures. It has something to do with the type of disk. So you risked your career for nothing."

J.C. felt incredibly grateful that she still had her job. But she felt equally distraught about the possibility that Special could be convicted of a crime she didn't commit. She couldn't leave it up to Jessup to find the real killer. *She* had to do it.

"Uh . . . I know I have some nerve asking this," she began, "but I think I'm close to breaking the case. Could I have just a couple of days to investigate this lead? I promise I'll pass on everything I find to Jessup."

The lieutenant gave her a flabbergasted look. "You're lucky you—"

"Lieutenant, my friend's about to be railroaded for a murder she didn't commit. If I don't have a suspect for you in a week, then I'm done."

"A week? I thought you just said a couple of days? That's forty-eight hours where I come from."

"How about a week?"

He frowned. "Here's the best I can do, Detective. Officially, you're still off the case. Now if you continue to investigate unbeknownst to me, you're on your own. So if things blow up in your face, my story will be that you disregarded a direct order."

J.C. smiled. "Thanks, Lieutenant."

"But a week from today, it's over. After that, you're to have nothing to do with the investigation. Officially or unofficially."

She nodded.

"I hope you can dig up something to clear your buddy. But keep it legal, Detective." He cracked his knuckles. "Now get outta here."

"Thank you, Lieutenant," she said rising.

"You're welcome."

J.C. was almost at the door. "So, I guess we're even now, huh?" the lieutenant said.

"Even?" J.C. looked back at him.

"Yeah, even," he replied. "The rumors about all the vics being sissies is finally hitting the streets and a couple of gay leaders are calling for an investigation. They claim the Department knew weeks ago that a killer was targeting homosexual men, but intentionally failed to notify the public because we didn't care if a few homos got killed. But, of course, you and I know that's not true."

Now J.C. understood why the lieutenant was being so lenient with her.

"I don't want or need any heat over this crap. And as far as I know, I'm the only one in the Department you discussed your little theory with. Am I right?"

She nodded.

"Okay, then," the lieutenant said with a smirk. "Here's the deal. I'll keep your transgressions a secret as long as you do the same regarding mine."

# CHAPTER 104

Don't look now," Jefferson said, "but your home girl just walked in."

Vernetta and Jefferson were standing near the bar at the Chart House restaurant in Marina Del Rey waiting for a table.

Vernetta did not bother to look. She could tell by the sarcasm in Jefferson's voice that whoever he had just spotted was probably someone she didn't want to see.

She took a sip of her Diet Coke. "And exactly who is my home girl?"

A smile stretched across Jefferson's face. "Golden Girl. The one who's rocking O'Reilly's world."

Haley was the last person Vernetta wanted to see. She finally turned and looked over her shoulder. Haley was talking to the maître d', probably trying to get a table without waiting her turn like everybody else, Vernetta thought. Standing next to her was a scrawny woman about a foot shorter than Haley with frilly hair and a bland, square face. Anybody who looked at the pair wouldn't even see the woman. Haley's shiny blond hair was perfectly coiffed and she was dressed in a slinky red wrap dress that accentuated her small waist.

Haley turned away from the maître d's stand and her eyes met Vernetta's. The look Haley conveyed was pure spite.

Vernetta turned back to her husband.

"Dang. She definitely gave you a look to kill," Jefferson said. "What was that all about?"

Vernetta couldn't help but smile. "I guess O'Reilly must have spilled the beans."

"About what?"

"I got a call from a company that was planning to hire Haley. They asked me what I thought of her and I told the truth. Maybe she didn't get the job."

"Aw, man, that's cold. You actually dogged the girl out?"

"I didn't do anything but tell the truth."

A man sitting at the end of the bar got up and Vernetta took his seat while Jefferson remained standing, resting his forearm on the bar.

"Uh-oh," Jefferson teased. "I think there's about to be some fireworks up in here. Golden Girl is on her way over."

Before Vernetta could brace herself, Haley was standing in front of her, up close and personal. Way too close.

"Thanks a lot," Haley said, swiping a curl behind her ear. "I guess you feel pretty good about yourself now."

Jefferson's face filled with amusement.

Vernetta had to fight to keep the smile off of her own face. It felt great knowing that she was the reason Haley was so rattled. "First, you need to back up out of my personal space. And second, I have no idea what you're talking about."

When Haley didn't move, her homely friend glanced about the crowded bar area, as if to assure herself that no one was paying attention to the mounting confrontation.

"I didn't appreciate you lying about me to Vista Electronics. You were probably just mad that they weren't trying to recruit you. But that's fine. I'll get another job."

"I didn't lie about you, Haley. I told the truth." Vernetta set her glass on the bar. "So, you didn't get the job? I'm really sorry to hear that."

Haley looked as if she wanted to swing on her and Vernetta secretly hoped that she did. She would love to have a reason to slug the girl. With all these witnesses, it would be a slam dunk case of self-defense.

"Like I said, I'll get another job," Haley repeated. "Just remember, it's a small world. You better hope I'm never in a position to recommend *you*."

Vernetta laughed genuinely. "I certainly doubt that will ever happen. I'm surprised that you left the firm before your offer from Vista Electronics was firm. That wasn't too smart."

"I had to leave right away because my father was ill. Unlike you, who left because you realized they'd never make you a partner. If my father hadn't gotten ill, I definitely would've made it."

The comment stung, but Vernetta took it in stride. "You're right, Haley. You definitely would've made partner. Giving the managing partner blow jobs in the office made you a shoo-in."

Haley gasped while her friend looked as if she was about to swallow her tongue.

Jefferson raised his glass to his lips and winked at the bartender. Both of them were psyched up for a girl fight.

"Just be glad I'm mature enough to ignore the vicious rumors people were spreading about me. I wondered who started them. Well, now, I guess I know."

"Get real. I have far better things to do than sit around talking about you. If you didn't want people gossiping about you, you should've chosen a less public place to carry on your affair."

Haley's cheeks were now the same rosy red as her puckered lips.

"Why don't we get a drink?" Haley's plain-Jane friend put a hand on her arm and tried to pull her away. Haley shook free.

Vernetta was actually surprised at Haley's bravado. If Special had been here, she would have jumped in by now and the two of them would've been rolling around on the floor. As much fun as she was having seeing Haley so upset, it was time to end this before things got out of hand.

"I'm trying to enjoy an evening out with my husband. So if you don't mind . . ."

Almost thirty seconds passed as they silently squared off at each other.

"Just remember, what goes around, comes around." Haley stalked off.

"That's a bold little white girl," Jefferson chuckled as he watched her walk away. "You better be glad y'all didn't meet up in an alley. She mighta kicked your ass."

"Yeah, right."

"Your average white girl wouldn't have had the balls to do that to a sister." Jefferson finished the last drop of his drink. "Dang. A white girl with a sister's ass and a sister's attitude. Where'd she grow up?"

Now, Vernetta was ready to slug her husband, too. "That wasn't funny, Jefferson."

He laughed. "Wasn't meant to be. Don't get mad at me because Golden Girl jumped all in your stuff."

"Be quiet."

Jefferson slid his empty glass toward the bartender. "How about a refill? And this time, can you put enough alcohol in it for me to taste?" He turned back to Vernetta. "I was serious. Where's Haley from? Jersey? Philly? Detroit? She definitely grew up around some black folks."

Before Vernetta could tell him she didn't want to hear another word about the girl, the maître d' called Haley's name. As Haley marched over, she whipped around and hurled an exaggerated smirk Vernetta's way.

"That's bull! We were here before her." Vernetta hopped off the bar stool, but Jefferson grabbed her by the arm.

"Just let it go."

"No, we were—"

"Golden Girl obviously has the kind of juice that we don't. Anyway, I wanna finish my drink."

Vernetta folded her arms. "Fine, then," she said, annoyed that she let Haley get under her skin.

But the encounter had served one good purpose. Vernetta no longer felt a shred of guilt about telling Vista Electronics the truth about Haley. She was glad the girl didn't get the job.

Vernetta smiled. At least one thing Haley said tonight turned out to be right on the mark. What goes around, most definitely comes around.

# CHAPTER 105

J.C. was in such a hurry to get back to her desk, she side-swiped another officer in the hallway.

"Sorry," she called out without slowing down.

With only a week before she'd be kicked off the case, J.C. had no time to waste. Lamont and Ken were still on her radar, but she was now convinced that the killer could very well be a minister at Ever Faithful.

J.C. resumed her research on Bishop Berry. Every article she printed from the Internet described him as the epitome of integrity. She even made a few calls which further confirmed that fact. She found very few articles about Reverend Hooks and Reverend Charles, but when she got to Reverend Sims, she felt like an idiot. His ties to the victims were so clear that the connection should have been made weeks ago. How had she missed it?

After only a few hours of research, J.C. had linked Reverend Sims to four of the six murdered men. According to Belynda, Eugene was a member of Ever Faithful and Reverend Sims had counseled him on at least a couple of occasions. The reverend served as team minister to the Fox Hill Tigers, Nathan Allen's junior college team. On Allen's MySpace page she found a photograph of the running back in the locker room with several other players. In the background she spotted a smiling Reverend Sims. Prior to becoming a full-time minister, the good reverend worked as an engineer at Raycom, the same company where the first victim worked. And not only was Reverend Sims a friend and neighbor of James Hill, the investment banker, he was the last person to see him alive. Even the car Special followed the night she trailed Eugene back to his house matched the reverend's car.

J.C. knew that if she kept digging, she'd probably find that Reverend Sims had ties to the remaining two murdered men: Dr. Banks, the Inglewood doctor, and the latest victim, a successful real estate broker who was discovered in the park across from Special's apartment.

Sims' connections to the four victims could not be dismissed as mere coincidence. It didn't prove that the reverend had killed the men, but his ties to so many of them were the first bread crumbs on a trail that J.C. was sure would lead straight to him.

She just needed some hard evidence before she could take her suspicions to the lieutenant. He wouldn't make a move to arrest Reverend Sims without a rock solid case against him.

She decided to show the reverend's picture to Carole, the sister-in-law of Dr. Banks, and to the clerk at the Marina Marriott to see if they recognized him. *Was Reverend Sims sleeping with the men, then killing them?* If so, they were dealing with a dangerous psychopath.

She copied a picture of Reverend Sims from the Internet, then went to Records and found photographs of men with similar physical traits and created a photographic lineup. If the two women picked out Reverend Sims, that would be enough to have him brought in for questioning. She just hoped the lieutenant agreed.

J.C. had just returned to her desk and grabbed her purse when her cell phone signaled that she had a message.

"We may've finally caught a big break in the Nelson case," she heard Detective Jessup say. "We got a call on the tip line. A waiter at the Marie Callender's Grill in the Howard Hughes Promenade claims Eugene and another man had dinner together the evening before he was killed. I'm stuck in the Valley interviewing a witness in another case. Get over there and talk to the guy. And remember, I'm only letting you in on this because I'm a nice guy. If you come up with something, it's mine, not yours."

J.C. hung up. "Prick."

As she drove to the restaurant, she struggled to keep her emotions in check, which was not something she had to do very often. The information she was about to gather could very well spring Special from jail. Before leaving the station, she had added a picture of Lamont, which she found on his MySpace page, to the photographic lineup that she now planned to also show to the waiter. Despite all the evidence pointing to Reverend Sims, J.C. wasn't ready to dismiss Lamont and his lover Ken from the list of suspects just yet.

When she arrived at the restaurant, she had to wait twenty minutes until the waiter's break. They walked outside to a lighted area underneath a street lamp. He pulled out a pack of Newports and lit one up.

Dean Mills had bright blue eyes and short blond hair that was moussed up into a weird geometric scramble. His hands fluttered about as he spoke. J.C. was certain he had never been in the closet.

"Can you give me a physical description of the man Eugene had dinner with?" J.C. didn't want to lead him in any way. If the man was Reverend Sims, she wanted a completely unbiased ID.

"I won't have to testify in court or anything, will I?" Mills asked warily.

"I can't say right now." She was anxious to get to the facts. If she had to lie to the man, she would.

"There's obviously a serial killer on the loose," Mills said. "I know they have some woman behind bars, but if she's not the real killer, I don't want to say anything that might cause this nut to come looking for me."

"Don't worry." She gave him a comforting smile. "I don't think you're in any danger. The killer seems to be targeting African-American men. So can you describe the guy for me?"

Mills took a long drag on his cigarette. "African-American, bearded, closely cropped hair. About your complexion."

"What about height and weight?"

"Five-nine, five-ten. One-eighty, maybe a little more. Older guy. At least forty-five or fifty."

He had just described Reverend Sims to a tee.

J.C. scribbled down the description on her notepad. "Did you think the two men were . . ." J.C. wasn't sure how to put this ". . . more than friends?"

He raised an eyebrow. "You mean, were they together together?"

"Yes."

Mills smiled. "That Nelson fella was a real hottie. They were certainly more than friends, if you know what I mean."

"What gave you that impression? Were they being intimate?"

He put his free hand on his hip and leaned his body weight to one side. "This isn't San Francisco or West Hollywood, Detective. They just seemed like more than friends. They talked nonstop, then ordered dessert to take back to Nelson's place."

Mills provided a boatload of additional information. From what they ate, to the fact that the reverend was married, to their racquetball game earlier in the day. He even recalled that Eugene paid with a Platinum

American Express Card. J.C. planned to watch her conversation the next time a waiter was lurking nearby. This guy was as good as a tape recorder.

Certain that she had exhausted Mills' database, J.C. opened a manila folder, revealing the photo lineup.

She held it up for Mills to examine. "Do you see the man who had dinner with Eugene Nelson?"

Mills studied the photos for a long time. So long that J.C. began to get worried. He flicked the stub of his cigarette to the ground and smashed it with the toe of his right foot. "This is the guy right here." He pointed to Reverend Sims. "He's the one who had dinner with that cutie Eugene Nelson."

Thrilled, J.C. was about to close the folder when Mills stopped her. "Hold on," he said. "I also saw Eugene the following night with this guy." He tapped his index finger on the photograph of Lamont.

"What?" J.C. looked from the picture to Mills. "Are you sure? Where?"

He pointed south. "In the parking structure. When I was leaving to go home. Just before ten o'clock on Saturday night."

# CHAPTER 106

Their regular booth at T.G.I. Friday's was taken so Vernetta and Nichelle took one near the front. They kept their eyes focused on the entrance, waiting for J.C. to arrive.

Vernetta had called J.C. an hour earlier and asked her to meet them at the restaurant. Since interviewing Belynda, J.C. had basically avoided them, which led Vernetta to suspect that she had uncovered some information about Special's case. Vernetta just hoped they could convince her to share it with them. She also prayed that it wasn't news she didn't want to hear.

Vernetta had just returned from the restroom when J.C. slid into the booth next to Nichelle.

"What's so urgent?" J.C. asked.

"We wanted to know if there's anything you can tell us about your interview with Belynda," Vernetta said.

J.C. didn't say anything.

"Well?" Vernetta prodded.

"You guys know that I can't do that. I shouldn't even be sitting in this restaurant with you."

"C'mon, J.C.," Nichelle begged. "Can't you tell us anything?"

"No, I can't. I'm in enough trouble as it is."

"Trouble for what?" Vernetta asked.

J.C. started to speak, then stopped. "For talking to Belynda," she said hesitantly. "She called the lieutenant and claimed I was harassing her."

Nichelle rubbed her forehead. "I'm sorry for asking you to go over there. Thank God you ignored my crazy suggestion about switching those cameras."

J.C. toyed with her napkin.

"Can you at least tell us which minister Belynda thinks was in that picture with Eugene?" Vernetta asked.

"I never said Belynda mentioned any of the ministers. Anyway, you'll find out soon enough."

"So one of the ministers at Ever Faithful *is* on the down low!" Nichelle gasped. "Oh, my Lord!"

"Please keep it down." J.C. looked over her shoulder. "I never said that."

Nichelle lowered her voice but not her anxiety level. "Is it Bishop Berry? Please tell me it's not Bishop Berry!"

"I'm not saying another word about the case. So please don't ask."

Nichelle started waving her hand back and forth, fanning her face as if she were having hot flashes. "I don't know if I can handle this." She flagged down a waitress. "I want the potato skins, the Jack Daniels ribs, a cup—no make that a bowl—of broccoli cheese soup, and the strawberry lemonade slush."

Vernetta and J.C. exchanged cryptic looks.

"And don't say a word about my diet," Nichelle snapped. "My stomach needs some real food."

"Can you at least tell us whether you expect to arrest another suspect?" Vernetta asked.

J.C. reached for her water glass. "That's very possible. Now please, let's change the subject."

Nichelle wrung her hands. "This is going to be a disgrace to the church."

Minutes later, the waitress returned with Nichelle's soup. She kept shaking her head between slurps. "I just can't believe this."

"There's something else I've been wanting to talk to you guys about," J.C. said. "And I guess now is as good a time as any."

Nichelle took another spoonful of her soup. "By the look on your face, the news isn't good. I need a real drink." She called the waitress back and substituted her slush for a strawberry margarita.

"You both have become really good friends, and I just wanted you to know that I—"

"Are you okay?" Nichelle anxiously interrupted. "Please don't tell us you're sick or—"

"Nichelle, will you please calm down. I'm fine."

Vernetta could tell that the topic was something serious. "What's the matter, J.C?"

"I just wanted you guys to know that . . . that I'm gay."

Nichelle dropped her spoon, splashing broccoli cheese soup all over the table. "Well . . . that's . . . uh . . . that's nice."

Vernetta nudged Nichelle underneath the table. Since she didn't know what to say either, she opted for keeping her mouth shut.

"Well?" J.C. said. "Say something."

"I know it wasn't easy for you to tell us this," Vernetta said finally. "Thanks for confiding in us. And obviously, it doesn't matter one way or the other. At least not to me."

The waitress placed Nichelle's potato skins on the table and she grabbed one in both hands. "Me, neither."

"I don't condone what Eugene did," J.C. said. "But I understand why he couldn't be who he was. Coming out isn't easy."

"Well, I'm glad you felt comfortable enough to tell us," Vernetta said.

Nobody knew what to say. Vernetta picked up a potato skin and started munching so she wouldn't have to talk.

"So are you going to tell Special?" Nichelle asked.

"Yeah," J.C. said wearily. "But coming out to her won't be easy."

# CHAPTER 107

J.C. waited in a small interrogation room at the county jail. All the way over, she had debated whether now was the right time to have this conversation with Special. She finally decided to just get it over with.

She constantly checked the display window of her cell phone, hoping for a message. She was waiting for a call from Detective Jessup. Any minute now, they were expecting to hear whether Lamont's fingerprints matched the ones found on the wineglass and windowsill at Eugene's place. Now that they had a witness who could place Lamont *and* Reverend Sims with Eugene within hours of his murder that made them both prime suspects. The fact that Lamont had lied about being with Eugene meant that he had something to hide. *Was it murder*?

J.C. was beginning to suspect that there might be two killers at work. Maybe Eugene was killed by someone he knew, possibly Lamont or even Ken, while the other shootings were the work of a different killer. Reverend Sims' ties to nearly all of the murdered men couldn't be ignored. Maybe he was a religious fanatic who befriended gay men, then killed them. As soon as she was done talking to Special, she planned to discuss her theory with the lieutenant. She prayed he didn't dismiss it.

When the deputy ushered Special into the room, she looked even more frail than she had on J.C.'s last visit.

"How about taking the chains off her wrists?" J.C. said to the deputy.

"Can't. She's a high risk inmate and—"

J.C. flashed her badge. "She's a good friend. Take 'em off." She smiled. "Pretty please?"

The deputy grunted, then complied, unlocking the chains. "If she makes a break for it, it's on you, not me."

Once the deputy left, the two friends embraced and sat down on opposite sides of a small table.

"How are you doing?" J.C. asked.

"I'm okay. Jail isn't as bad as everybody makes it out to be. I've had a lot of time to meditate and read the Bible. The food sucks, but I haven't had to fight off any dykes."

J.C. was starting to have second thoughts about coming out to Special. "I have a lot of friends who promised me they'd look out for you."

"Thanks." She traced a scratch in the table with her index finger. "Got any good news for me? Did the police find the real killer yet?"

"You're not supposed to be talking to me about your case. I'm on the other side, remember? But we're working on it. I just dropped by to check on you."

"It's good to get out of my cell. You can keep me here for as long as you want. And next time, if you want to sneak in a Fat Burger, I'll love you for life."

They chatted for a while as J.C. gathered the courage to get to the real purpose of her visit. Except for Eugene and other men on the down low, J.C. had never heard Special express any animosity toward gays. Still, she wasn't certain of her true feelings.

"You know," Special said, "that counseling session I had with Reverend Sims was really helpful. Can you ask Nichelle to see if he can visit me?"

J.C. twitched and Special noticed. "What's the matter?"

"Nothing." J.C. had no plans to pass on Special's request, which she found quite ironic. Special had been counseled by the man who may be responsible for the murders everyone thought she had committed.

"I have some good news," Special said.

"What's that?"

"Clayton called Vernetta last night to see how I was doing." She smiled for the first time. "I called him collect this morning and we had a good talk. Thanks for getting me the extra phone privileges. He says he's going to write me."

"That's great." J.C. fingered a long scratch on the table. "I came down here because there's something I wanted to tell you."

"What is it? I don't know if I can handle any more bad news."

"It's not bad news. At least I hope you don't think it is. It's about me."

"You're scaring me, J.C. What's going on?"

J.C. didn't know how to begin, so she just blurted it out. "Special, I'm gay."

Special jerked backwards. "What? Since when?"

"Since forever."

Special stared at her in disbelief, then her eyes narrowed in alarm. "Uh . . . I hope you're not telling me this 'cause you wanna get with me. Because I like dudes."

J.C. laughed. "No, Special, I'm not hitting on you. I'm telling you because you're my friend and I wanted you to know."

Special relaxed, but couldn't stop staring at her. "I've heard that a lot of female cops are gay. Did you get turned out by another cop?"

J.C. tried to remember that Special had become one of her closest friends. "Special, I didn't get turned out. I've always been gay."

"Re-al-ly?" Special stretched the word into three syllables.

"Yes, really."

"Well, I don't have a problem with it if you don't. My cousin Thomas is gay and I'm cool with him. But how do you know for sure that you don't like men?"

J.C. chuckled softly. "Special, I'm sure."

"Have you been with guys before?"

"Yeah."

"And you didn't like it?"

"No, I didn't."

"Really?" Special said again. "So do you have a . . . uh . . . a girl-friend?"

"Not at the moment."

"You ever had one?"

J.C. shrugged. "Yeah."

"So how do y'all determine which one is the man in the relation-ship?"

"There is no man, Special."

"Really?" She propped up her elbow on the table and cupped her chin in her hand. "Is it true that when y'all have sex one of you straps on a—"

J.C. held up her hand. "I think this conversation has gone as far as it needs to go. I just wanted you to know."

"Well, thanks for telling me. Have you told Vernetta and Nichelle?"

J.C. nodded.

"I bet they were as shocked as I was."

"Yeah, I guess they were." J.C. grinned.

"You probably thought I was going to freak out, huh?"

"Kinda."

"Nah, girl. You're cool with me. It makes me so mad when the media calls me homophobic. I don't have nothing against gay men or lesbians, as long as they ain't trying to hit on me. It's these deceitful ass, down low brothers I have a problem with."

# CHAPTER 108

Confident that she was about to convince a killer to crack, J.C. boldly entered the vestibule of Ever Faithful.

To her surprise, after telling the lieutenant about the waiter's identification of Lamont and Reverend Sims, he had given her the go-ahead to interview the reverend. She was still anxiously waiting to find out if Lamont's fingerprints were found at Eugene's place.

While Lieutenant Wilson okayed her trip to Ever Faithful, he made it clear that she was on her own. And she knew why. If it turned out that J.C. was on the wrong trail and the reverend was not the killer, he would deny any knowledge of her actions and brand her a renegade cop who had ignored a direct order.

The church secretary asked her to have a seat, then left to tell the reverend she was waiting.

J.C. was mulling over how she planned to approach the reverend when he came out to greet her. "What can I do for you, ma'am?"

"It's Detective," she said gently. "Detective J.C. Sparks."

"I'm sorry, Detective. How can I help you?"

"Perhaps we should talk in the privacy of your office."

"It's that serious, huh?" His levity sounded forced. "Hope I'm not about to be arrested."

J.C. intentionally didn't respond, but followed him inside. She barely gave him a chance to get seated behind his desk. "I'm investigating the murder of—"

"I've already talked to the police about the murder of my friend James Hill," he said, twirling an ink pen back and forth between two fingers. "I hope we don't have to do that all over again."

"I'm here regarding a different murder. The murder of Eugene Nelson."

He scratched his bearded jaw and sat back in his chair. "I can't imagine why you would possibly need to speak to me about that case."

"We typically interview people who knew the victim. Sometimes information people think is insignificant can end up being very important. I just have a few questions."

"Okay, then, ask away." He gently rocked back and forth in his chair.

"Can you tell me how you met Mr. Nelson?"

The reverend explained that Eugene had joined Ever Faithful a few weeks before his death and had come to him for counseling.

"Counseling regarding what?"

"I can't disclose that, Detective. There's a pastoral privilege. Our discussions are confidential."

"I understand. Did you ever socialize with Eugene?"

The reverend abruptly stopped rocking. "Uh . . . no. Not really."

"Is it *no* or is it *not really*?"

Reverend Sims seemed to be rehearsing his answer in his head.

"Uh . . . it's no."

Detective Jessup had followed up on the information from the waiter at Marie Callender's Grill and confirmed that Reverend Sims and Eugene played racquetball at the Spectrum Club right before dinner. *So why is he lying?*

She changed tactics and asked a series of questions ostensibly intended to put him at ease. They talked about how long he had been in the ministry, his work at Raycom and the other churches where he had served. All of his seemingly innocuous answers were confirming his link to the murdered men.

The reverend lamented the death of his neighbor James Hill and eagerly talked about serving as the minister for the football and basketball teams at Fox Hills Junior College.

"Sounds like you had a lot of contact with the football players."

"Yep. I was right there in the locker room, praying with them before the games. Got two free tickets on the fifty-yard line for every home game. Some of the players even came to me privately for counseling."

*And I bet you counseled them, alright.* "Did you ever meet Nathaniel Hall, one of the team's star players?"

"As a matter fact I did," Reverend Sims said. "What a tragedy to be struck down in life with so much ahead of him."

After he described the kind of work he'd done at Raycom, J.C. asked if he knew Marcus Patterson, the slain engineer. "That's not a name I remember, but it's possible I may have—" He stopped talking.

J.C. could tell by the spark of alarm in his eyes that Reverend Sims had just put the pieces together.

"Detective Sparks, why are you asking me these questions?"

"Because they're relevant to my investigation."

"How?"

"I'm not at liberty to divulge that right now."

His face turned angry.

"Would you mind providing us with a set of your fingerprints?" J.C. asked.

The reverend leaned over his desk. "Why would you need my prints?"

"Eugene had a visitor the night of his murder. We have some fingerprints we took from his home. We'd like to exclude yours."

Beads of sweat lined his upper lip. "Are you telling me that I'm a suspect, Detective? I understand that there's already somebody in custody for his murder."

"Is there some reason you don't want to provide your prints? You never mentioned anything about being at Eugene's home."

"I . . . I don't have time to get down to the station to provide prints. I'm very busy here and I— "

J.C. pulled a small package from her jacket pocket. "I have an ink pad and fingerprint card right here. I can fingerprint you right now."

The reverend's face went flush and he seemed unable to speak.

"Are you okay, Reverend?"

"Yes, I'm fine. I just . . . can you give me a second to go grab some water?"

"Sure."

J.C. hoped the man wasn't going to make a run for it. Just when she was about to think that maybe he had, the reverend returned to his desk. Without water.

"I don't think it's a good idea to give you my fingerprints. If you're asking me to do that, you obviously think I'm a suspect. I had better get legal counsel. I have nothing more to say."

J.C. stood up and peered down at him, a move intended to intimidate. "Reverend, it's been my experience that when someone lawyers up, it's usually because they have something to hide."

"As I just said, I don't have anything else to say, Detective." He got to his feet.

J.C. saw guilt in the man's eyes.

"Please leave my office."

Pumped with adrenalin, J.C. stepped into the hallway, closing the door behind her. The reverend's evasiveness and his bold-faced lies moved him straight to the top of the prime suspects' list. She wanted to bring him down to the station for further questioning right this minute, but she wasn't about to make that move without Lieutenant Wilson's okay. She flipped open her cell phone. Before she could dial his number, the phone rang. It was Detective Jessup.

"I've got some good news," he said. "We have a match on the prints we found on that wineglass."

"Are they Lamont's?" J.C. asked anxiously.

"Yep. But I don't think he's our killer."

"I agree." She started to tell him about her interview with Reverend Sims, but decided to wait until after her call to the lieutenant. "What about the windowsill?"

"Unfortunately for you, those belong to your buddy Special Moore."

J.C. wanted to cry. "I still don't think she killed Eugene," she said finally.

"Neither do I. I think Lamont's live-in lover, Ken, iced Nelson. Seems he's been picked up a few times in Griffith Park for lewd and lascivious conduct."

"I don't get the connection. That doesn't make him a killer."

"Nope, it doesn't. I only mentioned that to explain why we had his prints on file. We also found Ken's prints on that windowsill. A few other places, too. We just brought him in and I'm about to start questioning him right now."

# Chapter 109

Vernetta had not expected to see J.C. stalking their way as she followed Nichelle into the vestibule of Ever Faithful.

J.C. skidded to a stop when she spotted them. "What are you guys doing here?"

Vernetta pointed at Nichelle. "She insisted on coming and I wasn't about to let her do this by herself."

"Do what?"

"She wants to talk to each of the ministers here. She thinks she'll be able to find out if they had anything to do with Eugene's murder."

"You can't do that!" J.C. ushered them back outside. "You'd be interfering with a police investigation."

"I'm not going to interfere with your investigation," Nichelle said snippily. "I'm representing my client. I have a right to interview anybody I want."

J.C. looked at Vernetta, then Nichelle. "You have to go home and leave this to the police. Trust me, Nichelle, I'm very close to solving this case. What you plan to do could blow it for me."

"I'm tired of waiting for the police to find the real killer while Special rots in jail. *I'll* find him." She marched back inside the church. "We all know he's one of the ministers in this church."

J.C. jumped in front of Nichelle, blocking her path. "He may not be. In fact, I just got some information that points to another suspect. Two of them, in fact. So I need both of you to leave. Now."

"You're just saying that to get us out of here."

"Nichelle, please don't make me take out my handcuffs. Because if I have to, I will."

Vernetta watched as they stared each other down, neither of them willing to budge. She put her arm around Nichelle's shoulder. "Let's just leave and let J.C. handle things."

"Okay, okay," Nichelle said stubbornly. "But I need to talk to Reverend Sims about something else. Special wants him to come down to the jail to counsel her. If he is the killer, I want him to look me in the eye knowing *she's* about to go on trial for murders *he* committed."

"You can't talk to Reverend Sims about *anything*," J.C. said. "The police will be talking to him soon enough."

"So it *is* him!" Nichelle pressed her hands to both cheeks.

"I didn't say that," J.C. said, glancing back over her shoulder. "And please keep your voice down."

"We're leaving." Vernetta grabbed Nichelle's arm and tried to tug her toward the door, but she wouldn't budge.

"I won't say anything about the case," Nichelle promised. "I just want to see how the man reacts when I tell him Special wants him to come down to the jail and pray with her. I bet he—" Nichelle stared down the hallway.

Vernetta looked back and saw Belynda stalking toward them.

"Perhaps you forgot," Belynda said, sarcastically, "but this is a church. I could hear you all the way at the other end of the building. What in the world is going on here?"

"I need to talk to Reverend Sims," Nichelle said.

Belynda hoisted the strap of her purse higher on her shoulder. "Do you have an appointment?"

"I don't need one."

They heard footsteps and turned around. Reverend Sims walked over to them. He shot J.C. a panicky look. "What's going on here, ladies?"

Nichelle pursed her lips. "I need to speak with you, Reverend."

"No, she doesn't," J.C. said.

The reverend's eyes were moist and red. "Well, now is not a good time."

"When *would* be a good time?" Nichelle demanded.

He looked at his watch. "The church secretary should be back from lunch shortly. You can check my schedule with her."

"This is extremely urgent. It won't take long."

J.C. stepped in front of Nichelle. "Reverend, why don't you go back to your office. I'll handle this."

Nichelle would not relent. "No. I want to—"

The reverend sighed heavily. "Perhaps we should discuss this in my office. "

J.C. shot Vernetta and Nichelle a burning look as they all followed him down the hall to his office.

Reverend Sims closed the door, then stepped behind his desk as if he needed to use it as a bunker. Belynda valiantly stood next to him.

"Would you like me to call the security guard, Reverend?" Belynda asked.

"No, I don't think that'll be necessary. Will it?" He eyed Nichelle.

"We know you killed Eugene," Nichelle blurted out.

"Nichelle!" J.C. and Vernetta screamed in unison.

The reverend gave J.C. a hard look. "Detective, I can't believe you've been spreading these vicious lies. I'm suing you and the LAPD for defamation!"

J.C. took Nichelle by her left arm. Vernetta grabbed the other one. "You're leaving. Now!" J.C. ordered.

Vernetta tried to pull Nichelle toward the door. She managed to break free from Vernetta, but couldn't shake off J.C.

"The police Department restored that picture Special took the night before Eugene was murdered," Nichelle bluffed. "It shows you in Eugene's kitchen kissing him. We know you killed him!"

The reverend's eyes expanded, but not half as wide as Belynda's. She took a dizzying step away from him and almost plowed into the wall.

"How could you? You're a man of God! What a disgrace!"

"It's not how it looks." The reverend's voice shook and he was close to tears. "Yes, I was at Eugene's house that night, but nothing like that happened. And I didn't kill him."

"You're a liar!" Belynda screamed.

"I had dinner with Eugene and later, at his house, he came on to me, but I pushed him away." The reverend absently rubbed his hands together. "And that's all that happened. I swear to God I didn't kill him."

"You should burn in hell!" Belynda yelled. She shrank away from him and stepped closer to the door. "You knew Eugene was trying to turn his life around and you seduced him anyway! I knew you'd been up to no good. But I didn't want to believe it."

"I swear I didn't kill him!" the reverend cried.

"What about this?" Belynda reached into her purse and took out the lapel pin. She held it toward J.C.

"I found this in Eugene's bedroom," she said, weeping now. "I gave it to the reverend and he wore it all the time. It ended up in Eugene's bedroom because the reverend was *in* Eugene's bedroom." She whipped around and faced Reverend Sims again. "Engaging in that perversion!"

"Are you crazy? What are you talking about!"

Belynda's eyes were ablaze with condemnation. "Then tell me, Reverend, just how did this pin end up in Eugene's bedroom?"

"I have no idea," the reverend whimpered.

"I don't believe you. You're a sick, sick man!"

"Everybody just calm down," J.C. commanded. "I want everybody out of here, except for the reverend."

This time Nichelle willingly headed for the door. Belynda and Vernetta followed.

J.C. pulled handcuffs from her back pocket. "Reverend Sims," she said, "You're under arrest for the murder of Eugene Nelson."

# CHAPTER 110

J.C. handcuffed Rev. Sims and forced him into one of the chairs in front of his desk.

"Good Lord, please have mercy on me!" Reverend Sims sobbed. "This is going to kill my wife. I swear to God I didn't kill Eugene!"

"I need all of you to leave the building," J.C. bellowed into the hallway where Vernetta, Nichelle, and Belynda stood staring into the office. "Right now!"

J.C. turned her back to them, pulled her cell phone from the pocket of her jacket and dialed Lieutenant Wilson.

"I'm coming in with a suspect," she said breathlessly. "It's Reverend Sims. He lied about not being at Eugene's place and—"

The lieutenant cut in. "You're off base. Way off base. We already have the killer. Ken Landers, the boyfriend of Lamont Wiley."

"What? Are you sure?"

J.C. stared over at Reverend Sims who continued to wail. She stepped into the hallway hoping the lieutenant couldn't hear his sobs. Despite evicting them, Vernetta, Nichelle and Belynda still hadn't left.

"Ken caught Lamont cheating on him with Nelson and he wasn't very happy about it. He admitted to breaking into the house through the kitchen window."

"So he admitted killing Eugene?"

"No, not yet. But he will." There was a cop's assurance in his voice. "He claims there was a big confrontation and Eugene was alive when he and Lamont left. But he's lying. We just picked Lamont up and we're bringing him in now. So Reverend Sims ain't our guy."

"But we can't be sure just yet, Lieutenant. I think there could actually be two killers at work. Reverend Sims lied about being at Eugene's place and—"

"Do you have any idea what kind of backlash we're going to get from the black community when they find out we arrested a minister from Ever Faithful? I'm not taking that heat. Not without some solid evidence."

J.C.'s mind was a jumble. "I think we should at least bring him in for questioning."

"No," the lieutenant barked. "You don't have nearly enough to bring him in."

"But Ken hasn't confessed yet and maybe he won't. What if you're wrong? What if another man dies in the meantime?"

Lieutenant Wilson didn't answer. She could feel his uncertainty. "I'll place him under 24-hour surveillance," he said finally. "We're not arresting him without more. Now get back to the station." He hung up before she could say another word.

J.C. stared at the phone before sliding it back into her pocket. She peered into the office at the still sobbing Reverend Sims. She finally walked over to him, bent down and removed the handcuffs.

Belynda approached the open doorway. "You're not arresting him?"

"No," J.C. said. "There's another suspect already in custody."

"I told you!" the reverend cried out. "I had nothing to do with Eugene's murder."

J.C. watched as he massaged his wrists. Something in her gut told her the lieutenant was wrong. Dead wrong. This man was a vicious killer.

"You're a sick, sick man!" Belynda shouted. She pulled a gun from her purse and pointed it in the direction of Reverend Sims and J.C.

In a flash, J.C. snatched her own gun from its holster, and when she did, Belynda swung her weapon in the direction of Vernetta and Nichelle. "Drop your gun, Detective, or I'll shoot both of them."

A frightened Reverend Sims stumbled backwards into a corner and slouched to the floor. "Belynda, please, please, put that gun away!"

"Shut up," Belynda screeched. "You deserve to die just like all those other perversions against God."

Vernetta and Nichelle were wrapped in each other's arms now, too scared to even breathe.

The crazed look in Belynda's eyes told J.C. that the woman could easily pull the trigger. "Please put the gun down," she said softly. J.C. kept her gun pointed at Belynda with one hand and her other raised, palm out, as if to keep her at bay. "There's no reason for anybody to get hurt. Just put the gun down."

Belynda glared at J.C., but her gun remained pointed at Vernetta and Nichelle. "Drop your gun, Detective, or I'll blow their heads off."

When J.C. failed to obey, Belynda took a step backward, out of J.C.'s line of vision. She fired a warning shot at the ceiling, then turned her gun back on the cowering women.

Vernetta and Nichelle screamed and collapsed into a clump on the floor.

"I said give me your gun!" Belynda's now-shrill voice reverberated down the hallway.

Moving slowly, J.C. bent down, set her gun on the floor and pushed it out into the hallway with her foot. "Belynda, don't do anything stupid. Nobody needs to get hurt."

J.C. moved into the hallway.

"Get back!" Belynda shouted.

J.C. stopped, but stayed planted just outside the open doorway. She was about five feet away from Belynda. "How did this happen, Belynda? So *you* killed all those men?"

"They deserved to die. Every single one of them."

Belynda stared past J.C. "You're lucky to be alive," she said to the reverend. "If I had known for sure that you were having an affair with Eugene, I would've killed you, too."

"You've got it all wrong," the reverend sputtered.

"Shut up! You're a liar!"

"So you killed Eugene, too?" J.C. asked

"Yes," Belynda said proudly. "After Special came to my house that morning and tried to show me that picture, I went straight to Eugene's place to tell him about it. When I got to the door I heard a man's voice, but it wasn't Eugene's. I went around back and peered into the kitchen window. When I saw a man wearing nothing but a towel, I knew Eugene had broken his promise to me. And to God. But I had no idea the other man was Reverend Sims."

"But it wasn't me!" the reverend cried.

"Shut up, you liar!" Tears streamed down Belynda's cheeks. "I went back home and prayed for the rest of the day. God ordered me to kill both of them. But by the time I got back to Eugene's house, it was after midnight and he was alone." She stared in disgust at the reverend. "All of you are sick, sick, sick." Her hand shook so violently it seemed the gun might easily go off.

"Belynda, please put the gun down." J.C.'s voice was as serene as she could make it. "There's no need to hurt anybody else. I understand how you feel."

"You don't understand how I feel!" Belynda shrieked. "Your mother didn't die because some scum gave her AIDS. Don't tell me you know how I feel. You couldn't possibly know how I feel."

"Killing more people isn't going to change anything. It's time for us to think about the goodness of God."

J.C.'s words seemed to reduce some of Belynda's rage, but only for a few seconds. "It's not right for these sick men to do this to us," she sobbed.

"You can't take the law into your own hands, Belynda. Let the police handle this."

Belynda wiped the sweat from her forehead with her free hand. "I was willing to give Eugene a second chance to turn his life around. But he spit in God's face and went right back to that perversion. He deserved to die."

"And you deserve to die, too!" She lunged toward the reverend.

"Belynda!" J.C. shouted. "Noooooo!"

Vernetta and Nichelle shrieked in unison as two ear-shattering gunshots rocked the building. They remained crouched together on the floor, bonded by fear.

Everything was completely still.

After seconds that seemed like minutes, Vernetta untangled herself from Nichelle, who was whimpering like a petrified puppy. "J.C., are you okay?"

J.C. stood staring down at Belynda, who lay on the floor in a pool of blood.

Vernetta walked over and put a hand on J.C.'s shoulder. "Are you okay?" she asked again.

"I've never shot anybody before," J.C. said in a whimper.

"How'd you get the gun away from her?"

"I wasn't able to. I had another gun in my ankle holster."

Vernetta turned and spotted Reverend Sims slouched in a corner of his office, blood splattered on the floor and walls. "Oh, Jesus!"

Vernetta's scream seemed to bring J.C. out of her trance. She knelt down and took Belynda's pulse. "She's dead."

J.C. then dashed into the office and examined Reverend Sims' limp body. "He's still alive!" she shouted, as she tried to stop the bleeding. "Call 9-1-1!"

# EPILOGUE

When J.C. escorted Special out of the county jail, Vernetta and Nichelle ran to embrace her, almost knocking her down. They were locked in a big emotional huddle for a good five minutes.

"Can we please just get out of here?" Special pleaded, as she tearfully reached out to hug her mother, then her father.

"We've planned a special celebration for you," Vernetta announced. She turned to Special's parents. "I hope that's okay."

"Sure it is," her father grinned. He was a tower of a man, while her stylishly dressed mother was barely five feet. "We're going to let you girls go out and have a good time. We owe our daughter's freedom to all of you. I can't thank you enough."

The four women made their way to J.C.'s Range Rover.

"I still can't believe Church Girl killed all those men," Special said. She sat in the backseat, sandwiched between Vernetta and Nichelle. "I told y'all that heffa was missing some screws. She had some nerve calling me the killer. She deserved a friggin' Academy Award for that performance she did for those TV cameras outside Eugene's house. She was setting me up big time."

They quickly filled Special in on everything that had happened at Ever Faithful.

"I can't believe she's dead." Special shook her head. "Thank God J.C. killed her before she killed y'all."

No one said anything. It still unnerved Vernetta to recall the image of Belynda aiming her gun at them. Nichelle had called her twice in the middle of the night after having nightmares about the shootings. J.C. had yet to talk about it, but Vernetta knew she was having a difficult time with her first shooting in the line of duty.

"So is Reverend Sims going to make it?" Special asked.

"Looks like it," Vernetta said. "He was really lucky. Belynda's bullet landed an inch from his heart."

"Not lucky," Nichelle corrected. "Blessed. Just like we were."

Special shook her head again. "There's still one thing I don't understand. If Church Girl was so in love with Eugene, why did she kill him?"

"I'm not sure she really was in love with him," J.C. said from the front seat. "From what she wrote in her journal, they never had an intimate relationship. She truly believed that gay men could be converted and that was her mission with Eugene. According to her journal, if a man refused to change, he deserved to die. When she saw Lamont half-dressed at Eugene's place, she felt Eugene had betrayed both her and God."

"Wait a minute," Special said. "So the man I saw in Eugene's kitchen was Lamont, not Reverend Sims?"

"No," Vernetta interrupted. "It *was* the reverend, but he swears nothing happened between them. He claims Eugene tried to kiss him, but he stopped him."

"It's possible," Special said. "As soon as I saw Eugene lean in to kiss the man, I snapped the picture and got the hell out of there. So Reverend Sims isn't gay?"

"Apparently not," J.C. clarified. "He swears he left Eugene's place not long after you took that picture. That squares with Lamont's story. He came over later that same night."

Special was still having trouble piecing the story together. "So why didn't Belynda kill Lamont, too?"

"Belynda went to Eugene's place twice on Saturday. The first time was right after you tried to show her that picture Saturday morning. That's when she saw Lamont. She ran back home and started praying. She wrote it all down in her journal."

"This is hella confusing," Special said. "So where does Lamont's boyfriend Ken fit in?"

J.C. chuckled. "Now this is where it gets even more confusing. Lamont and Eugene spent Friday night and most of Saturday together. They went to a movie at the Howard Hughes Promenade Saturday night. Someone saw them together and called Ken. He drove over there and followed them back to Eugene's place. He climbed in through the kitchen window, and made such a scene that Lamont ended up leaving with him. Belynda came over about an hour later, after they had gone. We think it was sometime after midnight. We're not quite sure whether she broke in or Eugene let her in."

"Lamont was lucky his boy Ken came over there and acted a fool," Special said. "If he'd still been there, Belynda would've killed his ass, too."

"You're probably right," J.C. said.

"Girl, nobody coulda written this script. How did Belynda know all those other men she killed were on the down low?"

"You wouldn't believe what we found at her house." J.C. glanced back over the seat. "She had pictures, driver's licenses and credit card numbers on all of her victims. She'd been following them for months. A lot of her information came from SADDDL, that fanatical group Nichelle spoke to. She was working as one of their investigators."

"I actually saw her at that luncheon," Nichelle said, "but I figured it was just somebody who looked like her."

"Once SADDDL gave her information about a man they suspected of being on the down low," J.C. continued, "Belynda began following them. For instance, a SADDDL member who worked at the post office noticed that James Hill, that investment banker from Ladera, received regular deliveries from gay porn sites at his post office box. We think Belynda killed him based on that information alone. She had no idea he was a friend of Reverend Sims. She had a list of eleven other men she was tracking. Including the guy she killed in the park across from your apartment."

"Her ass was stone crazy."

"The *Times* story said she was mentally ill," Nichelle said sympathetically. "Schizophrenic. She was extremely close to her mother, who was infected with HIV by a man she'd been dating. We lost Maya, but can you imagine losing your *mother* to AIDS?"

"Like I said," Special repeated, "the heffa was crazy."

"Enough of this depressing talk." Vernetta clasped her hands. "We have some good news. Not only did the prosecutor drop the murder *and* assault charges, Eugene's law firm isn't going to pursue criminal charges against you for hacking into their computer system."

"Nobody can prove I had anything to do with sending that email," Special said, as self-righteous as ever.

"Actually, I think they *can* prove it," Vernetta corrected her. "But the firm isn't interested in having the media jump back on this story and drag its name through the mud again. Frankly, they're embarrassed that their computer system was so susceptible to attack."

"So count your blessings," Nichelle said.

Vernetta squeezed Special's hand. "And there's more. Eugene's estate is settling the wrongful death case. Maya's mother is going to get a very nice settlement."

Special looked more than pleased. "This is the best day of my life."

When J.C. made a left turn off Crenshaw onto Martin Luther King Boulevard, Special's face clouded. "Where are we going?"

Vernetta smiled. "To your place."

"I know I've been on lock down for a while, but I do remember where I live, and I don't live over here. I wish I did, though."

"Then your wish has been granted."

"I finally got Maya's estate settled," Nichelle explained. "She left her house to you. And the mortgage is way less than you're currently paying in rent."

Special started to cry. "You serious?" She reached out and hugged them simultaneously.

By the time they pulled into the driveway of her new home, Special's cries had turned into dry-eyed excitement. "I can't believe this is *my* house." She bolted from the car.

A bright yellow banner that read *Welcome Home, Special!* hung across the front door.

Special stepped into the living room and looked around as if it were her first time seeing the place. "You guys even brought my furniture over here! Everything looks so nice. And I can't wait to taste whatever I'm smelling from the kitchen," she said. "I'm not sure my taste buds will recognize edible food. So what's cooking?"

Jefferson walked out of the kitchen, followed by Clayton draped in an apron.

Special stared at him as if he were a mirage.

"I'm what's cooking," Clayton said grinning. "I figured you'd enjoy some of my jambalaya on your first day as a homeowner."

Vernetta had expected Special to run straight into Clayton's arms, but she just stood there in shock. Clayton finally walked over and gave her a hug.

Special buried her face in his chest and wept. "I'm so glad you're here."

Clayton still wasn't quite ready to forgive or forget what Special had taken him through. Vernetta was just glad she'd been able to convince him to fly out for Special's homecoming. She prayed time would mend their relationship.

Special finally pulled away from him, then turned around to face her friends. "Thanks, everybody," she said, overcome with emotion. "I wouldn't be standing here if it weren't for all of you. This has been such an unbelievable ordeal. I felt like I was in the middle of a nightmare, but now I'm living a dream."

"We're just glad you're back home." Vernetta threw an arm across her friend's shoulders. "Now let's eat."

Everybody headed into the dining room where the table had been set with Maya's colorful African-print dishes.

"Clayton, the table looks wonderful," Vernetta said.

Jefferson embraced his wife. "Excuse me, but this is *my* handiwork. I do have a few domestic skills."

"Looks like he's been holding out on you," J.C. said.

They all sat down at the table and for the next two hours, ate and drank and laughed and cried.

Just as Nichelle placed a banana crème pie in the middle of the table, Special abruptly stood up.

"I have a speech I'd like to make," she began. "I've been through a lot these last few weeks and I want to thank all of you again for standing by me. Jail is not a fun place to be and I never wanna be on lock down again. Ever. So I'm promising all of you, right here and now, that I'm not going to do *anything* that might cause a cop to even look sideways at me." She made eye contact with J.C. "Including running a red light or driving faster than sixty-five or letting a parking meter expire."

Vernetta and Nichelle traded cynical looks, then spoke in unison. "Can we get that in writing?"

# Author's Note

I often have a hard time recalling exactly when or how the idea for a particular novel originated. For the most part, the concept simply pops into my head from some unknown place. That's not the case with this book.

I have a crystal clear recollection of watching an *Oprah* show featuring J.L. King, author of *On the Down Low*. As I listened to his insider's account of the mindset of men on the down low, I was completely stunned. My emotions during that sixty-minute program, went from shock to anger to fear.

As a writer of fiction, my goal is to entertain. Writing this book, however, has given me an opportunity to both entertain and raise awareness about this important topic. The statistics mentioned in *Murder on the Down Low* are fact, not fiction. While African-American and Latina women make up only 24% of the female population in the U.S., we account for more than 80% of the total AIDS diagnoses for women, according to the latest statistics published by the U.S. Centers for Disease Control.

Unfortunately, these shocking numbers are not likely to decline until we—the victims—decide to do something about them. HIV may not be curable, but it is completely preventable. We can't continue to sit back and wait for someone else to tackle this crisis. This is our fight.

We must begin this battle by pulling our heads out of the sand. While there are indeed men whose conduct puts our lives at risk, we also do our own share of harm to ourselves. We place our own lives at risk by not getting tested. We place our own lives at risk when we fail to use protection. We place our own lives at risk when we behave in ways which dishonor our bodies. These are areas we can fix. Today.

While African-Americans are among the most religious people on the planet, we tend not to extended our spiritual teachings of love and compassion toward our gay brothers and sisters. That, too, must change.

A wealth of information about HIV/AIDS is available via the Internet. For more information, please visit The National Black Leadership Commission on AIDS, Inc. (www.nblca.org), The Black AIDS Institute (www.BlackAIDS.org) and the U.S. Centers for Disease Control and Prevention (www.cdc.org).

In the meantime, stay safe.

# Acknowledgements

Writing and publishing my third novel was very much like giving birth. Some pain here and there, but by delivery time, all I could remember was the joy. As always, I was blessed to have a ton of people helping me though this process in one way or another.

First, to my many friends and colleagues who served as my focus group for this book. Your feedback was invaluable. A big thanks to my big brother, Jerry Samuels, Sr., my cousins, Donny Wilson and James White, my newest homie, Robert Flowers, Jerome Norris (the deepest, most committed brother I know), Rafael Medina, Rev. J.L. Armstrong, Karey Keenan, Molly Byock, Ann Adame, Nellie Burhanan, Kathy Fairbrother, Marsha Silady, Ellen Farrell, Diane Mackin, Sophy Woodhouse, Debbie Diffendal, Netra Brown, Charles Zacharie, James Barlow, Patricia Lasarte, Dorothy Baynes, Jewelle Johnson, Cynthia Hebron, Russana Rowles, Olivia Smith, Terrie Robinson, Tonya Jenerette, Nancy Larson, Cythina Betz, Pat Penny, Karen Williams, Ginger Heyman, Star Atchison, Dawn Sutherland, Daisy Bates, Kenn Stokes, Faye Gipson, Antoinette Tutt, Waverly Crenshaw, Jonathan (aka "Big Baller") Deveaux of the Savoy in Inglewood and Kelly-Ann Henry (also known personally to me as JustAskKelly-Ann.com). I must extend an extra-special thank you to Erica Zacharie, who forced me to face my own biases and ignorance about HIV/AIDS. Thanks for the education.

To my parents and those friends, old and new, who constantly encourage me and demonstrate their support in immeasurable ways, Laurie Robinson, Stephanie Winlock, Roosevelt Womble, Sara Finney-Johnson, Colleen Higgs, Monique Brandon, Syna Dennis, Renee Cunningham, Cheryl Mason, Doris Shelby, Felicia Henderson, Alisa Covington, Ana Segobia Masters, Karen Copeland, Bobbie Copeland, Greg Sawyer, Eric Sawyer, Tommy Tolbert, Roosevelt Womble, Merverllyn Vaughn, Clarise Wilkins, Jackie Hilson, Alva Mason, Lynda Martin, Robin Smith, Robyn Brown, Gail Herring, and Fesia Davenport, your enthusiastic support keeps me going.

Thank you all my writer-friends who shared both their time, resources and encouragement, Linda Beed, Tina Brooks McKinney, Cheryl Questell, Barbara Wright Sykes, Linda Coleman-Willis, Angela Henry, Gene Cartwright, Staci Robinson, Fon James, Patryce Banks, Renee Morgan Hampton, Marti Tucker, Charles Chatmon, and especially Victoria Christopher Murray, a highly successful author who always finds time to help and encourage those who seek to follow in her footsteps. And to my writing group members, Adrienne Byers, Jane Howard-Martin, and Nefertiti Austin, thanks for your expert guidance in helping me shape this novel.

To Maleta Wilson of Book Sellin' Sistahs, thanks for your encouragement and advice, and for literally taking me under your wing and teaching me the ins and outs of the book business. To Mother Rose of Underground Books in Sacramento, California, thanks for your passionate support. Writers like me need bookstores like yours.

Thank you to the Los Angeles Chapter of Sisters in Crime, especially fellow writers, Ashley Baker and Gayle Bartos-Pool, whose tireless work on behalf of the Speakers Bureau turned out to be a true blessing for me.

To the girls at two of my favorite salons, Doña Grant, Brooke Bass and Tammy Griffin (the baddest hair stylist I know!) at Kristen Laurenz in Altadena, California; and Veronica Myers, Darlene Williams and Shawnta Ellis (the baddest braider I know!) at The Emerald Chateau in Inglewood, California, thanks for pumping my books to your clients.

A big thank you to Professor Sandra Adell of the Afro-American Studies Department at the University of Madison, Wisconsin. Girlfriend, you have no idea how happy I am to have you on my team. Thanks so much for your incredible hospitality during my first trip to Madison, Wisconsin and for your insightful feedback regarding this book.

To Power Couple Eric and Daisy Bates, who showed me what Southern hospitality really means. I can't wait to return to Atlanta to hang out at your fabulous crib.

Thank you to fellow attorney Debra Brown, who literally picked me up off the highway and made my first trip to Jackson, Mississippi so much fun, and Cyrus Webb of Conversations Book Club, a serious book lover who is making it happen in Jackson.

To my wonderful Las Vegas Crew, Helen Mingleton, Deborah Thornton, Ellen Brown, Wilma Pinder, Doris Robinson, Sharon Thomas, Jani Jeppe, the Las Vegas Alumnae Chapter of Delta Sigma Theta Sorority, the Las Vegas African-American Authors Book Club, and the West Las Vegas Library, thanks so much for the support. You really rolled out the red carpet for me in the town that never sleeps. I cannot wait to come back!

Without a doubt, book clubs have been my lifeblood. I have so enjoyed my afternoons conversing and dining with my sisters. To all of you who hosted me, thank you. I must extend a special thank you to the Jazzy Ladies of Pasadena, California, in particular, Virgie Edwards, Lois Richard, Joyce Robinson, Joyce Streator, Bettye Holliday, Sandy Bourne, Julie Woodyard and Mamie Grant; and the Reading Circle of Friends in Upper Marlboro, Maryland, especially Karen Murrell, Shebbie Rice, Deborah Crimes, and Melissa Hinkson. Thanks for your feedback on this book and for your continued support long after your book club meeting ended. You rallied behind me in a way that warms my heart every time I think about it. Readers like you are the reason I write.

A super special thanks to my talented team. First, to my tenacious publicist, Pamela Johnson of the Johnson Agency in San Francisco, California. Most authors would agree that a good publicist is hard to find. I am blessed to have a great one. Thanks also to my Atlanta-based publicist/promoter Shunda Leigh of Booking Matters magazine, book cover designer Keith Saunders of Marion Designs, web designer Milton Ellis of Onegistics Systems Solutions (thanks for always taking care of my Internet needs with lickety-split timing), web designer Tyora Moody of Tywebbin Creations, editors/proofreaders Lynel Johnson Washington, Dawn Dowdle of Sleuth Editing and Virginia Lee Gonzales of WordPlay Editing Services, book layout designer Jessica Tilles of The Writers Assistant, my fantastic virtual assistant, Eydie Stumpf of Eydie's Office, and finally, my super-creative graphic designer Lisa Zachery of Papered Wonders (Girl, your promotional materials are the bomb!). I couldn't have done it without all of you.

And finally, to anyone and everyone who read this book, thanks for your support. I'll keep writing if you keep reading!

Discussion Questions for *Murder on the Down Low*

1. Could you identify with Special's rage over her cousin's death or did you feel it was unwarranted?

2. What did you think of Jefferson's views about gays and men on the down low?

3. Once confronted with J.C.'s theory about the murder victims being on the down low, do you think Lieutenant Wilson should have immediately warned the public?

4. Why do you think it took Vernetta so long to make the decision to leave O'Reilly & Finney?

5. Do you believe the issue of men on the down low is more likely to occur in the African-American community than in other communities? Why or why not?

6. Do you agree with Professor Michaels' view that we live in a culture of sexual promiscuity?

7. African-American and Hispanic women face a significantly higher risk of HIV infection than other women. What will it take to reverse this trend?

8. Do you think sex education in schools could help reduce the transmission rates of HIV and other sexually transmitted diseases? Why or why not?

9. Did *Murder on the Down Low* raise questions and concerns about HIV/AIDS that you had not previously considered?

10. What did you like/dislike about *Murder on the Down Low*?